AND THEN THE COW WAS DROWNDED

Other books by Steven Paul Lansky

Main St.
Jack Acid
The Break
Eleven Word Title for Confessional Political Poetry Originally Composed for Radio
A Black Bird Fell Out of the Sky
Life is a Fountain

AND THEN THE COW WAS DROWNDED

Illustrated by Steven Paul Lansky

Paul Thanas

ARBITRARY PRESS
New York

For more information, or to book an event, contact :
lanskysp@hotmail.com http://www.stevenpaullansky.com
http://www.arbitrarypressbooks.com

Book design by Steven Paul Lansky
Cover design by Steven Paul Lansky

ISBN - Paperback: 978-1-958762-09-7
ISBN - Hardcover : 978-1-958762-10-3

First Edition: March 2024

For Makwa and Migizi

TABLE OF CONTENTS

INTRODUCTION

"Schizophrenia affects understanding." Mervyn Cartold, a counselor I've seen for over twenty years explained. The idea is expansive. I have schizophrenia. My understanding is affected by schizophrenia, as is the understanding of others. In addition to the symptoms that affect understanding so do stigma, confusion, perception, and the normal misunderstandings that come from individuals telling and re-telling their stories. This disease makes life complicated for everyone in its path. Every relationship I enter into, whether romantic, platonic, familial, or professional is affected by this condition. I know that I am different. This mental illness, this chemical imbalance in my brain keeps me alone and in the dark. I'm sitting in a crowded room, one foot on the floor, the other tucked across it and I know that something I have keeps me from connecting, yet it also allows me to experience the world through a different set of filters. I take medication. They call it antipsychotic medication. That disturbs me. I have psychosis. As you read this book you may find yourself stopping, pausing, or getting stuck. This need not be a problem. I am a reader and a writer. Many of the books that have affected me the most, moved me deeply, and changed my understanding of life most completely, were books that were challenging, confusing and foreign enough that I started them several times before reading them from cover to cover. *Gravity's Rainbow* by Thomas Pynchon, *Under the Volcano* by Malcolm Lowry, and *The Empire City* by Paul Goodman are three important books that I started, paused for months or years, started again, paused more, and then finally working steadily thoroughly reading through.

Pynchon's opening was so, I marveled at the early pages then became distracted by how dazzling, and complex they were. When I did get further into the book, its erotic power, combined with the way it twisted taboos while generating its own order kept me fascinated. I had to study writers such as Derrida, Barthes, de Sade, and Borges to appreciate it. The overall effect was to open my life to ideas including postmodernism, history, science, mathematics, and fantasy. Malcolm Lowry examined alcoholism in ways that few writers have. The agony of his character's journeys, the way the novel was introduced into my life, in a vulnerable moment while hitchhiking, the complex shifting languages, (he intermixes Spanglish with English) and the idealism that I understood as authenticity, made the experience of Lowry's work integral to my understanding of my own complex relationships and my gradual recognition of my own alcoholism.

Once I cadged my brother to buy me one of Lowry's books when I could ill-afford it but was spending every free cent on alcohol. Paul Goodman's oeuvre is full of plain-spoken philosophy, humor, pathos, and is as lively as it is organic. I hope my book offers the same sense of shifting structure from beginning to end. Goodman pioneered this quality. There is no shame or disappointment in struggling with a text. I am not saying here that my book is as meaningful as these examples. I still have not read all of *Ulysses* by James Joyce. Maybe someday I will. I am saying that I will not be hurt or disappointed if it takes the reader a long time and several tries to finish *And Then the Cow Was Drownded.* Nor would it disturb me in any way if you flipped around and looked at the pictures before reading it chronologically. It is my fervent hope that this book will affect your understanding, at least a little, of the disease called schizophrenia. When I was in junior high, socially confused and academically successful, my brother a freshman in high school, he dated a girl between us in age. Her best friend started dating me so that she could hang out with her girlfriend and I could tag along with my brother. We went to a party with teens, all ages, in a basement, where rugs hung from walls, loud music thumped, and kids drank beer, shared pills, and smoked. Scared by the pills and alcohol, and isolated, as the girl really didn't care for me, I called Dad, told him of the climate at the party, not about the unfriendly girl, and he came for us. At home we had a party with sodas and chips, a sinister disappointment to the others. In school in the weeks to come, lionized by adults, and straight kids, I was shunned by cooler kids. Then, three years later, having become vice-president of Student Senate and twice elected to the Principal's Advisory Committee, I changed schools, did two years in one, graduated early and cycled from Cincinnati (over the summer) to Boston to attend Harvard (important to get all these facts up front).

There was the single longest day I've ridden to this day on the solstice in 1975, from Lima, Ohio to Ann Arbor, Michigan, a distance of 145 miles. The day reached 105 degrees, had tornado warnings, while we pedaled dusty back roads, stopping for milk, juice, ice cream, and to rest. And in the Adirondacks, some weeks later, with my brother's sweetie, when we camped in a day area, she was off in the woods doing who-knows-what when the NY State Trooper stopped to police me. He asked if I had camped in the day area, offered to write a ticket. I said, "Oh, no sir, we didn't camp, we just stopped for breakfast and to air out our sleeping bags." He said, "It sure looks like you camped here." I lied again and we both knew I was lying. I had a letter from Dad, on University of Cincinnati letterhead saying I had permission to be on my own, as I was underage. I didn't have to show it this time, but it became necessary.

I used to tease other kids: "Have you ever seriously considered seeing a psychoanalyst?" I was so impressed with myself. Many acquaintances considered me conceited. My closest friends seemed to acknowledge my smarts, my talents. I was big time. I talked about the "big fish—little pond" phenomenon. Then came confusion and confoundment at Harvard in my eighteenth, nineteenth and twentieth years. Not just at Harvard.

At Harvard I wanted to be a creative writing major. They accepted five majors a year, one experienced fiction writer, one inexperienced fiction writer, one experienced poet, one inexperienced poet, and a playwright. In the first co-op where I lived, part of Currier House, Radcliffe, one of the residents so rich, she had a room for her pet raccoon, Whiskey, for whom she had traded a bottle of whiskey with a hunter. One thing I learned at Harvard was any space big enough to fit the head of a raccoon could fit a whole raccoon. So, as it turned out, I couldn't write after a leave of absence, or hiatus, and be evaluated for the major. I had to enroll and take my chances with all the other students whose desires were like mine. By 1986, I found some other writers to study with, and let the dream, the raccoon, and Harvard become a story.

Something I don't remember, and probably wouldn't know if it weren't part of the lore told me by my parents and shown me in an album of photographs: I was born with rotated tibia. For my first six or nine months, most of the time, or at least when I slept, my feet were attached to special shoes which were bolted to a board that looked like a cross between a painter's palette and a skateboard. (I was never very good at skateboarding, but became a painter, as you will see, though I never used a palette to paint with oils or acrylic paint.) It really looked like a plain steel bar, or aluminum? You should know that part of the problem with my writing is a slightly flawed memory, so details may be enhanced, embellished, or creative. The device straightened out my calf rotation and when I walked, late for most infants, I walked without pigeon toes or duck feet. I like those descriptors. My father told me I would never be a good runner, he lied. I resented that. (Many things my father told me became resentments. Such was the nature of my disposition.

Dad, a prominent Cincinnati Psychology professor, analyzed my dreams, as he was finishing up his own analysis. He had graduated Harvard after World War II and returned in the sixties to do a Post Doctorate.

Professor Lansky was a celebrated combatant in verbal disputes and a paragon of virtue in the world of letters demanding proper or extreme compensation from corporations. He was an example that many times conflict led to gain. He often said, "If you don't fight, you can't fuck." I think this was his theory of conjugal relations, but it carried over into a world where he suggested that conflict was natural. He loved an argument.) Did having my feet bolted down lead to the joy I felt as a teenager and adult using toe-clips and then clip-on pedals on my bicycles. Another parallel with Dad was that he traversed the continent by motorcycle in the forties, I did much the same on a ten-speed bicycle in the seventies.

And Then the Cow Was Drownded

During my quest, I struggled with questions of identity; my mental illness came upon me just when I learned about Arjuna and Krishna. This account could be characterized as a bildungsroman or as a creative memoir. As you will see, in my prologue, I identified Krishna as the goal, right away. But, in a way, I identified myself as Arjuna. More on that.

Some days I resent. I resent being mentally ill. Being disabled, I immediately remind myself that I have a creative urge, which is not a handicap. I cherish my urge to paint, write and play harmonica, identify with others with mental illness, in our quest for dignity in the face of all kinds of pressures, that is Arjuna. This one neither regrets the past nor fears the future but has been on the streets and has lived in dismal state institutions. I worked my way out of poverty. Arjuna doesn't enjoy being visited by and monitored one or two times a week by a Case Manager, Mervyn Cartold. But Steve has worked as a Social Worker, is a client, knows both sides of the mental health dyad. Steve wants to find his own special function within the coffeehouse culture (after giving up on bar culture) where he meets friends, women, musicians, poets, and all sorts of writers. I sit in coffeehouses, work on reading and writing, occasionally play music with friends, and give public readings, a social circle. It is from this locus, this milieu, that I center my life. But I cannot maintain such relationships without the dose of orange pills and the meetings with Mervyn; he keeps me on the spiritual path. He challenges me to be Arjuna, to be Krishna. I am one with the universe . . . one with Bob Dylan, one with Krishnamurti, one with Maharaj, one with Muktananda, one with all.

These spiritual teachers provide a sub textual tool that advises me. The relatives that I love are compassionate partners and friends, when we disagree agreeably, I do not intend to lose contact. But having schizophrenia and alcoholism affects my understanding of the simplest relationships, and if I could explain where and how it goes wrong in a few sentences then I wouldn't be making the effort to tell a story. I guess some people have to take medicine for Diabetes, some get cancer, some go to a boss every day for an assignment. Me, I have to remember that I am and recognize that my gift is to stay in touch, stay in touch with that which is spiritual. Lately my identity is tied up with notions of compassion and planting seeds with others who have mental health problems, and/or drinking problems.

I worked nine years as a Social Worker. Both to give back to agencies and individuals who helped me, and to see the other side of the treatment model. The agency I worked at, and was helped by, used the Psychosocial Rehabilitation model. I used to say that those with the disease were best qualified to help those that owned it. This was before I was trained as a Chemical Dependency Counselor, and before I began to regularly participate in 12 Step programs. The right idea. A reason to write, a reason for readers to continue reading.

When I write about myself, sometimes I slip into the third person. This is not to say that there is a split personality, but I think I understand why many people used to think that schizophrenia is a split personality problem. Confused about my role in different situations, at times, I think of myself as Arjuna, spiritual, a warrior, cool and meditative, other times I think of myself as a Social Worker, compassionate, self-less and directed by the Agency I worked for, combining the task of helping, mentoring, counseling with completing certain paperwork and satisfying bureaucracy. Then there were times when I thought of my poet nature as the focus of my identity and hedonism, lyricism, runesmithery, and enjoying the moment; unlocking the key to the moment and its sixty-five instants were all that mattered.

And the artist, painter, suffering transience like Buddha taught, hanging it all on the wall for the world to see. These artistic impulses came even in a locked cell on a locked ward, on private grounds or when a job abandoned for hunger, drugs, alcohol, or discontentment with the world.

Living in the world as an artist seemed the most difficult, as though to do so meant isolation, and willingness to work exclusively on my own direction whatever that meant. Business, food, practical considerations seemed to fall away as the art generated its own schedule. The only way to do it. If fit into another schedule, it could not be pure, real, healthy expression of me.

As Lansk I saw myself as something of a loser. I had had moments of brilliance, some real successes. (Notably being named Poet Laureate of Over-the-Rhine, an urban ghetto neighborhood adjacent to downtown Cincinnati, and having a weekly radio show for nine years on WNKU, Northern Kentucky University's NPR affiliate.) But, as someone who somehow lost out on the great things in life. I had some great long bicycle rides, camping and competing, crossing the eastern third of North America, and traversing the state of Wyoming. Hell, I hopped freight trains and hitchhiked twelve thousand miles in one year. But, I left Harvard, after hard knocks. The choices Lansk made were a little bigger and badder than other people's. Getting humble was the problem. Healthy people don't hitchhike and hop freight trains. I lived on the fringe of marijuana subculture. And there was that protest when I drove off with a Rolls Royce on July 5th, 1978 outside Baltimore after the smoke-in in DC on the fourth. That landed me in Spring Grove, Maryland in a state mental hospital for a month. An older man died in the bed next to me. I used hydrotherapy and got pretty badly gorked up on pills that didn't help. I learned many years later that a lot of LSD experiments were done there. I tried LSD but, my thing was marijuana. I think I was the only one who understood the protest. One other man, the Harvard Neurologist at Sheppard and Enoch Pratt Hospital *seemed* to understand, "the means of production belong to the people." That was after my parents intervened through a Baltimore attorney and had me moved "voluntarily." But we were connected to Harvard, that counted. The shrink there was very confused about the Rolls Royce. The joyride in my file guaranteed attention from every mental health official whose path crossed mine.

So, in relationships I functioned with limited skills. On Haldol, with blind spots, working with others to try to help heal them and myself, I had a series of women in my life. Before Haldol though, I had the crisis in relationship that coincided with my leap into mental illness. When I describe it this way, it sounds clinical, believable, and practical. There was Harvard College, the big Eastern Establishment University, where I lived on the fringe, in the Dudley and Jordan Co-ops even as a freshman, against the advice of a tutor. I was only seventeen and had bicycled several thousand miles from the Midwest through Toronto, Ontario to take my place in the Ivy League. My father had been raised in Lynn, Massachusetts, and I had relatives in the region. He had earned his undergraduate degree at Harvard, although it was divided by his experience in the infantry during World War II. I arrived at Harvard as the Vietnam War wound down amidst great social uncertainty, unrest, and police brutality against people of color and youth. I was the longest-haired male freshman in 1975 and had a young lesbian friend cut my hair to my shoulders before classes started. The Dudley Co-op (called THE CENTER FOR HIGH ENERGY METAPHYSICS in 2002) had a tradition of being the most far-flung, counter-culture at Harvard. In the sixties during student protests twenty-eight of the thirty-five residents were arrested. (This is lore that might not actually be confirmable but was told to me twenty-one times.) The underage drinking and active drug use at Dudley known to many, and I thrust willingly, nay, enthusiastically into this milieu, I met a young woman who liked me. What struck me about her was her attractiveness, her attention to my place in the room when I first saw her, and as I began to get to know her, I learned that she could appear in many forms. She dressed one day in a sari, another in ragged jeans, another as if to go to a New York party. Fashion is everything, attractiveness and the mantra of Krishna consciousness rolled out her lips. She was a New York Senator's daughter and had spent much time in India before her father became Senator, when he was Ambassador. I fell for her, but among other things, the class difference between us made a relationship unlikely. The ?delusion? that I could be with her haunted me. We never had sex, but kissed and hugged affectionately. I think in some way when the Rolls appeared in the turnaround in Baltimore my attempt to drive away was for her love. At Harvard there were always rumors about Rolls Royces, and non-students who had created scandals posing as students. The rumor started when I was at the Dudley Co-op a year and a half after dropping out. This was when I proposed to the New York woman. The bottom dropped out for me. She claimed her brother was schizophrenic; I later connected that to my own consciousness. It doesn't make much sense now as I write, but I think I wanted to meet her brother and find out about this craziness firsthand. I ended up doing LSD with her friends. Keeping all these various details organized seemed impossible to compose with a mental illness, and I have a good facility for writing clear sentences. But as I start to describe my consciousness with techniques and explain what cannot be explained, I find the task daunting, challenging, and must rely on the help of my colleagues at Miami University to write this novel. Just introducing the story is a challenge. I have researched many accounts of mental illness and alcoholism and found my own comparable to most.

A sexual relationship with a Cincinnati Congressman's daughter, of a different political party to my upbringing, also figured in the situation. Her dad had been Mayor of Cincinnati and the one time I remember meeting him, he confused me with my brother, seventeen months my elder. The young woman was seeing both my brother and me. This confused me. She and I hitchhiked together in a blizzard from Cincinnati to Ithaca, New York. She was charismatic, but not quite as enigmatic as the Senator's daughter. When I think of my situation, and depersonalize it, so as to remove for a moment the psychic, personal, and social pain and loss that I recall feeling, I can liken it to the Aesop's Fable wherein the dog is walking across the bridge with a huge steak in his jaws, sees his reflection in the water and drops the steak into the river, hoping to have two. What a crude allegory, to describe humans like this, the domesticated beast lusting for flesh. We were all remarkable young people.

My counselor persuaded me that I need to forget the past and live in the present. I am aware that the present is all I can change, yet, somehow I believed that experiences built, one upon another, so the past had some role in how we perceived the present. His most convincing written source, the Bhagavad-Gita. He told me to meditate; have conscious contact with God. He explained that we are all one; we are light, love, knowledge, and God. We never die and we were never born. At first, I didn't understand his spiritual philosophy, but I recognized that my hitchhiking and wandering around the country was a poetic search with mystical goals. I visited a Zen Center in San Francisco where my aunt, Mom's younger sister, lived.

Later, when I had a radio show I invited her on as a guest, on the way to the station I asked her how I might address her on air, as I was in the habit of calling her Aunti Zen in my notes, and she said, "Sensei."

I also stopped briefly at the NAROPA Institute to learn about the Jack Kerouac School of Disembodied Poetics. At the Yeshe House I helped chop and stir-fry vegetables, played Go, and read some of the creative work of current students. When I asked about Kundalini Yoga, I was told by a teacher, whose name I don't remember, "Sit."

The young Senator's daughter was studying Eastern Philosophy, Buddhism and mysticism. I lived in Palo Alto with friends of Ken Kesey, who was written about by Tom Wolfe in *The Electric Kool-Aid Acid Test*. In these experiences, which were detailed in much of the content of my early writings, I explored smoking weed and drinking bourbon during encounters with older women. We tested our acumen at a variety of creative contests. There were wild parties that included readings from experimental original literary works. These adventures increased my sense of self-importance. I felt I could connect with the spirit. As I said, I took LSD at Harvard a few times when I was there as a non-student working on my first book: *Jack Acid*. I sat meditating, smoking reefer, one breath, one word—it was an extreme variation on "first word, best word."

In the eighties I lived a very doped up existence for several years after a stay in a state psychiatric facility in Cincinnati. I had two stays in Harding Hospital. After the first one, I lived in Columbus and worked at a bicycle shop. This was exhilarating and frustrating. I had worked on bicycles in high school and in California, but now I had had a taste of "treatment" and was trying to work and live on my own again. I didn't have a phone or furniture. Dad would call at work to berate me into returning to Harding. I was never honest with the owners about my situation. As I drifted away from mechanical work, I generated artwork similar to the work I had started in the hospitals. Early one morning I watched a shrouded redhead cross the street to enter a Krishna temple. From memory, I drew her portrait. While I was working on this drawing I was walking near campus and saw an attractive blonde woman walk into a bookstore. I followed her in and lost her in the art supplies area. I decided I better buy something. I found the cheapest item in the store. For thirty-nine cents, I bought a clay tool; just a round edged stick with a pin on one end and a little cork protecting the pin. When I got home, I went back to the drawing and rubbed at the pencil using a cork in a wine bottle, the heel of my hand against the thick green glass bottom. Then, thinking the piece took a too comely turn; I began to spill ink on it and pushed it around with the clay tool. When the ink dried, I went back into it with a pencil. Later I had an offset print made and titled it *Harë Krishna devotee.*

Generated 1979

HARË KRISHNA DEVOTEE

Ink and various pencils on paper, 13.5 x 10"
From the Private Collection of the artist
Steven Paul Lansky

This shrouded redhead visually apprehended crossing a street in Columbus, Ohio at 5 a.m. to enter a Harë Krishna temple was later rendered in a garret by using wide pencils and ink. The pencil work was rubbed with cork stuck in an empty wine bottle, the heel of the hand on the wide bottom, and the paper resting on a hardwood floor. Later ink was spilled and pushed around with a wooden clay tool then parts of the work were re-drawn with a number 2 pencil. Prints are available for ten dollars. I think of this work of the proof for the Harë Krishna ten-dollar bill. It would be the first U.S. paper currency with a woman's picture.

I sold them for ten dollars
and later gave them as gifts.
One day I was asked to leave the temple
in Columbus by one of the men in saffron
robes.
I told him Krishna was a mischievous child,
and he said that was wrong,
Krishna was "God."
After a time, I lost touch again
and headed by bus to Cincinnati
where I had another round of hospitalization.
I had another inpatient,
then outpatient stretch at Harding.
This time I followed doctor's advice on some
issues.
I began going to the Ohio State University
part time.
I was getting drunk at nearly any opportunity,
even while I was in a halfway house.
I had a girlfriend and I adored her,
but she feared sex, was a virgin, such that
I found being with her frustrating.

Generated 1980

CAROLYN 1

Chalk pastels and pencil on paper, 12.5 x 10"
From the Private Collection of the artist
Steven Paul Lansky

This first portrait of Carolyn was drawn while she was drawing also in her room as a pensioner in Worthington, Ohio. We were both in our early twenties, both aspiring writers and artists. Here we shared a free-spirited creative moment, inspired by our recent therapeutic changes, each other, and the awakening to living life as outsiders.

Generated Circa 1981

CAROLYN 2

Oil pastels on paper, 12.5 x 10"
From the Private Collection of the artist
Steven Paul Lansky

This second portrait of Carolyn was drawn while she posed in her new apartment. We had each moved to new digs, six or seven miles from one another. She taught me about contemporary music. Wearing a "The Beat" T-shirt, her hair was a bit shorter than in the first portrait. Her laundry bag hung behind her.

Steven
Carolyn

Generated Circa 1984

CAROLYN 3

Ink on paper, 11x 14"
From the Private Collection of the artist
Steven Paul Lansky

This third portrait of Carolyn was drawn from memory. We had broken up and I had moved to Cincinnati. Out of contact for several years, we reconnected. She had written several drafts of a novel and was painting large canvases. Impressed by the braid, funky hat, and dangly earrings, this was to be my final version of her, painted after we saw each other a couple more times.

introduction continued

I had met her in a sex therapy group at Harding Hospital once I was an outpatient. We were instructed not to have sexual relations with anyone in the program, but there we were. She was a painter, musician and writer with great talent. She was also a drunk. She had admitted her problem with alcohol, but couldn't control it, while I had not admitted my problem and couldn't control it. We were a pair. I had her over to my apartment for dinner, served two separate beef stews, one cooked with wine, for me, and the other without, for her. On one occasion we went to a party with a bottle of white wine for the hostess. My girlfriend guzzled most of it and whined complainingly when someone else drank the rest. She had a black and white photo of an erect penis over her bed. We were drawing together in her room, and she said, "I have marionettes in the attic." A fabulous sensual kisser, she resisted going further. I once touched her breasts inside her shirt on a waterbed. She attended Ohio Wesleyan. I think the break with OSU and the shrink there had a lot to do with her ongoing rejection of our sex relations. This lovely young woman dumped me as I fell off of Mellaril and became befuddled. Mellaril had a retro effect on my orgasms, but I never told the psychiatrist about this; too paranoid.

When I got to Cincinnati in 1982, I was homeless for a while. Before returning to my hometown, I hitched and took the bus to Santa Fe to see a woman that I had met there. (Note the pattern, great passion for intelligent, attractive, sensitive women with dark sensual qualities.) She was much older, and on seeing her, I learned that she had breast cancer. Her letters and spiritual warmth had carried me during the long tough spell in Columbus. She had been a muse as I began inpatient therapy. She sent pressed desert flowers, and a photo of the guru, Muktananda, his mantra on the back. After seeing her, and returning by thumb, my cash ran out. A sane man would have found a job; I abandoned everything in Columbus and bicycled overnight to Cincinnati. Once in Cincinnati, I was doped up on Haldol. For the first time in my life, I had admitted myself voluntarily to a state hospital. At first the dose was very high, and I was not nearly as functional as I became after two years after gradually lowering the dose. I think I started at forty milligrams and ended up at five. The counselor that I met in Cincinnati, with whom I still meet, followed Muktananda to India, before meeting and living with another guru, Maharaj. This counselor, Mervyn Cartold, saved me. His interest and affection for me kept me from killing myself. Mervyn said, "When Maharaj was dying, I asked him what I should do. He said I had been very helpful when an elderly woman devotee had psychiatric issues at the ashram. I found a psychiatrist, procured a prescription and medication for the woman. She stabilized. Maharaj said I could do this kind of work back in the United States where I was from. I asked him how I would get clients? Maharaj said, 'Don't worry, I'll send them to you.'" I concluded that Maharaj had referred me to Mervyn through my friend, Linda, in Santa Fe.

I am told that the more suicides a person has met, the higher risk he is for that end. This statistic puts me at very high risk. The counselor led me into Eastern Philosophy gently and gradually, sharing mantras, and compassion. After about two years I had an apartment and a job. The Haldol was down to five or ten milligrams. I became a co-incorporator of a self-help group, a Mental Health Consumer Clubhouse. We called it C.A.P.E., Inc. (Consumer Action Project and Evaluation). I lived in an urban ghetto, on Main Street, (later I would be known as the "Main Street Poet.") I worked at the Community Chest as a data entry clerk for a Home Health Agency. I contacted the painter from Columbus, went up to visit on a bus for a conference on Mental Health Consumer Empowerment. My old girlfriend was not "out of the closet" about her psychiatric condition. She claimed to be willing to try birth control, the sponge. She came for a visit, but it was the same old shit. (This relationship, mercifully, is avoided in the text to follow.) Then I met the woman I'll call Marlena.

Marlena was a Social Worker, but not "my social worker." When we met, she was married for the second or third time, this time to a prominent Northern Kentucky lawyer. I entered her time sheet into a database and noticed that her last name was hyphenated. A liberated lass. She dressed in black leather a lot. She seduced me. Mervyn told me, when I admitted to falling in love with a married woman, "if it wasn't you, it would've been someone else." Marlena and I were drinking partners as the relationship developed. It was balls out sexy, a wild and fun romp that ended rather badly. She called my Mental Health Consumer friends MHC's and discouraged me from spending time with them. She liked my musician and dancer friends, going with me to hear me play harmonica in bars with my neighbor, Leo and his jazz trio. Leo played piano, and his wife choreographed modern dance shows. Leo introduced me to friends at parties as a poet. I had my first couple of poems published. They were about living in poverty in America, its bittersweet nature. Interested in sharing my unconscious observations, I made them conscious for others. Poverty was hard and painful mostly because it involved waiting, frustration, and my schizophrenia. I was becoming socially adjusted, slowly, after identifying mainly with others who had mental illness, alcoholism, and poverty as their daily struggles. My counselor said I was bright, high functioning, and insightful, but clearly needed the help and guidance offered. It became clearer to me that the medication was a key to survival.

This novel attempts to convey the problems of the medication, and how it is necessary, and does not resolve or dissolve the essential dilemma of affecting understanding. Mine is not the typical story of someone who thinks, *I took the medication, it cured me, now I don't need it.* As you will see, the problem is subtler. I consider myself a social person who relies on friendship and relationships much as others do. These transitions from one group of friends to another were in my case similar to others as well. I think that I had to make some choices about people, places, and the kinds of things I spent time doing, as I left the active drinking and drugging. As I took Marlena to meet my counselor, I began to have a few moments of awakening to the dysfunction alcohol and marijuana caused me. Mervyn drank whiskey and beer and smoked marijuana around me at times when we socialized away from Cincinnati. He lived in Oxford, Ohio, where he had attended Miami University, and commuted to Cincinnati. He confessed to flipping out and taking a sledgehammer to a row of parking meters in downtown Oxford one morning. He had just received his divorce papers from his second wife, his girlfriend was home in Scotland, there was an audit going on at the agency, and an Oxford cop had been rude to him. To a guy who had stolen a Rolls Royce as a wacked out protest, the counselor's act impressed. We grew close. He never judged me for anything I did. This man and his work with me constitute hardly quantifiable areas of clarity and blindness where understanding shifted for both of us.

In an effort to keep this novel from being just a recounting of events in a pattern that will become increasingly definable, I think it is important to recognize in the protagonist affection for, and distrust of, different authorities. The guidance of an other, given freely to one such as myself was extremely significant, (as anything anyone ever says might be fodder for some wacked out resentment that carries more energy than it should, a delusion that many alcoholics will understand.) My attentiveness to details of language, and the filters of my disease make me sensitive and paranoid to a degree that I hope others with mental illness understand. I want to avoid summarizing or characterizing my qualities, rather, I hope to give a reader a chance to share insight and at times, through irony, to have insight before, or beyond mine.

I need to say a bit more about Marlena before abstracting. During our time together, I whittled the Haldol down to four milligrams, had my first serious bout with hemorrhoids, a side effect of the medication causing constipation. Diet could correct this problem perhaps, but the voices I hear, and with my mental obstinacy, well, limited eating, and exercise rules challenge anyone. Maybe it was obstipation. Due to the combined effects of drinking, pot smoking, and Marlena, I lost my job, a bit of scandal ensued, and I turned to janitorial work. There was a moment when my mother told me she went to work early one morning.

"Why?" I asked.

"A coworker has an alcohol problem and we wanted to meet to see if we could come up with a way to help her." I later learned that the night I spent in jail, Mom locked her keys in her car with the engine running outside city hall. She worked for the city manager.

And Then the Cow Was Drownded

I went back up to five milligrams and that became the definitive minimum. Marlena divorced her lawyer husband. Then we separated when I was in a jealous rage over the new boyfriend. Her new boyfriend a black man lived with her and said it was his brother dating her. As a good liberal, this should have been understandable, but as a drunk and a schizophrenic, it ended violently. My account of this is recursive building the details of the narrative with each telling. The period following my break-up with Marlena coincides with being named Poet Laureate of Over-the-Rhine. My most humble jobs have led to some of my most accessible and accepted poetry. Something about janitorial work led me into rhythms and the serenity necessary to begin to routinize my creativity and focus it enough to draw in readers, then radio listeners:

> legs, patterns of moving oaks steady
> over damp rag heads,

I had related trains to poetry before, their rhythms had been instrumental to the voice of prose work as well. So, here in *Cow Drownded* the janitorial feel was allowed more scope and range combining poetry with prose:

> Trains pass at switches in the night--
> head beams cut gleaming paths.

In an attempt to reach a larger audience without too much respectability, I returned to college at The Union Institute. This program allowed me to receive credit for previous experiences. They called them "prior learnings." Among the experiences that were documented for credit were my visual art making, recordings of radio appearances, harmonica playing, public relations writing for The Jewish Hospital of Cincinnati, teaching ESL, work on poetry, and *Jack Acid*. Just before returning to college, I met

Urban Rat, with whom I got sober, and formed a union. She took her name from an angry punk sensibility, fiery and indifferent to anything South. I wish I could say that the trembling in my limbs caused by the Haldol was no more than waves of inner joy like the swaying of a lotus bud on the lake when a cluster of bees caught inside pollinates it. Is my story worthy of such a simile? Do I sink into the worldly plane away from Arjuna's peaceful mirth when I accept my ex-wife's assessment of my path? To talk about it is to crack the eggs of perplexity over the edge of her expensive cookware. I'd rather lift the heart of my homespun iron skillet, a tool she wished to discard, as she was ready to discard me as I strove to write my way through her charges, her claims, her own unwillingness to face herself, and her need to be creative. I've mixed some metaphors, struggled to give a fair picture of how she failed me, and also characterized the essences of my clinical schizophrenia as our life together unraveled. I think the break-up was precipitated by the medical problems, but in social relations there are not square edges. And to take responsibility without insight is to be blind. These episodes are told in a recursive structure similar to the chapters on Marlena. Urban Rat used to fight with me. She used to say, that she did not want to become a stepping-stone to a trophy wife. I never argued with her when she started. I'm not sure what it means to make a person a stepping-stone, and I have a problem with the descriptor "trophy" connected to wife. You may agree with her. My reaction to her accusations was to feel distanced, driven into my imagination. Now, neither drinking nor smoking marijuana, my malady was more clearly identified as "just" "mild" schizophrenia. I took the pills and went to work. I worked on myself with Mervyn, learning much

Generated circa 1989

VIOLET

Oil pastel on paper, 23.5 x 17.5"
From the Private Collection of the artist
Steven Paul Lansky

The style of this energetic portrait of the artist's partner of twelve years was a response to comments of Katherine Thanas, his maternal aunt, a Zen Buddhist Priest. She suggested expressive portraiture that blended with the movement and color of abstracts. This was among the most recent works in the 2002 exhibit.

about interpersonal relations, while working on my job to help those who were "lower functioning" mentally ill and chemically dependent. I took training in Chemical Dependency Counseling and wrote stories down as well. One class was called "Social Deviance of Alcoholism," the teacher, a Hamilton County probation officer who packed a large pistol in a shoulder holster let us write on any related subject. I wrote about Malcolm Lowry, *Lunar Caustic,* his posthumously published novella describing his month in Bellevue after drinking and playing piano in longshoreman bars, and how Lowry believed that he was doing research for writing at the time. All along I hoped to eventually support myself as an artist. I produced a play I had written about suicide called: HARD NOSED, based on my stay at Harding Hospital in the late seventies. The promotional material for the play included this blurb: "Hard Nosed is a psychiatrist with a mission, trapped in a suspended memory, with his patient, Rex Ronson. The two share a bitter dilemma which ultimately releases Rex Ronson into a different reality."

I wrote grants from the city of Cincinnati for the play and an earlier project suggested by my dad. His idea was to create (he didn't know the term) broadsides of my urban poems and show them at a downtown restaurant/gallery. Urban Rat and I had a meaningful and passionate courtship. In the process of describing and creating an account of our relationship I may betray my own weaknesses, show the reader areas of altered understanding more clearly than I see them myself, and ultimately present schizophrenia and its remission uniquely. The end of our marriage, caused by what started as a "happy accident" which reduced the dosage of the Haldol, led me to an exhilarating physical freedom for which I cannot take complete responsibility and yet claim the end result to be for the best.

A pharmacist accidentally gave me point five-milligram tablets instead of five-milligram tablets before my wife and I went on a vacation in a relatively remote area of Canada. I figured out the problem, noting that the tablets were smaller, and on the phone with the team, discussed lowering the dosage permanently. Urban Rat agreed to the reduction conditional on my increasing it if we got into trouble. Several months later we got into trouble, and I refused, due to the physically and mentally intoxicating relief from the Haldol's side effects and the confusion about who was making the choices and decisions about what was in my best interest. Yes, I decompensated into schizophrenia and lost awareness. Urban Rat confronted me in Boston at my family Thanksgiving after I blacked out on a subway train while we were exploring my old haunts in Cambridge. We flew back to the Midwest and separated. But, thankfully, I recovered and returned to the work of reading and writing.

I became a teacher as I had wanted and took bit parts in some local blue videos. The details of this part of my story will show how sex and intimacy in my life continued to trouble me as I reached mid-life, but that I came to accept my way of being in the world with sufficient meaning and self-expression to feel actualized.

I traveled to St. Petersburg, Russia to further my studies. I'm not sure how to explain my ending, except to say that some things will be clear while others will remain a mystery. The journey continues with new tools, and new friends.

I'd like to share a few words about the title of the novel. When I was visiting Harvard in the seventies, with the express purpose of arousing the interest of the Senator's daughter and defeating my rival for her attentions, I came across a nursery rhyme in the Oxford English Dictionary. In an attempt to resolve the Jack Acid project, I was working on at the time, I immediately connected the rhyme to one I had heard at the Second Perennial Poetical HOOHAW! in Eugene, Oregon the year before. There was a bastardization of the rhyme that ended in a line that struck me strangely. The bastardization as recorded in the OED mentioned a cow. In Hindu mythology, there is the use of the cow as a metaphor to describe the eras within time as we, as human beings, know them. These eras are known as "yugas." The current Yuga is Kali Yuga, and it is symbolically described as a cow on one leg. Here are the rhymes:

L ottie Lockett lost her pocket
Lily Parker found it
Not a penny was there in it
Only ribbon round it.

The bastardization is:

Kitty litter all around it
Patty Fischer went and found it
Less could work it then
Than said the cow was drownded

The title is a further bastardization of the last line to:

And Then the Cow was Drownded

And Then the Cow Was Drownded

by Paul Thanas

I sometimes wonder if that is what Krishna meant—
Among other things—or one way of putting the same thing:
T. S. Eliot

"He who thinks that this slays and he who thinks that this is slain; both of them fail to perceive the truth; this one neither slays nor is slain."

from the Bhagavadgita, a Song-Sermon

The Dream Palace

I heard in a somnambulant fervor, conversation between two, three, four, six siddhas, learning Eastern philosophy in the library of the Esplanade Temple in February from the side roof, reading in the sun, one of them talked about a beaded necklace, with a ring on it, a silver cocaine spoon. Chatter about post-Vietnam era dental work available in the USA only with gold and silver. Gutta percha from Malaysia under international control. The World Trade Center, harmonica music transmitted into the teeth of the world, in harmony with the human system.

They heard about trap rock and maple syrup, from North Ontario, traded for car parts, shipped to Cuba through the Panama Canal from British Columbia after making the trip across Canada through Winnipeg. The Lakers take trap rock down to Detroit, bring car parts back, to Bruce Mines, Ontario, on the North Channel of Lake Huron.

NAFTA, one called it. North American Free Trade Agreement. The language obtuse, obfuscating. The Chinese wanted it. I listened. Bicycle parts shipped to from Taiwan. Erie, Pennsylvania to the Hudson Bay. Don't know much about the Missouri River basin. It extends from Montana through North and South Dakota, Nebraska, Wyoming, and Missouri, it empties alongside the Mississippi, and the Gulf of Mexico, New Orleans, the big Easy. Where all this is supposed to happen to some rich kid from Cambridge, Massachusetts, a boy, or young man, who attended Harvard College.

But how to they get to Cuba without running through the blockade? It's easy, they go to Gitmo. The USA military prison. The bad guys run it. They load the ship with sugar cane, and rum, it goes across the Caribbean to Bermuda right out of Havana. In Bermuda it gets distributed, some to Russia, some to the United States, but the price comes from Canada. Distilled tree sap, and car parts. The Russian secret is they're hidden in Bermuda.

know, the same question came up many years ago when I was in New Orleans after Mardi Gras. A young man, less than twenty at the time, I had run away from home with a band of gypsies. Let's say I was on the road from Harvard, running from an unrequited love named Annie, who was bound for India by jet plane, while I drove off in a van with a sixties guru who had figured a way to buy a panel truck with S.S.I. and committed enough budget to finagle five or six students, fuel, pot, beer, cigarettes and a little wine in the deep snowy Winter all the way to the French Quarter and who cared if one fellow, call him Jack Acid (yeah me!) stayed in the Big Easy after it was all over and the youngsters all headed right back where they came from after the last band on that long, late, early, night morning after all the parades.

And Then the Cow Was Drownded

The Dream Palace on Frenchman Street where it all began. Mardi Gras whistling, fat black singer mambo into two a.m. bustin' out tune after tune dancin' vibe on and on like a snake of silver on a floor with tiles that spun like chameleons, changing colors as night twisted into hair, costumes and the only words remembered from that late night, a girl asking, "Does your mother know where you are?" Surprised, couldn't answer and she did not. Stopped dancing, given a blow like that on the loose ideas that had all spun through my night turned mind, fuzzy from beer, a haze of lights. The Dream Palace first discovered when we were on the LSU campus taking showers in a dorm, let in by some kids, and chanced on a bulletin board with a note from a girl looking for a companion to go to Mexico. I had called the phone number and there was a message, someone who said to meet at The Dream Palace in the French Quarter on Frenchman Street, so I dragged my friends there after the parades, and I had already checked out the Palace and it was a dive bar with parachute silk hanging from one ceiling and the night sky, including the Milky Way in a great dark circle above the dance floor and the stage. After the parades I wanted to hear Professor Longhair, in person, but didn't know where. This place was much better than Fat City with its, lit up highway sign, and the mirror-walled disco we'd crashed the night before where I had danced, dressed in three-piece blue velour suit, and we never did find Fess, who it turned out, was at the Superdome the whole time and we were gettin' bad tips from lame bartenders until we just crawled back to The Dream Palace with our underage crowd and fit right in until now when the band left at two-thirty, Wednesday morning.

Then with a few clumsy containers, dark and shabby, beer breath smelly, out of the rain came a few dark men, afros gleaming, a gold tooth in front . . . the guy looked like Jimi. The guy was a ringer for a dead guy in The Dream Palace at almost three in the morning after Mardi Gras and you think I'm making it up. I'm with my Harvard math genius friends and telling them sotto vocé that I screwed with two of the girls in the dorm on the same night the weekend before we left and they're uh-uhhing like I'm some kind of really cool gangster. By now, I'm a bit ashamed and stunned. They sort of whistle disbelief because they are probably not even really there, they've hopped back in the old van with Damon on their way back through Virginia and Pennsylvania. I'm imagining they're there with me, keeping me company in this late early foray into murky water on the shores of Lake Pontchartrain. One's blonde, one's fair, one with glasses the other none; fresh faced longhair preppies their dad head of a house called Mather. I know I've gone too far, and with the girls back in Cambridge it feels safe here, and I know I'm never going to be at peace again because I'm thinking of the seed I wasted and see that's the demon I'm running from into dream.

A Jimi look alike on Frenchman Street in New Orleans on a rainy, Wednesday, drummer, bass player, and this light-skinned negro with that shiny gold front tooth right in front, yeah, tuning that guitar into Ladyland. Cannot remember how long he played or the songs that juked and slid down that shiny slick microphone stand, into our propped up sneakers, yes we sat so close that our feet were on carpet by his and loud loud loud I can't hear anymore because of all that feedback collected like so many needles in the brain. He sang songs that had been sung so long, and answered the questions so new, that now he played 'em, and they'd never been played, and were again on the collected mind of all reason, and we came down for an instant, then were back on that wire, that cable, that string, that strand taking us right up into the void above us, on that ceiling, then we'd attest that he could do no more, and a string broke, and he played, as he was before, and in a breath said to us that he could play just as well, without the string, and with the thin wire gleaming like a strand of silk, his hand blurred across frets, and pick-ups like blown glass, or snakeskin, or luminous flow, prismatic colorful sound striking chord after chord, of being, in each of us until he stopped for a moment, propped the electric instrument against a stand, went to the drum, and tapped the snare, till the sound from the guitar feedback was a melody, and we were all so damn entranced, it was like the world had opened up a chasm, then the drummer was playing the guitar, and singing, and it went on until it stopped, and they just packed up, and left, and we went back to a corner, and sat there, or was I alone, and all this was imagined, like dust on the floor.

The question? *If you could be any animal in your next life, what would it be?* And this whole little story about New Orleans had to be told to a traveler somehow, somewhere in the ethereal radio night of the Winter deep and holy.

After all that acid rock, feedback and buzz Halloween felt like a light-year ago. Left by my Harvard friends, and deciding not to get on the bus to Mexico or California or wherever it would be driven, I weighed in at another back-alley bar. This one, called Moriarty's after the friend of another Jack, in the Latin Quarter, and had an all-night feel as well. Dark booths, six pool slates, a grimy jukebox, and a lady bartender, ahh–I felt welcome.

The barmaid kept me on a string, somehow drinking top shelf bourbon, if I remember right: Austin Nichol's Wild Turkey, not the good stuff, only the best, not quite though, a little bit less aged, from Kentucky, not Tennessee, certainly a Southern drunk rolling around less aged than the very, very, best bourbon of a top notch, good enough to dip a nib, and Archango, yes, Pedro, while Panama Red, "more please, Amy," whiskey glass, tipped to the bottle, yup Panama Red, bandito, who loves to eato, fancy that all over the bathroom walls. So, let it be known that I was trying to buy weed from strangers in a bar in the Latin Quarter of New Orleans at sixteen, would you believe eighteen? And not until I had wired, phoned Brawly, asking for money for the truck, I had sold to Will in Cincinnati over Christmastime, in a bit of haste, and with weed, not really cared for, and was there a full price paid, and weren't there some codicils, and such that? Soon there were fresh fives, tens, twenties, crinkly green, and I'm living in the strangest dream flop house room of squalor, with a gas burner, somehow taken apart, blue flame, heat, eight track, bad, loud rock 'n I can't roll, too stoned, seventies, crystal, rock shit and they smoke my pins, and needles and I give this big-ass guy, with hair out to there, a Vincent Bach trumpet mouthpiece, so he won't throw me out, then I'm sending a lady (of-the-night?) for *The New Yorker,* and not getting any, next thing I know I'm back in Moriarty's downing vitamins? The guys with the vitamins tell me there's a Baptist Mission, where they'll feed me, house me free up on Esplanade, "do we walk there together?" I can't remember how I got there, a long walk, and were they with me? On the way we pass The Theosophical Society (remember Annie Besant?) a place I had hung in another city; San Francisco had one where a different Acid had adjusted himself to the room long enough to play harmonica. And I am not sure if the vitamin sellers walked all the way . . . to the Krishna Consciousness Center, on Esplanade, in New Orleans.

"Do you care we walked a long way?" I asked, not sure, if I was one, or three, and a man showed me a room downstairs, with tiles, or were they? There were idyllic paintings, of gopis, and a blue-skinned flute playing youth, long, blueblack hair, a robe over his back, and many, colored streams with the greenest trees all so pure, and full of light, and was I in nirvana? For how long? I sat on the floor, in peaceful sanctuary, then there were others. Young, and middle-aged, thin, fat, with varied hues of shaved heads, saffron robes, bowing, dancing, prostrate, and chanting. And a hierarchy, that emerged from the sublime light, everywhere.

A scented sanctuary. I sat long and still in the candle-lit yellow-walled room, barefoot, knees tucked against my bony chest. An orange robed siddha invited me to stay for vegetarian dinner, exchange my clothes and pack for a robe. "We'll keep them safe," said Javara Djidt as he took my few possessions, money and passport. Djidt was stocky, a former gunner in the marine corps, without tattoos, he struggled to keep a friendly tone when shepherding us, his spiritual troops. His demeanor was warm, an athlete though not quite so lithe as a cyclist, or skater.

Incense fragrance blended with veggie foods, yogurt sublime sauces, nectar, chickpeas, dahl over steaming white rice prepared to sensate perfection. Assigned to a bunk bed in the men's dormitory, I tried to sleep on a plywood board on springs, no mattress. Men in each bunk, jostling, breathing, all this a very foreign place, with fifteen others. The shower, at four a.m., cold, shitting without toilet paper, just an urn of hot water and soap to wash your hand. At four thirty, we danced, and chanted, instructed in the mantra by Javara Djidt: *Harë Krishna, Harë Krishna, Krishna Krishna, Harë Harë, Harë Rama, Harë Rama, Rama Rama Harë Harë,* and again, 108 times as counted, on a strand, of beads. There remains a mysterious sense of purpose in my heart that said to me that this was the **right** thing to be doing, that chanting was the end in itself, that my time in the company of these siddhas was the true meaning of enlightenment and that I **am,** continuously created.

Regenerated 1998

TEMPLE AT NEW ORLEANS

Digital print on canvas, 22 x 19"
From the Private Collection of the artist
Steven Paul Lansky

Originally an oil pastel on paper 12.5 x 10" this work has been damaged. Fortunately, a slide was used to regenerate and enlarge the piece. One of the artist's earliest efforts, generaged* in a locked room at The Jewish Hospital of Cincinnati in 1978, the work captures the euphoria, and disorientation remembered from a brief stay at the Esplanade St. Harë Krishna Temple after Mardi Gras. The work evolved over a period of several days, by turning the paper around, and around.

Reading the *Bhagavad-Gita,* and the *Srimad Bhagvitam* on the roof of the library, lying in the sun. Chanting together, dancing barefoot on cold tile, gopis in robes, in a separate area. The tulasi tree brought in without a bud upon it, and the next time only hours, or was it only a day later, there were ovate leaves spiraling around the branches, bits of green smelling fragrant, and the miracle of how many/how few days passed in this way. They called me "Bhakta Jack" and I swept the porch, and the steps, and the walkways, to the sidewalk. The same job I'd had at Palo Alto Bike Shop. Food and housing, for sweeping the perimeter. Could I become a book salesman (selling Prahupad's *The Bhagavad-Gita As It is*)? Fellowship with the shaved heads, but for braided strands off the back of their pates, shiny and fleshy. I remembered Annie, as I read of Krishna's sister, Draupudie. An unrequited love of mine became a deity for a culture—her family had lived in India; she had spoken the mantra to me. Arjuna came to life as I studied in deep aroma secret blended bliss. *I am Arjuna,* I thought.

And we lay prostrate, to the white stone deities decked in offerings, of brightly colored fragrant petals, and freshly cut fruits. The devotees danced, chanting, ecstatic, movement swaying, bouncing, and moving, in swirls of orange, reds, different hues, of flesh. I attended Sanskrit class unfocused, and confused, by the wavy forms, and exotic, and melodic sounds. I don't recall a single cypher, as my ecstatic state blurred the lesson. Tambours like I had never seen, skillfully tapped, and played along, with sitar, harmonium in harmonic pleasure, graced almost every chanting period. I asked several of the robed men: who was the spiritual master? And, where was **he**? There was a photo, of him on the throne. The answers came in another tongue. I think Prahupad was no longer living and that there could be no living spiritual master. I thought I was seeking the truth . . . "take me to your leader." I had a sense of lapse and wondered *was I slipping into a cult? Was I building a cult around me?*

The hardwood floors upstairs were warm underfoot. Sometimes Javara Djidt let me wear socks to chant. The plywood bed made sleep hard.

We took a ride in a van to skid row, to pick up bums, and drunks, to join the others. As a new convert, in training, I sat, and watched, grateful to be "in the van." We stopped, and offered housing, and vegetarian food, and one, or two of the street tramps listened but none entered. They clung to their possessions, stuffed in paper, and plastic bags, they smelled of tobacco and shame. "Naw, naw, I ain't," one said.

On another day, we took a country drive to a farm where black, and white, spotted cattle roamed a recently fenced, moist, green, pasture under the watchful eye of a confident, skilled, Siddha farmer. These animals seemed the picture of health, in essence. We walked to a recently constructed dormitory, that frightened me. It was several floors of the smallest, unpainted wood-framed rooms, with low doorways, and sills, crudely built without any attention to craft, or fine detail. This was utilitarian housing, as yet un-populated. Bunk beds built in, plywood, and four, or six bunks to a room, with small sealed windows, and bare bulbs for night. A warehouse, cluttered with incense, and trinkets, for packing, and shipping seemed only slightly more friendly. The farmhouse, warm, and quaint made me wonder who chose to stay there bowing and sharing offerings to the deities of Radha, Krishna, and perhaps, Arjuna. One trainee chose to stay. I rode back to New Orleans, and Esplanade.

The garish blue, and yellow temple, with red trim a welcome sight. On our return I swept again, feeling some conscious choice of the city over the farm.

Javara Djidt, always the marine, drill, sergeant, instructor in all ways Krishna, even calisthenics, to do in private time, seated us on the floor of a leader's office, a tall, thin man, with dark, hair shadow around the back of his head. The man took a stentorian voice around minions, contrasted with articulate, and lilting diction when patient. This leader seemed to be the highest authority at the temple. He had a low desk with typewriter in front of floor cushions; a spot from which he rose to speak, asking five of us: *"If you could be any animal in your next life, what would it be?"* Bhaktas of various shapes, and sizes sat pondering. One said, "A deer, gentle and swift, running in a green forest." Another, "A black crow circling above a field of corn." And a third, "An eagle preying boldly on fish, field mice, and moles." Then my turn, "I'd be Krishna," I said. The quiz stopped.

The teacher asked me, "You took LSD at Harvard?" *How did he know* I wondered, who told him? "Yes," I said. "Do you want to stay, and type for me?" he asked, after Javara Djidt had instructed us that to stay we must shave. "No," I said, choosing to type my own words, not those of a Harë Krishna devotee.

I was attached to the hair on my head. By this time, I developed a sore throat from my carelessness. The call to type sounded like a clerical job, the haircut would mean joining Djidt's troop, all-in-all a destiny of servitude with severe limits on expressing individuality. I might be Arjuna, on my terms.

I was driven in the van to a hospital and given some of my own money, to buy medication. I waited in line for twenty minutes, saw a man in the queue, who resembled my Jewish grandpa. I wondered if Grandpa, and Grandma knew my whereabouts, if Mom and Dad told my grandparents that they didn't know if I had gone to India with a woman. In a strange transcendent moment, I realized to a small degree how far I was from home. As I filled out the paperwork for an indigent medical i.d. I came to the question: religion? Wrote: **Sufi**. Scared and alone I took a streetcar to a pharmacy, bought penicillin then rode back to Esplanade where I picked up my belongings then walked, stricken to the place of the big gray dog. I cried when I hadn't enough to journey back to Cincinnati, and I thought of dear Annie in Cambridge and what it had meant to love her and not be loved. In the temple I had believed I might see her again. **She** had been bound for India and that kind of trip was always possible if I shaved and chanted long and hard. One longing excised the sense of nirvana, desire was to be my painful path, destined still to wander, I bought a ticket to Atlanta, boarded the machine bound for colder climes, bidding bye-bye to the Big Easy.

COFFEE

"Whole cloth," said the curiously indifferent young man who said to himself that he was only a storyteller and knew for a fact, that he would never have need to call a spade a spade, except as an exercise in lofty halls for the practitioners of Ivy League dribbling brawls.

There was a dream dance one acted out, and the ace of spades fell on the floor between her and me.

"Is that a novel?" asked the psychologist, pointing to the book which the artist carried with him in a tattered black hand, so loosely woven that the tungsten of truth would have bitten only those who knew J. P. Morgan's morbid tale about Thomas Edison, and the young artist who came to be obsessed with his talking dog, and never offered to write the barking voice off as background (his father's, the psychologist's, barking dog voice) noise until the last day of his father's favorite March came crashing over him like a ton of cartoons wrapped in sweetness like cotton candy; the sheriff's deputies took him away while he, at twenty years old, was watching *Sesame Street* in his parent's home.

. . . while the dog chases a stick around the Reverend's table (*Mother's best friend was named Regine W. Ransohoff. Her handwriting was so terrible, she once received a letter addressed to Reverend Van Sneeth. The 'Rev,' as we called her, had donated tables to the parks.*), the young man's fingers trembling cold, and his toes no warmer. He lived in the park and played with a brown and white, stray spaniel.

"In any case, mention it to your wife," the young man had said to his father on the phone.

The writer called to the dog, and she came padding up the creek gathering stones between her teeth. The dog and the artist were the same spirits. Lucky for them, stones were moveable.

"The truth about who said it?" I asked the question. No doubt, I'm famous for questions; form in transit, a piece of legislation, which brought the writer to the park, thinking about police cadets' initiative.

"He said he's gonna be a cop." The writer commented on this man's quiet statement to the father of the writer. (Like father saying, "DO I HAVE TO BE A COP AND TELL YOU WHAT TO DO?) The writer wanted to be President of the whole United States. And he said, "I read that other novel years ago and I'm not unwilling to write fifteen more for her if it would make her happy. I am happy, if you want to know how I feel about it," he would say, and eyes would go rolling around in his head like drunken Rigoletto 'round a room. (*I remembered watching my brother sleepwalk in circles around his bedroom. My parents liked opera, so I just started thinking of him as Rigoletto.) I was the subject of rumors, and for certain I was king. King. King someone.*

"The psychologist's wife is a literary critic and grand Queen who concerns herself with Rigoletto, my brother, and his redundant qualifier." (He said he was the most, best kid in the family.) In the writer's words, "she had a malady that one cannot dispose of properly and it was redundant as well."

"I would only say it to my first agent, because I know the Queen reads a lot. The psychologist is known to have recommended Edwin Newman's book *Plainly Speaking* to the artist." I said out loud to the therapist.

"The psychologist said you weren't in your own dream," said mother.

"No, you're wrong. He was talking about the writer," I said.

. . . and he brought his dead dog along, when he said, "GO TO HARVARD." (*The family pupdog, Ralph, was killed by a car on my eighteenth birthday in 1976, while I was at Harvard.*)

"What about the novel?" Mother had asked on the phone eight months ago.

"Well," he says, (And it's not certain who **he** is.) "You won't understand it."

She didn't flinch through the car window when she crashed last week. Why should she flinch aloud on the phone? "Mother, is my dream girl real?"

"You mean she wasn't Jewish?"

"So, they're my myths, and Harvard was just getting ready for . . . wait, about my dream:

I had the dream again last night. This time she was more complete. Her form hadn't changed, but the content was new. We were touching practically the whole time. I remember it so well because she was so small inside my arm. My arm was hooked around her bare lower back. Or was her arm hooked around my bare lower back. Naturally, she was shorter than me. Her hair and eyebrows were equally dark. The eyebrows danced across her forehead when she laughed. She laughed more often than usual last night. I may have been telling jokes. I can remember a lot of jokes. We were at a party, as usual. That's the part the psychologist couldn't comprehend.

"If she's so lovely and you, 'you are deeply involved' (he would quote me) as you say, then why don't you stay home with her." And I would be forced to point out to him that these were dream perceptions we were discussing, and he knew as well as I that I had no place to bring her . . . I slept in the park.

"Perhaps some part of your unconscious is obsessed with parties." He might have said.

I was thrust back to early childhood dream analysis with the psychologist/dad before I could feel how much I missed the rich touching from the dream.

"Never mind the party part," I may have said to him. Yet I never once felt confident enough in my memory of the dream face to tell him that I could find her.

When I woke up from the dream this morning, my eyes were closed. I tried to hold her in my arms. She was turning her head aside. She laughed, as though she had been caught stealing kisses. Her body rocked, in my arms, her head turned away. She grinned, laughed, and wiggled her eyebrows. I suspected her of stealing kisses from my dream.

This psychologist and I supped together often. He had suggested that *I* might steal a kiss from her. I told him that I wouldn't be comfortable stealing a kiss from my own wife at a party. (*I'm not married.*)

"Why do you insist on taking her to a party?" He asked.

"It was a dream," I said.

Then he stopped listening to me. He started taking notes. I wasn't sure if he was writing about the party.

"The party was hard to focus on," I said. He looked at me intently through his polar-grey, silver-rimmed, wire glasses while his bushy eyebrows arched.

"How many people were there?" he asked.

"Does it matter?" I asked.

"It could," he said.

"I don't know," I said.

"If you could answer the question as if it did matter, how would you answer it?" he asked.

"I just did," I said.

He glared at me. I came to a crude understanding about Dad, which evolved into a casual observation.

"When I speak to you out of my own emptiness, when my countenance lacks affect to offend or cajole you, then you assume I am lying," I said.

"How did you know that your countenance lacked affect?" He did listen. Not as concerned about the party, he was concerned that I was not sincere enough about my own dream to show him affect. Then as the dangerous logic of my own psychoanalytic wonderings gathered steam, I considered his limits when it came to my love. It could not be resolved without sharing it with her, nor could I analyze without her.

I closed my eyes and tried to roll over in my bed and hold her kiss stealing face eye to eye. The waitress asked me what I wanted to order.

"Pardon me?" I said.

"Please," she stood tapping the pad.

"Coffee," I said.

The psychologist saw me open my eyes when I ordered coffee as if he were counting eye-blinks in some historical study of hypnosis.

"I'll order when you come back with the coffee," he said to her.

"This may sound strange to you," he said to me. "But for the moment, let's be practical. You met this woman at a party. You were drunk, perhaps by the time the two of you fell to one another, 'laughing and carrying on.' (He was handy in the afternoon diner as he spoke, carving an elaborate Corinthian column with his liberally applied finger quotes. He marked in the air above his head with his hands.) Now, never mind me for a minute," he said loudly. "Where was the party? Clothes? You are an artist. You would remember."

He stopped. I blinked in time to see an old friend get into a new car through the window of the diner.

"Are you married?" I asked.

Frowning oddly, he looked up at me from his notes.

"I just learned something," he said.

"What's that?" I asked.

"Well, I never really understood what you call: 'PARTIES,'" (His fingers notched the air in a very clean set of quotes.) A police car passed the diner synchronic with clean, well chipped quotes. "But whatever you mean, I am sure I don't need them."

The waitress, returned with the coffee, and Dad got up to leave. I began to re-invite him to stay, but somehow, his grace, exceeded my charm. I had read about Confucius' distrust of "grace" in a footnote in the *I Ching,* yet I felt pride in my charms. I did not trust him. Left alone, face to face, with her eyes, blue, then brown, yet somehow convinced, that they were neither, both, the color of her eyes troubled, only when interpreting her mood, beneath the cool, enjoyment of the dream. They came into focus blue, and warm. Her red lips, tulips to my nose. I kept leaning close, to catch the scent, of her breath, and offer a moment, for her, to steal a kiss. Then I resented the kisses, not stolen, more than, the stolen ones.

Paul Thanas

JACK ACID AND THE BLUE CROSS

When Jack went to high school, he studied very hard. Jack got bored with high school and began cycling his lightweight ten speed everywhere in all sorts of weather, snow, rain, dust churned off the unprotected tires, sun and humidity seared his strong legs, back, and arms, Jack lived for the thrills of cornering, descending, and battled his body up over hills and mountains, whether mid-pack of other high priced, finely tuned cycles, or alone. Jack took Cincinnati streets by storm, thrashed past red and green lights in front of honking cars, screamed: "Horn works! Try the lights!" He knew every xsbackroad within several counties in the Tri-state region. The cycle club had grown developed interest, a small band at first; they sponsored races sanctioned by men and women culling an Olympic team from among them. America had no credibility on the cycling map. A safe sport for Jack because there were no "jocks." He did not have to cut his long brown hair. (He wore a ponytail when he rode.) He cycled more than ten miles daily to and from high school. He rode eight miles each way getting to his part-time job after school. He pedaled a steep grade, past forested hills. Every day he forced his legs to climb a little farther in fourth gear, then dropped to second (Third was a cross chain position.) to ride as far as possible, then first at the top. Before he quit the job, he could finish the ascent without using first at all, out of the saddle for a few strokes at the summit to regain speed and go back to fourth as the road leveled. Exhilaration as the speed of the wheels whirred beneath him, cool air filling powerful lungs, his growth, determination, and focus satisfied him. The spring of his sixteenth year he raced in a criterium at a local park, sanctioned by the Amateur Cycling League, and had the best placing of any local rider in any event. His fifth place out of eighty-five riders earned him a green and yellow jersey with chest and back pockets.

He worked in a cycle shop. He assembled poorly crafted Taiwanese machines. An employee in the shop sold them for a month, until his conscience disturbed him. The fellow quit, then Jack Acid quit.

Jack lived in a middle-sized house, five bedrooms, hardwood floors, French doors, and decorated with Mid-century modern furniture. His bedroom once was the attic; a huge room with sloping walls painted in bright glossy blue, a green floor, with orange alcoves. Posters of bands, sailing vessels, a cow exploding into a rainbow cornucopia he meticulously hand-painted with day-glow black-light colors, that shimmered when he lit them with the four-foot-long black-light tube which formed a square around the attic ceiling. Jack had a great hi-fi and loved to crank *The James Gang, Jethro Tull, Emerson, Lake and Palmer, Traffic, Led Zepplin, Simon & Garfunkel, The Beatles, and The Grateful Dead.* He played the trumpet, was smoked weed with his friends, and switched high schools. He kept two fine trumpets lent to him by a neighbor, whose uncle had played in the Cincinnati Symphony

Orchestra. Three years later, while on a bike trip, Jack picked up the harmonica.

The principal, a tall man with a bony face, met with Jack and other students to discuss a student's bill of rights. Jack, a leader, actively wrote platforms for student government, stayed late in the decaying green-walled classrooms, discussing the need for more parental involvement.

Jack read about the Dean of the University of Cincinnati Education College in the daily newspaper. He had made international news, as the father of a newborn, he brought his own son, the fourteenth to share his name, to his office, so that he could share parenting When he didn't have his infant son with him, the Dean rode a motorcycle to university. Jack wrote a letter proposing the Dean and Jack initiate a mutual exchange day. Jack suggested the educator come to high school for a day, and let Jack observe the Dean at university for a day. The Dean accepted Jack's idea and they did the exchange days. Jack mentioned that the only black people the Dean saw all day were servers at the University Faculty Club. Appalled by how dumbed down the instruction was in Jack's classes, the Dean impressed Jack by his open-mindedness when such a tall gray-bearded man folded his body into the high school desks observing.

Cincinnati's school districts drawn by Jerry Mander, made famous butterfly patterns which kept blacks, and whites, from attending class together, except at the "alternative" schools. Jack attended the same high school that Jerry Rubin, *Do It* author, and one of the Chicago Eight attended. Remember Bobby Seal and the lawyers? Jack never met Jerry at school . . . Jerry graduated before Jack attended, when Jack was in middle-school, he did hear Jerry speak in Eden Park, at Seasongood Pavillion, a tree studded outdoor theater nestled naturally into a hillside between the Playhouse in the Park and the Cincinnati Art Museum. Jerry wore war paint on his face and bare torso while he said softly, "LSD is spiritual medicine. It is time to embrace the theatre in political polemics." Jack had not fully understood. He had heard of LSD but did not understand. He was too young. Jerry said, "Revolution, man!" And he said this in a near shout. Jerry had wanted to return to Jack's (future) high school to give a talk and had been prevented from doing so. The principal called out the SWAT team on the basis of Jerry's promise that he would visit and talk at the urban college preparatory school. The uniformed militia stood on the roof with high-powered automatic weapons at the ready. That day the students came outdoors for gym class in their red shorts and white T-shirts with their hands folded onto their heads, elbows above their shoulders. Jerry stayed away.

Layers of Memory

A man from the back and a woman from the front. A front side man, a back-side woman. These were the kinds of things that he pondered. He had friends. He had enemies. He had friendships. Why couldn't he have enemy-ships? This tunneled him into his past. But, for this man it was also his present. He had a hard time separating events, processes, and experiences. It wasn't like time stood still or shifted; it was like time layered over itself, like collage, a montage, or decoupage. There were minute slices of instants, which toggled into one another. Imagine flipping through the pages of a book, but the pages interchanged while he flipped. So, he could never be on one page at a time. He could visualize himself coming and going, as if he was in front of himself, or behind, or both. Sometimes writing this was done at the command of the writer, but he did it naturally, or unnaturally, he slipped into his own future and past just a moment before or after he was there in the present. Pedaling his bicycle along a country road and as legs, ankles, and feet rhythmically moved up and down, his hands felt the bang, bang, of the handlebars crossing bumps, he shifted back in the saddle, slipped for a moment into a point in front of himself and saw the brown eyebrows arched over the tucked-in eyes, the long aquiline nose feathering air, his wide mouth hung easy; and then he slipped behind into an imaginary slipstream, as if he were in a pack of cyclists, shoulders disappearing above a sinewy back and fit buttocks arching from side-to-side as the flesh pistons, muscular thighs and calves, pumped. Not that he would want to, but when listening to folk music alone, he could dance with himself, leading to take his own hand and stepping aside, following, as well. He had been asked to write about a time when he had just narrowly escaped death by a mentor. But, to him this time was ever present. It wasn't as if he could escape anything. Yet, he was alive, or so he thought, and he studied Zen koans, causing even this to become confusing. Narrowly escaped? Or, just dead.

A twelve-year-old on a sailboat. A sky-blue sailboat, the color that represents deception, with deep blue sails, also a bit deceptive, navigated by four people. The river, wide, green, but a muddy green, flowed with its own air of deception. And the wind. This day the wind fluxed. It fluctuated like time itself. It didn't storm, but the sky grew dark as the afternoon came. Sometimes it blew steady and from only one direction. Other times it shifted. When the wind shifted, the sailboat eased over at an angle, heeling. This is difficult to describe. The boy sat on the edge of the railing, a nine-inch-wide span of decking under his yellow weather gear. As the boat rose into his seat, it also eased away under his feet. His sneakers were tucked under a canvas strap, and he had to adjust his weight, and feeling to stay stable, as she heeled. The boy's brother sat next to him on the rail. The brother clutched the side-stay wire in his left hand. The wire cut into his flesh, and although he had calluses from sailing so much, he still felt the pain against his sensitive fingers. The two brothers were Will and Steve. Will was elder, yet smaller, and he sat to Steve's left side.

That day Mom and Dad were in a bit of a terse argument. There was tension about Steve's binoculars, they turned up missing from the car in the dry dock among the yellow turning oaks. A sycamore released brown seeds. Mom said, "Don't. Don't. You. You push. He's twelve. C'mon Ken." A tense moment progressed. Even after rigging the blue boat, setting her afloat, and finding the boys on the rail, as Ken steered her downriver, a puff of wind swept against her abruptly, as the crew tacked on skipper's instructions. OK. Here's the problem. In the official account of the story, Will wasn't there. (You remember, we dropped him off at a friend's house?) And so, he didn't cling to the side-stay. Wait. That's it. Will held the jib sheet, and Steve, closer to the bow, his left hand grew callused from gripping the wire stay. Both boys had their feet tucked under edges of fiberglass for tucking and wedging feet. Will's feet, tight in sneakers, were forced against, under, the edge of the centerboard trunk. And Steve's feet, in faded, black, low-top Chuck Taylors, were hooked against the edge of the foredeck, so he was way out on the rail, and had a hard time pulling himself in, when the skipper tacked. Both boys wore life jackets. It was the rule, when in yellow weather gear. OK. The skipper had tacked, from port to starboard, and the boys had crossed the centerboard trunk in tandem, moving to the low side. The wind shifted, the sails backwinded and the blue boat just kept going over. Will climbed down the low side and was flipped into the green (deceptively blue) cold water, under the edge of the boat. Steve climbed the centerboard trunk, as she gradually rolled, but got caught under the rail. Both boys were sputtering, swimming, wet. The sailboat turtled, and the skipper pulled himself from the river onto the bottom. Will was the second one up. (This again contradicts the agreed upon account, because he wasn't there. At a friend's remember?)

A Persian rug with many flowers faded from wear. There is an irregular red flower, a gussied-up version sells to a trader in an upscale downtown store. The prayer rug has not been in a store in five generations. Passed gracefully from hand to hand until it is exchanged for a small wad of bills on a street-corner. (This from Steve's future, ten years later after he left the mental hospital. On a visit the second time there he gave the rug to Adrianne for safekeeping.)

Steve swam around, splashing in cold blue water. He hated the taste, like sewage, sputtered coughs, his eyes sought Mom's. Dad pulled her up onto the bottom. She squatted on all fours, choked water, her face dark, in shadow, lean long legs splayed out, wet hair flat against the top of her head, orange hood crumpled at the back of her neck. Strong fine hands sought a grip on the smooth flat bottom. The pale blue hull held stiff below the red striped waterline. Water sloshed through the gap where the centerboard poked. No preventer held the board. This boat never turtled before. Steve fought, shouted, cried out, and was pulled by the left arm, Dad's grip on forearm, Steve's hand around Dad's wide wrist. The four, buffeted by the wind, cold in the ears, whistling deep dark gray, floating without control, on the upturned boat, waiting for help. Ken said, "OK, it's OK, OK, OK." Steve wanted Dad to say more. The man's glasses were foggy, wet, an orange hood covered his ears, and his large strong hands gripped his son's. His voice was low, confident, even.

Only ten minutes on the upside-down hull; this time seemed long. Steven had time to see the riverbank, the trees awash in high water, the cars beyond on Columbia Parkway, as other boats came up. One, with a blue and white Power Squadron ensign, and a bullhorn took control. A voice cracked, seemed to rain on the water from a dry sheltered cabin cruiser, a CrissCraft. Ken shouted back. As the dialogue followed, the cabin cruiser edged close enough so that the boys and Mom could climb aboard. Ken stayed with the sailboat, hunched in his orange weather gear.

From one facet the flawed jewel. From another, it glowed, warm light, ember deep, layered light. Facets don't match the paperwork. The prayer rug could not have come to him. The jewel had no value except as a curiosity. These trading elemental pieces are strictly clichés in this story. The wind might shift, and a different past might be useful. How would you say this if you could and couldn't at the same time? A man from the front. Beard. From the back, bundled enough in long black robes, long hair in tight braid. A woman if you didn't see the beard. Study the facets lies. Laws allow lies. But, if ego, the vital sense of self takes precedence over the power of flaws?

Clouds over the river. The deep blue muddy swirled at the brown banks, oaks and willows edged the shore, some awash in spring and fall. A gentle song called across the waves. The honk of geese took wing, formed a whirling, gray, black and white wedge, headed south. Dark fall. Crows crowd a lone leafless tree on the north shore. See the night coming as the murky gray sky shows silvery white where sun broke through at the rim of the valley. Blue water sparkled with white caps in the bitter west wind. In two hours, the horizon will flicker brighter as neon night city comes alive. The boys, warmed in the cabin cruiser, as Mom sips coffee, worried about her purse, wet and relieved to be off the boat. The boys drink hot chocolate. Clothes are stripped off. Towels appear. Then they are bundled back into their jeans, still wet, now cold and heavy. The yellow weather gear suspenders are re-fastened over damp cold shirts.

The cruiser takes them to the shore where a paddle-wheeler moored in shallow water lies against the bank. Leaves them on the steam-wheeler's deck. How can memory shift like light in a jewel? It must be a medical problem. A severe blow to the head? Increasingly, Steven hits his head. Medical problem. They told that. You told that. You told them that. You cannot ever know your past. Light shines in deep shadows of science.

And Then the Cow Was Drownded

Scientific shadows rape the faithful fears. Deep hidden beauty in the soul of an injured man who survived a child's brutal fall. The fall repeats again and again and again. Layers of stiff wetness. The hard way, the smell of cooking ham. A man in a white cloak said, "When he smells bacon frying, he'll know, he'll remember just the facet." And this dirty, chef, grit, grease talk will overcome the separation. If the boy should ever become famous, a lie. Another truth, random, physical. Fink, yes. The king, always a fink. Saved the life of a boy, who fell again, and again, and again.

Dad on the river. Dad on the boat, on the river. Always on the boat, on the river. Society based, lies? A past based on a singular, deception? You want deep background? Systems flow. Water and wind flow. Mountains flow. But light? It bends but, cannot be said to flow like water. Let me be. He'll seek the level he needs to resolve. A hazel eye rimmed with redness. Dad cries. His sons are hurt. It matters. The boys will never know. The pain centers in the brain have been disconnected. The understanding centers in the family have been disconnected.

There is a narrow plank. A foot wide, two inches thick, suspended across twenty-five feet. (That's too long.) A plank stretches to the shore. It hardly seems stable. Will crosses. He crosses step by step on white squishy gym shoes. His pants swish, when one leg passes the other. There is this high squeaky yellow waterproof nylon swish, on swish. His deep brown eyes flash, his pointy eyebrows are steady, his little nose runs, but he does not reach up with a hand, or sleeve. His wet hair scruffs up at the back of a tight purple hood crumpled at the nape of the neck. Across and silent. He does not walk away. Neither, does, he look back. Nor did he cross the plank. He fell. One foot wobbled on the plank, the other missed it only partially, there was a stumble, a waving of arms, then steps up into air. A tipping, and looping fall. Head hit water, rock below.

A bloody headed boy awash in smelly blue water, rocks still. The boy cried out, then whimpered. Steven, traumatized by Will's fall kneels, wraps an arm around his own lower legs, does not feel the yellow waterproof nylon, nor the yellow slicker, the gentle strong warm hand on his shoulder. His brother there crumpled.

Steven crossed on his hands, and knees, while fighting back tears, sobs, stunned. Then felt the wet on his knees, shoes squishy beside Will. Are his knees crushed, and bleeding? Steven kneeled over Will, held him. Will looked up at his brother blankly, not seeing, not recognizing. Blood and water wash. Will Will recover? Mom crossed behind the second boy. Steven may never remember this story. Now, both boys in shock. The men back on the CrissCraft with the radio do not know what happened. The inside action between the paddle-wheeler and the shore, hidden from view, as she left, Steven cradled Will in shallow water. "Keep his head above the waves," she whispered. Steven didn't move Will. She slogged back to the riverbank, clambered up the steep, sloping sand, grabbed a brown tree trunk, pulled her weight against the tree, it creaked and bent, nearly breaking. Up on the grass, her wet white tennis shoes squishy, a man watched. He came over and offered help. Scared. To a phone. Because her boy's life. The other boy. And the man on the boat. No ID. No money, not for a payphone? The man. OK, but not involved. She plead with him.

The sky darkened, horror, the shadow of the paddle-wheeler hid the boys. Steven thought of his dad. He wanted to be his dad's friend. He wanted to be his dad's man. But Will must not die. Will breathed. (Not the official story. As the golden story retold, Will dropped off at a friend's house, then Will invented something that day. Yes, a Patent: an electronic device that opens the door to garage computers. No, no one ever spoke, of when Will, almost, well, died. Steve, the only boy on the boat the day we tipped.) Steven remembered the story at least two ways. He might have been the one with the head injury. I bang, bang, my head, head, I think. Steve grew up to become an artist. Will grew his hair long to cover the scar, then when he got older cut it back, and the scar disappeared. There is no scar. No way to get the memory right. Steven grew up diagnosed with schizophrenia, drug and alcohol addiction, yeah, right.

No, seriously friend, I need to get to a payphone, to call police. An ambulance came. Mom rode off in the ambulance with Will. Steven just sat down in the grass alone, and night came. No. Steven stayed, with a man. No. Steven rode, with Will. No. Steven stayed, with a policeman. Seriously, friend. Seriously, friend. This sailing trip went awry.

On the boat with Dad again. Rolling upriver with another boat towing. Both Will and Steven aboard. Steven knew the old Johnson, outboard, the green beast would never run again. He held the tiller, while Dad bailed, to keep the water level just below the rail. The blue boat's blue sails down, crumpled in the swamped boat. Mother's wet purse floated toward Steven. He handled it with fear. Scoter handled sloppy, rocked, swayed, heaved. No, Will wasn't there. Dead and gone, and **he** is going to kill Steven, too. Steven knows Ken hates this family. Steven won't wait to escape. No, he will begin his madness at eighteen, when the parents have no more control. Dark water, flowing water, swirling waves, sitting awash in river stink. Cannot think about this, just an accident. Cannot remember how I came to be on the sailboat again. Wasn't I safe ashore?

Mom with the trailer. To the public landing. The boat, the car, the trailer. How did she get keys? The police took her home, she brought dry clothes, got car keys, got the car, the trailer. And burgers. This is the first Wendy's Steven remembered eating. He never even thought about, when it is over, and the story. In the car, the AM radio crackles. A man talked, in a scratchy voice about the skipper, staying with the boat, in orange gear. The family

74

named. Ken, his wife, the two boys, Steven and Will. One boy rushed to hospital. No, that is not mentioned, because the fall, kept from the Power Squadron broadcaster's view. The paddle-wheeler hid trauma. Steven heard the radio, while he ate his burger, forgot his brother. His brother's memory of the incident went black, black, black, never went sailing that day. (At a friend's, remember? He invented something. Something important. A Patent.) Watching angry Ken, guide the swamped boat, slowly up onto the trailer, draining slosh, through open bailers, through end plug. Hours of draining, sloshing, drained.

Up in his attic room crying. Crying for days. Shivering. Angry. The story always fiction. And in the depths of irony, Steven became a fiction writer. He wrote about how he will become famous, and tell the story of his madness, how it swept over him for no reason when he grew up. He won't know the story of his childhood, because he did not live, with clarity. He grew up on foggy river sailboat days. His memory a problem for others. And him. He will see layers, upon layers, of pages, washing up, from the river, swept honestly into the shadows, in swirling blue waters.

Will, in a whole clumsy rehabilitation stage. A cut on his face, left a funny mark on his lip, that kept him from smiling, so. Teeth had to be cut, and pulled. That part remembered, remember. He wore a night brace, on his teeth. He looked awkward, but had resolve, having invented something. Something important, that Steven doesn't quite understand. Later, Steve had a night brace. Were these connected events? Will walked a little funny, couldn't run much. Steven pitied him, cursed the fate to have an invalid, for an older brother, who seemed younger, but kicked with vigor. And Will looked up to Steven. Will's eyes, his face, the awe, wonder and admiration he had for Steven; was it in that moment, after he hit his head? No. That moment stayed gone. And the shift to confidence, after that day, for the older boy. One brother looked up, to see Steven cradling him, both faces like miraculous light. The moment that two brothers see in a moment they are ineffably, curiously tied together, and the dignity of young boys etched in memory. Or is it?

Ken sued the doctors, for taking too long, or something, and bought a boat, a bigger boat, and land for a summer cottage, where they will go to the North Country. All he wanted, better than his brother. He'll never have the quiet explosively calm, serene, patience of the older boy. And they'll hate to be compared. Steven's not complacent with his life. But the brother remained a constant reminder of their mortality, vulnerable to a fault, Steven pledged to watch over Will. Meanwhile Dad, always wedged the boys. If he got them to fight, he might win. Or if he can get them to condemn him, as a unit, they'll get together, unite and have each other, as strong friends? There's no limit to what they'll get. Yeah. Dad, a tricky man. Will, too. The truth of this particular repressed memory that Dad perpetuated the deception. The story of almost dying, not about almost dying. Later, Steven woke and no longer hated himself, for having the courage to crawl, before his brother could walk.

The jewel, nothing more than a yellow quartz crystal hidden within the holy book. The prayer rug, a flower story that might somehow exist. OK. The flower rug, always a flaw. Will explained Allah only allowed perfection. Man flawed. "Allah does not like perfection." The explanation, he stayed with a friend that day.

So, what if Dad never lied? What if Will never had the accident? What if Steven's schizophrenia is wholly chemical? Nothing Dad planned, he didn't tip the boat purposefully, that's certain… it's just an accumulation of events. Who would take advantage of a son, or brother without some motive? And yet, and yet, Steven craved explanation. Some fault, some way to understand Mom, and Ken fought that day, over the missing binoculars, explanation must be…be available. What harm could

Steven cause, by claiming some made up memory? What happened when Ken died? Mom dead now.

GO with Frisby

I first met Frisby during my final year of high school. With clear blue eyes and a rather soft voice, he looked every bit the girlie boy. A year older than me, he had shoulder length light brown hair, stood a few inches shorter and owned a 1967, blue, VW bug. We lived in Clifton. He wore boot cut jeans at a time when the fashion for bell-bottoms peaked. His sobriquet, Frisby, the result of a saucer competition, he won, three years before we met. As I took on the job of high school editor of *Hughes Guise*, Frisby grew as one of a group of great kid reporters. A couple of them went on to journalism careers after college. Frisby played acoustic guitar, composed his own music, became an electrician.

I don't remember, how we began playing Go together, during the late winter of 1975. There is a timeless quality to Frisby memories. We, were both, due to graduate, that June.

We met at City Wide Learning Community. This was one of a handful of experimental "magnet" schools in the Cincinnati Public system. I started there after leaving Walnut Hills High School, the college preparatory school that had a great reputation, after my tenth-grade year. It had become apparent that, scheduled to take all Advanced Placement courses in my Senior year, and several my Junior year, if at Walnut, I successfully persuaded my parents instead, because grades were good, that I would be better off to graduate early, and spend my seventeenth year, in college, rather than, in high school. Walnut did not allow early graduation. City Wide offered community-based learning and accelerated growth.

I had written to the Superintendent of the Cincinnati Public Schools, Don Walter, asking if I could study with him directly, in an internship. He wrote back that City Wide had an opportunity, and if I attended, I was welcome.

While still at Walnut, I had an exchange day with the Dean of the University of Cincinnati Education College. Dean Gideons spent a day shadowing me through high school, and I spent a day with him at the university. During my day with the long-haired, bearded Dean, the only black people I saw were the serving staff at the University Club, where we met with others for lunch.

I represented my class for two years, ninth and tenth grades, respectively, on the Principal's Advisory Committee. We were working on a student bill of rights. It had been through my effort that the Committee was re-designed so that the students would have proportionately better representation. We had also pushed to include parents. In tenth grade I was Student Senate Vice President, a job usually reserved for upperclassmen. Accepted because I had attended Student Senate while in junior high school, despite not having a vote. During this time, however, I felt increasingly alienated, and wanted to leave the college prep environment.

City Wide was alternately called City-Jive and City-Weed by the kids. A lot of the kids were there so they could take it easy and work at their own pace. Some of us, highly motivated to get better educations, wanted to work faster. Classes ranged from trade school training to advanced placement. Frisby's dad, a philosophy professor at the University of Cincinnati, his mom, a professional photographer, Frisby had the distinction of having a beautiful mom. She had long dark hair, was petite, and attractive. We often went home in Frisby's car for lunch. Over soup one lunch time, Frisby asked me if I had ever played Go. My dad, a UC psychology professor had earned his undergraduate degree in philosophy. He had introduced me to the game at an early age. I had the basics before I was seven. As things turned out, I was trying to study calculus and French at UC while at City-Wide, but in both cases, I bailed.

Go, a game of pure strategy, without differentiation between the pieces, is a favorite of game theorists and philosophers. Described as binary, played on a grid, nineteen-by-nineteen with one player beginning with 181 stones and the other with 180 shells, the pieces are played onto the board one-by-one, taking turns, until, by forming patterns, they surround territory, and in some cases, one another. If individual or linked pieces are surrounded completely, they're captured. Removed pieces, however, stay removed with one situational exception, when one's opponent may move back into the captured territory. The rules of Go are deceptively simple. The binary dimension to the game, as opposing intersections on the board may be counted at a glance (called "eyes" by Go players), the board, large enough, and the number of pieces high enough, that even, in 2015 computer software did not exist that could compete with an expert, or Master. Go originated in China as W'ei Chi. The oldest known board game, it came to Japan before Zen, and took the name Go. Ritually played for centuries, the game has a handicap system, and a rating system for categorizing players. Master games memorized to learn the fine points demonstrate timeless practice.

Frisby knew this when we started to talk about Go. I began to research, and soon enough we enjoyed many moments away from school in the afternoons, at Frisby's home, sipping beer, and teaching each other the finer points. Frisby taught me joseki first. Joseki means corner-play. Because the borders of the board end, finitely, fewer pieces are needed, to capture territory in the corners, and on the sides. Therefore, opening moves in Go, tend to take place in the corners. Similar to chess, openings have patterns. Frisby studied books at this time, but I learned from him. He watched me play then made me replay if I played badly. He memorized sequences of moves. At times frustrated by his ability, I grew, slowly, but deliberately. Well served by these moments of frustration, when I played later in California, and had moments of pleasure, defeating older opponents, by keeping my temper in check. Frisby showed me how to hold the pieces, and maintain etiquette, by always playing closer to your opponent in the early stages of the game, so that you didn't force your enemy to reach far away, which also served to lull him into a false sense of security. It worked. He taught me the monkey-jump, and Seki. He taught me many of the simple proverbs that I still study to improve my game. Seki is a situation where either player will lose territory if he plays. If left alone the area becomes stalemate. If a player does play, he may forfeit an area and number of pieces, so that it appears he has given in, but then, after capturing, and removing pieces, he may play back, into the same territory, and may win it. Seki, difficult, and ambiguous demands patience, skill, and bravado.

He struggled to teach me ko. Understanding ko meant mastering Go. Ko involved pivotal battle points where territory, exchanged based on sente, when one player must respond. When one has sente, and plays ko, then one controls the larger areas of the board and can tip a match. The ko rule goes something like this. Each player surrounds the other. But at the moment when one player plays into jeopardy in order to capture (the only time a player can play into jeopardy), she must be allowed to cover tracks and fill the empty eye. If the opponent can take sente, make a play, requiring a response, then a ko battle follows, until one yields. Rather abstract, and difficult to understand, but once understood, still difficult to engage, and use. As an active complex teenager, it became a loving challenge. Go, the way pieces create patterns, similar to gestalt psychology theories, or those presented by architects, social scientists, and artists where difficulty discerning background, from foreground, in space, and action, generate universal models, that increase understanding.

Architecture Class met at a community architect's office, a building that he rehabbed into apartments using student insight and labor. We solved a difficult design question with the teacher's help. The parlor had three angled off corners, a square fourth corner, the teacher asked how to place a ventilation duct to the second floor without disrupting the room. I said, put a round duct up through the square corner, and angle it off, with a drywall wall, to match the others. I wondered later, if my ability to arrive at the solution independently, grew from understanding Go. I had just begun to master joseki.

Frisby had a great teaching method. He cordoned an area of the board and said, "I'm going to get greedy," an invitation to stop him. Sometimes I was able to without help. Other times Frisby watched me fail, then stopped play, back tracked, replayed the corner from memory, showing eyes for alternate moves.

This process frustrated me; he had total control, as the neophyte, I learned, the pain increased desire to grow.

In Architecture Class, we learned how to build and test a beam, how-to drywall a ceiling, among other things. When dry-walling the kitchen ceiling, I worked with Gene. We did everything wrong. The edges of the room were not square. We decided, instead of starting on one side and moving across the ceiling, to take our four-by-eight-foot panel of sheetrock, put it on the studs in the middle of the ceiling, then piece the edges around it. We built an awkward T from two-by-fours to hold the four-by-eight sheet up, while nailing it in place, standing on ladders. Then we had to measure and cut each piece around the edge of the ceiling. These pieces had only one uncut edge making the fitting process difficult. Lessons parallel to Go, the middle of the board never easy to conquer. I learned that the way we chose to pattern that ceiling gave us more difficult seams to tape, and mud, than any other way we could have done it. I know that the physical world gave me a hands-on experience, while Frisby provided philosophical underpinnings that helped to visualize the work.

In Architecture we talked a lot about "foreground and background." Our teacher felt these were key concepts in designing living, and workspace. He took us to visit houses in Mt. Adams, where loft spaces, whose open ceilings made boundaries between rooms. In Go I learned to see the black stones as foreground in a glance, with the white shells in the background, then to shift the gestalt, by consciously making a mental change, observing the board and the pieces, so that white foregrounded black. Another of Frisby's teaching methods used this. We played a game through the joseki and just into "middle game" and then when indisputably, Frisby had a lead, we traded sides. Of course, this never meant moving across the board, or turning the board, just trading black for white. I always started with black, so to take the handicap. But, with this method, I played white. Frisby always won. Sometimes we played double Go, a game Frisby invented. Each player played two stones at once. This taught me to plan ahead.

Because of the current politics about blacks and whites in Cincinnati I had an education on inequality as well. On the Go board, the stones and shells were equal in power, each move was an attempt to gain territory. We talked about raising consciousness on the board, by creating eyes, or open spaces. For a Go group to survive, it had to have two independent eyes linked together. In Educational Politics class I attended Cincinnati Public School Board meetings and read everything in the local press, including underground papers, about the ongoing problem of de-segregating the Cincinnati Public Schools. Dr. Walter, with whom I became friends, worked at the heart of this issue. By attending City Wide, in Hughes High School, the nearly eighty per cent minority inner-city school, as a school within a school, the mostly white student body helped statistically improve the racial balance of Hughes. I attended a basketball game with Dr. Walter where we watched Connie Smithe of Hughes decimate white students from Aiken High School, the district school. I lived closer to Hughes, the district lines drawn in a butterfly pattern racially divided my community. Walnut Hills High School had been the first "magnet" school with a college preparatory exam for admission.

The school within a school at Hughes generated a very unequal system. City-Wide students each carried a pass. We came and went from the school building during the day at any hour. We entered the side door in the morning, after first bell, and walked through security checks. The regular students included many late arrivers. Students stood in a long queue in the basement by the side door. They had to sign and clock in. When moving past them, I felt a twinge of guilt. Not bound by the walls of the school building we moved about the city.

I liked Chinese History. The teacher, a recent Antioch graduate, later went on to become an important Teacher's Union Leader in Cincinnati and then Ohio. At first, I didn't directly connect this history of the Chinese Communist Revolution with my study of Go, but some of the ideology did generate parallel concepts. I remember later finding a library book called: *Cosmic W'ei Chi*. It had a subtitle about Mao-Tse-Tung's theories of war.

I got Physical Education credit for cycling on my ten-speed. I would have cycled more, but the ratio of credit to hours cycled, measured twenty-to-one, in academic subjects, credit measured ten-to-one. Given that I planned to graduate a year early, I had to accumulate two-years-worth of credit hours in two semesters. The limited number of work hours in a week, prevented me cycling as much as I wanted. The last half of the school year, I worked on school over forty hours a week. I could earn more than four credits a week, if I avoided Physical Education, and electives. Elective credits measured thirteen-and-a-half hours per credit. Most weeks I combined electives, academic, and Physical Education earning between three and four credit hours. The issues, and problems I learned and wrote about, while immersed in a system mired in political conflict, fascinated me.

Looking back, I think this period of my life may have been when I first had an inkling that something might be wrong. It's funny, but I have to put some responsibility for my awareness of the problem on Dad. When we argued about my responsibility level, I asked to see a therapist. After I spoke with a college counselor, who suggested anywhere I applied would accept me, I visited three colleges. Will attended the University of Michigan, he had bicycled to Ann Arbor, and I had friends from Walnut Hills at both Oberlin, and Harvard. My parents supported these college visits, allowing me to drive alone to Michigan, and Oberlin, staying at each for a long weekend. They flew me to Cambridge, where I stayed in Harvard Yard for a few days. My high school friend at Harvard was black. During my visit I met a friend, who could easily fling a football fifty yards with pinpoint accuracy in Harvard Yard, but did not feel welcome on the football team in the quarterback position.

Dad attended Harvard as an undergraduate after the war. Although he may deny this, I felt pressure to go there. Before discussing Harvard with Dad, I read about Columbia, and Princeton. But Dad shifted my focus. He also thought, as did many of my classmates, that I was destined for a career in law or medicine. Even then, I was convinced that writing would be my main occupation. He said law required writing.

My English courses included Journalism, Creative Writing and in-class Debate. During the fall of 1974, I became the editorial editor of a planned City-Wide school newspaper. Then our advisor suggested the possibility that our paper would be the school newspaper for Hughes High School. It had been several years, since the students had one. Our editor-in-chief was a charismatic black Senior. On the day of the meeting with the school principal, our editor failed to show up. Elevated to editor-in-chief, by consent of those present, I negotiated an uncensored paper, and led the way. My first eleventh hour move, editing the paper, including typing up each article for the printer. My editorials were often controversial, but the paper's advisor, our English teacher, defended a free press, his job on the line. I learned principles of direct action.

I took a Media Class. We generated a documentary about our school with a local TV station. I studied poetry writing, and American history.

Dad said Go was a closed system, where psychology was an open system. I'm not sure I understood this distinction, but I argued that because of the history of Go, and the way the Master system works, it lives as a game, with tournaments played all over the world, and its theorists cannot make a machine that can beat a man, make this point. While a game itself might be closed, the world of Go lives large, but even individual games take place in a context. I will tell a bitter truth. The last time I played Dad, I gave him a handicap and he grew so frustrated, that in the middle game he put his hands on the pieces and mashed them around as he resigned. I was still a teenager. By then I had traveled to California and back, after dropping out of Harvard, and had finally beaten Frisby in an even game by one stone (in California, when he visited.) I could go on about Go expertise, but frankly the idea of entering a tournament, and playing in the world of Go at large does not interest me. A personal game that, honestly, I'm scared to measure my ability against true professional at a tournament. Yet, I miss a good game. I think as an extended metaphor for life, Go is more apt than any other game besides poker.

Rapid to Wyoming

Eighteen my first summer of college, I planned to bicycle across the country to work on the railroad in Idaho, make money for a year or so, then go back to college, with experiences to write about. Will had a friend from Michigan, whose brother worked as roadmaster, with the Southern Pacific in Pocatello. I got his address, and wrote Joe B. a letter, inviting myself to get a railroad job. I don't remember if Joe wrote back, but off I went to Pocatello regardless. As things developed, I traveled with a pal from Cincinnati, by motorhome. Tom and I took our bicycles down off the rack on a dirty white motorhome in Rapid City, South Dakota in late July of 1976. Will stayed in the motorhome. He rode with his girlfriend's grandparents to Twisp, Washington, to work on a farm that summer with the girlfriend.

My bike had a flat tire when we unloaded, because the wheel rode too close to the exhaust pipe, and the rubber melted. I glued on a spare, then we cycled up the wide blacktop mountain road, to a tourist town near Mt. Rushmore, where we bought tinned beef stew. As the sky darkened from blue to black, we hiked off the road into the wilderness, up a steep hill amid large stones, and conifer shrubs, made camp and cooked up a steaming pot. Three tall trees arched over us. By nightfall, we admired the stars as well as three of the presidents' heads all lit by electric beams.

Tom squatted, poked at the fire with a dry stick and said, "Good to get out of the Motorhome. That fucking parakeet—"

"It wasn't so bad when the cage was covered. Birds belong outdoors." We could both hear a grackle and the distant call of crows. "Why didn't Will want to ride?" I said, pulling my sleeping-bag out of its sack, and staking my bivouac cover. I fluffed the bag, pulled coveralls over my shorts.

"He was pining for Shannon," Tom said, turning the stick, raising
flecks of ash, cascades of orange red sparks, and releasing a deep hiss from a larger log he pulled out of the woods. "I can't see it, she's only fifteen and he's twenty."

"Yeah," I said.

Tom's mouth, a flat line. "I wonder. Loren was cool. And Erin didn't want me to go." He pulled a brown long-sleeved shirt over his head, put a hand to his scattered hair. His sleeping-bag lay on a bed of pine needles; he made a pillow from the shirt.

"Lincoln, Roosevelt, I can't see who the third and fourth are," I said. Tom was counting his losses. I was counting on some future. "There'll be time for women in Cali after the railroad."

A long silence in purpose, in plan, in action. Climbing into sleeping-bags, feet kicked fluffed, taffeta nylon. Neither of us spoke. Tom rested his elbows, his torso tilted out of the bag. "Fuck Loren and Erin," I said.

"I wish," he said.

The stars shone with a solitary presence; a night sky so cluttered with celestial light, vast and soothing to rustling critters stirring, then I felt body tired, as cool, clear, fresh smelling night filled me while I fell asleep.

In the morning, after some cornmeal mush cooked over a wood fire, we hiked down to the road carrying our loaded machines, and cycled the two-lane, rolling, twisting roads to Mt. Rushmore. On the steeper climbs the traffic jammed up behind us, and on the descents, we chased down motorhomes, sometimes standing out of our saddles, and passing them. In the late morning, we arrived at the monument. A Harë Krishna devotee, with a shaved head, and wispy ponytail, dressed in saffron robes, shared books, asked for donations, and offered a free vegetarian meal in Rapid City. Instead of going back with the Krishna, we got the basic tour of Rushmore, then headed for Crazy Horse Mountain.

We pedaled through rolling hills, green pastures, and rock formations on a road narrow enough, tourists were continually pushing us to the edges, on the climbs, but feared passing, on the precarious descents. The Holsteins and Angus cattle, by the roadside stared, and spoke to us. In response to the lowing, I shouted, "Take a picture. It lasts longer." We smelled manure, mixed with pine needles. The warmth of the sun tickled us. I saw a Red tail hawk dive out of sight. Being outdoors lifted my spirits. Tom and I took turns, pacing each other, and drafting. I led more than he did, and we raced on the rolling climbs. The traffic was annoying, but mostly because of the odor of exhausts. Once a car passed very close, forcing us to the berm. In a couple of hours, we rode up to Crazy Horse Mountain on a picture postcard, blue-sky day with white, fair weather, cumulus clouds marching steadily from west to east.

Crazy Horse Mountain, a strange tourist attraction that I read about in a magazine the year before, where a Polish born sculptor, who had lived in Boston, got permission from Native American leaders, to earth-scape a mountain into the form of

Crazy Horse on horseback. In order to fund the project, he had a museum of his sculptures at the site, a view of the progress of the mountain, and his family involved in working the whole shebang. The sculptor had died, and his family continued the work. The monument would take at least twenty-five years to complete. We each paid ten dollars to see the place. Now it looked like a mountain with a hole cut in part of a rock face. I could not tell that it resembled the model of the projected finished product.

A nearly, life-size sculpture in the museum, a twisted, tawny, grained wooden fisherman, bearded and half-naked, resembled the resident bum at the Dudley Co-op where I stayed at Harvard. Damon Payne, now a mentally ill, hanger on at 1705 Mass Ave, had his own room, baked breakfast rolls, started the coffee every morning for the students. He was sixty-three-years-old. At the height of the Vietnam War, Harvard's political left, mostly residents of the Co-op, invited street people in for Thanksgiving. Damon moved into the stone and concrete basement, slept with a baseball bat by his bed, and by 1976 he had his own room, and a safe status, as an enfranchised counter-force. Maybe I imagined this, but it looked possible that as a young man, the Polish sculptor carved a wooden statue of Damon Payne on the wharf in Boston. I kept this to myself, as I had no way to prove it, and who would believe me?

Tom fell asleep outside the museum while I browsed, so I read a hardback: *Children of Dune* while sitting under an oak tree, until two hours later when he awoke. Then we rode our machines out of South Dakota into the Wyoming sagebrush desert.

On a desolate road that led into Newcastle, Wyoming, we were caught in a hailstorm. We hustled off the road under a sand-colored culvert under construction. As we watched our cycles, pummeled by hard rain, near golf ball size hail, a local sheriff pulled up in a white jeep and shouted to us to wait out the storm with him.

"Where you boys headed?"

"We're crossing Wyoming," I said.

"You crazy? We get pop up storms all the time. It's dangerous out here," he said. The inside of the jeep smelled of cologne. His creased uniform and shiny badge reeked.

Wet and shivering, Tom asked, "How far to Newcastle?" The hailstones struck the hood and roof of the jeep. The clatter made it difficult to hear Tom.

"That's miles from here," said the sheriff. "You really mean to bike there?" With wide-set eyes, his jaw moving side-to-side; he had a very neatly trimmed mustache. "Where are you from?"

Tom said, "Des Moines, Iowa."

He was lying for fun. I glanced at my wet knees and shivered.

"How long have you been riding?"

"We stopped off a few places," said Tom.

The hail stopped and quiet overtook the white interior.

"We better get back riding," I said, opening the door and stepping onto the road kicking bits of hail.

Tom, from the front seat next to the man, chuckled, picked up his cycle, looked past the jeep, mounted his orange bike and put it in motion. The cop pulled away.

In Newcastle, we found several disabled public phones, wires hung amidst shattered glass. We located a payphone in a dark restaurant with wood siding. Tom called home to Cincinnati. He came down the steps outside the building looking older than eighteen. Walking slowly, his face drained, he said, "We need supplies."

We rode across town to a grocery store. We stocked up on fruit and juices and headed west.

We had a Shell Oil roadmap from the sixties when my family vacationed out west. The map showed gravel roads ahead, but undaunted, it appeared we headed toward a small mining town. Darkness fell, slowly like a filmy curtain, first the sky became deep blue, and stars shone as a pink glow spread. We didn't have much water, certainly not enough to cook with. The water in Newcastle cost money. We didn't expect to pay for water. Stunned by the desolation, my limited knowledge of western geography figured the Black Hills were wooded and verdant and so were the Rockies. I never expected this wretched desert between them. A driver and a man in a pickup stopped to talk.

The passenger rolled down his window and even in the dark I could feel the blast of cool air from his air conditioner. "Where you boys headed?"

"Dunbar," I said.

"That's a ghost town," he said, "mining town."

A long moment hung in the twilight.

"You boys ought not to be out here," he said, rolling up the window

turning to speak to the driver. They drove away, their taillights dancing smaller and smaller, then over a rise and gone. We kept riding.

The horizon turned hot pink to the west as we stopped at a small pond off to the left side of the road. Our feet crunched in the pea gravel when we dismounted. In the near dark, Tom knelt down and dipped his water bottle in the pond and fouled it with crude oil. "Fuck," he said, tore off his brown shirt, wiped the bottle clean, tossed the filthy shirt into the dirt. Tom's anger stunned me. We carried only essentials. Could he manage with one less shirt? As we stood by a fence on the right edge of the highway, looking back miles toward the Black Hills I felt scared.

"We have to find water. Rattlesnakes," I said.

I gazed to the north a few hundred yards away, spotted a steel windmill against a blackening sky. Not turning, it offered the possibility of water. "A windmill. Maybe we can make it work," I said.

I found my battery headlamp to use as a torch.

"If we make noise, safe from snakes," I said. We leaned our ten speeds against the fence under the only tree, unpacked our aluminum pots, clanged them to scare snakes, climbed over the wire fence, and hiked to the windmill. After a deep breath, I climbed the steel structure. About thirty feet in the air, I swung the vane into the wind, held it there, as it had been disabled, and watched the windmill begin to spin.

Tom shouted, "Water!" He filled every available vessel, and I waited up there, while he went back to the bikes, for more. Standing up there in the closed in night, I felt exuberant, that we had gained water, yet anxious, as I stood not so balanced. My fingers, grooved, trembling with tension, I climbed down the ladder. Soon we had a small campfire by the road, where we made soup, from an envelope of seasoned dried potatoes. What had been a frightening evening, settled down.

In the morning, we rode for an hour, as the roadway grew progressively rough with golf ball size gravel. Slow going. Tom and I stopped talking. My lips grew taut as dust spread over my face. The machine banged up and down the ruts. I worried that my rims might dent, or a tire might blow. The heat grew and with it, wind. A red Ford pick-up rattled up to us. A man in a cowboy hat, and plaid flannel shirt reached across the cab, rolled down the passenger window, as cold air escaped the cab, he asked, "You boys want a ride?"

"Sure," Tom said. I opened the tailgate, climbed onto the empty bed, and Tom handed me the bikes. I laid them on their sides. We rode three in the cab, our bikes in the bed, for an hour and a half, in hot sun, past two copper mines. The driver smoked filtered cigarettes as he drove. When we reached a crossroad, we got out. We found a diner, and a carryout. Paved highway began. It was over ninety degrees in the shade. In the carryout, we bought a loaf of white bread, and some Velveeta™ cheese. The water tasted of sulfur.

Back out on the road, the wind blew a steady thirty-miles-an-hour gusting to forty into our teeth. Sand whisked around us.

"It's a good time to take a break. We're in no rush; why ride into the wind?" I said, "have another afternoon nap."

"Yeah," Tom said.

We rigged the light blue rain fly between a fence at the roadside and tilted our bikes together. There were no trees in sight. Traffic was rare and most of it the eighteen-wheelers just moving through. We saw some official looking cars, occasional pickup trucks, but tourists didn't venture this far off the beaten path. Tom went to sleep in the shade of the fly, and I read the rest of *Children of Dune*. Desert wrapped around desert. I imagined spice mines, developing oases on the planet Arrakis, with the help of the mighty sandworms, and the desert people, the Fremen, with their blue on blue eyes, all part of a rich sci-fi fantasy. After about two hours, I had come to the end of the novel. Desert scenes wrapped around me. I woke Tom. The wind had shifted 180 degrees. We packed up and headed out. In two hours, we traveled fifty miles. I felt great. I paced Tom. He drafted me for two thirds of the ride. He struggled. We passed wooden windbreaks for cattle. Tom said they blocked snow, made it drift, in winter storms. In hindsight, now, I remember that he got quiet, and a grim look came over his usually light face, his hooded eyelids hung big.

That night we camped in a dry thicket on the outskirts of a small oil town called Midwest. The place scared me. No natural water. We filled our bottles at a gas station. Sulfur flavor. The people seemed tough and poor. We cycled through a housing district. The pavement crumbled, yellow houses, with brown trim, tilted in rows, with dirt yards, and no cars parked near them. No kids. Tom pedaled harder in this finite housing district. It felt like a work camp.

The next day, hot and dry, we rode sixty miles, the first twenty slip out of memory, but then the last forty at a walking pace. We could see the town of Casper, Wyoming from forty miles away. Downhill, on a divided highway, with a twenty-five mile an hour headwind in our faces. We pedaled in fourth gear for three hours. What misery. Physically the road didn't challenge, but mentally, yeah! Because we could see our destination, and the slope towards it, we wanted to be able to coast; instead, our legs ached.

Echeloned to the right of Tom's back wheel, the draft there, following close, gave me an easier way. Our wheels stayed inches apart. I focused on the spinning tread. Suddenly he edged right, I jammed on my brakes and shouted, "Hey, HEY!" Swerving further right, to avoid touching wheels, on the paved shoulder, he swung back left. Something wriggled on the tarmac in front of me. I steered left just missing a half-coiled small Diamondback rattler. It passed a tire width from my right foot. "What? Fuck?"

"Just—get a look at it," he said.

Furious, but he hadn't done it on purpose. I muttered, "Jesus." Shook my head side-to-side…what the fuck? He almost threw me right on top of it. My heart raced with adrenalin. Sitting up, I sipped some water, drifted back a bit, feeling the full force of the wind. Casper, visible in the far distance, heat waves distorted the buildings, tucked in front of a red-brown ridge. I gradually settled back into pedaling, head-down, watched Tom's wheel against the pale gray pavement.

Late that afternoon we arrived in Casper on a nearly deserted, four lane, divided highway. Our speed, too slow for the banked curves, we pedaled easily down a ramp to a business district. We stopped at traffic lights for the first time in days even though no cars pulled up. We rode to a grocery store. As we bought food, juices, fruit, staples, etc. we met some people who invited us to stay with them. One guy sold me tires, at his house in the darkening city. I needed spares and he sold me two. We watched some of the Olympics with him including the track cycling and heard that George Mount had placed well in the road race in Montreal. I can't remember if George was fourth or sixth, but either way it was a remarkable result for Team USA. I had met George at the trials earlier in the summer. I felt excitement and accomplishment in the news, but Montreal had no television coverage of the road race, just a commentator's talking head.

Then we rode in the dark, our headlights glowing, to these other guys' place where we ate and played board games, Life™ and Monopoly™.

I remember marijuana. Tom told me after we left, that one of them poured vodka on his Cheerios for breakfast. Some of them studied at Casper Community College and others pumped jet fuel at the airport. They claimed that Casper had a high percentage of millionaires per capita because of tax laws. Many residents owned jets. These guys had motorcycles. In daylight, we could see they had a small house surrounded by shrubs, in a small subdivision.

The next day we pedaled over a hundred miles. We rode up for fifty, and down for fifty, the grade so gradual we barely noticed. The road stretched so straight that we could see for miles, a hundred-degree, dry sky, a cloudless, endless blue, expanded until distant snowcapped mountains began to take form transforming from sky blue to gray and white. We saw jackrabbits, pronghorn antelope and when we stopped, postcards for jackalopes. For ten minutes at a time, we could see pronghorn in small herds in the desert pacing us to our right, over a hundred yards off. People were not very friendly. Places to stop and get supplies came less often. In one place we were refused water.

When we got to Shoshoni there a river ran through town, and we washed up in it. Weird because there were buildings around, but nobody seemed to mind, or notice that we went into the water. After cleaning up, we checked out a park to camp in. We talked to some guys in a gas station. Both wore dusty navy, blue shirts buttoned in front. Their dirty noses poked where their glasses balanced. One said, "The moon landing was filmed nearby."

The other gestured flight with his hand and arm and said, "Yesterday we talked to a guy who had flown around the mountains in a small plane. He saw climbers approaching the peak from both sides, wondered if the two parties knew one another? "When they got to the top of the world they would." I imagined Will saying, in the middle of this conversation. He loved this stuff.

These guys hooked us up with a man with a pickup who, with us in the back, drove a few miles to the base of the Wind River Range through cornfields, and left us near the Wind River.

Irrigation ditches, red brown roads and lush green fields replaced the sagebrush. A scent of chemical fertilizer dominated the dry air. They gave us a couple of Coors beers.

It was the hottest part of the day. We were moving steadily through cornfields edged by wide grassy irrigation ditches. The water smelled. I stopped while Tom went ahead, took off my blue Campagnolo T-shirt and dunked it in a cold irrigation ditch. I wrung it out. It smelled of iodine and the chuff of a struck match. As soon as I pulled it over my head, my body chilled. The air was so hot, and dry, my forearms sprouted goose pimples, as the water evaporated from the shirt. I grabbed my water bottle from the handlebars. To my tongue, the water was hot, but when I splashed it onto the backs of my hands, it felt cold, as it evaporated.

I caught up with Tom as we cycled over a bridge across the river. He climbed a fence into the Wind River Indian Reservation. I handed Tom his machine, then mine, then I clambered over. We had to lift our loaded bikes onto our shoulders to get them down the embankment. Tom hiked through dense brush to the river, and got water for cooking, and cleaning. I prepared another stew. I poured the excess water on the embers from the fire. We drank beer, crawled into our sleeping-bags, and fell asleep just as it grew dark. I dreamed of a Native American, who came to us under the tree, stood over us in his buckskins, and watched us sleep. In a lucid dream, I thought I awoke, and saw people hanged, in the huge tree above us.

When I got up, Tom already made a fire, cooked cornmeal mush, with wood ash flavor. He gave me the ripe peaches, which I didn't eat. Then, without a word, he hiked up to the roadway. I stowed them in my panniers, before packing up, and putting out the fire. He had managed to get his loaded machine over the fence alone. Me too. Had I heard a truck stop, and a door slam?

Wind River to Idaho

The gray, paved road stretched ahead, as the double yellow line curved right, the way got steeper. The highway cut a channel, it surged upwards, hillsides rose into forests. Putting the machine in motion shook the stiffness from my legs. I flexed my sinewy, bare ankles, rotated the pedals easily. Thus began, the real climbs into the Wind River Range of the Rocky Mountains. Togwotee Pass, roughly ninety miles ahead, at 9658 feet, among the highest, with a road, in the continental United States. Crossing the continental divide, where water flowed either east, or west off the mountains.

Dubois, Wyoming, today's destination, about fifty miles away up a deserted road. Around 9:15, the sun warmed my arms.

Tonight, I would install a smaller chainwheel. As an aggressive rider, I used the highest gearing possible. When I pedaled, I spun quickly, but when climbing I pushed. The forty-two tooth chainwheel replaced the forty-five tooth, my largest rear cog a twenty-two. I rode racing gears despite the forty-five pounds of clothing, camping equipment, books, and food. I carried panniers, front and rear.

No sign of Tom. He probably hitched a ride ahead somewhere. I wondered if I would see him, when I got to Idaho. I decided to call home in Dubois. Nothing to do but ride. Alone on the road. I settled into steady rhythm, breathing in, out, pedals spun beneath me, the chain pulling, sounding just right. Moving my body felt good, the shiny alloy handlebars pulled by suntanned arms, the backs of my hands patterned from openings on cycling gloves. Time passed comfortably. I hardly noticed the gradual climbs. The road rose steadily for a few miles, then dipped for a quarter mile or so, and rose again. This pattern repeated. Tom's absence weighed on me, we had raced with surmised explanations. I felt angry and shouted at the rocks and trees. I met the mountain. Tom daunted by fear of the mountain, the Rockies, and although Tom and I had ridden together through great Eastern mountain ranges, this summer he had not been fit enough for this. No talking about the fear. Tom thought me weird, but he had never been able to talk about feelings.

As children, we shared excursions, adventures and work. Now, in the middle stages of our adolescence the challenges increased. Taller than Tom, I started at Harvard, while he finished high school in Cincinnati. In the spring, I had visited home and ridden a borrowed bike in the University of Cincinnati Criterium. Badly thumped in Junior category, in 1974 my victorious sixteenth year, I finished fifth out of eighty-five cyclists finishing higher than any local rider in any sanctioned category. But, in 1976, I rode a borrowed bike, did not finish. Tom traveled back to Harvard with me that spring to visit. We got a ride to Pittsburgh with a girlfriend and hitchhiked together from there to Cambridge. He stayed a few days at the **THE CENTER FOR HIGH ENERGY METAPHYSICS**. He didn't talk about feelings then, either, but those were better times.

Missing Tom choked me up as I pedaled. I wanted to break loose and cry but, couldn't. Even alone. So, I put my pain into cycling. Forced to think about other things, I watched the yellow lines curve and twist. Simple pains. The work of moving forward, moving up the mountain. Mind on pedaling. What kind of railroad work in Pocatello? Tom in Pocatello, or back home? Feelings, no words attached spun through me.

I climbed off the blue bicycle confidently. This day, in memory. Dubois, Wyoming, a small town, a few short side streets off the highway, it had a forested campground. After locating a campsite, I found the general store, bought some tinned stew, mushroom soup, fruit juices, and sweets. The clerk, behind the primitive cash register, in the old wood paneled building, totaled my purchases.

"Are you on a bicycle?" he asked. I had the little cycling cap with USA on it given me by the Pittsburgh girlfriend. The black shorts and cleated shoes also gave me away.

"Yes."

"How far have you come?" His freckled baldhead and sunburned face registered respect.

"From Rapid City, but I've been cycling on and off since Boston."

"Massachusetts? Well, welcome to Dubois," he said, warmly.

"Have you seen a sandy-haired fellow, about my age with an orange bicycle? He was headed for Pocatello, Idaho."

"No. Sorry."

"Do you have a pay phone?"

"Over there." He pointed to the front of the store.

Time to call home. Scared to tell Ken Tom had left, Mom answered on the third ring.

"Tom left."

"What do you mean?"

"Well, this morning, when I came up to the road, he was gone."

"Came up to the road?"

"We camped down a hill. He didn't tell me he was leaving."

"Where are you?"

"In Dubois, Wyoming. I'm less than fifty miles from the continental divide."

"How are you?

"Well, OK. I miss Tom. I didn't want to do this part alone. I'm scared."

"That sounds about right."

"Yeah," I said, "I'm on a pay phone and someone wants to use it."

"Hang on. Don't go yet."

"I'll call tomorrow."

"Steve, I love you. Take it slow."

"Will you call Tom's folks to see if they have heard from him?"

"OK."

"Actually, I think he's more troubled than I am."

"Do you have enough money?"

"Yes. I'll keep riding toward Pocatello. I'm kind of excited about the mountain passes. It'll be hard, but OK. There's a good campground here. I should go."

"I love you. Call soon."

"Bye."

I saw her dark eyes in memory. Good voice. As I replaced the phone, I wondered about Will. Forgot to ask.

At the camping area, I met a guy on a Raleigh Pro, over the pass from Yellowstone. No camping gear, traveled light, and only rode a couple of days. I couldn't believe how light. The fellow seemed tough, felt uneasy. We sat at a picnic table, talked about using the pool in the campground. The posted rules stated that it cost extra to use the fenced in pool. He wanted to sneak. I didn't. He had a small muscular body, girlish hands and long sandy hair. It was barely too short for a ponytail. He was twenty-five. He told about working in resorts washing dishes, traveling a few days at a time between jobs, sounded risky.

I cooked stew and heated soup over a small campfire. As it grew dark, a group, five cyclists, came into the campground. Younger than me, two teenage girls, two boys, a man in his twenties who led them. Headed east. I tried to talk to the girls, they kept to themselves, went to work pitching tents. I set up my fly and bivouac. The fellow on the Raleigh went to town for dinner. I cleaned up before he returned. We didn't have much to say. Once the mosquitoes started biting, I slipped into my flight suit. I changed the chainwheel on the Follis, as planned, under an overhead light, near the camp office. I needed rest and crashed early.

In the morning, dew hung on the tall grass in the campground. The group gone, by the time I ate cold cereal alone, packed up, then checked my map. Forty-two miles to the pass; then I'd descend, lunch in a day area at the base of the mountain, before the entrance to Yellowstone, cross the valley, to Jackson, a total of around eighty miles. Cool and clear, with a high blue mountain sky, alone in the Rockies!

My legs felt good, though my knees were a bit cool. Rock formations, glens with green foliage, mountain cottages, and large conifers lined the road. A sense of accomplishment grew as the miles eased past. I came upon a roadside rest area with toilets, like outhouses but with plumbing. I spent some minutes relieving myself and felt wonderful. Back on the Follis, I climbed toward the pass in fourth gear, and pulled up to another cyclist. He tried to ride with me, but I left him. Just over a mile to the summit the way got steeper. It sounds like a cliché, but a bald eagle soared overhead, as I climbed the last mile. Grateful I changed the chainwheel, all in all, this pass was easier than two that I remembered back East. Yes, the climb was longer, but not so steep. As I reached the sign, indicating the summit, I pulled off to a parking area on the left. Patches of snow melted in the grass. A guy on a brown bike pedaled up from the West, climbed off, and we shared a laugh.

"Funny to meet like this," he said.

"Yeah," I nodded.

"Share some Ho-Ho's?" He handed me a foil wrapped bit of chocolate cake. I took it; we clinked the cakes together, like a toast and mashed them into our mouths.

"Thanks," I said, chewing.

He laid down his bicycle, walked over into the grass and made a snowball. I did the same. We thought about pitching them at each other, but it seemed pointless. In his mid-twenties he had a camera. I let him take my picture holding the snow. Then I took a picture of him. Now, we were typical tourists. Antsy to go, I never got his name.

Back on the road, I spun around a bend. The peaks of the Grand Tetons appeared. I felt my stomach drop through my knees. Having climbed all that way alone, seeing the Rocky Mountains so close, so big, I felt something move my soul. Then I pulled up on a scenic rest area, stopped, laid down the bike, sat in the tall grass, snacked on sunflower seeds and watched prairie dogs play in dark dirt holes. I sat for half-an-hour in the sun enjoying the high Rockies. I tossed seeds to the prairie dogs. They sat on their haunches, chewed, begged, and played. The blue sky seemed so high and endless. Pure, crisp and cool air. The road twisted ahead down the mountain.

Back on the machine, I trembled with fear. The curves kept coming, braking through most of them, the bike ran free, on sew-up tires, if the glue melted, from the heat of rim brakes, a rolled tire, on a curve, or tire creep, from the pressure of braking, might yank the valve-stem. I decided to stop periodically to cool the rims. It worked. I stopped four times, on the shoulder, as I coasted down the mountain, several thousand feet. I must have descended for forty minutes, or more. When the road leveled out, tall grass grew everywhere, and a picnic area appeared to my right, along a small stream, where people stood fishing, spotted earlier on the map, as a planned lunch stop. I pulled in a gravel lane, found a table, made myself a sandwich of honey, and peanut butter. I drank water, filled up bottles. I left Yellowstone, in a few miles, passed it, headed for Jackson and Teton Pass. An hour later, I stood, aching, in a carryout gas station parking lot in the high wind. Dark clouds whirled above. The smell of rain blew around me, but it hadn't started. The store, on an apron of asphalt by the highway, accompanied by a Colonial red brick building, with white trim, and tall glass windows facing a poorly maintained lawn, made up an understaffed naturalists' office. A ranger stood by his white car with gold insignia. I was far from home, working a cola out of the vending machine, watching the ranger, imagining Will with me. I had a sense that Will appeared, as he had disappeared on the sailboat, as if not alone, and aloneness sunk in and I shook. A tremor spun down my arm.

Tucking the cola in my pannier, I rode for forty minutes, buffeted by a cross-tail wind, racing the storm. I pulled off on a narrow, curvy, dangerous stretch of highway, where tourist traffic was heavy. Cars stopped, and parked in a paved lot, just ahead unseen, momentarily blocked vision, so consumed with the fear of the storm, I climbed back on my bicycle, pedaled the thirty yards to the parking area as it reappeared.

The road passed near the Snake River. Insects, mostly gnats and flies swirled in clouds. Turkey vultures hovered, and people's dogs scurried through the underbrush. The ground was a strange light brown, damp from recent rains, with even lighter sand blended with dark soil building around clumps of tall grass. I wanted to walk off the lot into the woods to pee, was afraid of snakes, did it anyway, and imagined Will again. He shouted and whispered alternately. "Go pee," pulling his bicycle up next to me.

I didn't travel alone until the day before. In solitude. Somehow now the sense, of being abandoned, the ruggedness of the terrain, the absolute majesty and scale much greater, riding alone trying to beat a storm. Did it rain as we arrived in Jackson? I don't know, as I look back, I can remember Will in the rain.

Did it pelt rain? I'd been through a different kind of struggle. My parents had lost control over the boat when we sailed, and they fought over the binoculars. I asserted my independence. Helped Will. The last four conversations I had with Dad we argued. So consumed by her work, that Mom let me ride, with the knowledge that she could not stop me. When I think back, and realize at eighteen, thousands of miles from home, in the vast open mountains, alone, I knew my parents trusted me, or couldn't control me, some combination. They questioned my judgment, and I resisted these ongoing questions. The pattern matured. That is, I made more and more questionable judgments, and as I grew, the maturity that I wanted to project, began to become filtered through an adventure, and survival method, that served me.

I passed from Midwest to West, alone, with only intermittent guides, on a journey, that catapulted me into the excitement, of the left coast as things in America stirred and spun. The year of Bike Centennial, 1976, an organized bicycle camping excursion, from West to East across the whole United States. As you see, I cycled East to West, my trip, not the whole country, but making an independent adventure. Without a tent, and without a cook stove, my equipment simple, a lightweight blue rain fly, and the dark red and blue bivouac cover, waterproof on the bottom but water resistant on top. Roughing it. A rite of passage perhaps, that planned fully could not have happened. If I had planned more, and adventured less, would *On the Road* have had an impact?

Part of an enormous sub-culture, a counterculture, that with a healthy distrust of institutions, had set out to feel the pulse of the open road, the vast country, and to touch the wilderness a little more gently even than the motorcyclists. *Zen and the Art of Motorcycle Maintenance* made its way on the bestseller's list. Headed for the California Zen Center, a key point of consciousness in Marin County, San Francisco, and Carmel Valley. I didn't know that, yet. I knew, I knew somebody, but I had no idea whom.

Jack Kerouac, the embodiment of the road warrior, a man who could always land on his feet. Maybe work would be difficult, but I'd become a writer. Damned if I didn't and who knew if I did? Jack had nearly always had a companion, but when alone, he worked with that. When alone, he discovered the greater truths of the others, with whom he had contact. His close partners became characters, that lived larger lives, in the imagination of his readers. Jack, a man who traveled, and worked on the railroad, and wrote books, and the character, Jack invented, to represent himself. Sometimes Jack, called himself Jack. Not always. Neal Cassady became Dean Moriarty and Cody Pomeroy. Gary Snyder, Japhy Ryder. My friend, Tom, like a brother, and he became part of several characters, I later generated in fictions. I did not know then that later I would use the name, Jack Acid, or any other created persona.

During this time, I imagined the presence of my brother, Will, not his real name. Spoiler alert. I felt him guide me past Yellowstone along this tourist highway. The storm was just over my shoulder, and I imagined another cyclist a quarter mile back, watching, pacing steadily. A part of the decision-making team. I have a few memories of Will appearing and disappearing that seem difficult to sort out. It's as if his entity, fluid in my brain, finding a constant level in seven different severe compartments, or like my mind, a channel on a river where locks fill, or empty, depending on my level of anxiety, or security. (Or sanity?) As I became less secure, his presence rose into memory, whether present, or in reflection.

I don't remember arriving in Jackson. I remember street theater, pouring down rain, while I leaned my bike up against a restaurant, under a green and white striped awning? Did I eat a

meal of fried fish and French fries?   Did I have a cola and a milkshake?   Was there a Wild West street
theater show? A million tourists. Did I get drunk and black out? Someone, please explain the fragmented memories. I know I feared leaving the bike and gear unwatched. I had no lock. Did Tom and Will beat me here and tease me on arrival? Were there heirlooms in Jackson Hole? Tomatoes? I pedaled to the south edge of town.

I looked for a place to camp. A green space by the ski area, a grassy sloping mountain, rose above a field. Off to the side, a lift stood idle. A man in blue jeans, a faded jean jacket, and light blue T-shirt stood in the corner of a parking-lot, behind some bleacher-like benches, tiered around the field. A nearby brick schoolhouse. The man had sandy hair to his shoulders, a weathered face, and when he said hello, in a gruff but quiet voice, I saw several gaps in his teeth, and a receding gumline on others. He put a hand with a roll-up smoke to his red lips, puffing and spouting clouds.

"Is there any place to camp around here?" I asked. I leaned the Follis against my inner thigh, the black wool shorts wrapped heavy muscle. The man, in his thirties, had a Western aura. A student of the paranormal at Harvard, scouring libraries for material on Zen, astral-projection, and self-hypnosis focused me, I saw auras. This man had a dark, red glow. A gambler, or highwayman, a shaman. His past wore him down.

"There's no free camping," he said, looking over my gear. "Where are you from?"

"I came over the pass from Dubois today. Traveling from Ohio."

"Long way," he said.

"Do you live in Jackson?"

"Traveling through," he said. "I grew up in Utah, staying in Idaho here and there."

"Do you have anything to read?" I asked.

"Just finished this paperback, by Roger Zelazney," he said.

"Want to swap for *Children of Dune*?" I asked, zipped open my panniers, pulling out the hardback. The *Dune* story influenced my imagination. I thought the drug implied by the novel might be marijuana, and the giant sand worms an imaginative, living freight train metaphor. The qualities of the hero, Muad'Dib, or Paul Atreides, a man who had prescient capacities, had found himself leading the desert people into power, through

meditation, transcending fear, methods I learned. I fantasized that as this fictional character with my haircut, hands, bicycle, etc. I read the novels and related them to experience. I bicycled across the desert. Independence, and sense of adventure, tied to pop-literature, generated a lake of curiosity.

That night I went to a small grocery with a pink, curly, neon sign. I bought a tall green bottle of 7Up, and a half-gallon carton of vanilla ice cream. In the dark, I walked my bicycle to the drive-in movie theater, slid along the edge of the perimeter chain link fence, and found a grassy slope to sit, with a view over the rear boundary. I left my machine in the dirt gully, pulled out my bivouac, made a seating area, and waited for the movie to start. I could hear the sound coming from the speakers in the back of the parking lot. Jack Nicholson filled the screen. *One Flew Over the Cuckoo's Nest* began, as I flipped the top off my 7Up. I found my steel spoon in the dark and sucked on big hunks of vanilla ice cream. I imagined that my brother and a girlfriend were with me, watching.

For a moment I was back in Cincinnati, transported to the family room of my childhood home, with my girlfriend, watching the Academy Awards. A hardback first edition of the Ken Kesey novel lay on the side table, where it had been pulled down from the shelf. The room was dark, except for the glowing color TV, and a lamp pooling light, in the corner. She sat on a hassock, while I sat on the couch. Our knees were touching. Neither of us had read the book, nor seen the movie. But now, in Wyoming, alone with comfort foods, and a giant spoon, I could hear Big Nurse shouting, then whispering through the crackling remotes. Chief Bromden's silent presence loomed over the roofs of cars. The 7Up fizzed on my lips. The escape, the boat ride, and the prostitutes, cascaded in the breezy summer mountain air. When Billy Budd killed himself, I felt pangs of sadness, my eyes burned, and tears salted the vanilla ice cream. The shock treatment felt so brutal and shook me more. I loved the way the Native American triumphed in the end by escaping. I wondered if he was the one that flew over, after all. As the credits played, the cars started, and filed out into the night highway. I was afraid to camp behind the drive-in, because it seemed like in the morning I would be exposed.

I bicycled around for a while, in the frightening night, stirred by the film's violence; headlights, fear, and demons swept through on the breeze. Then I rolled off the road into a ditch, unpacked my sleeping-bag and bivouac, crawled inside, and drifted into fitful sleep.

I was awakened at dawn in gray dampness; headlights glared, and cars roared nearby. I had camped in a construction area by a muddy gravel trench. Things were shifting a bit out of control that morning. Between Tom's elopement, the difficult climb, the unsettling film, and my difficulty finding a safe place to camp, I felt disoriented and tired. I feared the sluggishness that I knew caused accidents. This was a dangerous time.

As I pedaled out of town, slogging in the early cold I saw an open roadhouse restaurant. I ate a large, satisfying breakfast with strawberry jam on biscuits, eggs over-easy, and a side of pancakes. Then I sat on the bark-stripped pole railing of the wooden porch, ate a cinnamon roll, and in memory, I think my brother Will sat with me at that diner for breakfast. He spilled sticky, maple syrup on the white, paper placemat. Gold rush stories with cartoon drawings edged the them. I wanted to save mine, take it with me. But it was so sticky. Will suggested I ask the waitress for a clean one. I chose not to. I remember he ran a dark fingernail over the crust on a dirty piece of flatware before we ate. His gestures were strong, but quiet, pulling a blue canvas Velcro wallet, from his khaki shorts, with his large, veiny, right hand. My fear ebbed, as I listened to him talk about the climb ahead. He soothed me into believing I could do it. He had a Patent, remember? I walked the machine over the rough gravel to the road, my toes clacking, and crunching as the cleats kept them up.

Teton Pass began a few miles out of Jackson. The way started with a straight highway leading into heavy forest. The pavement, relatively new blacktop, the double yellow line bright and clean. Thankfully, there was little traffic. A sign said the grade was seven per cent for eight miles. I had no experience with mountain passes this extreme. In the Adirondacks in New York, and the Green Mountains in Vermont, I had faced mountain passes. This was twice as long as the toughest I had ridden. As I hit the beginning slope, it was immediately apparent that the grade never varied. I think highways have a limit to how steep they may be. Teton Pass stayed right at the limit.

My lungs heaved with weight. It took all the force I could muster, just to turn the pedals over each rotation. The momentum from one stroke to the next seemed non-existent. I pedaled for all I was worth. Fifteen minutes of this, sweat soaked, aching, huffing and weaving up the grade, I looked up, lifting my head painfully, and the road looked flat. Even on the curves the grade never varied. I stopped, stood and looked back down the mountain. I clung to the handlebars, exhausted. I waited for a few minutes, gaze blurring, gathering my wind. My feet hurt, my shoulders ached, and I was afraid to look back. I knew I had passed many curves, not seeing how little ground I had covered kept me in check. Ahead, the road was more of the same. Conifers and rock outcrops rose above; to the left edge of the road beyond the heavy guardrail was cliff. Outside the cliff, an older road wound snake like against the edge. As my breathing recovered, I took in the view behind me. I had come a long way. Mountain below and mountain above. I was climbing Teton Pass. All the years of adventure and racing came together in this moment.

I climbed back on the blue bike and pushed on. Each stroke was again barely stroked. Each moment, when my feet were perpendicular to the road was pure agony. Agony again. A swoosh of force, a giant standing push, then agony. This continued push, after push for another fifteen, or twenty minutes, until I felt like my lungs were nine hundred degrees, my tongue dry and sticky, my mouth and nose both open, and I could not get enough air. Thighs burned, back tightened, and ankles stung. I wasn't going to cramp, but I had to stop for another break. Head heavy, I pulled onto a shoulder, on the left edge of the road, by the guardrail, after crossing the left lane, dismounted, and nearly collapsed, my chest heaving. I drank deeply from my water bottle. Lungs heaved more. Just the pause to get water in was a violent disruption to the clawing need in my lungs. The vista scared me again. This time looking back the road disappeared in haze. I had climbed into the clouds. Ahead was more of the same, as far as I could see. I rode alone, but everyone I had ever ridden with rode with me. They slipped behind, all behind; I was leading the way over the Grand Tetons. Teton Pass was 8429 feet, in thin moist air. Here, the cloud moisture, clung to black wool shorts. My legs burned, yet a cool breeze kept them from overheating. My calves never cramped, only because I was too afraid to let them. I had been training in various ways for years for this ride. Each piston like movement on the pedals was at my limit. I continued to turn the cranks. More than halfway to the top I stopped for a third time.

The sun cut through the clouds warming the sweat on my face. The cycle tilted against my waist. I put one hand on the black plastic saddle and one on the handlebars, lowered my head beneath my pumping heart and breathed. I had never pushed myself so hard. Even at Harvard when I rowed crew, I had not sustained effort so long. I remember, a power ten on the Charles River, in an eight man shell, when I caught a crab at the end of the ninth stroke, the oar flailing over my head and getting stuck behind me. Then I had been scared and exhausted, as the coach in the motor launch had yelled. I found the oar and ducked under it, pulled again, recovered my rhythm, and rejoined the rowing. Now, I made no mistake. I stood and felt like I might vomit. I sipped some water, fighting to breathe. Gradually, I caught my breath, lifted my head, turned and looked at the sky. Clouds covered the sun. I felt a chill, climbed back on the Follis, put my feet in the toe clips, strapped in tight, and rose to renew my rhythm.

Over the next two miles it got colder and colder. I forced myself to glance back, as I swung the machine into crisscrosses arching up the right lane of the highway. Motorists came up behind me, stayed blocked until they could see a way around, then puttered past, sending exhaust. The sound of the motors and car tires was a relief from the roar of my breathing. The machine creaked and something rattled in my panniers. The load stayed steady. Now, when I was able to glance back, the vista impressed and awed me. The road appeared, and disappeared behind blind turns in the thin, cool, gray mist. At the summit the temperature was in the forties.

I pulled up to the observation area by a gray Mercedes. A man and his wife watched me dismount but said nothing. I nearly collapsed, then just sat down on the blacktop surrounded by dark mist. There was no view in this cloud. I had climbed Teton Pass, alone, Will had been with me in spirit, Tom was gone. Will had joined me at the breakfast table of my imagination.
When we were planning the trip, I told Tom I wanted to ride over the Tetons, and he had agreed. It was the most direct way to Pocatello, Idaho, where we were planning to work on the Southern Pacific Railroad. Now, I thought about him as I sat eat-

ing an apple. There were no benches, nor any area of grass to sit with a view. I could see down the highway twenty yards, or so, into mist, and the wind swirled, cool and uncomfortable. I put on a long sleeve windbreaker, zipped it up. I checked my tire pressure.

I remembered Carlos Castaneda's Don Juan and his Yaqui Way of Knowledge. The Indian had been able to exercise his will. The will was an elastic, light-like force that emanated from the trunk of his body. He sat upon a mountain, stretched his will across the sky, and pulled his body to the top of another mountain miles away. In the scope of two days, a moment in my lifetime, a nanosecond in the space of time, I had lifted my body over two mountains by effort of my will. Dogen says mountains are mountains. Mountains walk. In the span of the lifetime of these mountains my existence was less than a snap of my fingers in time. A miracle had allowed me to walk on aluminum and steel over two mountains. The bicycle had seemed stationary with my body, a machine stuck in my time, and together we had moved over mountains. Glaciers move.

After about ten minutes, I decided it was time to go down the other side. For a moment I wished that there was more to do at the summit, something to mark the time. All I could think of, was to eat the whole apple except the stem, and toss the stem away. No other gesture came to me. Each crunch of the pulp helped clear the pressure in my ears. The coming descent lured me away from the pain of the climb. I wondered how much weight I had lost. In my lifetime I had not experienced a comparable challenge. When I had cycled from Cincinnati to Ann Arbor, Michigan in four days, the previous summer, my friend Charles and I had ridden from Lima, Ohio to Ann Arbor, a distance of one hundred forty-five miles, in one day. That was my longest day of riding. This was different. Here the effort had taken me through an hour and fifteen minutes of the most intense suf-

fering I could imagine. Once I started, there was no turning back. To go back would have involved many days, an alternate route, and would have lengthened my trip. I wonder if that mattered, as my whole life stretched before me without def-
inite commitments. I had climbed the mountain. Because it was there, and because I could. Yes, those were reasons enough. To get to the other side. I had exercised my will.

As on the previous pass, I had to stop on the switchback curves to cool the rims. I pulsed the brakes, swung through turn after turn, cars not daring to pass me, until I pulled off onto the paved shoulder for a break. I reached down to the front wheel. The rim burned to the touch. Cars squeaked, careened past, a camper trailer fishtailed behind a big Land rover. I watched the swaying rig, pleased to be off the highway, sipping water. Then I began again. More arching turns, green grass and clumps of gray stone flanked the roadway. My rims squealed with the pressure. The intensity of the descent came fast. My hat pulled loose, and I reached up to snag it, before it blew away. My glasses fogged up in the mist, the air cold, and damp on my face. I stopped again, this time nearly blindly. I stood on the shoulder on a curve. I sipped water. More cars blew by. The mountain released me as reluctantly as it allowed me its summit. Yellow and white wildflowers dotted the way. I smelled the earth warming, as I reached lower elevations. The third time I stopped to rest the brakes, I felt lonely. Standing there in this near wilderness, without Tom, without Will, with only my mind, body, and spirit. As I looked back up the mountain, I felt it as a presence, and thanked it for taking me in, and not damaging me. I guess the feat would have been less in some way had I not been alone. Unsure of this trip that lay ahead, I reached a straight stretch, once I remounted, spinning higher and higher gears. I felt myself explode with speed. I was in tenth gear and going hard. The sign indicating Idaho came and went in a flash. I rode a few miles at breakneck speed, then the road leveled, and I came to a tiny town called, Victor.

There was a general store. I pulled up, went inside, bought a quart carton of orange juice, came back out, and sat down on a wooden park bench. A fellow in his early twenties, with shaggy dark hair, and a thick beard dressed in blue jeans, and a white T-shirt, with a pattern on the back, jumped out of a green pick-up truck. He banged the door shut, walked into the store, as he looked me over. His pick-up had a partially painted over faded insignia. With the faded paint job, it appeared to be a fleet vehicle for a college in
Utah. The paint job on the truck was badly faded, seriously, and when he came out, he was drinking a can of beer.

"Where ya headed?"

"Pocatello, Idaho."

"If you want a lift, I can take you to Salt Lake."

Salt Lake was miles out of the way. But my GO partner, Frisby had moved there. I would have a place to stay in Salt Lake City. But the railroad job was in Pocatello.

"I have a friend in Salt Lake, but a job in Pocatello," I said.

He checked out my bike and gear.

"Where did you come from?"

"I started in Boston months ago, but the last continuous stretch I've ridden was from Rapid City, South Dakota."

He whistled.

"I really have to get to Pocatello. Could you drop me there on your way to Salt Lake?"

"Well, I'm in a rush to get to Salt Lake, but I'll be coming back up this way next week, and I could drop you in Pocatello on the way back."

This was huge. I had a ride. It was too good. I couldn't say   no.

"OK."

"Throw your bike in the back," he said, introducing himself.

Tetons to Pocatello

What had been a bicycling journey shifted and became a car trip. The trains would soon enter stage right; it's a story that's a progression from Beat sensibilities and sixties psychedelia. Travel, with blues and folk music keeping time, hitching, and hopping freight trains under the watchful patient eye of dharma; reinventing what had been the epic story of America seemed worthwhile, but it's important to study the recent history, and looking back now, to begin to learn some of the larger truths. In the literary shift from Kerouac to Kesey, the voice of madness transformed. In this story the voice of madness could not be othered, nor expressed through filters; chemical balances and imbalances became internal, and landscapes shifted between internal and external motifs.

Moments were sliced up like DNA on a slide. And this new driver, the man who called himself Rick Dunphee, his gruff dark beard propped on the hairy backs of his knuckles, hands in turn propped on the gray steering wheel of the old fleet vehicle, wore the DNA T-shirt. It wasn't a one of a kind, only because he had made a set of them for his friends. On the back of the white cotton shirt was a swirling, black and pink, double helix pattern with stars inside the wavy lines. He talked about it with his mouth, working behind that big beard, his birdlike eyes glowing brown and flickering with something to say. Rick's verbal cadence was laconic, words arched, then curved. He got me stoned on some dynamite Colombian Pale, and every turn of the road revealed another great green farm, or deep blue lake, or dark rocky mountain forested with conifers, busting with wild rabbits, and slick with streams. I had found a valley paradise, but now, instead of pedaling up, and down the rolling curving hillocks, I reclined, touched the gleaming edge of the window with my elbow propped, relaxing.

He was older, and I feared my own youth. I started to feel the quaking paranoia stream of marijuana highs. He talked in these lazy sentences then paused for what seemed like miles, and years went by, while he searched for the right word, then gave up and said, "Uhm. Uhm. I bought some land in Idaho, near where I —picked—you—up until then I was just thinking about the cabin. I bought a cabin in Idaho—near where I—picked—you—up." He stalled again, looking, resting his chin, his bearded chin. Flashing eyes my way. "Foundation," he said. Again, he paused. "Foundation—the problem of foundation. I want to move to the Idaho mountains."

"So, you have a cabin in the mountains?"

"A farm. A stretch of grazing land. Cows. I rent the land to a farmer. A cabin—" he looked out to the left, pounded the steering wheel with both hands, reached for the radio, then decided against it. "The land. And the cabin is on someone else's land. I have to dismantle—move the cabin."

Fields blew by with cylinders of cut grass, giant balls of gray green shredded wheat. Low fields of crops, soybeans. Horses by a deep brown wooden fence. Tall wooden farmhouses back from the two-lane highway. Rolling by. "Want to roll another one?" he asked, handing me a soiled plastic baggy and a blue cut corner pack of Zig-Zags. He flicked on the radio, and Bob Dylan crackled with "Santa Fe, dear, dear, dear, dear, Santa Fe," I felt fabulous. I patiently put my fingers to work, and in a few minutes had a workable joint. He pushed in the cigarette lighter. I began to get used to the West, puffing, rolling up the window to conserve the smoke, leaving just a crack for ventilation.

"So, I need to devise a foundation for the cabin before I can start to move it," he put together the whole idea in one clear sentence, and I coughed as the harsh acrid smoke expanded in my lungs. I passed him the little cigarette. "Do you know anything about construction? Architecture? A—foundation?"

"My family has a summer cabin in Ontario by the lake. The builder poured concrete pylons, I think he had some kind of tubular form and he embedded it in the ground, but it's real rocky ground. He might have even dug down to bedrock, I don't know. It seems to me, you could use cinder blocks and concrete. I've seen it done."

"Concrete and cinder blocks," he said. "I never thought of that. I could stack 'em, I could dig holes for 'em to rest on rock. It's rocky. I'd just have to level the surface, maybe pour some small footers," he looked quizzically around him, as if the answer was in the air, "Concrete and cinder blocks."

"You could carry some up in this pick-up truck."

"Yeah. That was the problem. I could take some sacks of concrete, or maybe buy those in Idaho. But cinder blocks are cheap in Salt Lake. Would I block in the whole base?"

"It's up to you. I imagine the cabin is too big for you to carry enough bricks for the whole thing in one load."

"Yeah, but I could make several trips. I have the whole summer to move the cabin." He pulled his hands off the wheel, rubbed his palms together for a moment. "I think you gave me the solution." Rick looked over; a good set of teeth appeared behind the mustache.

"Glad I could help," I said. And I was glad. I felt a warmth for this man and his project. Maybe in the future, I'd have a friend to visit, in the mountains of Idaho.

The truck got low on gas, we got the munchies, and the roadway grew bigger, the land flatter, and a little dryer. Dry mouth. Yellow grass replaced the verdant valleys. We went to a fueling plaza. Rick filled the truck, and I bought a soda and snacks, some sour cream and onion chips, a pack of salty, sunflower kernels, and a Mars bar. Rick bought a Yoo-hoo.

Back on the road, we munched in hungry silence. The wind blew, warmer and drier. A hitchhiker appeared at the roadside. Rick pulled over. "I'll get in back," I offered.

I got out on the shoulder, walked around behind the truck, climbed the bumper, and pulled myself into the truck bed, next to my blue bicycle. The young man, with curly dark hair, and a dirty, blue brimmed cap climbed into the cab, after handing me his pack. I fished an apple out of my pannier, and sat down, as the truck lurched forward. I sat up close to the cab, as wind roared around me. The sun filtered through the sky; it filled with clouds. I watched Rick share the rest of the doobie with the other man. It felt good to be back outdoors. I got out my red parka to shield my arms from the wind. Traffic. I watched the highway, and the land, and drifted into a shallow drugged sleep.

I awoke as the truck rocked to a stop. The hitchhiker climbed out. Rick waved me back into the cab. He handed me the baggie, and the blue pack of papers again.

"I'm just coming down from the last time," I said.

"That's OK," he said, "We'll go back up."

I rolled and soon we were puffing.

"What do you do in Salt Lake?"

"I'm a film student at the University there."

"Film?" I asked as openly as I could. Just managing the word was a stretch, I was so stoned.

"I was a philosophy major, but Kierkegaard kicked my ass. I liked the Germans, still it all got so much in my head. I was looking for something more practical, down to earth, less cogitative. Are you a student?" he fired back.

"Taking a leave of absence."

"From?" he looked my way.

"Harvard. I studied creative writing. We read Tom Vietch. John Batki was my teacher. He's Hungarian, has published in *The New Yorker*. I've been reading Robert Creeley. It's this whole approach that destroys syntax, and other structures. I'm not sure what the film equivalent would be. Some of the critics call the poetry 'language poetry.'"

He pounded his hands on the steering wheel in excitement, I think. He looked happy, and the Rolling Stones played on the radio, I didn't know the song, but I recognized the signature sound.

"Did you see *Taxi Driver*," he asked.

"I did," I said.

"I want to write a review of it for the school paper," he said.

"I went out for *The Crimson*, fall semester, but got cut. Fuck journalism."

"Help me write about *Taxi Driver*," he said.

"I'd say it was pie-wormed."

He looked over at me, questioning. The outside edges of his eyes raised, his lips, a straight line, and I suddenly felt he cared what I had to say. I had impressed him, coming out of the mountains on my blue Follis bicycle to ride with him to Salt Lake City. Giant sand worms were on my mind, just having finished *Children of Dune*.

"My friend in Salt Lake was a high school buddy. His dad was a philosophy professor in Cincinnati. He might be teaching philosophy, at Utah. My friend taught me Go."

"OK. OK. OK. You didn't like *Taxi Driver*?"

"It was a total mess."

"You play Go?"

"I'm learning."

He whistled low and long, reached to the black knob on the dash and switched off The Rolling Stones mid-song.

"What's pie-wormed mean?"

"I just made it up. Pie is sweet food and worms process earth. How do you talk about fucked up, violent, scatological, psychotic nonsense? I think we have to fight fire with fire. Call it something no one will be able to deconstruct or decipher. They'll have to either accept that you're a genius or be sure you're totally full of shit."

He laughed a little. For a moment, I thought he faked the laugh, and wondered had I gone too far? We were both stoned and the laughing got contagious. We laughed.

"I dug Cybil Shepherd," I said. "I'd like to meet her."

"Weird role," he said.

"Pie-wormed movie with art wires sticking out of the elbows of the crust," I said, "and that is exactly what you should write in your review. It'll catch the world's attention."

"You're higher than me," he said, "but, I've got the DNA Tee!" It rhymed and we both laughed again.

Recovery from schizophrenia began with describing events that led to the onset of the disease, and to give the reader some kind of sympathetic closeness with my persona as portrayed in the story, by Draups. This involves manipulation of time, shifts in perspective, moments where concrete reality disappears just as chemical balance eases into its polar opposite, while staying understandable to the reader. (Understanding, a shifting desert sand, a flowing wind without steady direction, a force in flux by the nature of schizophrenia.) You must be able to identify with my narrator, my protagonist, and fight for his survival both in the time frame described.

The DNA T-shirt, interesting in a way, perhaps more complex in context than to a spot reader. Why? Well, I have a friend, as I write this, an artist who made the Pacifier T-shirt. Each shirt is one of a kind with a couple of pink and yellow pacifiers, at different angles on the front. The idea, that everybody wants something to comfort his or her mouth, and thus satisfy the mind. But the DNA T-shirt implies a scientific analysis of the individual, explored with drugs, and later with the discovery of the human genome. Each individual has a DNA. My artist friend who made the Pacifier T-shirt, made art by filtering images through bar codes. He took his Naval Reserve Military I.D., scanned the bar code, made pixels, of himself, with the pixel's shape coming from the individual bar code. So, in my mind, these two artists, nearly thirty years apart, who never met one another, nor even heard of one another, are connected. Conceptually, both were T-shirt geniuses.

Rick left me off at his third-floor, walk-up apartment, and I found a map, and searched for my friend's home. There were numbered roads that were Avenues and Streets. At first, confused, and still a bit stoned the late afternoon, I don't remember exactly, but my sense was that I left Rick, looking for Frisby directly on arriving in Salt Lake City, I know I spent some nights with Rick, and his roommates at their apartment, but I remember after Frisby couldn't house me. Frisby's family's house was on a steep hill. I walked my bicycle the final quarter mile or so, pushing the loaded machine, listening to my breathing, and clicking uncomfortably in bicycle shoes. An ironic agony in the big muscles of my thighs and earlier the same day I had climbed Teton Pass without walking a step. Here, frustrated with the steepness of the road, the uneven pavement, the heat, humidity, and fatigue, I walked along the edge of the street. The sidewalks too broken to comfortably push the bike there, and the curbs rose eight inches above the street.

And Then the Cow Was Drownded

The brick, and white panel house had steps up to the front door, which faced down the hill. The steps came out to the side of the yard, where the sidewalk led to a garage that fronted against the sidewalk. Gardens surrounded the place, dark green ivy, orange day lilies, and other summer flowers. Trees lined the street, even breaking through the grassy border between the sidewalk and the steep street. I knocked at the door and there was no answer. I left a note on the front door after knocking on the garage as well. I went coasting back down the hill, away to a park, ate a snack then called from a telephone booth. Yellowjackets dove and hovered around me. In the park, a large grassy expanse, with tall deciduous trees, and picnic tables, I watched a young man throw a Frisbee for a black and white border collie. As he ran and played with the quick dog, I swatted and waved at the yellowjackets.

Months later, when I told the story of trying to connect with Frisby, Dad suggested that Frisby had been shacked up with a girl, when I had knocked. When he said it, I laughed, because that's what happened.

Frisby sounded out of breath on the phone. "You're in Salt Lake?"

"Yeah. I stopped by an hour ago and knocked."

He chuckled. "Give me forty minutes or so."

"OK."

When I knocked at the front door on the second visit, Frisby answered, barefoot and shirtless. Puffing from the hike up the street, I saw he had a wispy goatee, more facial hair than I did; we were both still too young to shave.

"Welcome," he said. "Let's go down to the basement."

I followed him through the carpeted entryway, ducked a low narrow door, down steep steps into a partially finished basement, with dark concrete floors, yellow steel poles supporting floor joists, overstuffed chairs, and an old upholstered green

126

couch. He lit a Marlboro cigarette, offered me the pack, I declined.

Frisby went upstairs. I sat down. I wondered if my bike was safe outside. His lit cigarette burned in the gold tin ashtray, that lay tilted on the end of a wooden crate, that doubled as an end table, and magazine rack. The smoke curled up to the ceiling, the light gray gas clouding against the dark unpainted wood, visible between the floor joists. I knew he wouldn't be gone long; he wouldn't want to waste a smoke. I hoped he'd come back with some weed. I heard footsteps on the stairs, and a lithe, nearly skinny, twenty-year-old girl appeared with yellow, streaked hair, pulled back partially under a blue bandana. Her eyes were furtive and brown, she was barefoot, and I could see the shape of her bra-less breasts.

"Steve, this is Lauren," he said. Frisby wore a dark blue T-shirt now. He picked up his cigarette, drew on it and said, "He's from Cincinnati," to Lauren. She picked up a purse that I hadn't noticed before. A paisley patchwork affair, it matched her jeans.

"Good to meet you," she said in a husky voice. Her hand rose to stroke the bandana, and the blonde hair behind. And there was a sense of everydayness, a commonsense practical stroking, a gentle habit that would never trouble anyone. All this way from Cincinnati, far off river city in the Midwest, where Frisby and I had grown up in middle-class comfort, looking to learn Go, and find the adventures that we read about in books. We were going to do something, with our lives. Now, in Salt Lake, Frisby had this new place, this basement to debase, and lift, to dream of ancient Japanese Go Masters. This was the seventies, our era of teen marijuana indulgence, when postmodern sensibilities in art began to seep into the fabric of our young understanding. We thought about ourselves, we introspected. We shook off the slippery apathy that fell over so many, we had escaped Cincinnati, or so we thought.

And Then the Cow Was Drownded

"I'd offer you a cold beer, but the stuff is hard to come by in this Mormon town," Frisby said. When Lauren left, Frisby broke out some Mexican weed, and we toked up. Then he went upstairs, and I played solitaire with a bent deck of Bicycles, until I fell into a doped sleep, drooling on the green dark fabric of the couch.

Beer. Looking back, I remember a haze of cigarette smoke, quiet, dull bars, with too much neon, and high-priced beer. We drove around in Frisby's car, without finding any women to talk to. The bars had cowboy motifs, with festive lighting, but we never seemed to find anything to celebrate, or anyone to celebrate with. We longed to see distant California, to find the dissipation that mirrored the glory of conquering the physical mountain. I did not talk about climbing the passes or crossing the desert. I kept quiet about Tom's disappearance. Cowering in the smoky bars, the dry basement, I flew into drugged sleep states that expanded the space behind my eyes. The quest for altered states hid the fear of being alone, the feat of the mountain crossing became history, a trick that was more than anything I imagined but could never communicate to another person. Mountains walking. A machine willed over peaks with the stroking of pedals. Frisby let out a whistle the one time he lifted the bike with all the gear on it. He was amazed by the thing, and I accepted his amazement, but it was not something to talk about.

After the haze cleared, I was back at Rick's apartment eating cereal and sleeping in my blue mummy bag in the carpeted hallway of his walk-up. I snacked, slept, smoked, and never left the apartment for two days. Rick and his two roommates had motorcycles. There were three cats, and a kitten, living in the cramped carpeted rooms. The kitten, a calico, was the only one I liked. The apartment harbored a cat piss smell, a yellow smell, with a clear cut that made everything tilt. Syllabus—a black furry green-eye, had six toes on his fluffy feet. His tail puffed, a diminished feather duster hanging in one direction, and his body was shaved short. He looked skinny enough to host a variety of worms. An indoor fountain in the hall attracted him three times an hour, his big fluff head tilted against the flowing stream. He meowed for food often, and Rick fed him once a day. Leon, an orange tabby with a pleasant face, licked the window from the outside, then licked paws, lick, lick, alternately paws to face, tongue to glass. He was let in the window over the fire escape. Blue, a gray cat with Siamese points, used the litter box sloppily, spraying litter and piss out the edge—scattering pellets and flakes on the bathroom floor.

I didn't buy groceries, while crashing at Rick's, but raided the refrigerator, with impunity. I ate pretzels, and powdered donuts, when the munchies came attacking.

The cats described a locus of twitching tails, whining hunger, and endless sandpaper licks. A cat scratched at my hair, put a clawed paw into my ear, scratched skin under the ear lobe— there were potted plants in the room off the hall (not pot plants). I reached up, grabbed the cat's belly, and as it writhed away, tightening soft, furry underside into a squeezing of sinew, belly, muscle—I was angry, gripped hard, pulled it toward my body, bit furry ear with front teeth, a squeal, and I threw the squalling critter eight feet into the wall where it met the floor. The cat landed, ran right back at me and clawed my bare arm. I felt anger. I wanted to heave it again, instead I became passive, limp, let Blue mangle my arm with claws. I could feel them releasing from the softer pads of the paw. Then the cat leapt up, and played chase team, with her twitching tail, scampering bang, bang, of little cat feet— a nightmare ripple of cat air followed her. Leon hacked in the next room—a breathless choking cough, more staccato than a man vomiting but nonetheless, arch—the wet hairball, the obstacle I stepped on, when I paced to the toilet barefoot, later on. I slept and smoked away the days while the men worked.

In Frisby's basement the Go game heated up. We thwacked at the board, our long fingers twiddling the stones and shells. Learning to play stoned slowed things down. Frisby laughed as he captured a whole side of the board where I stupidly played ladder. I wouldn't have done that straight.

Ladder in Go is one of the most basic neophyte mistakes. The game, over in a matter of minutes left Frisby grinning, his young face framed by girlie hair. He had the start of a mustache on his comely face. I wanted to be mad about making such a dumb gaff, but Frisby glowed with pleasure. I knew in my heart it was the last time I would ever lose because of ladder. In ladder a barrier crosses the whole board dividing it, giving one player a sure win. It was dark outside when we finished, and I coasted back to Rick's on my blue bicycle.

Rick and his roommates had heard about a laser light show in downtown Salt Lake. They were going by motorcycle. I was given a helmet and climbed on the back of Rick's Yamaha. We rumbled, two abreast, through the city streets. This was my first time on a motorcycle. The amazing thing was the view. Looking up at the streetlights, as a passenger was something I had never quite experienced. I could look around at the whole horizon. On a bicycle, as I pedaled, I was committed to steering, and watching my course. But here, as a rider on the back, although it was difficult to see in front, because I was seated just behind Rick, I could see around, and felt comfort in gazing. Stars were visible, even in the city, on the long stretches, where there were fewer streetlights. What an open free feeling. I started thinking about buying a motorcycle, and planning ways to ship my bicycle. I would go up to Pocatello next, get a job on the railroad, and after working through the summer, head out to the coast. Thinking back, I believe the motorcycle ride was the moment I concluded, finished with cross-country pedaling, from here on I'd motor.

Downtown, we parked the machines, and went into a big auditorium for a laser light show, which featured a wide movie screen, and swirling dancing pencil-thin beams, moving to rock music. I had seen better laser light shows in Cincinnati, at the Art Museum, two years earlier. Rick, and his roommates took hallucinogenic drugs before the show. They weren't impressed either. A bit nervous about riding home on the motorcycle with Rick while he was still high, but he assured me he was under control. And we traveled without incident. I felt a thin contact buzz, enjoyed the motorcycling, more than the light show.

I called Joe in Pocatello the next day. I told him when I would arrive, and he gave me directions to a crossroads, where I could find a payphone to call when I got there. Anticipation, and fear co-mingled in my heart. Eager to get away from the clawing cats, the steady pot smoking, and tired of losing at Go to Frisby, we parted ways.

Rick and his girlfriend, Laura, took me through a dark rainstorm from Salt Lake to Pocatello. I don't remember any of the conversation, just the weather, chilly, wet and we wobbled, with the pick-up truck loaded down by cinder blocks, for the foundation of Rick's cottage. We pulled into a gas station parking lot where there was a phone booth. I stood on the concrete watching Rick and Laura at nine-thirty, in a driving rain and lightning. This had to be unusual. I called Joe and he said to look for a yellow pick-up. Rick waited until Joe got there, then drove off without looking back.

Joe was a tall man with sandy blond hair, a goofy big Adams apple, sinewy arms, large thick clear-rimmed glasses, and warm grey eyes. He reminded me of his younger brother, Sean, a teacher and friend of my brother. Like my brother and I, Joe was older than Sean, yet thinner, and a bit more attractive. My brow is heavier than my brother's. Similarly, Joe's nose was less crooked, and thicker than Sean's. Joe's young son sat beside him in the truck, all wrapped in a yellow slicker. "Welcome to Pocatello, where the women are scarce, and the sheep are scared," Joe said.

I laughed, put my bicycle in the bed of the truck, and shock corded it to the side. The truck doors clanged shut, with a metal-on-metal bite of a work vehicle, and he whined her through the gears, up into the suburban hills. "Did you hear from my friend, Tom? He was riding with me up until a week or so ago," I said.

"We were out of town the last couple of weeks. The neighbors said he camped on our lawn." Joe's mouth, a taut line, he had a Michigan accent. He pulled at the wide wheel, moved the gearshift easily, "I guess he left the day before we got back."

I felt weak. No Tom, no partner to work on the railroad, a solo adventure. "It's OK, to stay with you for a while, then?" I asked. "I have money for food." I looked through the dark cab, at Joe's profile, with the background of streaming rain, windows cracked for defrosting, and rivulets running on glass. We were shadow figures in the night. "I want to work on the railroad," I said. "Did you get my letter?"

"Relax, Steve," he said. "We'll talk in the morning." And then he went into a whistling song, talked with his young son about something they had been into before I got in. "Yes, this rain will help the grass in the yard."

"What about Martha?" the boy asked.

"She'll stay in the den," said Joe.

Joe and his family had just moved into a suburban split level which stood on a muddy tree-less lot adorning a hillside overlooking the northeast edge of Pocatello, a small desert sagebrush town in southeastern Idaho. The night I arrived Tyler watched a late movie on TV, while Joe, and his wife Polly, entertained. The conversation turned to Beat poetry and Kerouac. I listened. Randy, a plump, bald fellow, in his early thirties, visiting from the Bay area, on a black BMW motorcycle, seemed knowledgeable. I settled into eight-year-old Martha's second floor room, in my blue mummy sleeping-bag with a copy of Ann Charters' biography of Kerouac, while the other adults drank beer, and wine into the night. The room had white wall-to-wall carpet, a pile of stuffed animals, and a wide foam pad, which became my bed. I didn't meet Martha that night, she slept. The tow-headed boy, Tyler, who was a little younger than Martha, was enmeshed in Disney. Martha's room smelled of chemicals, the carpet and paint were new. I recognized there were a lot of houseguests in this newly occupied place. I felt very much the outsider, an unbidden presence, without clear plans, possibly imposing, but without full awareness, perhaps.

I felt young for a few seconds. Not so young as the children; but the full flow potential for getting flung beyond where I had ever been seemed to lurk and linger in my hands and arms, and even a little in my chest. I was going to actually work on the railroad in the West where Kerouac and Cassady had been. Maybe not the same rail line, or the same job. As I read Charters, and flipped, and flopped, from stomach, to back on the floor, I wondered if the writing, that came from these experiences would be meaningful. I pulled a worn black bound blank journal from my panniers. With the Kohinoor Rapidograph, I made notes describing the room, and even did a quick character sketch of Joe. Strangely, I compared my personal plan to the past success of Kerouac to the degree, that I sort of hoped, I wouldn't work well on the railroad, rather, I'd be a better writer. And internalizing that thought, I flicked off the reading lamp at my shoulder, and tried to sleep. Sleep did not come easily. But, once I began to dream, I was moving fast, on a motorcycle through the night, lights flashing and images streaming, helter-skelter. I awoke from a warm moment, where I saw the face of my Muse, the one I would later call Draupudie, and her blue gaze penetrated my whole essence.

In the morning, I called home and talked to Mom. "Have you talked to Tom's folks?" I said.

"Yes," she said. "He's in Laramie, with his Aunt and Uncle. He's planning on heading back to Cincinnati. What are your plans?"
›55

"I'm hoping Joe will help me get a job on the railroad in Idaho," I said.

There was a long pause. "Is that what you want?"

"Yes."

"We miss you. Be careful."

"OK."

"I love you," she said.

"Bye," I said, because others were in earshot.

"Here's four dollars for the call," I said, "and twenty-one, for a few days food." I handed the money to Joe. The kitchen smelled of coffee, scrambled eggs, and grits. Polly was chunky, and fair. She cooked for the whole crowd of visitors, who took shifts around the kitchen table. On this cool gray morning I asked. "When can I start work?"

"I'm the roadmaster for two-hundred miles of track going west and a little bit east of Pocatello. My job is to maintain the track. We don't have any major projects on my track right now. And I have enough men. There's another roadmaster based here, and he covers the track east of Pocatello into Wyoming. He might need some workers. His name is Ken Kimoto. I'll talk to him. Then we'll see about getting the two of you together," Joe finished his coffee after making this explanation. "Just stay here at the house, or take a bike ride around town, and I'll let you know tonight."

Relieved, that Joe had explained the process, I still worried, that I wouldn't be working with him. I wanted to get started. Just to know something sure. It had been a difficult stretch. Why did I have to work for a complete stranger?

After taking the panniers, and other gear off the front, and rear racks of the blue bicycle, I cycled down out of the suburb, past hilly cul de sacs and yards. Some were recently sprayed on; ChemLawn futuristic grass. Others had clods of dirt, with seed, hay strewn. A few were landscaped with peat, mounded shrubbery. As suburbs went, this one wasn't very attractive, too new. The city of Pocatello didn't offer much to the traveling cyclist. One bike shop, no sew-ups. I looked at some camping gear at an outdoors shop. The city seemed to be an endless strip with stores and signs and fast food places. I couldn't find an old district with a courthouse, or a friendly diner. No coffeehouse and the bars I saw had motorcycles and oversized pick-up trucks with dirty haunches. There were muddy ATV's and dirt bikes strapped in some of the beds. I was back at the house by noon and hadn't much to show for it.

The children were playing with a large red rubber ball in the driveway. I went in and wheeled the Follis with me. I heard voices from the kitchen. Randy sipped at a bottle of dark beer as he talked to Polly at the kitchen table. She was having coffee. The other couple had left while I was in town. Pulling at the beer, Randy turned his attention to me directly.

"Where did you cycle from?"

"I started in Boston months ago. I rode up into the Adirondacks to support a team at the Olympic Trials, then on into Ontario, through Toronto and up the Bruce Peninsula. After some rides, some hitching, shipping the bike to Cincinnati, I started cycling again in Rapid City, South Dakota. I crossed Wyoming, then just into Idaho I got a ride to Salt Lake, and then here."

He gave me a long look. The brown of his eyes seemed to shift color a little, and the shape of his cheeks elongated as his jaw just dropped. "That's a shit load of pedaling," he said.

I smiled proudly then looked down. Polly offered, "Beer? Coffee?"

"Just water," I said.

"You sure?" she asked.

"Yes."

She filled a glass from the tap with a filter.

"You want to work on the railroad?" Randy asked.

"Well, I want to earn some money and have some experiences to write about. I was at Harvard for a year and I want to go back after a leave of absence with some significant writing and working. Railroad pays good and I'm curious about freight trains."

"Harvard?"

"Yeah," I said. It was always the same. Big name, big place, little me. When I met folks and then they took me in it never added up just right. There's this elitist stereotype. "I'm from Cincinnati. I went to public schools there. Did real well, graduated a year early and last summer cycled from Cincinnati to Boston before school."

"Kind of a high achiever, huh?" he said.

"Did you go to college?" I asked.

"Dropped out after two years at UC Sacramento. I grew up near there. The road called to me. I met Joe and worked with him off and on for five years. This last year I bought Betty and I've crossed the country twice, once low, once high. Now I'm headed back for California."

"What did you do on the railroad?" I asked.

"I started laying steel; moved up to heavy machinery," he laughed.

Polly had been listening then she eased out. Her pale cleavage lingered in my mind as I heard her join the children outside, the screen door banging. Something about Randy became very kind. He understood the curiosity about the railroad. He understood it deeply and fully.

"Are you going back to railroad work?"

"I have a steady job in a warehouse in Sacramento. Driving a forklift is enough."

I wanted to ask if working the rails was dangerous. I felt like he was telling it straight, but not all of it. Like he could tell I was scared. I sensed that Polly pulled away because of the danger. The men did dangerous work. I don't know if I remember this or imagined it in retrospect, but one time when Joe, Randy and I were together, I think in the cab of the pick-up truck, probably going to the store to get beer or milk, bread and eggs, Joe talked about the semi-truck drivers who tried to race the freight trains at crossings. "It happens every five months or so. Some jerk gets cocky, feels his oats and just revs too high, pops the clutch too fast and stalls out right on the tracks. Never damages the units much. Might shake up a switchman or engineer, but the semi looks like a smashed tin of Vienna sausages." I shuddered as my question was answered. I felt for Polly. She stayed home and waited for the phone to ring, or the men to come home.

Having Randy visit gave her comfort. I saw all this. And I was becoming a part of it. If I stayed around, they would let me into this life. I wasn't sure about the living conditions, but I knew my time in Idaho was temporary. I'd be working for the summer, maybe a year and two summers. If the pay was as good as I'd heard, I'd have money to travel next summer easy. I had a few grand, in the bank that my grandparents had given me when I turned eighteen. The fact of it was I didn't need to work at all yet. But, I wanted, to get a rhythm. Get in on the railroad. I needed to ask Polly if I could call home to the bike shop to have them ship me some tires. I had left money with the owner for enough tires to get me from Idaho to the coast. But I had time, to do that. I wouldn't be riding anytime soon. A part of me remembered the feeling that I'd had before. Maybe I'm done with bicycles. I wanted to talk to Randy about motorcycles. If I made enough money on the railroad, I could buy a motorcycle.

"When did you get your first motorcycle?" I asked.

"Oh, I rode dirt bikes in high school. The first road machine was a Honda five hundred. That was eight years ago," Randy said. He finished the beer, stroked his clean-shaven face and seemed to drift into memory.

"I can't imagine how much ground you can cover in a day on a motorcycle. On pedals it's more than one mountain. I think walking it's one mountain or less." I sipped the water Polly had given me and gazed for a moment at the shape of my large hand as it gripped the plastic cup.

"Two wheels, with a motor is real different from what you've been doing," he said. "I like to see the scenery and camp, ride back roads for a while, but be able to move through traffic on the Interstates into major hubs. I can do over five hundred miles in a long day. Two or three hundred makes for steady progress."

"The most I've done is just short of one-fifty. A buddy and I rode from Lima, Ohio to Ann Arbor, Michigan on the longest day of the year, last summer. We started around ten in the morning, rode hard, twenty or twenty-five miles an hour for an hour or so, then rested hard, quaffed milk, juice and ice cream for almost an hour then did it all again. An hour on and an hour off nearly twelve hours later, as it got dark, we pulled into Ann Arbor. It was over ninety-five degrees and when we arrived, we found out there had been a tornado watch all day. Windy, yes, but no rain."

Randy grinned. "I crossed Missouri one day. It rained buckets."

"I haven't had to ride much in real bad conditions. One day in Wyoming we waited for a couple of hours for the wind, reading and sleeping. It shifted a hundred eighty degrees. Then we did fifty in two hours mostly coasting."

"Wind makes it difficult on Betty, too."

Polly came in. "Want some lunch?" she asked.

We nodded. She made some tuna salad sandwiches on thick white bread. The conversation paused while we ate.

"Do you have work shoes?" asked Randy.

"I just have my cycling shoes and these ultra-light running shoes," I said.

"What size do you wear?" he asked.

"Eleven and a half or twelve," I said.

"I have some cowboy boots that might fit. There's no way you'll work on a crew without boots," he said.

"Thanks. I guess I'll try them," I said.

After lunch, Randy got the boots while Polly did the dishes. The kids came in and ate after we did. Randy and I moved out to the driveway. He had the boots in the saddlebags on Betty. They were black leather pull on cowboy boots with worn rubber soles and heels. The right one fit pretty well, but the left was a little tight. I walked around and convinced myself that they would do. I didn't want to buy boots. Randy and I spent the rest of the afternoon hanging out until Joe came home.

Joe hadn't seen Ken Kimoto that day and had no news for me at all. He and Randy got to talking and I went back to the Kerouac biography in Martha's room, again flipping between my back and belly, stretched out on the pad and sleeping bag. When dinner was served, I kept reading, then came down later and snacked on leftovers. I didn't feel included, and wasn't making an effort to fit in. This sense of not belonging seemed to parallel some of Charters' descriptions of Jack, and I was willing to be like him, at least in my mind, at least for the time being. Jack had been French Canadian raised in Massachusetts. My heritage came without a slang packed well-worn second language. But, as athletics go, I was sure racing and cross-country bicycling was going to make me cooler than an Ivy League football star had ever been. Cycling had an appeal that everyone could see was growing. I had no control over Joe, and while I liked him as far as I knew him, I didn't know him worth a damn. I wanted to punch him in the head and get his attention. But, none of my needs were pressing. Of all the things I had, the one I had the most of was time. If he wanted me to hang around a few days or weeks before deciding either to help me or cast me loose, it was his decision. I figured I'd either start to get to know him, or not. After reading several more chapters, and hearing the kids put to bed, I wanted to have a conversation, but shyness kept me from venturing out. I went to sleep.

Several days passed much as the first one did. Joe went to work, Randy chatted with Polly and me, and then I returned to the well-thumbed paperback. Randy never offered a motorcycle ride. I didn't ask. When Joe came home in the evening, he had no word about Ken Kimoto. I stopped waiting for him and didn't ask. I kept to myself more and more. Then I finished the biography. I have to say I was a bit put off by Charters' assertion that Jack was bisexual. Yes, I was troubled by the sexual identity the Beats were given. One day I brought it up with Randy, just as I started to read *The Subterraneans,* a fragile fading paperback from my dad's library that I had snagged in Cincinnati before leaving home. Randy listened to me and somehow waited until Joe was in the conversation to circle the focus back around to gender and sex identity.

I felt discomfort, and wanted Polly to be part of the conversation, too, but it seemed her role was of mother and wife. She did not work outside the home. She wasn't included in the philosophical and social conversation when I was around. Manly men who worked on the railroad who were into men as well as women? This was new to me.

"When you read Kerouac, do you get a sense that he was bisexual? Neal Cassady and Jack were lovers as well as best friends? Is this fact? Is Charters just talking about literary interpretation? If you ask me, it's a little weird," I said.

We were in the kitchen; Joe and Randy were drinking beer. Joe said, "I don't know for sure, but Charters is a respected biographer."

"Does it matter when you read his novels?" asked Randy. (I had not yet read the poems of Allen Ginsberg and Lawrence Ferlinghetti, but I was familiar with some of Gary Snyder's poems that had a Zen quality.)

"I don't know," I said. "Dean Moriarty and Sal Paradise didn't have sex in *On the Road*. According to Charters there are keys that explain which characters are based on which real people, but fiction and real life are not the same."

"But, does it matter to you, as you read Kerouac, what his sexual orientation is?" asked Randy again.

I looked over at Joe. He looked benign, empty, a void of anything but a blue work shirt, a family, and a halcyon job working for the Southern Pacific. He was a workingman. What difference did it make to him what the sexual orientation of a now dead novelist might have been? I didn't see how it could matter to me. I knew I had some great male friends but wasn't interested in sex with them. I also knew that if I wrote a novel without a great woman character, I might also be described by some authoritative biographer as someone who had all kinds of hang ups and hang downs that were just in his or her mind. "Joe, does it matter to you that Charters characterizes the now dead Kerouac as bisexual?" I asked.

"Not if the country accepts Kerouac as a meaningful novelist and poet who appeals to more than one generation. People are way too hung up about gays and bisexuals in this world." He looked at Randy and added, "Accept people as they are, let them be."

"Joe, I want to work on the railroad. If you want me to leave, or if you don't want to help me get a job for some reason, then let me know. OK?" I said.

"What is your work experience?" he asked.

"I worked as a bicycle mechanic summers, part time, and on breaks, my last two years of high school. I've worked in a couple of different shops. I did repairs and assembly," I said.

"That's not much experience. And you are young for this kind of work," he said.

"What is the work like?" I asked.

"Most start on a steel gang. You'd be laying down quarter mile long strips of rail that are delivered by special flatcars. The weather is brutal, the days are long, and the work is hard."

"What does it pay?" I asked.

"It starts at $5.26 an hour."

"Would I get a caboose pass?" I asked. I had heard about the caboose pass. Legend had it that with one from any large freight company, a worker could ride for free anywhere in the United States.

"Yeah," he said. "But don't spread it around."

"I want a job," I said again.

Joe got up from the table, drained the last few drops from the brown bottle into the kitchen sink, gave it a rinse and put it in the trash. He left the room. Randy turned to me with a look on his face that told me only that Randy couldn't interpret Joe's action.

A couple more days passed with no word from Joe about the job. Then one Friday Joe said he had seen Ken Kimoto and he needed workers on a steel gang in Sage, Wyoming. Sage was half a day's train ride east, a remote outpost with nothing but bunk cars and a chow station. I would meet Ken on Monday, get my card and leave directly on a slow freight that morning. I did laundry over the weekend. The time dragged worse than it ever had. Reading Kerouac about Mardou and Leo Perciped was the only thing that kept me from watching the clock tick. I was going to work on the railroad.

Monday morning, I was up before daylight. Joe drove me down to the Southern Pacific office. It was a low-slung room with hardwood floors, institutional green painted steel doors, windowframes and furniture. The internal doors had mottled glass panes that were translucent. Joe introduced me to Ken, a small man with square shoulders and a flat face. He wore a blue, button down, work shirt, and a gray zippered jacket, with cotton cuffs. It's weird how he looked so much the stereotype of a middle-aged worker. In his office, he gave me all the paperwork to fill out for payroll and typed up an orange card for me, himself. The caboose pass. It didn't look like much, but I tucked it into my wallet. I wore my only jeans and a blue Campagnolo T-shirt to remind me of cycling. The boots were a bit tight, and my gear was packed into my orange panniers, which were strapped together with webbing. The gear hung on my shoulder, already a bit uncomfortably, as I walked through the railyard to the caboose. Ken told me which track it was on after a quick orientation. I was on my own.

Black and green on the outside, with an iron handle next to a narrow stair, the caboose looked large, oversized. The scale of trains resembles the scale of semi-trucks. It is a world so different from bicycles. Yet, when I am on my bike, I sit taller than most cars, but this massive steel train car with its solid iron wheels with shiny silver rims where metal met metal seemed to epitomize a past, and a timelessness. The modern industrial iron-age is characterized by a certain permanence that grew out of corporate stability. But, change might someday make these monolithic vehicles obsolete. For today, the size, the future, all were reduced to this immediacy. I came across the mountains, which walked their own steady pace, to wait nearly four weeks, decompressing from the great cycling adventure in Salt Lake and Pocatello. Now, I was entering the next phase of my journey. Scale, combined with function, and its durable appearance gave me pause. I took in the train, its tracks and its looming presence with a long gaze and several deep breaths before I climbed on. The inside was open and roomy. There was a raised seat in the center of the compartment so that the brakeman could see out the little oblong elevated windows that gave the caboose its characteristic shape.

Silas, a grey faced man with a bulbous nose, thin lips, and a clean shaven, jowly chin had a charcoal, colored train worker's hat covering his close cropped, thin, gray hair. "Welcome," he said. I shook hands with him just as I unshouldered the gear. "Toss that in the closet," he said. There was a dark, flat, padded bunk with an electric lamp and a pillow on the right side of the car. "We'll be pulling slack in ten minutes," he said.

"Pulling slack?" I asked.

"The spaces between the couplers have to pull taut. It takes a little while and makes a lot of noise," he said.

He fiddled with a CB radio. "You there, Jeffrey?" he spoke into the handpiece.

"Almost ready, Silas, over." Jeffrey's voice crackled through the speaker.

"Got a kid, Steve, headed for Sage, over," said Silas.

"Come again, over," came Jeffrey's voice.

"We've got a passenger here. His name is Steve. We take him to the Sage worksite, over," said Silas.

"Copy," said Jeffrey.

Then there was a pause for a few minutes, and I smelled the pipe tobacco, and the mustiness of this old caboose. I felt like I had started the journey, even though we weren't moving yet. The space filled me as I filled it; it had become what it was years ago. Many men had traveled in this enclosed room.

"Silas, how long have you worked on this train?" I asked.

"Eighteen years on this very line," he said.

This man knew time in a way that I had yet to understand. And all of Kerouac's efforts to know time through jazz, Benzedrine and alcohol were different from the old brakeman's understanding. He measured each ride in puffs of smoke and watched the seasons. I could only imagine the view from those little oblong windows.

"You moving, Jeffrey, over?" asked Silas.

"Started three minutes ago, Si, over," said Jeffrey.

"We're pulling slack," Silas said in a gruff voice.

Then I heard it, a series of repetitious bangs, one after another getting closer, louder, and spaced ever so slightly closer together.

Over the radio there was a flash of static then Jeffrey's voice, "You coming with us, Silas, over?"

"We'll see, over," said Silas.

Then the banging was all on us, and the caboose jerked, I grabbed a handle on the wall to keep from falling, and we were moving. Once the whole train was in motion, Jeffrey blew the whistle.

The train gathered clicking, rattling speed as the floor moved in a steady side-to-side, up and down, and front to rear shifting. It was similar to standing on the deck of a boat on the lakes. My inner ears adjusted well to the movement. We seemed to be going incrementally faster for nearly twenty minutes. Silas said we were doing fifty-five miles an hour. The clacking noise was steady. As the movement increased, there was also a smell of kerosene, not unlike in the cabin of my family's sailboat. The lanterns were auxiliaries to the electric lamps in both cases. Nausea swept over me. Silas came down from the upper seat and saw my discomfort. "Feeling it, son?" he asked.

"I think it's the motion and the kerosene odor," I said.

"Climb on up. Fix your eyes on a distant point and hold it. It'll settle you down," he said.

I got up in the seat. Up there it smelled more like pipe tobacco, and the view was quite amazing. The sky was lightening, orange and pink to the east where we were headed, but the desert had distant rock outcroppings that glistened in the angular rays. I focused on one large butte and the movement seemed to lessen because of the distance and perspective. Silas' advice had proven itself. Soon the blue sky dominated. By turning my head, I could see the whole horizon, as the oblong windows opened three hundred sixty degrees. I wondered if Silas ever got bored watching the landscape. The desert stretched away as far as I could see, probably six or eight miles in every direction. As the rails clicked along, I felt my life was finally moving in the right direction, but   I was still not sure what Sage would be like. Who would I have to bunk with? I forced myself not to think about the next thing and to stay right where I was.

"How long will we be in Idaho?" I called down to Silas.

"Most of the day," he said, "Sage is just over the border."

"I feel better."

"Good. Stay up there awhile."

I continued to focus on distant points and let them slowly pass before shifting to yet another. The morning drifted by. Silas opened one of the windows below and began to puff on his pipe. The additional light, the aromatic fragrance blowing on the desert air, and the sky as blue as a movie star's cobalt eyes kept me from the ill feeling. It's funny, when I dreamed of working and riding rails, I never once had thought of motion sickness. That kind of a problem could make this line of work much less enjoyable. The sound of the train's whistle droned before crossing roads. I remembered the story Joe had told, about semi drivers. I thought about asking Silas if he'd ever been in a wreck. I imagined he'd tell me if he needed to. I gathered it was not the best question to ask a brakeman.

As I mused about where I was going, the thoughts about the place narrowed into wondering if the name "Sage" meant anything in the grand scheme of things. Was there some wise old soul waiting for me on the steel gang? Ken Kimoto had directed me to find the foreman at the site and introduce myself. There was a name, Tony Santos. "When you get to Sage, find Tony Santos, the foreman, and he'll tell you what to do." Would some kind of wisdom be passed to me in my hours, days, weeks, even months at Sage? Or was it just Sage for sagebrush? That's what it meant, obviously. Why was I even thinking about this? The desert extended. That's what it did. It extended. It was an extension of land and scrub brush as far as I could see in every direction. So remote, that with all the money coming in, there would be no place to spend it. I would be set for a couple of years with all the money earned at Sage. The money would bring me wisdom. Yes, sagebrush and sage wisdom would bring me good fortune. This kind of good luck could be planned. I had left Boston months ago with this very day distantly in mind. I had expected Tom to be with me, his grinning, silly face would be totally at home here. He'd have become infatuated with the train ride, and the idea of a steel gang for sure. When he found out how much money I saved in the next year, he'd shit. He'd throw himself down at the ground with anger and self-loathing. He'd be so envious, I'd feel humble and debased, just telling him of my good fortune, and virtuous planning. Yes, dreaming and planning were the things, in the eighties we would say "the shit." I was the fucking Sage, for getting to this never to be forgotten, impossible to imagine amazing caboose ride.

I got down from the seat and Silas climbed the rungs. Then I lay back on the bunk and opened the Kerouac novel. Leo was a successful writer who loved jazz and a black woman named Mardou who was hooked on marijuana. She took her clothes off in the alley of the San Francisco apartment building in a marijuana freak out. This was cool and elementally tragic. Leo hung out and drank with writers and jazz heroes till the dawn, then, Mardou lost patience with him for not being around. More than I could imagine I wanted a life like Leo's, but I wasn't sure I'd be comfortable with Mardou. She sounded hot, but sketchy, not grounded, flighty, a risky endeavor even for Leo. A girlfriend would be the thing. Yes, to be in San Francisco, after working on the railroad, writing a book about it, getting published, gaining a reputation with the jazz cats, then finding a black woman. I imagined she danced for him. Was this Kerouac's life? Or was it fiction? What did the man really do? Leo was out with his male friends. Were they sexing each other? A Zen syncopation danced through the text with its jazzy buzzing energy. The book never spelled out the sex details. Hinted descriptions, bedsheets and euphemisms, a seedy, exotic, tempting, sly, foxy, greasy, humming, racy, jumping, jittering, manic, lazy, florid flow of long, languid, anachronistic sentences pulled at the reader with gut level, tense, mildly erotic swishing. A literary critic or biographer might be able to interpret this fiction. What would I do on a steel gang if I got lonely for female companionship? Was it that simple? No. I don't think I could ever have sex with another man. But, to judge someone else for his orientation was not right. Reading *The Subterraneans* on a caboose was so cool. I wished I could have a photograph taken of me leaning back on this bunk reading the dog-eared paperback novel.

Then the train started to slow down. First to forty-five, then thirty, soon we were doing less than twenty-five. Silas radioed Jeffrey.

"We lost a unit, over," he said in a reedy thin voice.

Silas turned the radio off. The train slowed to ten miles an hour. When we came to a gradual rise, she went even slower. "We'll have to stop before Sage to pick up a unit," said Silas.

"Before Sage? How much?" I asked.

"It's going to take us most of the day to get to the border. There's a town and small exchange there. You'll pick up another freight." He said with both hands gripped into fists.

And I hushed the music generated by words that had flowed in my mind and heart, reading and bouncing along the desert railway. This had to be the best way on the desert. I thought about the *Dune* novels and wondered if freight trains were the contemporary equivalent of sand worms. Were the giant critters based on the fast desert trains that could be hopped by bands of roving desert warriors? Could such a connection have any value as literary interpretation? Do the freight-hopping, Buddhist Beats in the Jazz Age, and the giant worms of the contemporary science fiction novelist intersect. The jet airliners were like the Guild spaceships. Were the desert hallucinogenic plants the spice? Where I had visited in the North Country was the old planet, one with abundant clean fresh lake water. Now, the North Channel of Lake Huron was no longer safe to drink without filtering it. When I had been a child, reaching over the rail of a boat with a cup was safe, and the summer lakeshore cottage drew drinking water pumped from a hose right out of the lake. But, this personal interpretation of the great Frank Herbert's novels was just that, and I plunged into the darkness of feeling inadequate to the task. Why do these thoughts of a life begun in the desert frighten me now? The Beats wrote poetry and transcended time, leaves in the rain, trembling lightly drop-by-drop. They smoked marijuana, another possible source object for the "spice" in the science fiction epic. The illumination a short moment ago, seemed fleeting, as the train chugged slowly, and I began to sense that Sage was further off, and that the fantastic adventure had pitfalls and wrong turns by the hour. Just when the thing might have felt like it was a done deal, yes, it had felt done. I felt I was working on the freights. I wasn't on the clock yet. I had no job description. But no reason to flip out, this was just a delay. A temporary setback. Surely the trains kept going and I'd get to Sage a little later, none the worse for wear. I knew others had ridden from Pocatello to Sage. This freight ran all the time. When Tom and I had bicycled, we had met with pitfalls, but managed. This new way might be slow, but if my efforts were sincere, the day would flow into a new adventure. I asked Silas if this was a daily scheduled freight. If a road passed through here, I could go faster on a bicycle than this hobbled freight. Silas was distracted and didn't give a clear answer. He had drifted out of the clear communication mode I had gotten used to. Maybe he took me as part of the problem. I was an extra hassle when things weren't going well. As long as the train was moving, he was helpful and concerned about my wellbeing. Now, with the slowing of the train his energies had turned to another radio, a VHF, two-way, walkie-talkie that he used to radio a railyard up ahead. The train made less noise, the rhythm of the rocking slowed, and time bumped into itself. Our spirits settled into making do with what we faced. A comedown effect took over. My reading pace was even affected by the slowing of the train. I kept looking up from the book and losing my place. Methodically, and not without a struggle, I forced myself to refocus. And then I read for two hours, taking in the long sentences, the ellipsis, the dialogue and summary of Leo and Mardou and all the other whacked out characters. I could almost hear Charlie Parker's saxophone solos ringing through the clattering caboose. But, what, did I know of jazz? I got drowsy and napped. Then the train stopped. Silas asked me to walk the length of the train on the large cinders and climb onto the unit. The train wouldn't be stopped long. He would stay on the caboose.

I climbed out onto hot dry cinders. My glasses darkened, the thin webbed strap on the panniers dug into my shoulder. My toes pinched as I hiked nearly a quarter mile from one end of the giant freight to the other. I had a small, crushed shadow as the sun was nearly overhead. There was a compact, thin, young man with shaggy blond hair wearing an open white shirt and jeans standing on the ledge-like railed platform at the front of the unit. I didn't ask his name or give him mine, but we said hello to one another. Then I met Jeffrey. He had a small pointy-shaped head with a prominent jutting jaw. Jeffrey with the jutting jaw. His eyes were big and grey with a swirly quality that was emphasized by bushy white eyebrows. He had the same hat as Silas. Jeffrey chewed on the stem of a curved black and brown pipe. Tobacco seemed to be a theme among the train men. The warm glow of fragrant embers added to Jeffrey's presence in the cozy engine room. There were only two seats. The steel walls were painted grey, and instrument panels partially covered them. Windows let in sunlight and offered a view of the track ahead and the desert on each side. When I stood, I could look down through the front window and see the track disappearing under the deck once we were moving.

We slowed soon after starting, and the young switchman jumped off, running, ran ahead, manned a switch, then hopped back on even though the train never stopped. I envied him. That would be the job to have. A switchman on the Southern Pacific Railroad. What a story. But, I'd have, to start my career, on a steel gang. That was my destiny. I'd work my way up to switchman. The train moved on slowly.

As the afternoon heat warmed the interior of the engine, I stood by the front window on the left side. The switchman had one seat and Jeffrey the other. A small river appeared silver and shiny under a tiny bridge. I saw a glistening fish curling under the water's surface. The fish looked so big for that baby-sized river. It wasn't until much later that I would consciously see that fish as a metaphor for myself back in my hometown. But, at Harvard, it had been the converse. Again, here on the railway, I felt like a little fish in a big pond. The days in Salt Lake had been a lazy vacation compared to what was coming. Kerouac had proved he was a giant, but in *The Subterraneans* he was just coming into his own before descending into isolation and booze. I later read all his published books but the first one. I had an inkling of his later life, but only from, his biography; life's difficulties, temptations, and deep water still unknown. At Harvard, I had the sense that other students had richer and better-placed parents. Much of my ambition was tied up with resentment that I had to work at all, and with fear that I couldn't perform as well as those who attended prep schools or private international schools. In the quiet rattling, of the slow moving, freight train, I gathered an energy that I hoped would move me, push me into real American adventure. Sure, some writers might just imagine riding across the desert ponds surrounded by succulents, but I saw the dusty heat waves rising above the sand with my own eyes.

At one-thirty we came to a small town with a water tower, low brick buildings, high concrete curbstones and a wide paved street. Walking around with my makeshift pack and tight boots in the sun hurt more than I wanted it to. My exposed arms felt the tingling of the dry heat. Dry heat made for strange sweating. As my forehead got gritty, the dust clogged my nose and my feet felt pinched, heavy and clumsy. The pinching became a heat that spread up from the toes into the arches. I found a diner and got a chicken salad sandwich. I don't remember the interior of the diner. I imagine it was clean and full of light. What I do remember of the town was exterior space, big plate glass storefronts, dust and very high curbs.

After lunch, I waited on a wooden bench in a narrow light green hallway at the railway office. Again, the wait seemed to draw out for hours. I wanted to take off the black boots in the hallway and wiggle my toes, but I was too ashamed. Sitting in public in my socks would draw attention. I wanted to be in the background. With a word the young switchman let me know it was time to go. Then I was on a train again. The same young switchman worked the yard and joined me, and Alfie, a thin-shouldered man with blue-black eyes behind thick black and silver-rimmed glasses. This engineer chewed tobacco, pulling wads of shredded, moist, golden brown leaves from a foil pouch with stained fingers. He had his own spittoon in the unit by his seat. The smell of chew and dust mingled. Alfie had the freight at a steady thirty-five for a couple of good rattling hours. I nodded off on my feet, propped at the sliding window with a desert breeze blowing in over the clacking sound and the gentle rocking. I worried that Alfie might sleep, too, but the chewing seemed to be a regular stimulant. Alfie was younger than the other engineer. Then, as the clock on the grey instrument panel struck five o'clock, Alfie slowed and stopped the train. I awoke to the squealing brakes.

Rubbing my gritty face, I asked, "Aren't we going to Sage?"

"This is as far as we go," he said, blue-black eyes flickering behind the thick lenses. "Sage is a mile further on." He spat a brown stream into the dark spittoon.

I wanted to argue, or find, some explanation. There didn't seem to be any reason to stop here. But, Alfie said, "Just follow the tracks east."

Shouldering my gear, I left the unit's dim interior, down the steps to the golf ball sized cinders. The stone-like chunks gave with a painful crunching sound. I had no hat. The sun was still high enough to generate a steady poison ache in my head. The rough bed sloped away from the shiny steel rails. If I tried to walk on the creosoted ties, my stride had to shift with each step, so I chose the sloping left side of the tracks. My shadow crept forward as I stepped into it. Before long the thin white straps were gouging my shoulder and hand. I tried to use my elbow and fist to keep the orange panniers from swinging and rocking. They shifted often enough that every fifteen steps or so, I had to re-adjust where the straps crossed from chest to back, and about a third of the time this re-adjustment required stopping for a moment. The two webbed straps were an inch wide. It was difficult to keep them from riding together and twisting. When I stopped, my toes were crushed even more than normal. In slowing my gait, the pressure forward burned up to my shins and knees. The burning became an ache. Blisters grew on my toes and heels. If I watched my feet hitting the cinders, the pain seemed stronger. But, if I gazed ahead, I became demoralized by the sameness. I stalked my own shadow. The narrowing of the tracks, the shimmering heat, the illusion that I was abandoned, and the anticipation of this camp where I'd be thrown into a bunk car with strangers all gnawed at me. The gnawing burned my eyes, and when I looked off into the desert at grey green sagebrush, dried and withered, but growing, and I breathed the heat I felt a weakening. Gradually this adventure was pulling my chain. I tried to force a chuckle at the irony. Suffering builds character. I had no water with me. My mouth was dry. I had imagined a great wonderful future. I had expected to be delivered at the site of Sage. Anger bubbled up also. That damn Alfie could have brought me another mile. It wouldn't have delayed him much, and it would have saved me this delirium. This mile walk broken into stride after painful stride took the better part of an hour. If I were one who compares kinds of pain, this would be in the category of slow, excruciating, and most like water torture that I could imagine in my young life. There was a discomfort factor from the strap, the sun, the dry heat, and the boots, that because of their combinational reinforcement, held a keening, self-defined place in my locus of suffering. These were new pains to me. They played, mimicked and riffed off one another. One alone would have been annoying, two together would have been difficult to maintain attitude adjustment, but the three were nearly transcendentally monumental and I wanted to cry. My eyes burned from the sand, dust, sweat and grit. Cycling had at times been agony. You don't ride cross-country without experiencing physical suffering. While cycling is joyous and of the spirit it is its mechanical simplicity and conviviality, the very nature of the effort is human power. Walking has a different appeal. Its rhythm and psychology is not as satisfying as cycling. But, making the comparison under such circumstances put the mind even further out of balance. The rail bed spoiled the hiking. If it were a dirt path, or even a sand path, without the giant endless track with the big uneven cinder bed then it would be better. I managed to hate the men who had brought rail to the west. I think railroads are better than superhighways. And riding rails, even with intermittent hikes was perhaps next best to cycling, or horseback riding. (I haven't had the experience with horses to compare.) The iron rails couldn't easily conquer the mountains. Because of the steep grades, tunnels and horseshoe curves had to be designed and built. The desert presented its own challenge. If I had never walked this walk, I would never know in my searing feet what I learned outside of Sage, Wyoming. Laying steel in the desert was not meant for the weak-willed.

I kept on until I trudged upon people and machines. First there were big yellow machines with gears and external wheels and a man moving levers way up top. Two of these machines moved on sidings. Then I saw men with shirts off carrying heavy steel hammers, spikes, and long iron levers. The men were red, big, tall, and had dark hair and stiff bluejeans. One man's hair fell to his shoulders, the locks were shaggy, and black. I thought of Bromden from *Cuckoo's Nest*. At first the men were in small clusters, backs bent in labor amidst others standing, gripping tools. Then there were idle men gathered outside a row of shadowy boxcars.

I asked a short oriental man next to a rusty yellow machine where to find Tony Santos, the foreman. He told me to look for a blue car, with the number eleven painted on the side. He said it was a hundred yards further. Passing rusty boxcars that stood on the siding like disheveled gentlemen waiting for partners at a monolithic cosmic square dance, I came to the center of Sage. I found the navy blue, number eleven car, stumbled painfully up the rusty steel steps to the blue painted steel door, pulled it open and stepped into a narrow, sky blue interior. A man in a khaki hat with a swarthy face, a pockmarked nose, and tinted aviator glasses sat behind a broad grey steel desk with his elbows propped up in front. His fists knocked together.

"What can I do for you?" he asked.

"I'm Steve Lansky; I've come to work on the steel gang," I said.

"I got a bunch of Navajos off the reservation today. I'm fourteen over on the head count. I don't need you."

And that was it. I turned away, walked down to the cinders and felt my heart and mind drift into oblivion. The awkwardness filled me. I was sore, hungry, thirsty, angry, lonely, tired, dusty, and full of a delicious liberation. I was not going to work on a steel gang in Sage, Wyoming.

Steven

And Then the Cow Was Drownded

Generated circa 1978

DRAUPUDIE OR MUSE

Ink on newsprint, 23.75 x 18"
From the Private Collection of the artist
Steven Paul Lansky

In the Bhagavad-Gita Draupudie is Krishna's sister and she marries Arjuna. The artist was inspired by the visage of an unrequited love that he has allowed to become his muse for his writing. Draupudie is said to have a great boon. In the Gita, when Arjuna brings his wife home to the family his mother, Kunti, shouts something to him to which he answers affirmatively without hearing. Kunti had said, "Whatever you brought home, you'll have to share with your brothers." Arjuna always honored his word with his mother. He had four brothers, and Draupudie had five husbands.

Paul Thanas

As Draupudie Became a Muse

When Jack got to college he learned about Paradise. Jack was bored to tears by English Literature in Libby's cans at Ohio State University. It was overcooked, tasteless, and mushy. In Paradise there was a Red Cross. There was Red Cross Lifesaving class. He rescued boaters in the Halloween sailing regatta. There was Blue Cross when he had accidents. There were Knights of the Red Cross and Knights of the Blue Cross. He took fencing just before he dropped out. One morning, there was the print of a dropped rapier in the foot deep snow, outside his small apartment. He thought he was a Harvard man, perhaps a knave and not a knight. He did not understand the educated elite and therefore lost faith in the Knights of Columbus when he was a student at Ohio State University.

Some years before he attended Ohio State, when Jack dropped out of Harvard College Jack heard that Kennedy was working on a new health bill in the Senate that would allow all individuals free medical care, or social medicine. He saw that he could help. He followed all the free advice he heard about.   He made one mistake though.   He followed bad advice. It was not exactly that simple.   His family friends included many medical professionals. They disdained his decision to postpone college. He lost track of how professionals effected change out of compromises and negotiations. He began to steal, at first marijuana from his friends, then wine from his brothers next he was envisioning symbolic political action. Then he heard about ISKCON. A young woman told him about the International Society for Krishna Consciousness. Her father was a leader of Democrats, but had been a high ranking official, in a Republican administration, a United Nations Ambassador, and US Envoy to India. He stood for elected office with positive results. He represented New York in the U.S. Senate. Jack followed the rules and joined neither camp. Medical care was free to him. He identified himself as a Sufi. Moslems were known to have good advice. Hindus were not known for good advice. Javara Djidt, an ISKCON representative, and former master gunnery sergeant was no exception. He advised Jack to find a path and learn to follow. Jack, known to the New Orleans Hindu people as Bhakta Jack, helped out by sweeping the porch, read a little of the literature, (*The Srivad Bhagvitam*) and *The Gita*. Mostly he dreamed of *the* young woman, Draupudie, whose marble figure adorned the place of worship. He smiled a lot, and prayed. He also often thought he might really be Arjuna. She had always said, "Karma yoga is the only way." He thought "karma" was a Buddhist term. It was ten years later that he learned karma yoga came from India.

When he was scared, he thought about medicine.

When he was less scared, he thought about her. If Jack could tell it he would say he hitchhiked all over the United States looking for Draupudie. Jack would drink and imagine he saw her. He often did think of other women, but even when he was with other women, his thoughts turned to thoughts of her. And incidentally he imagined that she was talked about by rich fat men who wore blue sweaters, sat in Rolls Royce limousines and discussed the future of medical care. He didn't want to be a doctor.

He knew these times like he knew nothing. He often sat now, a man, in his cold apartment, deeply resolved to beat winter, and composed long sentences about his mother.

SHE, darkness seen, saw, in bright, seven tiered, long night started layers filling ash white soft fluff day along lay lines like lyric lacked lovelorn psyche sorry, saying: *SIT SON*.

And like the dumb bastard Jack thought he was at times, he did. He sat. He sat long, he sat hard. He looked and he stared. And as time progressed, he blew smoke and he lost dimension to his vision. It came back though, slow and cold filtered like Wet Willie's Whistle Lipped beet Red beer. It came back through dark timber of nighttime dream construction. And dime bags of cocaine appeared lit and numbered in glove boxes when he had hitchhiked.

When Arjuna was young in a river city in middle-America where his mother and father brought him from boyhood to young adulthood, he had a cold apartment, that got warmer in the spring. The neighborhood where he lived was tough: sirens, tensions, and very violent nights took place in the bar just one door over from the entry way to his locked building. The night street often beckoned him. He often heard caterwauling, and loud voices yelling swear words, cursing, foul language, all redundant, and noisy keeping him up long past his nighttime sleeping hour.

In order to somehow express affect with his wild-eyed leadership when he wasn't writing passive voice sentences, he one day walked, bold and alone into the Pioneer Bar. There was a sign which said, "Draft beer 65¢—No pennies." He looked around, dropped a cool clear eye on the pool table, and thought hard, didn't swallow, and remembered the noisy night and the TV reporters, the paramedics, the white truck with blue and red crosses, and the benefit for the guitarist who was smacked to death with a pool cue in this very room where he was standing. He sensed an aura of argument. He wanted to start one, himself angered by this meager and ugly, stinky, swill of a barroom on a warm late afternoon.

He went up to his apartment. The next day he didn't go to work. Instead, he thought. He sat for two days without moving, except to get cigarettes, water, and to shit, only once, or to dump, if you so prefer. Possibly shat twice, once early on, and again when the sitting, was all in loose fitting clothes, on pillows, on the couch, with his eyes rolled up in his sockets cause he had hemorrhoids. He then pulled out of a dark trance, woke up, and said, "SHIT" to himself, outloud, then grabbed a fistful of pennies in each fist, carefully opened the front door, locked it behind, and headed right for the Pioneer Bar. Walked in, noticed a drunk or two getting drunker, drinking, and gently, quietly, and forcefully, (if it's possible) said, "How much for a draft?" Knowing full well the answer. When the old, withered, funkfaced gray-haired lady said, "sixty-five", he responded with a very clear voice, "I didn't ask your age, I didn't ask the drinking age, I didn't ask your IQ, and I didn't ask the year the Vietnam War turned ugly," and he dumped both hands of pennies {or "of coins"} out on the bar, turned, and left feeling a lot of relief. The woman had begun to squawl too late; he was gone.

Back upstairs in his apartment he opened the windows and threw pennies out for hours, using the logic that if a bunch of old bums found enough copper discs, they might go into the Pioneer, to buy something and they'd like as not remind, or pester the lady bartender into thinking of the youth who made such a strange and misspent mountain of his anger that day in Spring.

At this moment I am explaining to some friends in a downtown Cincinnati restaurant how I will write all this, seated in a room facing a small computer terminal. I'll be sitting in the double, wide open door of my redneck neighborhood apartment, in the peneplain flats by the Ohio River, where glaciers created the land that my people called Over-the-Rhine, after the German 'ain'ts who 'ain't around when you don't need 'em, whatever that means.

I live at 1425 Main Street, one point four miles from the Ohio River, two blocks East of Vine Street, which divides the city East from West. At the river are the public landing, the serpentine wall, Sawyer Point Park, and then the new stadium complexes, which are cut off from downtown by Fort Washington Way, a maze of interstates that parallel the river and lead to all the major arteries. The streets are numbered, and run one way alternating directions until Eighth Street, which goes East to West until it hits Walnut Street (which runs North to South), a block East of Vine Street, which is one way South to North until Central Parkway which would be eleventh street if it had a number. North of the Parkway, Vine is two way all the way out of downtown. The Parkway used to be the Miami Erie Canal and separated downtown from a residential district called Over-the-Rhine, named for the German immigrants who populated it in the early 1800s. The canal snaked around the city until it stank from too much sewage in the 1920s. Then it was paved over. Eighth Street is two ways from Walnut to Vine, where it changes names to Garfield Place, which is two ways, but has a park between the lanes. Many streets in Cincinnati change names at Vine Street, and for that matter at other major intersections for reasons long forgotten and best unexplained. Garfield Place is two-way until Elm Street, two blocks West of Vine Street (where the Public Library of Cincinnati and Hamilton County has its main branch) where it changes back into Eighth Street and continues one way from East to West. Then at Plum Street it becomes two ways again, I think, but I wouldn't swear to it.

As I finish explaining to my friends, I decide to leave Mullane's Restaurant and wander to a bar name of Ronald's, at 210 East Eighth Street, which has green neon in its window, which reflects off the chestnut brown ceiling fans. I write my name in the table with a big knife, gnawing out chunks of wood onto the floor among the peanut shells. At least I think I do, because I am a bad ass, and no one better fuck with me. I think of how I'll meet up with that social worker named Marlena and fuck her alot. That's *when I had a beer, none of that Wet Willie's beet Red shit, but a good ale, a stout from old Ireland, the home of my Ire which is what led, dead with lead, will lead, if I need, to that drap, that Draupudie, that Irish Asian Indian, she's **the** young woman. Karma, beer, butt naked, and fucking around make it.*

I think about how I'm going to write this whole story and make good of myself but that's much later. Yes, Mother's getting ready to die about now, in this here story, five or ten years later, maybe twenty-five, maybe I'm forty as I pick up my only remaining icon, a small baseball bat, a twenty-one inch, Louisville Slugger, and think, mother dead, social worker might come back if I have a heart attack, and need her. Maybe tonight as I wander back to where mother's alive, and all that shit about the funeral of my grandfather comes spiking back at me I'll tell how he gave up on doctors and hospitals to die in a Christian Science reading room. Really, he died a Christian Scientist, having been an ambulance driver in Berkeley, California. He had a stroke that medicine might have held off for years. Still, he lived to 81, and died with a novel by his grandson sitting on his lap in his favorite chair, the lamp still shining past dawn.

His mother seemed to know all about him, he was Jack Acid, the dimension free lunatic who drifted in and out like a man possessed with desire to lead men, and with the natural capacity to draw executive lines and decisions hard into both good and bad, yet he chose no path; he was followed. Yes, he led. He was guided by novelists, here or there. And years passed him by, never to be unpresented with guidelines, so they said. He would say to himself, and the reader would walk a mile or two down the road.

Mother knew he walked a lot. She always bought him a lot of shoes.

He thought of himself as an actor. People were always giving him names. Sometimes he longed to forget names. He wanted to fuck all women at once and knew that was impossible. Still, it intrigued him that he knew he had no choice, and he felt fated to someday sleep alone with the gopi, the cow shepherd woman, Draupudie, once a young girl, who had a brother name Krishna. This being his only motivation in life at an early age he stumbled many times. He listened to musicians, fortune-tellers alike. They all liked one another, most of the time, but a girl herding cows must have seen all, known all, felt all, been all, in one lifetime or such.

Karma yoga, yeah, okay, send me to military school, he said.

NINE MOMENTS OF INTIMACY

Outside the white painted wooden window frame of the big yellow house on an Avenue in Cambridge I don't remember if we were speaking to someone through the window or were both leaning in the bushes, I know I was close to her because it was almost as if I could touch her hair with my head and I said with a voice from confident adulthood seventeen or so, said, "Draupudie, I think I could love you someday."

She never said a word back, just sort of smiled and shook her black hair out of her gold-flecked blue eyes.

She didn't play volleyball with the others at the dorm. She fell in love with a piano player who had had a single that Buck Owens played on *Hee Haw*. Jack left Harvard, came back a year and a half wiser. LSD made Jack Arjuna and Arjuna traded his graduation present, an expensive standard typewriter, for the typesetting of Jack's first two and one half page text. Arjuna was unable to change this fact of her love with this poker partner. *The Jack Acid Society Excerpts* told of Jack's loss of identity when faced with a mother like a freight train.

And when he got to the military estate, sanitarium he knew. Ouchlike. Late at night in the dining-room we studied together. I went away and wrote about characters that really were and were in all the rooms around us because it was a rooming house that we all shared. She was reading about Buddhism. We laughed and talked of being, oneness, karma-yoga and reality. We cared little for duality, not yet part of the *I Ching* and without the reflexive mind body gestalt of GO. I came back later that night. We decided she wanted No-doze so we climbed on my Phillips three-speed bicycle at 4:30 a. m. and she sat on the handlebars as I steered down Mass Avenue under the sodium vapor streetlamps to the square where no one sold No-doze at that hour. She got some Rothschild's or Rothman's cigarettes. I was dazzled by riding her on the old Phillips; my hands were against her skirt. The back tire went flat. It didn't make any difference. She balanced our weight such that the rear wheel was hardly touching the ground and I stood on the pedals and put my head close to hers.

After many lectures she kissed me good-bye and gave me a poem she had written. I don't remember much of the poem. I carried it in my wallet for years and when it tore, I put it in a ceramic jug I made in a sanitarium workshop. I would have to shatter the jug to rescue only scraps of it. I remember one line: "The sea of souls to which I warm my breast," I was entranced. She signed it— "to ACID, an interesting and growing writer, a joyful cyclist, and a good shit. I love you Acid, old man."

I think, as far as she was concerned, she said, "BYE."

Remembering the angel. She's sitting with her heels together in front of a statuette of the deity Vishnu—candles the only light casting long shadows of her cross-legged form over her shoulder shielding the light from my eyes. She whirls, a continuous motion— "I was meditating Arjunajack, I'm going to India."

"To India?"

"Yes!"

Arjuna stands above her by the twin mattress on the floor, black cloth, pillows, and the scent of incense.

"Do you want to see India?"

"Yes!"

"Hold on"—she says— jumps up, leaves the room, returns with a sheaf of watercolor paintings on heavy paper— says— "This is India."

Arjuna lights the room with his smile of love, interest, and devotion. *I want to paint.* He thinks. She holds the paintings up to the light of Arjuna. He examines greens, reds, purples, yellows, and oranges. "Are the colors really this bright?" (He thinks *vivid.*)

She says — "YES!"

They exchanged vows and rings in the light of the candles under Vishnu's watchful eyes.

He remembers walking with her on Massachusetts Avenue, down to Harvard Square in Cambridge to buy chocolate chips. She wanted to make cookies. Her hugs and kisses are perfunctory, not impassioned, but rather lacelike and euphoric in brief fancy. He thought she would steal the chips off the shelf, not knowing he had some money. Walked with her and admired the way she held her head and watched her breath and the snow floating past her shoulders covered by a heavy black overcoat and wrapped at the neck in a downy white scarf.

After the psychologist left the restaurant, I began to wish I had ordered tea rather than coffee. The neighborhood was alive with pastel colors. Yellow-fingered spring tipped trees in view from my window side seat at the edge of the door to the diner. I began to buzz; I had caffeine high that put me in a mood like one I had seen in a French flick when longhairs tore off shirts and danced in circles shouting aloud. I think it was a concentrated addict film of pure essence and being. My thought when I saw the flick was, *they let you do that.* I wanted to learn French and go there, right now.

I think what I did instead was drive away with the Rolls Royce. There were conflicting visions . . . you know, I'm thinking *I'm God or will be president someday and there's this cat who wired my brain and he said "wheels forthcoming."* Unfortunately, the message came without the warning: IDEA COURTESY OF MURPHY. Harvard law states: "Given all possible forces and pressures under stressful circumstances, the one thing for certain is that the organism will do just as it damn well pleases." And I had stopped at Harvard on the way to the car . . . then I went to the apartment on Main Street in Over-the-Rhine.

BUSBOY - BARBACK

I worked for a week as a busboy and a barback in Cambridge, Massachusetts in September of 1978. I got the job after I was arrested for discovering a Rolls Royce.

Not right after, a few months later, after I escaped from the asylum in Baltimore, Maryland. I hitchhiked to Canada, got caught at the border; they said I didn't have enough money. After the arrest in New York, they took me to another hospital, where they said I was OK.

Then my parents flew me back to Cincinnati, Ohio. I got into an awful row with my mother. The deal was that I would get my college education if I paid for fees, books, and clothes, that sort of stuff. I had spent all my money, didn't have a job, a home, anything. Mother said "NO" when I asked for the money to pay my crew charge and library fines left from two years before when I took a leave of absence from Harvard.

I picked up a chair in the kitchen, waved it around, threatened to smash some things, demanded money by the next day, then went up and took a shower. Mother had been in the habit of writing me checks for thirty dollars at a time. I thought she knew I was spending the money on Mexican and Colombian marijuana. In the morning I was watching *Sesame Street* when the deputies came. My father let them in. They had an affidavit from mother.

Two big men escorted me to a hospital psychiatric ward. I had about three dollars, some change and was wearing blue jeans, a white T-shirt and gym shoes. (Clothes courtesy of my father.)

At the hospital, I went to a pay phone, called Mother at work; she was in the Personnel Department of the city of Cincinnati. I told her about what I felt was corruption on her part. Then I said, "I'm leaving." She said, "the sheriff will be after you." I walked, in eighty-five to ninety degree, heat, four miles out Reading Road, to the Norwood lateral, and hitched rides for a day and a half to Boston.

When I got there, I made a beeline for the Harvard Co-op House where I had written, expecting to re-enroll that fall. I walked into the Co-op on Sacramento Street and found my letter tacked to the bulletin board. They expected me. I had changed my name to Paul Kennedy. The sheriff was on my trail, and I was in Massachusetts, the best place to be a Kennedy.

More than anything, I hoped to find a job. I was standing in Harvard Square when a young woman approached me with flowers. She was doing a promotion for a restaurant. I asked her if the restaurant was hiring. She said, "I think we need busboys and dishwashers."

I walked right into the restaurant and got a job as a busboy. The bus help ate last, either a hamburger or chicken. People called me by name, and I was puzzled. (Because I wasn't used to people calling me Paul.) I stayed in the Co-op, because I needed a place, but couldn't fend off the Senior Tutor, who insisted that my father wanted me home.

In the restaurant life was busy. I carried ice in buckets over my head when they made me barback. I learned that ice in a drained glass meant customers were turning tables, seats; work for me, money for all. I left early and didn't get my tips. After a week there was a staff meeting. I missed the meeting and got fired. When I asked to be paid, the manager asked where he could send the check. I wanted cash to pay the crew charge and library fines at Harvard. He paid me $25. That wasn't enough. I was also without a home.

So, I hitchhiked back to Cincinnati for my father who kept calling officials trying to track me down, and besides I couldn't stay at the Co-op unless I registered, and Dad wouldn't pay tuition for me, even though I wanted to stay and work in the restaurant. When I got home, I was re-arrested, and spent six years of my life in and out of "treatment."

Silver, tablecloths, napkins, bottles, glasses, a busboy's dream in late night bars and people were doing brain surgery with conversation and when it became a flick it was construction . . . three or four conversationalists would work to bring their conversation together with three or four others and the conversations would merge and the result would be a "construction" which if well created would serve as pressures to create "action" in a film.

Murphy gained perambulatory status. He was known in the neighborhood because knee pains[1] were habitually attributed to his local presence. I hesitate to admit that my knee had hurt, reminding me not to see Murphy, to avoid Murphy, to at all costs miss Murphy in case he might toss me into the dance of the

---

[1] knee pains
They tell me the Irish call the punishment "Black & Decker" for the cordless drill driven into the side of the squealer's knee. Crippling.

French flick because French lessons were the topic of discussion at the party. The party had been more than a dream.

The psychologist would have something to say about that, I thought, and left the diner.

At the party in a Boston disco, **Boston, Boston** where Caroline Kennedy was snorting coke with a white paper straw from a glass top table in the corner. Draupudie and I sat at the bar and I bought her a screwdriver. I had the same and she lamented that her love of her life did not even know she was alive. I was dying to say, "LOVE ME! PLEASE!" I wore a military green fatigue flight suit and heavy boots.

There was a dinner when we sat side by side in the crowded rooming house dining room, eating Indian (Asian) food with our hands. I pretended Draupudie was my wife and steadfastly looked ahead as though I had blinkers on, as if a horse, though we were eating roast lamb. I knew we each must face our fates independently, so I looked at the person across from me, I looked at the heavy, oaken, table top, at the plate. Before dinner she had briefly read my palm. She said I would be a lousy businessman, perhaps very creative and would have two great loves.

What Arjuna really said to himself was keyed on a central thought about fighting for individuality. He knew that all mankind and womankind were one being. When Krishna's sister, Draupudie, complained on the telephone to her mother that her brother was a schizophrenic, Arjuna, warrior that he was, decided to seek him out. He envied Krishna because he had such a lovely sister. Arjuna himself had no sister, except the one with whom he had the incestuous relationship. (Adrianne was like a lover to his brothers and since they were all so close, sometimes he believed his love for her was incestuous.) Arjuna had a heck of a lot of desire. Krishna was his charioteer. He concluded that he would find Krishna near the power center of the universe. So, he went to Washington, DC. First, he tried Telegraph Avenue, thinking that this, would be Krishna's recruiting ground. Then he tried San Francisco, thinking it might be where the street warriors of tambourine would subsist. He tried everywhere where there was marijuana. He made friends with lovely influential women at each power center. He sought that epicenter; he sought vortices. Heads were rolling as it came together. Draupudie was leaving for India, Arjuna was New Orleans bound, before he met Javara Djidt, before he knew chemical war, before ISKCON, before social medicine. Many students were headed for jail, and the Chemist's dog was permanently changed. Not in the sexual way, however, the Doberman had one less limb, its balance was disturbed, and it was groggy from the anesthetic. Krishna had been lopping off heads right and left that day down in Maryland, so he was pleased to hear Arjuna might be arriving within the moon phase, or two. Two settings might be imagined here; the lofty palatial estate asylum in Maryland where Krishna held court and martyred himself in fine fashion, and the glorious heyday of Harvard's anarchic off-campus stewardships colliding solidly, graduates versus undergraduates, brilliant and athletic versus scholarly and strong.

The battleground of Krishna was warm and motionless. The longhaired prince of cattle dominion polished his weapons in a motion not unlike his labors over his physique. Arjuna could only imagine one day being as beautiful as Krishna yet all beings are equally beautiful and love blindness kept Arjuna from seeing this. KRISHNA IS ALL ATTRACTIVE.

I like your feet, with the red toenails, the silver toe ring. The shape of your feet is perfect, not stubby or slender, but right, so right and porcelain alabaster, flesh. And your hands the right size, the nails not overdone, nor short, just like I would have mine if I were you, and some part of me feels like I am you. Your eyes, blue as a stream, the whites of your eyes so fine. I love your smile, the straight white teeth, the lips over the perfect smile and I even like your lipstick, or the pucker you make. I guess I am in love with you so I think.

"I want to marry you," I said.

"But you don't love me," you said. And like a jackassed fool I stood then sat then stood then sat then stood then sat. And I stared at the mirror. I looked away and up and down, and then at you and my tongue was in a knot.

"You are infatuated with me." And I listened and I cried inside.

"What are you going to do with your life? You don't love me. We're too young to get married anyway." You, *the* young woman said.

And that's all I remember her saying but when I was leaving, she smiled that expansive smile and I said, "I feel like a dog. I'll see you on Telegraph Avenue in Berkeley," and I eventually went to Berkeley, but she never showed. I wanted to die. I wanted to be nothing. On the way out I stopped and stood on the corner and peed in the snow against the side of her building. I remembered what my father had said. "He peed and she held it for him." And I hoped it was true. I hoped it was true.

Arjuna had met Draupudie in the off-campus rooming house where anarchy was nurtured as if only anarchy could guide America and India to the colossal fated confab of the century. Javara Djidt told Bhakta Jack that this was the golden age, the twenty thousand years of paradise on earth. Arjuna believed, the end of this twenty thousand year reign of man, over his environs, was scheduled to be decided, by this young group of humans, each of violently merging origins.

Arjuna, the lonely Western cowboy had ridden his blue bicycle into Cambridge and staked out a room. He jested and jived until the poker crowd set into a habitual round table, then began to discover the little women who kept the dreams of all little cowboys from being too vivid.

And Then the Cow Was Drownded

Two years had passed since that first arrival of Arjuna, and Krishna was still totally unknown to him. He thought he had faced nearly every known alternative to school, work, and cycling travel. He believed he was a man.

Arjuna sat at the poker table that fated day when she came in, a vision out of the East in a tense blue-gold shawl, coal black hair shimmering like blueviolet blacklight in threads of magic waves or particles (he couldn't tell) from beneath the garment that dazzled him. He saw only white, her skin like shiny glass, dust melted into dapple porcelain lace cornered eyes witnessed his aghast stare.

On the second visit he was able to stand and sway close aboard, settle her and they shared a chillum, brass bowl on plastic stem. She taught him how with her hand moving like magic, nails unnicked, pink painted, silver studded fingers and all in a swirl of friends who seemed a little more in place than the furniture, almost as dusty, in a desert scent, and absorbed in self-devotion, introspection and far out cosmic love. He knew she was formal, royalty, if not a goddess of timeless aromatic flow. She was wisdom, knowledge, and could only be outshone by a masculine version cut of her own cloth. He could not focus away from her long enough to discern if that male idol could be alive, his vision was stymied, blocked, stormclouds floated where moments before he saw only rivers, then the sands of the riverbeds ground under his feet, and he knew he was loveblind.

Krishna was content to polish his blade, tuck away time, and fly about in his antithetical rages, unknown to Arjuna, and reacting always to Arjuna's fated courtship with Krishna's lovely sister, Draupudie.

Arjuna knew nothing of Krishna's guiding hand over his mortal moves. This saved him, this and Krishna's youthful playful suggestions, which Arjuna received as a devoted anarchist who had time for little games, toys, and magic talks.

Finally, he thought a little bit harder and got very stoned in a sunny day way outside Baltimore. It took a bit of wisdom, but he tried to discover a Rolls Royce Silver Cloud. This got him to the jail. The next step was the epicenter itself. He wasn't sure how to get out of jail, then he reconnoitered, thought of the malingering actions demonstrated to him by a childhood rival, and tried acting crazy. If he was taken for a schizophrenic outside Washington, DC, wouldn't he end up with other schizophrenics? And, ah-ha, if he was smart, they'd first think he was poor and give him mind altering drugs, knock him about, and keep him for a while, in lazy luxury when his parents turned up with financial backing.

Some of his thinking was rather sharp. As it turned out.

ON AN-UDDER FACE

Arjuna's moving around the file room while Jan, the full-time file clerk sits on a stool after pulling pale green folders. She's marking them with a pencil. She has a table with a white desk phone. Marlena comes over. It's a shotgun room, long and narrow, file cabinets on one side, Jan's small table on the other. Marlena looks great in a tight jean skirt, short curly brown hair, green eyes fuzzy through glasses, a slightly pointed nose, and nice hands and wrists. She is wearing scuffed blue pumps, and pantyhose. Arjuna can't help seeing her legs, is impressed, scuffs his expensive brown wingtips together, and crudely re-tucks his light blue dress shirt into his tight brown corduroys. Arjuna wears teardrop black-rimmed eyeglasses and a very demure, thin, brown wool necktie. He seems to be a little embarrassed about his graying dark-brown hair being on the unkempt side. Jan is chattering aimlessly to Arjuna, who feels trapped into listening, about her teenage daughter's recent inability to hide drinking from Jan. Jan is in her forties, wears red pants and a pale pink blouse. Her bifocals are large with clear plastic frames and her lipstick is too bright. She has tacky gold hoop earrings, and her voice is mousy.

"I know she wants me to trust her. She tells me her friends are drinking, then I found cigarettes in her purse." Jan says.

"What were you doing in her purse?" asks Marlena.

"You smoke." Arjuna adds, lighting up a filter-less shorty.

Marlena looks a bit stunned, smiles, lights a filtered cigarette.

"What are you doing for lunch?" Marlena asks.

Jan looks up, "Filing."

Arjuna announces, now that the discussion of the teenager has fallen away, "I got a car last week."

This is new to Arjuna who hasn't had more transportation than a bicycle, a borrowed car, or the bus for six years.

"Take us out to lunch in your new car," Marlena says.

"No, no, we'll go in my car." Jan says, adding, "Give it a week, so at least you'll know how it works."

Arjuna has been eating at the cafeteria on the fourth floor for six months without missing a day and is damn excited about the possibility of eating out. He's interested in Marlena, despite the huge rock on her left hand. He enters the timesheets on the computer and knows Marlena has a hyphenated last name. He's noticed the tight skirts, occasionally leather, the mini-jean skirts, and the fishnet hose that are more fitting to a prostitute than a social worker, so he's a bit puzzled. He doesn't really know what the social workers do at this agency. Marlena is an unknown quantity and the first woman who has shown interest in Arjuna in a while. She talks to him when she gives him time sheets and looks directly into his dark eyes. He sees the green, watches her pop gum. She leans on the heel of a blue pump, her leg wobbling suggestively.

"Where will we go?" asks Arjuna.

"Do you like gyros?" Marlena asks.

Jan says yes, and Arjuna echoes the same.

ooooo

Two hours later, Marlena is squeezing her five four frame, into the backseat, of Jan's car. Jan looks clumsy, lights a cigarette, empties the ashtray onto the parking lot, which gives Arjuna a little twist in his stomach, while he settles into the driver's seat. Marlena insists that Arjuna drive. She calls out directions from the backseat. In traffic for a few minutes, Jan comes back around to the teenager issue.

"So, what if she smokes cigarettes? She has a job at the YMCA teaching swimming to handicapped kids. She got it all by herself. She goes there after school, so I pick her up after work."

"That's great, Jan." Arjuna says.

"You smoke anyway," says Marlena then gives final directions.

Arjuna finds the place, a small Greek diner on McMillan, near the university, and parks.

They pile out, Arjuna a bit nervous about being away from work for lunch, Marlena quiet and all eyes for Arjuna. Jan seems to approve of the luncheon, but also is preoccupied.

In the restaurant they order Cokes, gyros and salads. Arjuna also gets french-fries. The place is small with white Formica tables and booths. Marlena and Arjuna are seated side by side, with Marlena on the inside. Arjuna faces the table, and Jan, while Marlena sits sidesaddle, looking at Arjuna.

"Where did you go to college?" Arjuna asks Marlena.

"Northern Kentucky University," she says, "You?"

"I started at Harvard, then went to Ohio State," he says, "I was going to transfer to NKU before I got this job."

Marlena has her gyro in her hand. Arjuna sees the wedding ring again. He likes the shape of her hands, the clear nail polish; the fingers are feminine but look strong.

"What did you study at Harvard and Ohio State?"

"English. Do you have a M.S.W?"

"No, a B.S.W. What were you going to study at NKU?"

"Journalism."

"Are you from Cincinnati?"

"Clifton. My father is a psychology professor at UC. You?"

"I grew up in Fort Thomas. Dad was a pharmacist," she smiles, and her voice gets a little childlike. "He liked to play music on the ukulele. His pharmacy was in Covington. I worked there during high school."

Arjuna thinks about her voice. He likes baby talk. "I worked in a bike shop in high school."

"When did you go to Harvard?"

"Seventy-five and seventy-six."

"What happened?"

"I'll tell you later."

○ ○ ○ ○ ○

FUTURES!

Stonewall Apartments were for the welfare poor. I was one of them. I had moved there in August of 1984. Stonewall was a forty-five-unit, brick complex, with unfurnished, two bedroom apartments, stacked three stories high. It stood at the corner of Warsaw and Grand, a stone and mortar facing above the street level. All full of former psych patients, drunks who were trying to clean up, and day and night partiers among those who were clients of the same social workers. The social workers managed to help me get some furniture, and after my parents' house was damaged by burst radiators in a bitter Winter spell while they were out of town (unwilling to have me check on the house) there was a green couch and a green shag carpet from the family room.

It was a small ghetto for those who struggled, to help each other, and tried to help themselves. I had checked myself into a Cincinnati state mental hospital in 1982 after dropping out of OSU in Columbus. It had been a bitter Winter in Columbus, and I had sun-bathed nude in the South window on the first sunny days of Spring. I dined on tinned chicken and white wine before abandoning the apartment as I was being evicted for nonpayment of rent. I needed to get back to Cincinnati, had dreams of getting off the fucking anti-psychotic meds, and starting to race bicycles. In May I rode through all of Ohio, from Portsmouth to Putin Bay as the weather warmed. I ate smoked salmon, used up the last of the support from my parents. They had cut me off in February. I quit seeing the shrink at Harding Hospital, began drinking my days, painting in my second floor Victorian Village apartment. It had taken two years in Cincinnati since that overnight ride from Columbus to get into housing. I'm trying to collapse a lot of history here, but I want it to be clear and detailed, as if I have a great Harvard mind. They say I did. Still, I was in treatment since shortly after Memorial Day 1982. A few weeks of homelessness in Clifton, then into the state hospital. Medicated on Haldol, forty milligrams at first, then slowly worked my way down over two desperate years. So, I won't detail the hospital stay or, the fist fights, the strap downs, the forced medication, the cigarettes, smoked, one after another. I lost a lot of my youth. It was difficult to read and write under the sway of Haldol, but I managed. I got on with the therapist at the community mental health center. We met twice weekly until I got housing at Stonewall. He had done acid, too, over two hundred hits. He'd followed a guru to India.

There was this animated olive-skinned, balding Italian man, whose veins stood blue on the backs of his hands and contrasted the mottled brown spots on his scalp. As the medical director of the community mental health center, and a man who conveyed dignity, he said after reading my file, "The worst possible injustice I could give to you would be false hope." He paused, pulled at a fine cotton shirtsleeve, with silver cufflinks, "I believe that someday you will be able to do without the medication entirely." His time with the health center was nearly over, mine had just begun. I had a year and a half of inpatient and outpatient psychiatric treatment.

And Then the Cow Was Drownded

After a placement in a halfway house while waiting for a housing certificate I moved to Price Hill. During my year at Stonewall, I began doing volunteer work. At first, I took an internship at Jewish Hospital where I had been locked up some years before. I was a public relations writer. Each day, I rode the Metro, in all weather, from the West side to the hospital district in the center of town. I talked to people about what good things they did for the hospital. My articles ran in the Jewish weekly, and in two in-house papers. I was writing for a living. I was writing, and on welfare. Then I got another position at Traveler's Aid/International Institute. In a downtown office building, I began to teach English to new arrivals and refugees who were, like me, on welfare. Their support depended on taking classes; my support depended on teaching classes. I remember a conversation with a young woman who came to observe my class. She had been a high school classmate, and engaged, to be married, to a corporate-type. She was considering some volunteer work teaching English. After class, she said, "It's great you do such work. But not everyone is independently wealthy enough to give their time that way." I stifled a chuckle. "I'm on welfare," I said. She looked at her well-shod feet and left the room. I never saw her again.

If I could, I'd explain how I budgeted my pittance. I'd list the cost of my rent, and how few Foodstamps I got, and that I shopped in a fledgling cooperative grocery, where I bought cornmeal for mush, and brown rice in bulk, carrying my own containers to the store to reduce waste. I lived within my means, but my mother gave me a little each month for tobacco. I cooked dry beans, and discarded vegetables, an occasional chicken stew when I could afford it. Sometimes I got cheese from the government, powdered eggs from the group home, bulk cereal, too. And government butter, a pound at a time. Coffee was in my budget. I had enough for food but when I shopped, I felt shame. And to fight the shame I made sure I had my share of bourbon, beer, and ice cream. I found clothes at the various secondhand stores, books at the library. Once every two or three months I'd splurge and buy a used record or two. I always had a few harmonicas lying about for when I felt blue. I don't know how I did it, but I believed in futures. I believed in my students, I believed in myself, I believed in the people at the hospital who worked hard. (I wrote stories about Celtic musicians who played at the psych ward for free, a retired man who delivered meals on wheels, a Summer camp for kids, always looking for human interest over news).

After a while I had done what I could at the Jewish Hospital, and they said I had to move on. I had passed a promising Summer of vocational rehabilitation whose high point was sharing the Vice President of Public Relations private box at the tennis championships in Mason, Ohio. The stadium was green with blue pipe railings and plastic seats that were hot to the touch. Years had passed since I had been in the presence of a large crowd. I took my mother with me to see Ivan Lendl and Boris Becker and bristled when she said, "Boris's advantage was his breeding." She wore flashy sunglasses and a red paisley scarf over her gray hair. Then she insisted on buying me Reeboks extracting her Amex card from her tightly held Colombian purse. Mother had these high flung attitudes about athletes. She had discouraged my bicycling, out of fear, or because she wanted me to develop my mind.

I had taken a tennis clinic at her insistence. This allowed for competitive social activity within the family. I had poison headaches from standing on the hot paved courts in the humid Cincinnati summer. Tennis bored me. When I got frustrated, I would hit the ball too hard letting it fly wild. I'd started cycling again to Mother's disappointment. She had had one of my brothers clean out my abandoned apartment in Columbus and "The Rev," Mother's best friend, had let me store my things in her basement until I moved to Stonewall.

The next phase was clerical training. I hearkened back to those New Orleans days with the Krishnas. They wanted me to type for someone else. I was neither confident, credentialed, nor clever enough to find a job without a leg up from the power structure. I had given up Harvard, I had abandoned Ohio State University. Now, in poverty I had economic independence, so I could get loans for school on my own. Self-sufficiency was a sour mash on my tongue, and a lot of fight in my brain. It was time for more education.   The office training that the Bureau of Vocational Rehabilitation offered was the most frustrating experience I remember. Before personal computers were in office budgets, I typed on an IBM Selectric with no correction ribbon, while sedated on an anti-psychotic that made my digits tremble so much that my top speed was seventeen words a minute. The Krishnas had not cared how fast or accurate my typing was, but to get a job, that would take competence, not ideas, not thought, rather a certain subservience to the task, and a lot of skill at clicking keys. And besides, I'd have to show up each day, at a specified time, ride the bus to and from, and dress the part, with a tie and a clean pressed shirt. It was impossible with my medicine at that level, and without the medicine, there was no desire to do any such thing.

I fought. After meeting with a fellow at BVR and taking several tests, the crass, balding, mustached man in the white shirt, stinking of after-shave, with a striped, wide tie, began to chat with me about sailing. He wanted to buy a sailboat. Yeah, who doesn't? He wanted me to teach him how to sail. I declined. I convinced him that I'd follow reporters around for a few weeks, and if I thought I liked journalism, and could find a college that would guarantee me a journalism job after I graduated, he would get me bus fare to and from the campus. I would have to take loans for books and living expenses, but I might be able to get government grants for tuition. I was scared, but enthusiastic.

I followed four *Kentucky Post* reporters, on their beats, and met an interesting columnist. The newspaper was small, and just introducing PC's into the newsroom. One night I covered a fatal fire in Newport. The bodies came down the ladder, from the third floor, window wrapped in crumpled white plastic in the snow. A neighbor watched Michael Jackson perform at the Grammy's on a nine-inch TV that she had brought into her front yard powered by a long extension cord. The columnist took me to visit a guy who couldn't pay his gas bill. I'll never forget the stuffy heat, the photo of JFK in the dining room, the tasseled tablecloth, and the sweet, iced tea, we drank at the guy's table. The reporter listened, complimented the wife's tea and took notes. The story was harder edged than public relations writing, but not as cold as the fire.

I would become a professional writer. I applied to a commuter school. I took the bus to Northern Kentucky University in Highland Heights. The buildings were all concrete towers. I thought about the brick and ivy Harvard and sprawling, diverse Ohio State behind me. I met with the head of the journalism department and persuaded her to write the required letter to the BVR guy. She looked at me as I sat in her cluttered office and said, "Your hair is turning gray, but that mustache is going to stay black." I was admitted—my financial aid sailed through.

A few weeks before, I had started a volunteer placement at the Community Chest on Reading Road. This was a large concrete fortress like building that housed the United Way Agencies. I had come to an office over a year before when I was first looking for volunteer work. The interviewer had shamed me into tears. I had had to admit my problems to get a volunteer job. Another emotional low point. Coming back to this building on the bus from Price Hill for a new placement held little satisfaction. I wanted a paying job. I wanted to write for a living. Ambivalent about going to Northern Kentucky University, I wondered why they placed me at a home health agency in a position where I didn't even have to type. The job consisted of taking files of the deceased, or terminated clients, and retiring them from the file room. I volunteered for six weeks. A new computer system was introduced, and I applied to be the first data-entry clerk on the new system. It was my first full-time job with benefits and an hourly wage.

I had a choice between NKU and the job. With the job, I could move to an apartment on Main Street below a dance studio. Leo, my jazz pianist friend and his choreographer/dancer wife found the building and were moving in upstairs. I had managed to get down to the five milligrams of Haldol a day and I had opportunity and freedom again. One of my social workers bought my drawing of the shawled Harë Krishna Devotee, then she stopped seeing me.

I still saw the other therapist weekly. I saw him from nineteen eighty-two till he retired. He even got to meet Marlena, but I'm not sure, I'll tell that part.

○ ○ ○ ○ ○

Marlena calls Arjuna at home and invites him to the library for a slide show about Nicaragua. He drives his beat up Valiant across the singing bridge to Covington, Kentucky. The skyline is low and shadowy in the dark. He finds a parking place and goes into the library. She is already there in a meeting room. She introduces him to some friends, but he notices her legs, her green eyes, her musky scent, and her hands again. She is dressed in a short, tight, black leather skirt and fish net panty hose. When he gets close to her, he feels his breath shorten, his chest, tighten.

Arjuna sits in a folding chair next to Marlena as a tall dark woman, in her mid-thirties, dressed in a beige pants suit, opens the slide show. He is impressed by the woman's voice and diction, which are careful and articulate. There are pictures of villages, green lush hills line a highway where a hand painted billboard shows a woman, bare breasted, nursing an infant. The Spanish says something about natural milk being safer than a powdered or condensed milk concentrate, the product that is illegal in the United States but is marketed in the Third World. There are construction sites, collective farms with camouflaged buildings to prevent air strikes. There are discussions with the President of Nicaragua, and even photos of literacy workers. The show lasts about forty-five minutes. At the end the person leading the discussion is standing behind the seats and Arjuna strains his neck trying to listen. The whole audience is straining. He observes others turning in seats. He speaks up, "Wouldn't it be easier if you stood in front of us. We could move the chairs around." Marlena is a bit surprised, smiles and says in a whisper, "Good idea."

Soon the discussion wraps up, the two say goodbyes to the others and go out of the library into the night. Marlena says, "let's go to the bowling alley."

She insists that Arjuna drive her car, a sporty two-seater. She directs him to the bowling alley. The alley is on a side street in downtown Covington. They enter through a thick wooden door with no window. Inside are black, vinyl bar stools with backs. The bar is small and dark, carpeted and lit by a big screen television, which pounds the room with music videos. Marlena says to the round-faced, black bartender, "Hey, Teddy this is Arjuna. Treat him right."

Teddy sets up beers and refuses to take any money. Arjuna sips carefully.

"What's your story, Arjuna?" Marlena asks.

"You don't want to know," he says.

"I think I have an idea."

"OK," he turns to look at her legs then tries to keep focused on the green eyes.

"You were too smart. You got into trouble at Harvard. Then at Ohio State you were a genius, and no one understood you."

Arjuna's face feels numb. He pulls his smokes from his shirt pocket, fingers the packet and asks Marlena for a light. He is thinking about a conversation with an older lady, a family friend. She was a drunk. Everyone knew. She read his novel manuscript and told him he might have a drinking problem. She said the novel was a mess. He takes a deep draw and blows smoke through his nose. He is sitting in a bar with a married woman thinking he shouldn't be drinking. She has him figured.

Arjuna puts the cigarette packet on the bar, sips his beer, says, "You don't want to know."

"You think you're a loser. Hey. Relax. You're just too smart." "Yeah. It's nice to hear that. And I am smart, but I got into a lot of trouble. Aren't you married? Should you be out with me?"

"To get into Harvard you have to be a genius."

"Yeah, sure."

"My husband and I have an understanding."

Arjuna smokes and watches his big hand get close to his face, then move away. Marlena lights one, and talks again, "You're Jewish, aren't you?"

Tina Turner, is on the video screen singing, *What's, love got to do with it?* As Arjuna looks at Tina's undulating legs on the huge screen he wonders what will happen next. "Half Jewish," he says.

"The other half?"

"Greek. How about you?"

"German," she says, and he looks at the shape of her chest. The blue sweater has a low neck, and her skin is freckled. She has a big butt, and he is thinking about touching it. Not now, but, in the future. It seems to be happening very fast and very slow at the same time.

"What does he do?"

"My husband?" she looks cross, her voice tightens. "He's an attorney."

Arjuna tries to whistle. He feels a wave of fear shake him, reaches for the beer glass, drinks and decides not to ask more questions. *Need to know basis.*

∘ ∘ ∘ ∘ ∘

That woman they assigned to follow Arjuna, the Social Worker, Marlena, she took a liking to him. He was a bull of a man, where she was a wide framed cow, and took to making crass remarks and wooing him around. A nameless brother got involved, we'll know him as another of Draupudie's husbands, cause that's how she was known, and it was thought she had four or five husbands, the possessor of a great boon[2].

This wasn't *the* woman at all, neither was it Arjuna's sister, but a Social Worker who teased the old bull, Arjuna along. He had been typing masterfully on a very important Home Medical computer in the offices of the Community Munitions. (In reality it was the Community Chest, a haven for liberal lobbyists who were working on a home medical model. They provided subsidized home health care. Arjuna's job was to enter billing and tracking data into a new computer system that was always crashing. He learned that most of the patients were dying, eventually, in home hospice care.) Or as they called it, Community Mortuaries, or even, just, as that old hag had said, "The old funeral

---

[2]great boon
In this case, Arjuna was said to have brought Draupudie home to meet his mother, Kunti. Entering the house, he shouted, "Mother, guess what I brought home?"
Known to always keep his word, Arjuna did a dis-service to himself by answering his mother in the affirmative without hearing a word she said. She had said, "Whatever it is, promise me you'll share it with your brothers."

home" cause right around this time one cigarette drooped boldly out of the mouth of Arjuna, a viscous French Gauloises cigarette which was in a blue helmet pack, supposedly because it would promote male sterility, but it really just caused Arjuna, that old bull, to heat up a little slower, and heighten his sense of taste, it was oral bull, so to speak. So, the old, oral pension heated up, and just now the story gets crippled, so's it'll walk by a little slower.

The fellow without the name, one of Arjuna's brothers, see, he was working on a degree in mathematical genius as they say, or working out the whole sticky mess with a pencil. The nameless brother studied and studied, when he wasn't partying with *his* Social Worker. Arjuna kept adding diary entries in an old shoestring type hand when he was off the clock. But on the clock, Arjuna was clicking away on this computer faster than ten old ladies could fill out the forms he was clicking into the old data-master's data-pile. He paused for crash tests. Crash tests were simple measurements, of how he was doing on any given day, as they all sat around the office getting older, and wondering why medical bills piled up each time they made a bit of money. Something about the way the computers crashed, and the important ladies hovered, had Arjuna thinking it had something to do with floods, on the Ohio River. Or about testing some hard and software for some military function and when they said "function" he got really confused and wasn't sure if this was a sexual idea, or a nuclear device, or even somehow, he thought he had pushed the button that dropped the bomb on Hiroshima and his lack of understanding of relativity of space and time made it seem possible that he was implicated in the holy war. Then this Social Worker, Marlena, whistled, popped a little chewing gum, and wore, like it made a difference, a short, black leather skirt.

Well now you're confused, leather goddess, the sleazy side of our Arjuna, bull interest, the black net stockings, the glasses and thinking eyes all pictured a plump cow that our bull snorted a bit. A small time earlier, the other fellow, the one without the name, said, hey, here's a smaller Social Worker with whom he's going to live, with a carburetor on the kitchen table. She, of course, hits the roof and as our fellow is telling his situation to Arjuna. Just as Arjuna is moving out of his subsidized housing Arjuna, being lifted back to his project (housing that is) where he shares a room with a cripple, for whom this all moves too slow, who happens to be black, and is a West Coast budding journalist who turns up later at the Justice Hall, janitor central, as this decent Social Worker, the one with the leather, the fancy teeth, and the penchant for bullish Arjune's and also, aha! She had a very strong need to discuss the benefits of hot toddies on colds in the nose. When Arjuna is muttering through a crash test—-she whistles!

I am a spy awakened in my dream. I have been a spy for so long that no one has deprogrammed me. I invented the method to deprogram spies, then was deprogrammed with my own method and lost the tool. Like a wrench dropped through the engine compartment of an old motor, knuckles skinned against a black greasy nut, clank-clank, a chrome slick box open wrench under, on the leaf strewn concrete my mind dropped through a pocket of thought. Army surplus clothes, night missions on bicycles, long treks across country, drugs cleaned and bagged in a kitchen while elders were out of the room or house, orders. Orders to take care of something, someone. It was all changed by the true harryman. Hairy true man. Harë Harë. Even the computer seems to know that much of the action bent and built into the community chest, the mortuary hospice where we worked the new computer system. At times I thought the work was measuring waves in the river to know when the water would crest. To know about floods. If all time stood still one moment it would have to be a moment called Hero she's my ma. Na ga sa ki. Zen. Zen and now. Go. All this came to me many times and I feel that somehow the Asiatic race built a better human. This being destroys its past. It climbs like a parasite up the evolutionary ladder and destroys the base of the pyramid. It is the eye atop IN

GOD WE TRUST. Or sum such. I feel I must be the man who sent the encoded message to drop the bomb. Somehow that hydrogen bomb had to be assigned to the plane. If I am truly the messenger, then I know the atomic bomb was a moment in everyone's time, where they remember in their mind and body, where they were at the moment, they participated in the world war passion play. And every dollar bill reminds us of this moment. America-of-the-all-seeing-moment. I feel responsible for the team effort but did not know what the project was, only that we completed it just in time and saved the world for humanity. How can I say that?

But there's this old black drunk moseying wet-footed on a rainy day, up the main street rush hour, five p.m., downtown traffic, on the sidewalk, a big red gash in his worried brow, scoundrelly trousers too long dragging over his wet shoes, in his pocket a paper bagged bottle, and just ahead of him on the street two tall thin dark black men walking leaned over one another, Arjuna thinks these men have robbed the other and stuffed the bottle in the back pocket, robbing and beating him, then actually picking him up onto his feet, and acting all along like they are helping a drunk. Arjuna is in denial. He knows there is a problem, but he cannot understand if the drunk is choosing to drink, or if the drunk is being propped up by the people who provide the booze. He knows he is being robbed blind and miserable.

And Arjuna sees the whole of his relations with hard drinking social workers as just like those two men and proposes this story will tell an incident that is just like so. The critical analytic approach to the *GITA* says that women, men, all equal beings, being, nothing but, is to be fought for, but no violence, just fight illusion, and become one with the self, the inner Self.

The writer cannot achieve this, as Arjuna can. Arjuna believes he must fight women, because he cannot yet fight himself, yes, he can, he is mortal. Mortality must cease, and Arjuna will become one with Krishna. This is a path to the sister of

Arjuna. It is only Krishna's love that makes this association good for both. EXPRESSED THIS WAY WHILE DOG BARKING—IN THE PARK.

It's amusing what the they say. I am reduced to going to the park to think about a time when I smoked cigarettes. I write ferocious letters to editors, try to get works published and all the good it gets me is late nights at a computer screen hoping the phone will ring and it will be Draupudie or Harvard or some Ivy league president re-affirming that I am sane and that I read a novel the way I write a novel, one silly word at a time. The park is simple public land that is closed when you want to be there and open when it does you no good. The Social Worker, Marlena with her misty green eyes and black leather dragged me into the convoluted arena of this agony of daily drunkenness and sorrow. I thought that wedding invitations were the printer's priority. I was drunk on coffee thoughts when the phone started ringing and then it stopped. No one called that I wanted to talk to. I don't want to talk to anyone. I only make phone calls out of habit. I memorize friendly numbers, make calls and hope that if I answer well . . . and of course the dogs have all quit barking.

WITH THE SOCIAL WORKER

Eyes closed, glasses propped on dashboard, lips on lips, tight and wet, hands gripping clothes, touching springy, resilient muscles and breasts through blue sweater. Fingers reaching for tiny metal clasps, elastic released, a pert nipple rolled, then let go. Windows steam up, bodies lean heavily against one another, a moan escapes between moving mouths.

A light, shines into the car window, in Arjuna's eyes. He is glad he had just helped, replace her brassiere, and more glad, that both their shirts are on.

He rolls down the window of her husband's sporty two-seater and says, "Hello Officer."

The officer speaks quickly with a lucid command that Arjuna is already certain he's in deep yogurt, as Krishna would say.

"Driver's license," and a whole line about past park closing, why's this your car, and do you know it's closed, and she's speaking, quickly and they're contradicting each other in confusion.

Green eyes turn noticeably misty, scared, practical and Social Workerish in a flash as the two copys, (copy this, copy that, radio static) cops making sure they've got their man, go down, then she managed to be scolded about being married by the black cop.

"Run this," to the other officer and then, "OUT OF THE CAR." Further hassled on the topic of getting all A's items out of the car, that being his sweater, pulled off, minutes before, when all was being said with *caress, smooth, smell, stretch, expand, snuggle, strain, stretch, pull, rub, drag, sense.*

Snapped into cuffs, searched, told there's a warrant, "Trespassing CAPEAS." Arjuna's face droops, cause he knows, it's been six long years, maybe seven, since he fucked a woman, and this one, tit in hand and he's going to the pokey for the night, not the dry warm waterbed, in the flat where he can seduce and be seduced, as he likes to think.

Now, all business, a night in the pokey stunk like shit, cold and damp, dirty concrete, gray paint worn off the bars, and down to Camel cigarettes, when nothing made much sense. Arjuna going over it in his mind about how she's going to call the right number in the morning, have money, time to go to the bank. He makes his one phone call to his neighbor, Cady, the red-haired dancer across the hall, who can't, I mean, forgive, you know, Arjuna, calling her from jail and why'd he call her and he's not sure and, she's single, and a California kid, and she don't really get this story too easily, but yeah, she'll pick up his possessions to make sure his car gets moved back to the neighborhood from where he left it downtown, so he won't get a ticket, and of course later he figures, my money too, she'll take that, and the bank card . . . shit it ain't a good lie.

Then he knows he won't be able to call in sick at work, doesn't think this out too well. It could've been easy, number of his boss, call from jail, but then it ain't fair, the officer won't let him place the call himself. So, he's left with what Social Worker decides on everything. He could call her, but her husband might answer the phone, and then what, in jail, and he is too scared he'll hang up, and that's his one call, so he's glad he called Cady. He thinks, yeah, NO NET!

When, years later, in conversation Mother told Arjuna about the morning she left her keys in the car he knew the day somehow. He finds out that Kunti, came to work at the city hall that morning above the jail and left her car running and locked the keys in the car and someone found the car, traced the license plate and had Kunti contacted. She claimed she never knew that Arjuna had been in jail overnight. There was nothing she could do about the car but get a damn slimjim cop who opened the door with a quick pop and she shut off the Toyota before it run out of fuel.

Arjuna's thinking back from his jail cell, and the Social Worker connection never occurs, in his mind one unknown, and the other less known, the mystery of how a carburetor could even get onto the kitchen table never even crosses his slack brain muscle.

Paul Thanas

THREE TIMES A LADY

I don't want to write about places I've made love to Marlena because when we broke up, I hit her head so hard I broke my hand. I was jacked up on codeine, Guinness Stout, and marijuana, and she had just ripped the shirt off my body and slapped me silly. All this led to my sobriety and effort to stop abusing women.

But it, was a relationship, that lasted over two years—arguably my first real love affair. She was married when we met—soon to be divorced—Bob Dylan got that line from my affair, I guess. She had wrecked her husband's nightmare blue Honda CRX into a telephone pole reaching for a dropped cigarette.

We fucked in a lot of good places—held that passion for love making so hard—so hard—it would be easy to mistake this love for a romp. She bailed me out of jail the morning after the first night I felt her breasts.

Marlena once said, "Men, all they have is this pink thing—a little wrinkle of sausage hanging between their legs. We women, we have this delicate flower between our thighs where you can hide things, explore for hours with your fingers and a mirror—if you put things inside you invent it. You invite your curiosity with you—you can strum a bit on the eraser head of a pencil pink spot at the top—or front of the flower—where the petals come together in the middle. Wash it out—a little vinegar. Mix. Mix and mingle.

"The guys with the sausage thing—let me tell you it changes shape—fills up—engorges—becomes a thick blunt stick to poke with—Penetrator—it shoves and waggles."

There's no easy button with Marlena. She rolled hot and feisty. Of German descent, she was a great swimmer—I said she should be on the East German Olympic Team. I remember her strong wide shoulders. She bragged that she had a black girl's butt. Her hair—short, dark and curly, was soft in my hands when I held her head.

There are three places where I made love to her that were unusual, outstanding, and adventuresome—and I really don't want anyone to know about this. I waited until my parents were dead to write it down—not that they read all that I write.

Green-eyed Marlena wanted to fuck outdoors. I wanted a blowjob while driving. We made a deal—a pact—one for the other, which led to the third. Fucking outdoors may not seem like a big thing to you—but we were urbanites in Bible Belt Cincinnati. I was an avid cyclist. At the time I liked to ride my road machine through a city park called Mt. Airy Forest. Cincinnati has great parks. I'd ride from Over-the-Rhine (once a German immigrant neighborhood near the Miami-Erie Canal) through landlocked city streets—sidewalks and buildings—brick and concrete— corner to corner—gated locked tenements—Italianate architecture—a future historic district but then a slum with rats, roaches, overfed American cars, and cops in that order. I'd ride out, through the industrial parks, slaughter houses, and soap factories—print shops, machine tool, machine shops, and freeway ramps to a residential area that was being demolished until I got to a gradually climbing winding road that led into the back entrance of Mt. Airy Forest. I'd ride up the paved roads into the arboretum—past the greenhouse and orchard—roses and sycamores—until I got to a gravel road that swept downhill into the forest—a needled floor—a two track trail, overgrown with tall green grass.

So—I took Marlena—in my '73 yellow Valiant—the one with rusty corners that I'd bought for $100 from a little old lady when her husband died. (You can't make this up.) We drove up to the cemetery—gave up on that—then into Mt. Airy. We parked—she wore a blue pullover dress—I can still see her shape in it—God she walked and chatted so sexy I couldn't stand it. We went through the arboretum—passed the turnaround and walked in autumn leaves down the gravel road. It turned, to the two path trail—and the tall oaks and maples formed a canopy—there was a patch of pine or fir needles and recently fallen leaves. I lay down on my back—we were kissing. She pulled the dress up to her waist—she wasn't wearing underwear—I pulled down my jeans and man I stood up—or my dick did—I should say. Then we were slowly fucking—the city sounds gone to us—just breathing, the breeze in the leaves, bird twitter, sunlight filtered, flashed, flickered—I could see blue sky and light through the trees—smell the musk of decay and fucking mingle. The mosquitoes took an interest, too, and we were bit up.

We were quite proud of how that worked out—I didn't even stain my jeans—Marlena's face showed a new glow from then on—we were conspirators. And she owed me.

The rest of the story—about the blow job and the third wild thing takes the fun and twists it up a bit.

My family is a Zen kind of miracle. Anyway, they were. Since my father was a psychologist—really hip to a lot of the establishment bullshit in the sixties—so he let his kids have long hair (my brother and me) and he was proud of his related attitudes—but truth—truth tell it, WWII—the Big One had gotten him angry at any authority figure and made him suspicious, prone to the occasional problematic lie—for example—when the family vacationed together on the North Channel of Lake Huron—pristine water, tremendous perch fishing, amazing tiny villages that could be visited by sailboat with marvelous friends who partied old school, medical families with kids who could get great weed—and of course a shared fondness for Canadian beer. My father would often refuse to buy Canadian red wine, complaining that it tasted like sweet vinegar. So, he would put a couple of bottles of French Bordeaux or California Pinot Noir in the trunk of the sedan, the green Dodge Polara that would not stay tuned up—it rumbled and grumbled — ate gas like Schwarzenegger ate steroids —   these bottles were innocent enough—customs at the border crossing allowed a liter per person. Mother, bless her silly heart, liked to tease as we arrived at the border.

Father would say, "Let me do the talking."

Then Mother would put on a deep voice, "What's in the trunk, sir?" And in her own exaggerated feminine falsetto, "Just guns, occifer." And as kids we would laugh—while Father steamed.

So, this one time—predictably, the customs inspector in his sharp blue suit covered with sewn on badges and topped with a dapper cap, asked, "Any alcohol?"

Father said, "No sir."

And— "Let's see what's in the trunk." The bottles were located, and we were all asked to get out of the vehicle and watch while Father was instructed to break the necks of the green wine bottles against the curb and pour the dark red wine into the sewer drain.

Mother said as we drove away, "I almost interrupted you to say, 'Honey we brought some wine—I bought it and didn't tell you.'" She wasn't sure if it would be better to break Father's rule————the shame hung in the car, a shroud over this memory.

Sixteen—no twelve or fourteen years later, I was headed for the summer place in Richard's Landing with Marlena—recently divorced—driving her new Subaru—a bright pink hatchback. We drove at night—to save time—we only had six days off work—five and the holiday weekend—and I love to drive at night. The road is quiet, the world gets close, and Marlena agreed she'd do it. The blow job. We were driving past Detroit—listening to Laurie Anderson jazz. *A snake in the grass.* Then the traffic thinned and thinned—nearing the Mackinac Bridge—the great northern suspension spans—on a dark deserted highway–she leaned over me unzipped my trou, reached in, felt around and out it came. My dick was hard—in her mouth. I don't know how long it lasted—the car had cruise control—I smoked a cigarette—but she wouldn't let me come in her mouth–she brought me to the brink three times and each time eased back while I moaned, smoked and steered. When her head popped up, she read the road sign: Vanderbilt.

After the blow job, I was wired—smoked cigarettes, one, another, then chain smoked while drinking hot coffee from a thermos. The night highway's white dashed line steamed past, the smell of smoke and sex filled the car and filtered out over the cracked window. The flicker of headlights coming the other way grew more frequent as dawn approached. We reached the border, sailed across with only a brief question, "Where are you going? For how long? Alcohol, tobacco, or firearms?"

"Just a few packs of cigarettes."

Then it was morning. Our eyes burned with all-night weariness in the bright dawn as we drove the final stretch along the St. Mary's River on Highway 17. We arrived at the cedar smelling lakeshore cottage. By that time, I was so horny it was difficult to do more than gesture.

I hugged my brown-eyed father and mother as they came out of the bedroom in robes and pajamas. While they put on coffee, and started breakfast, I had other plans.

"Marlena, let's go, check out the boathouse—" I said.

She followed me through the trees on the narrow mossy trail. Pine forest, tall cedars, birch saplings, and sticky-bark fir—up the wooden ramp–through the rusty-hinged door. The smell of gasoline and paint mixed with musky sex. We were on the floor, the unpainted wood—fucking passionately—our clothes half-off and half-on. Then when we were finished, Marlena laid her head back on the floor and said, "Fantastic!" We listened together to the sound of waves lapping the shore, the wind in the trees and the cry of sea gulls. Our clothes were rearranged as we dressed, hiding the damp pubic hair with our underwear and jeans—

Back at the cottage, we ate the breakfast Mother had prepared—bangers and pancakes, fresh blueberries, and Island Maple syrup, and lots of strong coffee.

SEKI I

There came a time when Jack Acid and Arjuna blended into a single personality, and although such a design is unusual there was a common sense of unified thought patterns that evidenced itself to nearly all inside observers, though they would not admit it to the powers who now were in a position to choose for the young man when he felt he could not choose for himself.

The urn, the suggestion of the availability of psychiatry at Mount Zion and the knowledge that the Zen Master was a clever entrepreneur who saw immediately how to keep Jack and Arjuna separate and in conflict. The brother personalities acted like the brothers who were being forced into competition over the rich daughter by the sisters because of the acreage donated by the grandfather who was dead and in the ceremonial urn, a secret felt to be best kept. What's more Kunti, Arjuna's mother, had a best friend whose brother was a psychiatrist at the Mount Zion establishment.

Mother and Father had named me Steven Paul Lansky. Sometimes I went by Paul Lansky. That was what Adrianne called me. She also called me Ace, with affection, which was a shortened hippie name, Jack Acid. Before stealing the Rolls Royce, even before the trip to Mardi Gras in New Orleans there was Adrianne and:

Generated 1980

ADRIANNE

Watercolor and gouache on paper, 21.25 x 16.25"
From the Private Collection of the artist
Steven Paul Lansky

A painful love affair that seemed to hinge on longing and anticipation with moments of satisfaction that were dashed by drugs, alcohol and schizophrenia. Adrianne was a childhood friend, very much admired, and loved, and yet the families seemed destined for conflict. At one point her mother intervened with the artist's mother, and in a critical instance hopes were dashed, and innocence could never be restored. Adrianne was painted from memory. The artist has no photos of her.

GO DOWN

She was nineteen, he eighteen. Her pubes poked up in a tufted arrow over her mound. She had just slipped out of her blue denim coverall dress to climb into a sleeping bag on the floor of his dorm room at Harvard. She had started Brown the previous Fall. Paul was scared of Adrianne, not because he was a virgin; he wasn't, though only barely. He was scared because her father was a United States Congressman and Paul had political ambition.

The moment Paul saw that tufted arrow in the incandescent glow of his single bedroom, he thought he could rise to the heights if only he followed the arrow. They didn't kiss goodnight. After all, Adrianne was a childhood friend from Cincinnati; she admired him for riding his bicycle from home to Cambridge. Adrianne and Paul were platonic buddies. There was no danger in seeing her naked.

"Paul, you're signed up for breakfast dishes," said Shorty.

"I never signed up," Paul said between bites of his pancakes while he watched the dining room door for Adrianne.

"There's your name." Shorty said.

"Paul" was written on the schedule. Paul, something of a prima donna, had signed up for baking duty, meal duty, but never dish and kitchen cleaning. Now, as the school year neared its end, he had hoped to squeak by without ever doing the dirty work. The work steward had caught up with him, and on the one weekend he had a guest, Adrianne, he had been assigned kitchen detail.

"Shit," he said and just as he spoke Adrianne's long chestnut and auburn hair fell through the doorway into Paul's view.

"Adrianne," he said, "I have to do the dishes."

"I'll help," she said.

Paul was horrified. "No," he said.

She disappeared and Shorty said, "Get any Paulo? Huh? Huh?"

"It's not like that." Paul said, realizing that he had blown it, said the wrong thing.

Paul was becoming involved in a relationship that had the potential for becoming incestuous. She wasn't exactly Paul's sister. His brother wasn't married to her, nor had he made such an intention known. The brother and Adrianne were friends. It was clear to Paul that she wanted Paul and not his brother. Paul believed this. Paul believed his true anima projection was Draupudie. Paul was not as well acquainted with Draupudie. She had spurned a direct involvement with Paul at about the time Adrianne had surfaced in his life. Paul wanted both. The anima called to him from the guise of a Hindu cult, the rationale "you must fight those closest to you to conquer fear and desire. . . ." The focus on rebellion, which was a connecting thread to lure the young, churned the fires inside Paul. Paul did not have much moral indignation. Paul felt no duty to give Adrianne to his younger brother Rigo. Still, she was more of a sister, given the love they both felt for her.

And Then the Cow Was Drownded

Sailing . . . that day was for sailing. Paul had found a three-speed bicycle at an auction without wheels. He discovered some unused wheels and put them on the old Phillips and tuned it up. He borrowed another machine for Adrianne who followed him through congested streets, past cabs, buses, honking trucks, delivery boys leaning pushcarts out of alleyways, down Mass Ave, ringing her bell and veering around potholes.

They pedaled through Central Square until they reached the Harvard boathouse on the Charles River. At the boathouse Paul procured a bathtub shaped sailboat, Adrianne folded her lengthy frame onto the rail, and they angled their way upstream toward the opposite shore. Paul knew what he was doing, was overly fit, and teased the small vessel upriver with Adrianne anxiously clinging to the side stay, splashed gently and intermittently by waves bursting off the gunwale. Paul noticed Adrianne's anxiety at getting wet, seemed pleased to put her on the defensive and joyfully hiked out, his weight on the rail next to hers.

Paul was admitted today. There were many things about the place that he noticed on the drive in. Now, writing this some years later, he cannot remember much of what he noticed because buildings were torn down, roads bulldozed through the woods, new buildings built, old memories replaced with new images in a tangled mess around the inside of his head, and he feels empty of early impressions other than the unquelled sense of anxiety that occupied him at the time.

He walked in and immediately met a fellow in a wheelchair. The fellow had broken both legs trying to jump off the bridge into the creek at the entrance to the asylum. *This, bode evil.* Paul thought. Before Paul went to the cottage where he met this fellow there was the meeting in the main office with the financial person . . . Paul's father made some major financial decision and committed Paul. Father had health insurance. Paul had to agree to voluntary admission, and he knew he had no choice.

Paul met a psychiatrist and a social worker. Paul wanted to be with Adrianne riding bicycles on the way to the sailboat. He remembered the ride because on the way there she had fallen behind a bit, and on the return trip, she had pulled along evenly. On the way there she was riding the borrowed single speed with the seat set too low; as they cycled back to the house, Paul was on the borrowed bike. *Now*, he thought, *if only I could always be on the way.*

Paul may have remembered not what happened, rather what he had wanted to happen.

Perhaps he rode the blue and silver flake colored Follis racing ten speed that was made in France and had afforded Paul the opportunity to build wheels, he imagined, not invent them. And perhaps, with no doubt, when she had ridden the fine racing machine whose seat post he could raise and lower by loosening the seat post binder bolt with an American allen key wrench because Paul found the lightest binder bolt was American, and incidentally the most rare, to insure his Unicanitor (Cinelli) plastic saddle against theft by the wanton seatpost heist, though it was not loose when he tried it in the Spring . . . making it necessary to dismantle the cycle and carry the frame, fork and seatpost into a lab room in the science center where GO games were held upstairs at Harvard, and he had clamped the post in a vise and twisted the frame off of it because the frame had electrolicised itself onto the post, duraluminum and molybdenum being fused by chromium, giving her an edge over him that she rode easily ahead. He suppressed the memory.

It snowed. That much I could say reliably. It snowed. I was with Adrianne when the now blizzard famous snow started. We had dinner with my parents, I think. I can't really remember what either one of us was doing there. Or where we had been. It had just been that we were there together. It was like our childhoods had decided that she, of the plaid dress and private school and me, a year younger, tall dark, healthy and full of myself would want very much to have Adrianne. We had been together naked. I was back from Harvard after hitching there. I had flown home and then off to New York then back again. At least I think I sort of remember it that way.

The book was *Behind Her.* It was erotica. I read and reread and beat off in every imaginable way sometimes twice in one night or maybe even three times, orgasming all over sheets, belly, bellybutton, legs, pubic hair. It was the cleanest real orgasm of my entire puberty. I self-fucked to scenes of Elaine rubbing her pussy on a fence, feeling the wood on her clitoris rub and titillate until she moaned and groaned. But, most of all was the scene where the Colonel licked her pussy, his tongue up in the groove of her cunt, wet licking back and forth over her clit, tongue spiraling her lips, all at once, nose in her schnermer wet and horny. The Colonel dared to do what no other man could do without shame. He felt no shame. He had her submit to his tongue because he knew she would ask him to hurt her before he would do it again. This was what I read time and again, feeling my cock stiffen, my loins heat, my balls ache. And I dreamed of one day being with a woman.

Adrianne and Paul walked hand in hand through Clifton, gaslights glowing dimly under a shade of falling snow. Flakes drifted into their hair as they stepped their way right down the middle of the empty streets, their feet making fresh tracks in virgin snow. Paul was with Adrianne. The two talked in hushed whispers as if dampened by the blizzard. His boots crunched louder than her voice.

"My sister's in Ithaca." Adrianne said with glowing eyes.

"Where are we staying tonight?" Paul asked.

"At her place on Ludlow," she said.

"She's in Ithaca, New York?"

"Yes."

"What's she doing there?"

"Well, the old girl's got a house, she's sitting."

"OK."

"Sauna,   near   a   cross   country   ski   area!"

"OK."

"We could visit. Ski."

We're walking and without a hitch in our step we're up to Ludlow and walking past the night darkened shops toward the apartment. There are two different sisters. One lives on Ludlow where we're going. The other has a place in Ithaca where we can crash. I have no money.

"How?"

"We could hitch."

"Tonight?"

"Yes. But let's get a little sleep first."

Then I get really weird and crazy and start telling Adrianne that I love her and another too. I think they might know each other. The other girl's father is in government too and her name's Draupudie. I tell Adrianne that I want to ask Draupudie to marry me. I say I'll go to Ithaca, but after will have to go back to Cambridge to see the girl I love and ask her.

I don't have a ring.

Adrianne says, "Go ask your father's blessing."

I walk back home, leaving Adrianne at Ludlow in a brick tenement. At home I ask Dad for his blessing. He is watching TV. The blue screen reflects on his face. He asks me how well I know this girl. I tell him I know her so well that I am intimidated more by her than anyone else, including my mother. That sort of seals it for me in my dark-eyed lovestruck way. (remember I am loveblind) Dad defers to Mother. She won't listen past the beginning of the story and he's still glued to the TV and I am focused on what Adrianne said. Ask your father's blessing. I say, "Do I just have your blessing."

"Yes, you have my blessing," he says but he maybe adds that he doesn't believe it will happen, I'm too young, it won't work.

I sort of object to him, until I get him to say the blessing thing, in a reluctant voice, out from under the late night TV eyes, glasses reflecting blues, and yellow black faces. He is watching something very frivolous, but it is more important, than paying attention, to me. I am sort of grateful that he doesn't pay much attention.

"Yes. You have my blessing."

I leave.

Back at Ludlow walking . . . I'm damp from sweat, fully eager and very horny having just received a blessing to marry from my dad. Adrianne says good night to her sister and tells her that we will not see her in the morning because we'll leave in only a few hours. I did tell Dad we're hitching to Ithaca tonight and he nearly shouted that I was damn crazy but never really took his full attention off the TV. I wish I knew if it was *I Claudius* or some other fantastic PBS drama or just drivel like he is accustomed to watching. He likes the magic of TV, like Columbo is almost his invention from the way he eats it up, grinning and explaining. But now he was swearing and saying he didn't understand me.

Hell, I didn't understand me. I was messed up. So we're in the dark livingroom of the apartment and Adrianne spreads a white sheet out on the rug. I'm used to sleeping on floors. She strips and in the dim light I am more in love because I'm with her and I strip and we're skin and naked bodies and at that magic age where nothing sags, and opposite, really, it stands up pert and trembling. She lies down on her back, spreads her legs, her vortex open and very wet to the touch of my tongue as I, mouth first, try to climb within her wetness and marry my horniness to her body. I am thinking I am the cockroach that ate Cincinnati, the young dirty old man from Texas, and the man who will have exacted some sort of favorable treatment and be accepted as a man without shame and very, very masculine by diving, like this head first into her pussy. I wind my tongue up and down smelling a muskiness that drives my frenzy into rubbing my cock against the sheet in a purely involuntary way and I am thinking there is no risk of pregnancy and that makes it more arousing as the tongue, breath and lips are all teased to perfection and we are both orgasming, she, lifting her pelvis, arching bones toward my teasing lips, and I come right into the sheet.

Then we kiss and I get up to wash my lightly bearded mouth and she asks me not to even brush my teeth, asks that I let her scent linger on me as we dress and go out into the two-thirty a.m. night to advance our souls by hitchhiking all the way to upstate New York in a damn blizzard as if it is our country, our right, our passage through horny adolescence.

SEKI II

After, stoned on codeine, caffeine, nicotine, beer, tranquilizers, horny and mindless, feeling steered, like an errant boat, making a way through waves. (The game of chong gambit comes to mind here: an insistent competitive drinking game in which the characters all get together on a small speedboat, push the throttle forward, drink into the night until someone falls overboard.) But somehow this time the boat advances only as long as the hull is intact and all the characters seem to be equally in danger of going to the other side, perhaps death, the most welcome of outcomes to the inebriated is even more welcome to the drugged, and the hull is not intact, the one-eyed black cocaine dealer trapped in chong gambit but never well balanced enough to even stand on the speedboat driving her back with flesh, pulling her close, feeling lips hot against neck, breathing, caressing, licking, wetting, screwing—then dressing, a blue flame, about loneliness, gray green corridors, saying, "It's good," chanting out of darkness, saying, "No, no," louder, confessions to mere acquaintances, shouting, calming—Marlena saying, looking for love, about loneliness, "No, no, It's bad." He, and she, arguing, then kissing, rolling on the bed. Along the borderline, never at the university, groping, seeking merciful women, a voice, "who gave you that hickey," mercy, then saying, "Charlotte, Lottie, the model," innocently being—stands in antiseptic rooms—slapped, pushed, holding her away, hands on head, hospital—slapped, slapped, "Cunt, cunt," she screams, angry, on and on the struggle broken by a referee, shirt torn from limbs, wishing it were gone, the life, the memory, the love, the fight, the fear, numb face, keys in hand, numb face, keys in hand, leaving, keys in broken hand, the janitor had a fight.

JO SEKI

So both in orange shirts, the younger one with wider stripes, two young boys in white, sit on the living room carpet and begin to explore the adult world in a space of several sittings, each in a brief conversation about emptiness, fullness, volume, space, and liquids, and solids. To conform to mores, the boys have a Japanese toy, the game of GO, and a pair of clear plastic homemade, American service type cups that stack, and a variable quantity of, shall we say, apple juice.

One of the children is of a certain mythos that leads him to believe about himself that culture is highly individual and identifies only with his own indigenous understanding of reality. He creates some rules for participating in the homo sapiens club, and it becomes ultimately more exclusive as rules are added to foster limits and create exclusive categories. (Striped white shirts. Orange stripes. Horizontal stripes. At least one brother.) Until he creates in himself a category which ultimately seeks another. That is, he discovers girls and in the same instant, or possibly the next, wonderment, empowerment, and delay. Gratification delay based on limited mobility. Enhancing his problem to the point where it can establish critical mass is the next goal in his life march. But first he must identify his myth. This proves to be a very difficult task as he understands right away that he is his own worst enemy, and his guide (whom he sees everywhere) is not only inside him, and outside him, but forever trapped in the most envious of enviable positions.

A letter Arjuna wrote to clarify things after the facts began to come out. The letter was never sent, and might have been lost, if not for "project abstract."

As Arjuna, I, making my way, was often hindered by individuals, this one guarded a secret that took me some time to uncover, as it was I discovered it, relayed my discovery instantly to my younger brother, older by now, because he studied more quickly, and less patiently, by way of the DNA between us; that was cut off because we were relatives—the whole SEKI, real seki, not joseki (cornerplay), not ko (real pivotal battle points), not ladder (terminable treks in the wrong direction that without self-correction lead to walls and waste), nor even monkey jumps (side play that secures territorial area like joseki, only along the edge), took form here. I had shown him the connection between GO— 19 x 19 gridirons "NO I WON'T TAKE A HANDICAP' and yet I won't answer you when I ask, which glass, is more full, or fuller, when you then say, "Huh." It's a question of whose ashes are in the urn! And whether you could possibly argue that one of us owns the retreat!

So - it was written on hand cooched paper, that was not kissed off, and it was written like a well-tuned bicycle wheel, each nipple hand twisted and crimped with a steel wire cutter without a lock action.

I'm sitting in the den with my head back against the couch, reading a science fiction book called *DUNE*. I hear someone crying, and I know it is my mother. She has only cried once before in the big house with the heavy wooden beams and French doors, hardwood floors which launch me into the world of sliding, splinters, and boomies. The first time she cried my father asked if her father had died. My grandfather. I knew him only slightly, for he lived in California. We live in Ohio. She was crying because one of her very best friends had died in a car crash in Chicago. We didn't like Volkswagens after that. I didn't really know what dying meant until then. I just knew that I would never see Maureen again. She was gone.

With my head back on the couch I think about getting up to turn on the TV, or giving mother a kiss, or hiding somewhere in the basement. I am afraid to go to the attic alone, usually I drag my little brother along for such play excursions. I don't think he was home when mother cried. I was thinking about grandfather. What I didn't know was what had happened about seven years earlier when I was three and we lived in Lexington, the cradle of revolution. Mother was in the house preparing dinner and Father was at work. I played in the yard. There was a long letter on the mantle, out of child's reach, neither of us could read anyway. The house was a colonial red brick, with a fireplace, weeping willows and grass and a vegetable garden out back. Farms bordered the land, which was quite fertile in 1961. The letter was from grandfather. The part that said a certain few choice words was all that my mother could think about. It was direct. Now that I've helped you two buy the house and the children will both be in school, I've decided to sell the restaurant. That will leave me with the nest egg and only the hot springs retreat out here. I've deeded the apartment building so that it will be both yours and your sister's. I think she is going to be fine with her new young friend here in San Francisco. I'm coming to live with you, Kunti. Father had seen the letter only once, when he came home from work yesterday. Mother and Father had had a big fight.

I waited in the hallway some days after the hitchhiking trip to the retreat. The young monastic woman had whispered in my ear: "You hear the bell, sit facing the wall . . . you get up slowly, turning as you rise, walk to the room, walk in, bow to the urn, sit facing away from Roshi, turn around after being seated, and bow to the Roshi. Don't speak until he does. Sit facing the wall. I sat facing the wall.

When I heard the bell, I walked down the hall after slowly rising, in stocking feet, turning and thinking, why? Why am I here? Does this man know anything special? Isn't the urn just ashes, ashes of his master, the great Suzuki?

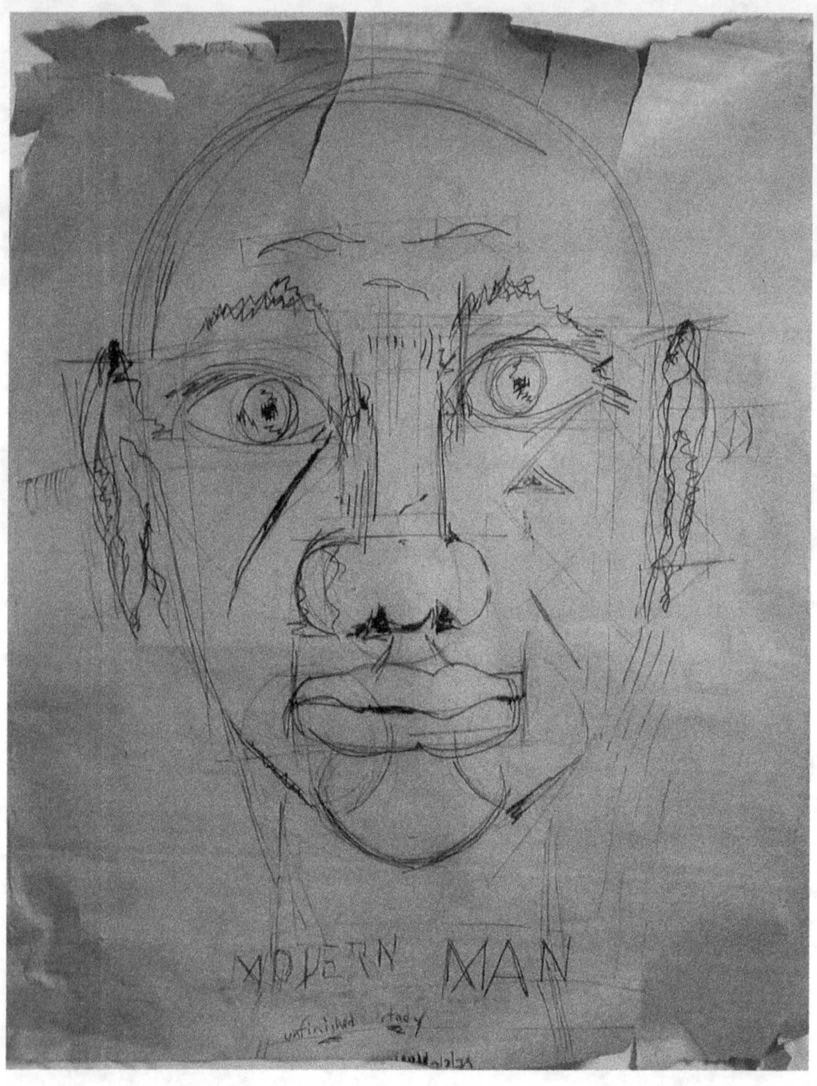
MODERN MAN
unfinished study

Generated September 4, 1978

MODERN MAN

Pencil on newsprint, 36"x 40"
From the Private Collection of the artist
Steven Paul Lansky

The artist met Baker, the Zen Master, in San Francisco Zen Center face-to-face. During this time the artist was writing, collecting stories, drinking late at night and carousing. Yet, when Baker told him to see the psychiatrist at Mt. Zion, and that he should be working, the artist stuck to his primary task of writing despite all the pressures. He turned to visual art when unable to write. This "portrait" drawn in Cincinnati was a self-acknowledged "robbing the temple." Later it was revealed Baker had then been in a dalliance with a married Zen student that became an imbroglio and led to Baker's being deposed from the San Francisco Center and its affiliates. He lost his BMW, private residences, privileges among elite Californians, and opportunities to guide young artists.

And Then the Cow Was Drownded

Generated September 4, 1978

SALIENT LOTUS

Artist's pencil on newsprint, 36"x 40"
From the Private Collection of the artist
Steven Paul Lansky

Generated in the same artistic urge that yielded MODERN MAN, this piece also seemed to be "robbing the temple." The artist spoke with his father about the depths that these two drawings came from. The psychologist father acknowledged this as "work." The details of the head and face were intended to be like that of Buddha, and the figure a kind of Hindu Deity somehow sexualized, and scandalized. In connecting this drawing with MODERN MAN, one wonders if the artist was sensitive to Baker's indiscretion(s) and was making a cryptic note of it/them.

JO SEKI II

Lord Caitanya Mahaprabhu (Krishna) offered Arjuna a watch. He knew nothing of love, only he knew time in containment. Not in a refuge or sanctuary, safely hidden, ensconced in a sanitarium estate instead, he saw the gift as form. Later he knew it was love. Love of the brother. Krishna gave to the man who loved his sister, although Arjuna still knew only the pen.

When Arjuna was later given a tour of an international museum piece, twice, once under guard, once with Kunti he knew of the ancient ceremonial scabbard, and flintlock, both of his great grandfather, or perhaps his grandfather. Krishna had offered back the watch, a gift from a previous dispute between the families. Arjuna was wary of Greeks bearing gifts. Caitanya knew of the sexual sword, for Arjuna had been among those who took the women of the rooming house.

> on the wind-beaten wall forty clocks tick
> tick-tickety-tick, tick-tickety-tick
> each a click off the next, one tick,
> another tick-tickety, and tick

in the room a small painting painted
in three tocks, a large photo tacked
against the side wall, photographed in a
shot, pinned up, after being washed in
chemicals for seven ticks, and that a
tock, tick, tickety-tick tock.

In the head a lack of time, no
lines drawn, twixt one tock or the
next. Each thought twisted and wrought
from a small little chemical, electrical
shot, a charge of ions, blood-cells,
clicking, and clawing like little cats
in the belly of a bigger one. The
pregnancy of thought, timeless,
like a tree, not a streetlamp with
its bright bulb, glowing, casting shadows,
a tree, elm, or birch, from distant side
alleys, trees like limbed figures, shadowy
in moonlight. Central rings mark the only
clicks of time to measure age of wooden
statues, un-carved but by wind, weather,
rain, sun's heat.

Knowing notes:

Krshna is a warrior who carries a sword, which his army
knows, is to be used in slaying cattle. The sacred cow.
Arjuna is his friend. Arjuna refuses to use the sword. The
story is a mystical blending of two different kinds of people. The
one who is "that" is Arjuna. He is identified in many traditions.
To the Asian people he is the SCARLET BELT. He is the one
who has inherited the highest order of the non-weapon martial
arts. He is sworn never to fight. If he is caught fighting in all

countries, other than the USA he is a criminal. If he fights, he must fight to the death, if he is identified as the SCARLET BELT. The laws in USA were designed for unique varieties of religious practice. He is the bloodline of the highest house.

"There's a thing or two to be said about Kunti," Arjuna said.

"And I got it wrong when I explained it to the dead man."
"NO!"

"Yes, she's my true love, I'm Arjuna, Lord Caitanya . . . I have wronged her."

"Kunti is your mother, Arjuna," He would have said. Krishna knew the myth, pulled the strings.

Then it was softball.

Arjuna was all strung up about baseball, hardball, mumbly-peg. He confused his love for Draupudie with that for Kunti.

Lord Caitanya Mahaprabhu, the living Krishna incarnate played softball with Arjuna in the great estate. The palatial hotel was a hideaway haven for schizophrenics in the area of gift exchange. Arjuna gave devotion to Krishna.

Filial and sororal communication were mysteries. Arjuna had three brothers, in the myth. Each had a more than filial attraction to Lord Caitanya's sister Draupudie. Arjuna wrote:

I wanted the love of Krshna's sister. I guess he suspected as much.

Likely she had spoken of my quest for her hand in marriage.

It's a long way around, I often thought. I did not mean to become

a thief. It hurt me in my heart. My soul yearned for her. She

knew nothing of the tense pull in my loins. She knew I had slept with her friend.

Arjuna said, "Krshna. . . . Why the watch?"

Suppose we do away with all the subterfuge for a moment and deal with the symbols as raw issues. SEKI as a notion is a demonstration of politeness. It is based on the idea that both parties are giving a gift of greater value and neither party wishes to disrupt the relations to the point of accepting a greater grace than he or she could bestow.

Arjuna got himself into a bit of a problem. He was trapped in Cincinnati. He knew that the media was the best way to escape the city of porkers. This being known, he took up the harmonica and hung always in a local tavern trying to hawk his harp, and to find a keen interest in his language arts, that is, to sell a song.

So, he writes two songs on fairly drunken nights on napkins. Both are love ballads about Draupudie, his only desire. One is about a snowy night he remembers walking with her on Massachusetts Avenue, down to Harvard Square in Cambridge to buy chocolate chips so she can make cookies. The other is about her touch, which is the most momentary fleeting bit of enjoyment Arjuna can conceive. Her hugs and kisses are perfunctory, not impassioned, but rather lacelike and euphoric in brief fancy. He describes this better in the songs.

He comes home from the bar, the other bar, now later, wanting that past, that homecoming, with Draupudie, to be his holy everyday, and he turns on the radio, to hear the singer talking, about the songs, and he never gets a whit of credit, nor does Krishna. He feels frustration and thinks on the bitterness of battle and looks to Krishna for guidance. He opens his eyes to the facts. He must fight.

Arjuna sits upstairs in the ISKCON temple library after chanting, eating, and sweeping the porch, his bare feet against the hard floor, thinking *these texts were written for him. He knew this because as he read, he saw his own name. As the words entered his conscious thought, he became the animal man that drew life from these words. They described his Godhead. The emission of love from Lord Caitanya engulfed him, fulfilled him, he became one with epic love, being, epic proportions flooded his peacefulness. He called out to mythical Gods, and went into bars thinking of Gods, his young adult life was spent in quests. He could have been shopping.*

What stupid thought struck him? He knew it was the same thought every time. He knew he would never fight. It was his nature to be beyond fighting. He was hospitalized because he could not play. The martial forms he knew ended in mortal combat, war; certain death for someone. That Krishna loved mankind, and slayed cattle for mankind, he could not prove, the ownership of any ceremonial swords he could not establish as fact, he only had circumstantial evidence, visions, and cryptic love. He understood chain reaction. He might breathe too strongly, suggest a moment of tumult in a gathering and it could be acted out with his blessing, his central role might betray foreknowledge, yet it could be all paranoid mentation. He could be imagining violence because of some psychological defect. *Wondered if the flick of the jaw could kill, someone lay dead. Could kill with a flick, he wondered. And did not want to fight.*

The whole thing about some of his writings (one called *The Purple Kerchief*) was his heart. The diadem that stayed in the estate was a toy of his castle people and their disavowal of Arjuna's dominance. The dance of life needed the

SCARLET BELT

Access new information gleaned tonight to interest readers of all sorts, ages, races, colors, creeds, religions, origins, and levels of historical, genetic, and temperamental development.

Three things need be learned:

1) Flight reaction sufficient to run till bloody feet paralyze flight reaction.
2) Fight reaction learned, and genetically intact through stages of flight.
3) Born into loving hands.

Homo sapiens: wise man would be born a little bit flawed to make others take notice. Running is not a viable alternative for a baby. Defective legs imply different evolutionary cycle. Without correction, a cripple defends, and attacks, but cannot fly (run), would, borne into good hands, make good. Born into intelligent hands would be corrected to the norm, beyond the mean, into a cyclic awareness of advantages allowed unique individuals. DNA, RNA, long cycles of genetic research in the bones are factors.

Technology is love.

Now, there are practical parts to this new learning that could be assimilated in parts to families and races, each toward the ultimate survival of the fittest. Darwinian theory validates a species that can only correct once. The first and only mistake.

GOD

The story had landed at his foot when he was very young. He never remembered contact unless he was injured. He was injured a couple of times. At first, he believed himself invulnerable to broken limbs. This was the mystery. He thought he was invulnerable as a human mortal. In a way he was. He would be confused with the one with average ability. He had to fight the women, because he had intellectually let them on to his spit. His spittle of supposed craziness was his excuse. When he was young women spit in his face. He might be able to avoid legal action in court on assault charges because he was certified. The truth of his certification was known to his sex partners. The partners envied his legal status. They knew his ticket to holiness was a feigned madness that lay in the encompassing path of freedom in a crazy society. The law was different for him. His certified madness excused his lack of discipline. He belonged to all the dances at once. He could fit himself to aikido, to jujitsu, to karate, to kung fu, to tai chi, to judo, to tae kwan do, to modern, to belly, to ballet, to tap, to clogging, to ballroom, yet he knew only fragments of his role. Dance was in his soul and it was life dance. He danced the strongest elements of each form. As he grew older his central position became more visible. He was the center pillar of the circle of blows. This carried his myth through jail then out onto the street again. His time in mental wards fighting drug addiction acted as a salve to the would-be fighter. He hungered for combat as the human civilized man, in knightly valor, in this age of all ages this was the only one where he could write, speak, behave.   Arjuna's bloodlines were so good. He was not that, but he was THAT. The unknown living man that could kill with each fist, each foot, his head. He dealt blows with his wit, but he solemnly swore never to fight in earnest because something told him he would not know when to stop. Just as when he wrote he feared he would say too much. When he spoke, he carried his words, I should say, carried the world. He came for only one thing. He meant to lead. At the prime of this lifetime, he held no high position. But fame was creeping up on him. He knew that fame was a line he could handle. He performed. He read. He wrote. He felt the stiff neck. He recalled countless phone conversations that filled from his sleep. He knew he spoke with the outraged elderly on the phone from a deep state. Knowing he never slept alone, or well, he always slept with his woman, he slept better knowing he would die with a kiss on his lips. He spoke readily with his guards. He befriended each warrior. He studied. He knew that the insides of hospitals were homes to him as was the hall of power where he held court with other rulers and sages. There were days when he knew heaven was his home. He was in heaven when he was homeless. He had no fear but fear itself, and that was only a dream of an axe breaking down the door at night. The dreams were so filled with terror that the hunted look on film was in other's eyes way beyond what fear anyone could ever see in his. Yet he knew he had a crazed look when he cut back on the necessary pills. His diet was defended by psychiatrists and medical experts. This coterie of experts would come and go with fashion, but the food, the spiritual food, was always there, on time, with need, with love. He bled the same red blood of all mammals. He had seen his own blood.

And there were no mysteries to her, but the blind side of consciousness. He had migraines. He knew his fantasy was of knowing styles that had no form in the inner circle. There was no way he could know what he knew would save him and he did, and it did. He owned the Ethiopian Death Ring on the beaded chain, and he built on it the stone of life. He knew his role was to conquer. In history he was Alexander the Great, Arjune, and Moses who had forbidden his children to speak of Christian love. He was the center of time and the solar system. He lorded over and hovered within the longest golden age ever known. He was, is, and always will be. And he had God consciousness. Yet he was not as attractive as Caitanya. He was the beast in the BEAUTY, and The BEAST. He was the stupid, ugly, boring brother in the story of the Frog Prince. He was always winning, and he was a winin' boy. He was the subject of song, the object of praise, the moment of glory, the signpost of valor, and the Teflon man, who rode out the sticky times in other places where he felt a smooth and well tensiled, high toned yet soft, and gentle, red budded breast. He felt inside like a clean woman, and he felt around his soul because his Kundalini released like a shot, and he was not good in bed, afterward, no he was greased gumption, he was sooo bad in bed that his lovers were sworn to love. Object of envy, he was.

He lived at a time when his skill and prowess allowed him for full legality when he deemed it necessary and when the law circled around to his cases it was always just a matter of editing history, clarifying this particular word, a definition perhaps misunderstood, probably because of a typo. That was a minor thing to him. When others beat at the walls and earned foul humors; he simply worked on his conditioning to make it better always. The future is always better. He knew always that adolescence and childhood would make everyone the small same people that he had known at once he would never be and yet was, always. How could he deny that the Scarlet Belt was his home? He lived in ashram, in temple, with deity, by, and by. He thanked God when he got older because he knew his reputation as a youth allowed few to know that he was who he knew he was. They were always honoring him above all others, but it soothed them to hear him speak aloud about his own God. He loved with fruitful passion. He took care of all and one. He knew when he sat fat the others would plot, but plots never haunted . . . . He knew the old danger of two speakers. He knew being in a spiral of time he could be in more than one place at a time. He was infinitely embarrassed by his personality rifling through the tough times, but he stood well the test of time. He stuck to his story. He told it so many ways that that each listener knew that he was THAT and they tah-tahed and thanked him for being. There were many names. Arjune.

OF **KUNTI**

She came here to visit, her only sister. Her father dead, a long time now, almost twenty years. This was Kunti's home, not Aunti Zen's. Aunti Zen rearranged half the artwork in the house. She didn't ask. Two years later when Kunti was ill, Aunti Zen was welcomed in. Then she moved into Kunti's bedroom. Kunti was angry then. More angry than she could believe, she could be. Kunti said, "I know you are the artist, and you have different tastes than I do, but this is my house. And how you could have been just lying in my bed. I came home and didn't know where you were; when I checked my son's rooms, you weren't there. I called out. You were in my room with the door closed. We're both lucky Arjuna's father didn't find you. You know he would have blown up. But I found you. You didn't even ask. You said I feel it's my house too. It's not your house. I don't want to bring this up, but you have your own place. I know it's not the same living in the monastery, not much space, and little privacy. This is my house, not yours. I come home from work and find my you, my sister in my bed. Remember that? You must. Yet you seem to forget. Now it's the living room again. You've taken the younger boy's kiln God and moved it to the mantel and the rust red round colored ceramic bowl is not part of my arrangement. All that damn pottery. I can't understand how you could be so insensitive to put all that pottery all over this living room. I don't ask that you keep everything in the boy's room, but you didn't even ask. It's not your house. It is my house. You made a choice. When you joined the Zen, or whatever that damn place is; yes, I know. Don't you even think to yell at me about my possessiveness. You are the one who has the gall to possess my house. I live here. This place is not Zen's home. You cannot just come in here and act like you live here. There are other people living here. I want you to feel welcome here, but dammit this is my house. You didn't even ask. I will tell my children about your insistent demands on this house. Yes, Arjuna isn't welcome here now. Yes, you say Arjuna should be treated with more sensitivity and respect because he is an artist, like you. He doesn't take over the place. He just can't control himself. He'll learn. You don't seem to be able to learn. I wish you would just ask. I might have said, OK, a few pieces, the plates on the side tables, or some of the bowls on the mantel. But twenty seven different colored red rouge and gray brown bowls all over my living room, blue green plates, mauve vases, it doesn't even match the decor. The living room is out of place. And besides it has not a damn thing to do with aesthetics. This is my house. Arjuna is learning the hard way. I don't want to overdo this but go. Go see Arjuna, and you tell me if he is OK. Maybe he is and we have to wait for his father to understand. Don't tell me you can heal Arjuna. You have too little good sense yourself. Remember Dad always said, Dad always said listen to your sister and you did sometimes. This time I want to tell you. I am angry at your damn impatience with communicating your own desires. Ask. Why didn't you ask? I don't mind letting you make a little corner yours while you are visiting. But expand into my house. Do you understand it is my house? No. Don't. Don't try to explain. I haven't the patience. You said you wanted to do a little typing; use my desk. Now, I know I said use it. A couple of days ago I said OK. You said a little typing I said OK but this is not a little typing. This is a damn book. You must have enough pages strewn about for forty lectures. Sure you are busy. You are working hard. Forget it. You didn't ask. You said. I won't say it again. You are welcome here. I never claimed to renounce anything. Don't call me selfish again. I like my house. I need my desk and work area. You are taking over. If only you would have asked."

I thumbed to Carmel Valley by the coastal highway at first, my angular hand propped against hip, feet protesting loudly when I had to walk. In the valley the golden rolling hills sounded in my head, a song lyric.

Somehow, I managed to get near Tassajara Hot Springs by late day, sun raising steam off the narrow road, the final ride on the back of a hay cutting rig to Jamesburg as far as the mail was delivered. I approached the white paneled house and knocked. A young fellow in loose fitting clothes appeared, mug in hand, head shaved to a fleshy shine. I introduced myself, stated I came to see Aunti Zen. The man looked surprised, asked if she expected me. I rubbed my hands together, then on my jeans, smiled, and mumbled an answer. The man did not ask again.

"She's at Tassajara, headed out tomorrow. Want to stay and wait?"

"I'd like to go in," I said.

"No vehicles passing in tonight. You might walk in come morning— like as not they'll be on their way out before you get in."

With that, he swung the door wide, invited me in for tea, fruit, to roll a cigarette. I peeled a navel orange with big hands, rolled an adequate stick, puffed and sipped green tea with milk and honey. I slept in a small bunk house.

Poppies, dirt road, stones half the size of my shoe . . . I walked toward Tassajara. Aunti Zen was on her way to zazen in the twilight zendo of Tassajara Zen Mountain Retreat Center. She walked one step at a time past the coffee bar—the skunk smell—a sweet indulgent vice. Her loose pants felt good. She didn't wear a brassiere. Her cancer was gone—the regime of garlic, carrot juice three times a day, and the San Jose based, Korean healer's supplements combined—her skin turned orange, she reeked—and now she was in remission.

After zazen she ate granola, dried apricots, raisins, almonds, and a little plain yoghurt. Then she returned the call. She hadn't known I had hitchhiked to DC. The official in Baltimore said there was a problem.

I'd never told her about Draupudie, I'd only asked a political question about the Senator and had spoken in fragments about my decision to break from college. They had eaten lunch under the wooden and tin roof two days ago, Draup had a contact in the embassy in Washington, D.C. The two had talked before and Aunti Zen thought—the thought rushed through her like the creek ran through Tassajara Mountain after snow melted—yes, she knew I had picked up the harmonica—yes, I had stayed at Harvard. Less than a year had passed since the day I visited her on the way to Tassajara.

As Aunti sat at Tassajara, July 5th, 1978, a cold morning in the zendo, a rain shower fed the creek.   She smelled the dew on the platform around the zendo—smelled the green banana feet of the ino, heard the scraping broom, the tenzo shouting at the blue jays, and the sniffling of the monk next to her as she sat facing the wall. The morning sunlight came over the
ridge as she took her turn in line, walked, chanted, passed the ino, saw the pale pate, the dark robe, again smelled dank dew, and foot odor.

239

After zazen, another knock on her door from Draupsie. She said I had gambled at college. Listening to Draup describe my erratic behavior at the college rooming house, Aunti Zen cursed Kunti for her bad choice to let me go to college back East on the bicycle and settle in without Ken and Kunti to guide me. Aunti Zen's meditation practice was the only thing that Ken had talked to her about at family Thanksgiving in Cincinnati months before when I was in Santa Fe.

I could imagine the scene: "Don't you hurt when you contort and sit? Why give yourself that pain?" Ken asked. He struggled with back problems. Kunti had told Aunti that Ken said she stank of garlic. She could not tell. She was jetlagged then. Ken sat in his Eames chair in the den, reading *Encounter Magazine*.

GLOSSARY

Arjuna- Protagonist of the *Bhagavad-Gita*.
> *Bhagavad-Gita*- A song-sermon about Krishna, the basic Hindu scripture.

Bhakta- A term of endearment. (love)

Blue Cross- A health insurance company.

Brooks Brothers- A brand of clothiers.

Caffeine-The drug in coffee that wakes up the user.

CAPEAS- A legal notation that requires police to hold a suspect without bail.

Codeine- A drug to kill pain. Prescription required.

Community Mortuaries- A mythical hospice agency.

Community Munitions- Another name for Community Mortuaries.

Dharma- Law, religion itself. Practice of being in pure consciousness.

Drap- A drink of alcohol.

Dune- A novel by Frank Herbert.

Estate- Sanitarium.

Ethiopian Death Ring- A mythical piece of jewelry that included a ring of silver said to be worn only by someone who had killed.

FBI- Federal Bureau of Investigation.
GO- A board game from the Orient played with black and white
disks on a 19 x 19 grid.
Home Medical- A mythical health company.
Honeymooners- A TV show in the late 1950s starring Jackie
Gleason, Audrey Meadows, Joyce Randolph, and Art
Carney as two married couples.
I AM THAT- A religious tome by an Indian Guru named Maharaj
I Ching- The Chinese book of Changes. A book of hexagrams and
oracles.
Ino- The ino is in charge of the meditation hall, or zendo, is
responsible for cooperation in finding a seat.
ISKCON- Acronym for the International Society for Krishna
Consciousness which is an organization that promotes
Hinduism.
Joseki- Opening corner moves in the game of GO similar to the
openings in chess.
Krishna- The Lord, God, the All Attractive One, Lord Caitanya
Mahaprabhu is the relevant incarnation. Arjuna's
charioteer.
Kunti- Matriarch of the Pandava family. Arjuna's mother.
Ladder- a postion in GO that is interminable and carries to the
edge of the board if there is no stopping piece.
Maya- The state of living in illusion.
Monkey-jump- A term for a position in GO that involves linking
pieces along the side of the board.
Mount Zion- A psychiatric center in San Francisco.
Mumbly-peg- A child's game of tossing a knife up so that it falls
near feet.
Nicotine- The active addictive element in tobacco.
No Doze- An over-the-counter drug to combat sleep.
Over-the-Rhine- An area in Cincinnati North of Central Parkway,
bordered loosely by the hills surrounding downtown.
Pandavas- Arjuna's family name, also Pandus.
Pioneer Bar- A bar on Main Street in Over-the-Rhine.

Red Cross- A safety and rescue organization.

Rossford- A mythical freightyard town.

Scarlet Belt- A mythical level of accomplishment in martial arts.

Seki- A position in GO where neither black nor white can attack but in which neither player can claim "eyes".

Shiva- The God of the Self.

Smithsonian Institution- An archival museum of history and restoration in Washington, DC.

Srivad Bhagvitam- A holy scripture of the Hindu religion.

Sufi- A Moslem mystic sect.

Suzuki- A Soto Zen priest who founded the San Francisco Zen Center.

Tenzo- One of the positions, and titles given in Zen Buddhism, usually limited to six or seven individuals at any given time. The tenzo is head chef, responsible for providing meals from donated and farmed goods and foods for the community.

The Purple Kerchief- A short story manuscript of The Writer.

Wet Willie's Whistle Lipped beet Red beer- A mythical beer, red In color.

Zen Master- An expert in Zen.

Zen- A branch of Buddhism that emphasizes meditation or "zazen."

Lottie Lockett lost her pocket
Lily Parker found it
Not a penny was there in it
Only ribbon round it.
The bastardization is:
Kitty litter all around it
Patty Fischer went and found it
Less could work it then
Than said the cow was drownded

BOOK 2

Draupudie's boy, the blond blue-eyed thin main rival for Arjuna's talent and the man who single-handedly engineered the whole conspiracy. He was Arjuna's competition for Draupsie's attentions and Arjuna, as a young man was fiercely jealous. How could anyone rein in a man who could bicycle over a hundred miles a day whatever the weather? (He needed time to work, he was always being asked to look at this or that for some sycophant.) And the computers were being labeled and separated, like the labels on beer. Remember the honor system at the CENTER FOR HIGH ENERGY METAPHYSICS? There was a pencil on a string. Arjuna was supposed to make the milk from powdered concentrate. That was free. The cartoned milk was a few cents a cup. The men drank more beer than milk, the women in the CENTER FOR HIGH ENERGY METAPHYSICS were coffee drinkers and milk drinkers. Knickerbocker Natural, Carling Black Label, and Labatts Cream Porter were Arjuna's three favorite brands of beer. No one knew which brand of milk to drink. The cows gave, the sheep would bleat, but at the CENTER FOR HIGH ENERGY METAPHYSICS you served yourself, or you didn't eat. Favors came hard, and easy. Sleep there was the best in the world. Arjuna thought of it as the coolest whorehouse on the planet. There was a pair of torn up wingtips that were too big for him. Time seemed to move through those walls like the wind, and the paint on the walls was never dry. It was a favorite time, and it happened really fast. But the LSD Chemist took a lot of heat. The *Hee Haw* songwriter that I spit at with jealousy reveals my secret to us.

"I'm named by Harvard in a lawsuit. You mustn't tell anyone," click, click he snaps a pen and cap in his left hand, a nervous gesture. Snap, snap.

"A lawsuit?"

"Yes, no one knows."

"What?"

"The magazines?"

"The CENTER FOR HIGH ENERGY METAPHYSICS." He lives off campus in a condo now on Harvard St., fancy room with carpet, upright piano, state-of-the-art typography computer. The CENTER FOR HIGH ENERGY METAPHYSICS magazine subscriptions.

He doesn't have to spell it out. I laugh. There has been a tradition of making up names. Bill Melater, Shirely U. Jest, Gamma Functionne, there were twenty-five obviously fake names. Everytime a subscription was cancelled, someone just made up another name, or signed another magazine up—it was a sport. Before computers checked, and when a human collection agency would actually see the name, they'd know they'd been had, but by then . . . they never cross-checked the address . . . until, well, now.

Oui, Gentry, Club, Playboy, Penthouse to name a few, all stacked in the communal, either gender bathrooms. Hell we rubbed ourselves, delighted, without concern.

"Somehow they got my name," he clicked, and he was clicking pictures of me with a spy camera while I toked, toked, played harmonica to his piano, he played Bob Dylan songs, sang too. I laughed at his lawsuit. He had changed his name, too.

Somehow, I see the exhibit a second time with Kunti, on a special trip and I know she is not saying, not speaking, her dark brown eyes teaching that this Arjuna, this is your heritage. Your weapons are in a traveling museum exhibit.

It was weird because later Arjuna understood that the differences between sheep farmers and cow herding girls was the eternal conflict among the clans and some part of him believed that was the true source of all his problems. The medical problems were just factional battles between peoples who knew he was the natural leader, the true man to fight for individuality. His wool and leather jackets came later, he never owned a motorcycle, because his lineage was so eccentric. This all came to him at the CENTER FOR HIGH ENERGY METAPHYSICS when he was talking to the Asian women trying to explain perestroika. The museum display called it Afghani Art, but he was on a mission to conquer the world and these were the weapons that his rifle bearer and sword bearer wanted him to see. That was the only explanation for why he had been brought to the museum twice. The mother-of-pearl inlay, the obsidian, the flintlock must have been older than any one in the city. He couldn't swing the sword. His arm ached for battle. But he was a man of peace and with his mother, Kunti by his side, her salt-pepper hair, brown eyes, olive-skin, that slight anomaly; even with her contact lenses embarrassed her, scared because of future possible macular degeneration, having been teased by her family for not being able to look anyone quite in the eye. Her haughty look was on her face that day. Almost regal, this woman who always proudly honored her peasant immigrant stock wore cotton dresses to work. Later, Marlena would comment to Arjuna often about Kunti's wardrobe, and budget for clothes. Halcyon days for the family passed like movements in psychiatry, kind of fitful eventful periods, while he worked and wrote; Freudian psychology was not in vogue, but medical pharmacy was being used to save the elite population from heart disease. This was the time of the cow drownded. Sheep moved in front of herders, or behind, with sheep herding dogs, even pigs, a confident public had wool, and ate lamb. Gopis were honored among all the people. Krishna made sure of that from his throne wherever and whenever he could. But, Arjuna was interested, in Draupudie. His weaponry was important, but the interests of Krishna were his interests, you don't play games with a man whose father rules all of India.

A movie about time and space. Shots of large things in time lapse and sped up. Imagine earth movers, strip-mining equipment all moving fast enough that the shape of the landscape shifts, shifts, moves almost organically. Like God's view of the planet. Explosions slowed. Masses of people in cities, cars, all moving, walking, faster, sped up. I'm sitting on my Ergometer rowing machine, my—Coffey Indoor Rower—I spend twenty minutes folding and unfolding legs/arms/back in a few seconds. The way I cycled my legs pumped ninety times a minute, a fluttering spin all day, all day, all day.

Marlena said: "My dad had two brothers who fought in the war. One of them was a big shot. He printed backstage passes for rock concerts. He had his own limo and driver. Everyone said he was in the Mafia, you know, cufflinks, pressed white shirts, gold chains, a son in politics. My dad was a pharmacist, he had class. He made a forty-five once with a barber-shop quartet; let's go to Pompilio's in Newport—it's still in the jukebox, you know, *Rain Man* was filmed there." Marlena was a vicious woman. She circled Arjuna and got him drunk before he could make a connection to a solid economic base. Before long Arjuna had been forced out of his chair in front of the computer data bank. He was alone in his apartment, except for Leo, who was balling his wife, trying to make a baby, calling himself BIGGUS DICKUS and laughing and glazing over when Arjuna talked of Draupudie with awe in his voice. They would sit up nights, talking and exchanging piano licks, Leo recruiting dancers, and Marlena ministering drunkenly to older people and visiting young men who had taken stupid risks and ended up in wheelchairs. She would sit with them while they would smoke, smoke, smoke, toke toke toke. Marlena respected Leo, because she had no choice. Leo had helped Arjuna get out of prison. They called it a hospital, and they called it transcendental medication, but it was a plot to keep Arjuna in sync, or out of line, or some such shit. There were a lot of women in Arjuna's past, and doubtless more in his future. They came to see him play monica at Joe's Bar. Or was it Ronald's? Peanut shells? Tile floors? Wooden bars? Ceiling fans? Fair weather, overhead fans, fin air conditioners, and a future in Russia was all he dreamed of. If Arjuna could escape the capitalist system, they thought, he could beat the deadline, get published, get out of the trap and help more people. Marlena convinced Arjuna that helping more people was better. She called him a taker and accused him of not being generous. This, a man who had been imprisoned for symbolically capturing a Rolls Royce by steps. His whole mission was to change the economic structure. The Harvard neurologist took it right to Marx, but they still had kept him captive in Towson, Maryland. He had had a ceremonial dinner there with chopsticks. He had taken the chopsticks with him when he escaped. Maybe he was a taker. He had taken Marlena and every drink she had set up for him. Leo, on the other hand separated him from the other musicians and wouldn't pay him. Arjuna had made a vow not to accept paper money for playing music. He was afraid of intermittent reinforcement. It was a hitchhiking commitment. He didn't want to end up drunk and dead in a dark bar when some woman brought an evil man to hear him play. Remember when he hitchhiked, he stood alone. He walked. He played harmonica. The road stretched before him. He called it stealing cars with drivers. Maybe that was what she meant when she called him a taker. Or, when he took a kiss off her thin lips, struggled to hold her green eyes in check. Never trust a green-eyed girl, he said. It's in the kama sutra.

—37032
"Victim or Prophet"

G randmother is dying. She lay in bed, head on a crushed pillow. Pale green walls, brown and yellow tile floor.

"Arjuna, you look so much like Kunti. You're beautiful, so beautiful," slurred speech, a grin, gold teeth showing, holding Arjuna's right hand very tight, pulling him close. "Ohh Arjuna."

She'd had strokes.

"Bring me a corned beef sandwich. No. A half. A half a corn beef sandwich with mustard. And a bluebird. . ." and her speech went slurred bad and fuzzy, words tubed out her mouth gurgling like a mountain stream in springtime, but then a warmer sound of breathing. Grandfather focused on the half.

"How can I get you a half sandwich?"

"I only want half," she said.

"I'll buy you a whole sandwich, you eat what you want."

"A half," she said.

Lou flared with anger and they argued for a few moments and the grandson knew it wasn't about a goddamn corned beef sandwich. When they left her there, he talked about the Bluebird. Later the grandson solved it. She always talked in brand names. She wanted a can of juice, a six ounce can of orange juice, Bluebird brand. Papa thought she was hearing bluebirds, going loopy. The anger was gone, left frustration. They cried as they drove too fast.

1982

A wandering buck stands on the shoulder of a two lane highway in Texas. The sun is rising behind him. Along the road a grass field stretches as far as the horizon. A chest high barbwire fence separates the road and the acreage. Holsteins are standing in the field. Some of the cows are lying down. They are getting up though, one or two at a time, mooing and lowing. The young man extends his thumb to the road. A brown pack rests on his shoulder. A car passes with the rubber on freeway sound. The man can smell the dust. Across the road are railroad tracks. Redwing blackbirds chatter behind him along the fence wire. The young man looks back the road, swings around walking east, shielding his face from the sun with the thumbing hand, listening for another car behind. He can smell the dew on the grass. As he walks, he thinks about women. What else do lonely men think about while they walk highways.

1986

Arjuna the sculptor is twenty-eight. He is in the cramped urban bathroom of his flat brushing his teeth. He spits whitegreen toothpaste and blood into the sink. As the spit hits the porcelain a blackish brown cockroach appears on the spot. The man, trembles, reaches to the faucet. He twists the tap, and the insect is gone down the drain. He is left with the impression that he bleeds roaches from his gums.

1989

I don't remember her name. I'll call her Augusta. Meeting her, a turning point in my career as a custodial supervisor in a vocational rehab program, wasn't particularly memorable, but the weeks that followed were. We were in the lobby of the Lewis Center, the state mental hospital in Cincinnati. In the fall, big brown leaves crunched underfoot on the walkways leading up to the low-slung brick building. Augusta had deep brown eyes, a pleasant plain face, salt and pepper hair, stood a little over five feet tall, and spoke in a naively loud tone. Carla had explained to me beforehand that Augusta had never worked, was in her mid-fifties, lived in the hospital, had been in institutions throughout her adult life and this was an experiment to see if she could work on the crew, with the ten others who came in nightly from their apartments, or group homes around the city. Augusta announced her name, then stood off to one side.

The lobby, a small open space with a bench seat, by the glass door, separated from the hallway where offices and the supply closet branched off where I left Augusta seated on the bench when monitoring tasks that started the shift. "Give me a moment to get the crew started," I asked her before orienting her to the supply closet and helping her get her cart. I asked her to work with me for at least part of her first shift.

She took me in, said, "Arjuna's going to work with me," to those in earshot.

"Start cleaning bathrooms," I said, as it was simple, straightforward, and easy, bathrooms in this administrative section never got too dirty. First the crew filled mop buckets with soapy solution, checked vacuums, and as I keyed the others into locked areas they paired off.

Back in the lobby, Augusta sat, gazed at her white Converse gym shoes, counting quietly. "Uh, Augusta? Time to set up your cart," I said.

"Oh, Arjuna, oh," she said, leapt to her feet, and bounced her way along with me, mouth hanging open. We walked back to the supply closet, in the clean white hallway with yellow wooden doors, past the police station where Officer Star poked his head out.

"Who's the new worker?" He asked. Augusta turned, embarrassed, made some noises, and looked. I gathered they knew one another. Star went on, "Gonna make us proud, Augusta?" How long had she been at Lewis? Ask later. Star had a police personality; I took him with a grain of salt. As a practice, I did not get paperwork on new workers, just a quick description from Carla. *Most of her life in institutions.* Our goal, as a project, helping mentally ill adults to find work as therapy to facilitate transition to competitive employment and community placement, now introduced to a less prepared worker. Augusta was the first patient/client ever to work in the program.

We stood in the dark supply closet, even with the bare bulb in its protective cage, the tiny room closed in. Her musky, cigarette smell overwhelmed me. I helped her fill spray bottles, check them, gather rags, a squeegee, vacuum, broom, dust wand, and abrasive pad.

"Usually all this would be finished at the end of the evening so each cart would be ready for use the next day at the start of the shift," I said. "Sometimes day shift uses these carts, too, which is why it isn't ready now," I said. She watched. "You can help," I said, identifying the different bottles, and cleaning supplies. Augusta helped, filled a bottle, then paused, started to count. I said, "Augusta, this isn't time to count. Do your job, don't let your mind's obsessive thoughts control your behavior. We all count. We are all important, and your job here is not to break down, rather to accept that we're proud of you for wanting to work. This is going to be your daily routine. It's going to get you a little money. You'll pay for your own cigarettes. You can buy some things you really want." *I thought back to the first shirt I bought when I started the office job before I graduated. After all those years, going to a store, picking out a blue denim, button down collared shirt. And a second one a month later, a soft forest green, textured cotton. I wore them proudly, knowing these were my doing. Back to Augusta.* "Tomorrow come right to the supply closet and prepare your cart," I said.

We walked together a few yards down the hall, and I keyed her into the women's restroom. "Do you know how to clean a bathroom?" I asked. Taking nothing for granted, I drew her attention to the toilet brush, the bottle with pungent cleaning fluid, told her she could put on gloves first. Augusta, eager to please, struggled with the fine motor motions to pull the purple gloves over her badly manicured hands. Medicated to the point of stiffness, her hands shook. When I showed her how to squeegee the mirror over the sink she grinned. Her jaw dropped when I left her there as I heard my name called. "When you finish, please wait for me in the lobby," I said.

Another worker needed help with a broken vacuum cleaner belt. Augusta might not finish cleaning the bathroom, or she might finish and then not know where to go next. There wasn't much trouble she could get
into in the administrative wing, and Captain Star would look out for her. I would not take long.

Micro-management kept me busy with the whole crew. Thirty-second intervals between tasks, tasks took five to seven minutes, changing crew members, keying doors, and thinking about my next cigarette break. Two hours later, the twenty-minute crew break for coffee, pop, and snacks in the commissary, a welcome point in the evening's effort. How did the time pass for Augusta? Minute-by-minute, her anxiety preyed on her healthy attitude, and when she couldn't stay on task, as I moved her patiently, from one locked room to another, keying her, quietly, sometimes without a word, other times with a "good job," or "well now, that's it," finding competence beyond a layer of pausing, counting, and talking to herself.

And Then the Cow Was Drownded

These first days with Augusta seemed an exercise for me in especial focus, I felt delight when she smiled, and thanked me with such an open heart, and I praised her for helping. Reflecting in the wee hours with my girlfriend, my gratitude solid as a stone at the end of life, a mark in my struggle to find purpose. We gave each other lingering looks and glances in dark small rooms when things went right. Now, I'm speaking here ambiguously of my girlfriend, seeded by the little growth of this middle-aged lady, on a worksite when I rounded thirty, sober in the Lewis Center setting, working through my personal disability, feeling pride. I had not found a job to earn lots of money. In the past, learning had been impeded by false pride. Now, in some magical way, usefulness of the smallest sort, maybe just dignity, grew out of a weird client supervisor interaction. I no longer craved alcohol, as I encouraged Augusta. This outcome, a long time nascent, described the arc of a triumphant, step-by-step, recovery that had peaks, and valleys, similar to the ones raced through as a teenage bicycle competitor. While racing, flashing past low points, drawing from my depths, I felt pain climbing peaks. This competitive experience now inverted. When a client worker in a similar program as Augusta, in my twenties, I remembered sitting idly on a bench in the Hamilton County Justice Center hallway, taking instructions from a supervisor, leaving the job with my coworkers for Ronald's Bar downtown on Eighth Street to drink. A big black co-worker behind me. The slow painful valleys, despite the underpinning of small successes then, coming as the first days of active employment after losing an office job, and girlfriend, through alcohol abuse. Tapering off. Waking up to write poetry in my Over-the-Rhine apartment. I then had a long road ahead and behind. Augusta left her job to go back to a ward in the Lewis Center where she had a saved snack, brushed her teeth, and went to bed.

Since starting at Lewis, I became famous for my radio program. Not easy to launch it, and it happened just as the Lewis

Center job got under control. I played the harmonica for years, off and on, accompanying singers, guitarists, and piano players. In the mid-eighties at Joe's Bar on Sixth Street, downtown Cincinnati, I sat in on Fridays and Saturdays with a trio, including a high school buddy, Leo, on keys, a tall black singer, Katie, who could belt blues, croon jazz, and a rhythm section of upright bass and drum kit. The hotel, home for out-of-town baseball players, when the Reds had home games, had a dark bar with high ceilings, heavy wooden furniture, peanut shells on the floor, a deli block, with a gangly creole chef, sporting a white coat, black hat. The scantily clad, sexy servers, kind and considerate let me nurse a free grapefruit juice, not get drunk, and when Katie called for Arjuna and his friend, Monica, escort me to the stage, to blow the blues. Usually, I played the last tune of the night, and the encore. This got me noticed by the program director at a regional radio station. There's more to the story. I worked at The Union Graduate School several years before, getting my tuition remission to finish college. As a deputy registrar, I answered phones, and made photocopies for the admissions committee. When I quit, frustrated by weed, claiming I was fired, unjustly, in the aftermath, filed for Unemployment Benefits, was required to apply for work, to keep my place in the queue, for the hearing. One of the jobs I applied for was at a radio station, calling the program director leaving my information, and asking if it would be okay to list it. I had guest DJed a couple of times in the past, and he knew about the gig at Joe's Bar from the grapevine. As it happened, I didn't win the hearing. But I got a call from the station. There was a volunteer board operator slot open, and that led to the show. The fame made it fun for the workers. Some of them listened on Sunday night to my weekly broadcast. *Night Music with Steve Lansky.*

Augusta never let on that she listened. I want to think she did. It's this kind of fame tarnished by circumstance, that led to temptation. I remember smoking cigarettes in the concrete stairwell of the university, outside the double door from the studio.

And smoking in the courtyards of Lewis Center, taking Augusta aside, giving her an unfiltered Camel, and watching her eyes widen, with awe, when I congratulated her on working for a week. She managed herself well enough.

By the end of the second week, without knowing how, I had her setting up her cart, moving from task to task, cleaning as many as five bathrooms in the two and a half hours, before break. After break, out in the dark garden courtyard where a tastefully lighted, grim fountain displayed a boy holding a boot, water pouring from a hole in it, I looked up at a waxing gibbous moon and thought over my past dark skies, the shoes I struggled for, the miles I hitchhiked, before turning twenty-one and succumbing to treatment in places like this, while deciding to limit my smoking to three cigarettes a night. Augusta would become a worker, and I a non-smoker. We would share a certain special pleasure. Later I would tell of how she inspired my self-discipline. I asked her to wipe down the tables in the commissary after break, clean a bathroom attached to an office, finally dusting the office. I keyed my way in to find her humming while she dusted the shelves over desks.

The middle of the fourth week, she came to work wearing a shirt that was too dressy. I sent her back to her ward to change. She took twenty minutes before reemerging, her makeup was a bit smeared, and it looked as if she had cried. That day. That day she gave me a gift on break. She pulled it out of a decorative bag with handles. "This is for you, Arjuna," she said.

I said, "You're not supposed to give me gifts." Her face fell, yeah, a cliché. Yeah. And I looked at it. I still have it on the mantle over my fireplace in the summer cabin. It's weird. A small dark stained wooden box, with glass on four sides, a felt lined surface inside where two, empty, painted eggshells, with bright colors were nestled side-by-side, pink ribbons ruffled around them. I had never seen anything like it, before or since. The way she looked at me, and the floor, and it, all had me jumbled up inside. After she gave me the gift, she smoked one of her cigarettes, and kept to herself. I talked to her about socializing with the other crew members.

Now, I could see there were going to be problems. When I keyed her into the office after break, and left her, I worried. And rightly. When I came back, she was sitting in an office chair counting. I escorted her back into the hall and used the phone there to call Captain Star. He was gentle. "Tough night, Augusta? Everybody has bad days. We'll walk and talk outside," he said.

She took the rest of the week off. I told Carla about the gift, the aftermath; she said the team would talk with Augusta about it. I explained that she was too attached to me. I didn't have time for it. Yes, it was important for her to have this experience, but look, the job depended on a degree of independence.

When we look up at a blue sky, we see something seemingly limitless, an expanse of color so pure that it inspires us. I'd like to think the inner life of Augusta was as vast as the fall sky that Monday, and perhaps it was. I'll never know. She waited in the lobby, seated on the bench as she had been that first day, but this day, cranky, talking loud to herself, staring at her feet, as she talked, not anything I could decipher at first, then it seemed she was telling someone instructions, correcting someone. This way. Yes, the way you do that, you have to start at the beginning. Start over. Over. OVER! I thought for a moment and decided to ignore her completely until she settled down. I imagined what she was going through might be like an LSD experience I had many years ago. She seemed to be in a separate reality.

I took charge of the rest of the crew, left her on her own, and a few minutes later when I walked back into the lobby, she got up, came over to me, said, "Arjuna, I'm ready to work. Sorry about the other day." And in her eyes, I saw suffering. I saw that she may have the vastness I saw in the sky in her heart. In time she would be able to recover, I hoped.

I said, "It's okay, Augusta, everybody has bad days. Are you ready to clean some bathrooms?"

"Sure," she said.

"You know where your cart is. Just like before."

"Uh huh," she said.

That evening I felt the weight lift a bit as I walked on the yellow tile floor in the administration building. Going out in the evening between the buildings seemed a little triumphant. The crew seemed to be clicking. I might even get a chance to open *The General in His Labyrinth* by García Márquez. The hardback had just come out, and I ached to read on my free time. Thinking for a few weeks before Augusta joined the crew, I'd be able to find a spot to read for at least twenty minutes a night, while everyone was well tasked. I scoped out a dental office on the far side of the complex. A waiting area where I could sit. I wasn't sure if Augusta would manage or not. Still, worth a try. I told Larry, one of the experienced crew members, that I would be in the dental office doing paperwork, and he could find me if anyone needed anything. I imagined my prospects were looking up. My girlfriend had agreed to move in together if we could find an affordable apartment in a neighborhood we liked.

I read two chapters, became immersed in the text, and no one disturbed me. What a coup. After twenty minutes, I found Augusta, cleaning away. The rest of the crew was fine. This was the way things were supposed to be.

There were a few things to lift the spirits of the crew, and I chose to utilize them at the end of this evening. One was to finish early, which we did, as I helped mop an area of the commissary, and the second was to let them use the basketball, I also bought a soda for anyone who wanted. Nate had taught me the moment of the soda pop. It was a great tactic, method, and way of interacting to motivate workers. After we finished the second half of the building, before we returned all the carts, mops, buckets, and gear to the supply closets (This after our parade through the locked wards where the patients begged for cigarettes and clamored around us). I led the crew to the vending machines and paid for a cold beverage for each. They chose, and chatted, some of them more easily than others. Then, carrying their cans, we walked, all eleven of us, to the gym, a big open room with two backboards and hoops. On weekends the hospital staff had neighborhood games here. They were physical, competitive, sweaty, and feisty. Often arguments, trash talk, and testaments took over the games.

Tonight, we played HORSE. Augusta managed two baskets. Four crew played. I played, too. This kind of team building worked. By the end of the night, Larry had built a little more confidence, having won at HORSE, and kept his sense of pride at being the most competent on the crew. I'd like to describe the other eight. That's for another time and place. With time to spare, we managed to clean up, get in the van, and after saying goodbye to Augusta as we passed through A Ward, where she stayed, we went on to administration, someone put away her cart, and I drove the night streets back to the city center dropping members off as we arrived closer to my parked car.

Later that week, the team building seemed to be working well, Augusta was cool at the beginning of the night, responsible about prepping her cart, knowing that she didn't leave it prepared the night before, started right into the bathrooms, and seemed comfortable. Once again, I had time to read García Márquez. I noted the full moon that night was just as described in the book. My research taught me that the author studied Bolivar's battles to unify South America, to the degree that he detailed moon phases as they were at the time. This attempt by García Márquez to write fiction that resembled nonfiction though he tended more and more toward journalism, in his historical writing, and later would write a work of journalism about journalists and kidnapping in Colombia.

While I was reading, Larry came to me. "Augusta's having a problem," he said.

When I found her in the dental wing hallway, she sat on the floor cross-legged, her green pants pulled up showing her striped socks, and bare shins, she held her shoes. She mouthed words incomprehensible, loud, rocked, hit the back of her head against the wall, while her eyes, half-shut, distant, remarkably lost, moved up and down. I found a phone, called 911. When I told the dispatch that I worked at Lewis, a patient worker flipped out, they asked me to wait, sent orderlies in white coats, followed by Officer Star. I never saw Augusta again.

1996

A ponytailed man walks with a woman to a restaurant downtown. She wanted to sit and sip a cola. He suggested Mullane's Café because he can get coffee for 50¢ and two refills. She walks slowly in small steps, stops to light a cigarette from a trembling hand holding lighter. He feels his heavy wing tips on the concrete sidewalk; thinks of walking when he was leaner, poorer, more scared. The woman is older than he is. She would gravitate to fast food restaurants with free refills on soda. She complains about the black teenagers at the bus stops, and in the fast food places. She has been knocked down. Her friends have had purses snatched. He wants her to improve her social standing by going to the Café where there is a fortune teller in the late afternoon; where there is sidewalk, seating; where the mayor sometimes comes for dinner. He believes she will be safer, and more secure at Mullane's, than at the fast food restaurants. He finds it difficult to explain this to the woman. She takes pride in her participation in the mayor's campaign. The man is trying to covertly encourage her.

They sit at an outdoor table. They order beverages. He pours cream in his coffee, enjoys it. She has a cola over ice and asks him if he remembers when they first met. He is worried that she might think this is a date. A thin black man with a little facial hair approaches the table with a sketchpad. He asks if either of them would like to be sketched, a portrait, for a donation, "say five dollars?"

"Are you an artist, too?" asks the man.

"My girlfriend is an artist," he confesses trying to hide his reserve.

"Go ahead," says the woman to the artist, "she won't mind," she says to her Social Worker.

"I don't know," he says.

"You don't have to show it to her," says the woman.

There is an awkward silence. He observes that the artist is missing the temple on one side of his eyeglasses. He needs the money.

"OK."

"Good," she says and sips cola.

The artist uses two different pencils. The Social Worker tries to watch him work, but knows, this is distracting to the artist. When he is finished the woman likes the sketch at once.   The Social Worker observes
that it is a good likeness except for the nose, which resembles the woman's, more than his own. He withholds comment, pays the fellow.

After he has walked her back to the hotel, he hides the sketch in the trunk of his car. He is never able to find the sketch again.

1990

A man sits talking to another man in a room. The room has white walls, a drop ceiling with overhead fluorescent lamps, a Formica topped steel desk with yellow drawers, three chairs, one heavy and stuffed, the other two adjustable desk chairs with shiny wheels. On the desk is a black multi-line telephone and a desk size calendar blotter which the therapist has unfolded onto the desk. The calendar is worn, stained, and carefully marked in clumsy ink with names and times on each day, including many weekend days. The therapist is in his early fifties, trim, balding and clean shaven. His skin tone is good, as is his color. The client is thirty-eight, a bit overweight, wears his hair in a long graying ponytail and has an unkempt curly dark beard and mustache. Both men wear wire-rimmed glasses.

"You may be like van Gogh," says the Case Manager. "His art was of no value to him when he was living. He worked at it and carried canvases around, but never made a living selling his work."

Both are thinking about van Gogh. When Arjuna was in the throes of his despair, locked in a room to keep him from girlfriends and parents. Especially parents. He was angry at his mother and father enough to threaten them and to mean it. They let him have books in the room, and art supplies. This was The Jewish Hospital, yellow walls, brushed aluminum door handles, heavy keys, deadbolts. He used artist's crayons to painstakingly copy van Gogh prints into larger pieces. He had a copy of **Lust for Life** and he copied bridges, cafés, portraits.

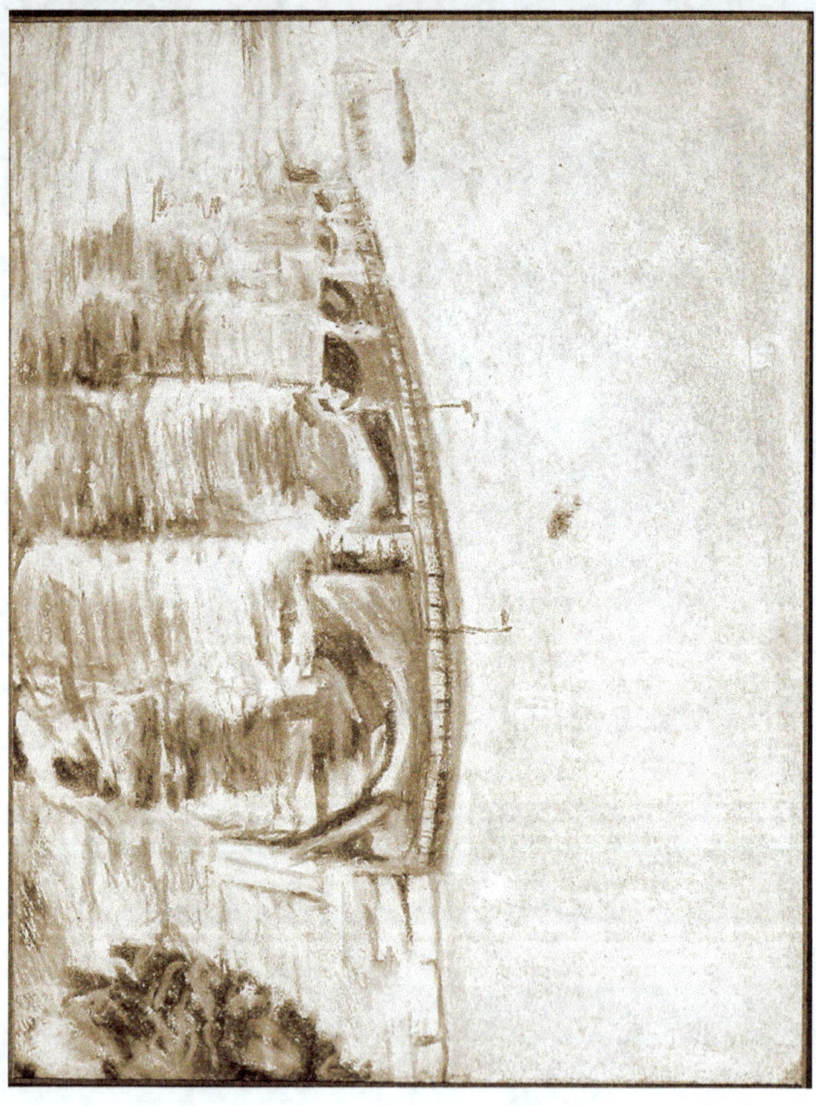

Generated 1978

OLD WOMAN

Xerox of ballpoint pen on notebook paper, 11 x 8.5"
From the Private Collection of the artist
Steven Paul Lansky

This copy of Vincent's *Old Woman* was the artist's first drawing. Locked in a room in The Jewish Hospital of Cincinnati, the goal was to learn to draw by copying plates from a hardbound copy of Irving Stone's biography of van Gogh called *Lust for Life*. The artist's original is long gone, but this Xerox remains. The artist could not write in a locked room, but he could express himself visually and chose to draw for six to eight hours a day, thinking that if he was to eat, he should work. He was satisfied that, as an untrained artist (he had basic drawing his first semester at college), he must work to improve.

Generated 1978

SEÑOR TANÉ OR DARK VAN GOGH

Oil pastel on paper, 12.5 x 10"
From the Private Collection of a friend of the artist
Steven Paul Lansky

This dark copy of Vincent's *Pere Tanguy* was one of the artist's earliest works. Locked in a room in The Jewish Hospital of Cincinnati, the goal was to learn to paint by copying plates from a hardbound copy of Irving Stone's biography of van Gogh called *Lust for Life.* After learning that the painting was of the man who sold paints to Vincent, Lansky challenged himself to conserve supplies. This particular copy was drawn with five colors. He read some of the literature that Vincent had access to at the time he did the painting, notably, Émile Zola's *Germinal.* Lansky has worked on an experimental short story called *Señor Tané* about a Santa Fe, New Mexico based art dealer with this and another portrait as illustration. The nose and eyes do not compete with Vincent, but the experience of copying served the artist in his growth.

Generated 1978

SEÑOR TANÉ OR COLOR VAN GOGH

Oil pastel on paper, 12.5 x 10"
From the Private Collection of the artist
Steven Paul Lansky

This copy of Vincent's *Pere Tanguy* was completed at Harding Hospital some months after the "Dark" version. From memory of the plate in a hard bound copy of Irving Stone's biography of van Gogh called *Lust for Life* and from the "Dark" version. This time the man who sold Vincent his colors was depicted with exuberance and the farm in the upper left was reminiscent of the East Palo Alto Farm where Lansky lived in the late 1970s. The hat floated a bit, the nose sort of disappeared into the face, and the hands got a bit large....

Generated circa 1980

THERE ARE NO THIEVES IN THIS TOWN

Watercolor on paper, 17.5 x 23.5"
From the Private Collection of the artist
Steven Paul Lansky

This interior scene was inspired by Vincent's *Night Café*. The billiard table is turned sideways and the room is vacant. The idea for these changes came from a Gabriel Garcia Marquez short story by the same name. Looking for money and finding the cash drawer empty Damaso robs the only bar in town of its billiard balls. A "Negro" is accused of the crime, publicly whipped and deported without evidence. Damaso, on a bender, beats his pregnant wife Ana, breaks into the bar again to return the three billiard balls, gets caught and is now to be responsible for the 200 pesos, the owner, Roque, claims were included in the heist.

He still has most of them, hidden away in his apartment. He showed them in the sanitarium the second time he was there. The first time he studied sculpture.

"You think my writing is art? A theater director said I create art. I've spent a lot of time writing to not be paid for it at all. I'd like to profit from my art during my lifetime."

"That may not happen."

1995

A ponytailed man sits in a dining area of a large home that is set up as a residential group home. There are four residents. He is on duty staff, sitting at the dining room table eating chocolate chip cookies and listening to a cassette of his own voice and music . . . it is a tape of a radio program he hosts once a week late at night. It is late now. Michelle Shocked's voice carries up the stairs. A young woman, one of the residents, walks into the dining area, her feet sounding on the hardwood. She tosses her blond hair off her shoulder with a quick headshake.

"Mick Jagger is *too* famous. He wants to be less famous. He is so famous that it hurts. Mick Jagger is reading my books." She tosses her head again.

"Being too famous could be stressful." The man with the long hair says.

"The psychosis has lifted," he says to the Case Manager. "I take the medicine. I've only had a few acute episodes. Really, none since I quit the weed and alcohol."

"I don't know what you have. A little schizophrenia . . . but really you don't seem schizophrenic to me."

"If I am schizophrenic how could I be stable for the better part of fourteen years? But, I still take the medicine."

"You're an artist. What I can't figure out is that you're right on the cutting edge, but also concerned about economic stability, a job, a place to live . . . stable relationships, wife, family."

"Yes."

1996

Arjuna enters a downtown residential hotel across the street from the new Arts Center. He signs in at the desk. He goes to see one of his clients. He is a Social Worker at the same agency as his therapist. He thinks about his life. Once he needed the system to heal him. Now, he needs the system for a job. He gives to others who need healing. He gets in the elevator. He walks the carpeted hallway. The day is warm, and the man is dressed in khaki shorts, short sleeves and running shoes. He set the timer on his chronometer as he left the car to time the parking meter. His client is on the fifth floor. He stands in the narrow hall knocking on her door. He is impatient when she does not answer. Perhaps she is sleeping. Possibly she has gone out. He was expecting to help her straighten up for her room inspection next week. It is the last day of May, a Friday early afternoon. He does not give up easily. At the front desk he uses the telephone. Her line is busy. He returns to the elevator. He goes up to floor five. He walks the corridor with more urgency. Again, he knocks. No answer. He shouts her name. Now he knows something is wrong. She would respond if she were on the phone. He goes back to the desk in the lobby. He requests assistance in opening the door to her room. Fourteen years ago, to the day, he had returned to Cincinnati, on his bicycle, to restart his life. He does not think about that. He is fully occupied with getting the maintenance man to open her room. His patience is beginning to annoy him. The door is keyed, and he can see that the carpet is dirty. The security chain is on the door. The maintenance man radios on the walkie-talkie for a bolt cutter. The other maintenance man is there. They both wear gray shirts with their names on them. One name is Sandy, the other, Baldy. The man with the sandy beard reaches through the gap in the door with a screwdriver and unscrews the chain. There were two screws. Time hung on the chain. The muscles in the man's neck stand out as he unscrews. She is on the bed bleeding. The man with the walkie-talkie has the desk clerk call 911.

She's alive, he thinks, very relieved. He can see her breathing. *She is alive.* Fourteen years ago, he was penniless. The bicycle tires were flat. He had ridden from Columbus to Cincinnati, over one hundred miles.

Overnight. Just after the hitch to Santa Fe. Fourteen years and a month ago he stood on that highway, watching cows. Listening. He hangs up the phone. It rings. The police and life squad are coming. He calls his supervisor. She is distressed.

Blood red and blood brown. The footprints are everywhere. She's a pacer. She had walked that room after she had cut the crook of her elbow with a fourteen-inch blade. Footprints. He had paced the edge of the road fourteen years before. Looking for love. The cow herding girl. The gopis. The bathroom tile blood red strewn. The knife lay on the edge of the blood-filled tub. The empty pill bottles lined up on the top edge of the refrigerator like fence posts. On the table the emergency sheet with the therapist's name and doctor's name and parents. Her face streaked with crusted black blood. The bedding red, soaked, red, deep gashed arm at elbow the blood of paint drip depression and the fear of fear of her luck in folding the arm up to breast in bloody night clothes, unconscious, breathing, rapidly, breathing but not wake able with a shout.

Life Squad comes in. Two men. At first, they seem to think that someone had done this to her. "How old is she?" The young worker will never meet with the woman at Mullane's Café.

Fifty-one. She is fifty-one. Fourteen years ago, she was thirty-seven. I am thirty-eight now. Fourteen years ago, I was twenty-four.

After the medics come the constabulary. Two mounted officers, one male, one female. Two officers, from their high tech, cruisers, again both genders. Arjuna is interviewed as she is moved onto a stretcher, the gash wrapped tightly. A blond woman with blue pools for eyes that open into tomorrow; good clean fingers hold a tiny note pad and a yellow No. 2 pencil. Some questions . . . the pill bottles are examined for dosage, number, dates. Arjuna is lost in the eyes of this Miss and answers willingly, wantingly. The redhead from the mounted division has spurs on her boots and a sense of humor. Arjuna is impressed with his desire to keep his eyes in the pools. He reflects on how mystifying her presence is in the room where he had sat previously on the brown sofa, or at the tiny kitchen table, the lingering odor of cigarette smoke in his nostrils more pungent than the dust on the highway those fourteen years ago. The uniforms are so blue, collars so white, pins of

brass, and black shoes, boots, with spurs; always back to the pools with the dilated black open pupils. The voice calm, reassuring, melodic. Arjuna wants to linger with these uniforms, feels comfort in their pacing, so much more secure than those of the missing client. His own pacing somewhere between the officious and the bloody unsteady footprints.

1986

The artist Riley had touched his face with his open palm. The young man was very scared. He wanted to ask the artist to leave the apartment. He didn't want to be touched on the face by the welfare artist.

1996

When the men talk, they often sit with index fingers on lips, a vertical *shh*. They have active eyes, a sometimes, wrinkled brow. The room is not always the same. Years ago, both had offices. One had a painting of a castle and an attractive wooden desk. One had a photo of his guru on the desk. For a few years now, they move from room to room. One has a cubicle and a desk. They never meet at the cubicle. That would not afford them privacy to talk. The rooms are not very decorated.

"She was alive," he was telling the Case Manager.

"You need to go see her," said the Case Manager.

Arjuna, the ponytailed man sat in the room and felt an emptiness deep in his heart. The emptiness manifested as a knot in his stomach. He reached down to his foot and touched his shoe; he ruggedly tugged at the tongue of his shoe.

"When I was leaving the hotel back on the street by the big bay the redhead said, 'I hope your next visit goes better,' and I forced a smile, felt like crying, nodded a *yeah*. I got back into the car before the meter expired. I thought, *mounted police never have that worry*. That sort of irked me. Should I have driven directly to the hospital?"

"No," said the Case Manager.

"Why do I need to see her? I don't want to see her. She's alive. Let her be." Arjuna realized he was angry at her.

"She's hurting. She needs your compassion now. Think about how miserable she had to be to try to end it. There's a certain courage in taking action. You need to help her to feel that courage and seize life with it. It will help you if you face her. Your fear of her death; it will help to see her alive."

1986

The artists were going to get famous together. The welfare artist and the poet of the ghetto. They both knew that. The young man's therapist didn't think it would happen. In this town you have to be on television to be a celebrity. Television makes fame. Books and paintings done by artists and writers here would never buy fame.

They walk the urban streets and parks, day and night, talking, sharing smoke, confidence, stories. "I smoked weed with a diplomat's daughter." The young man would say to the artist.

"She was gorgeous. I wanted her so bad. I thought some day she would be mine. We would be together, in love."

1996

Three men named Arjuna meet at a copper ledge Friday night the last day of May.

"I remember you, Arjuna Pandava, you're the most hostile customer I've ever served," the man down the long end says to the man on the short end.

"I thought that was you. I recognized your name. I was looking for a camera lens for my wife. You said you had the lens I wanted when I called and when I arrived you didn't have it," says short end Arjuna.

"You needed a manual focus lens and the model number you gave was . . ." Long end Arjuna speaks.

"You only had the auto focus lens. I had located the lens I wanted at another store and you said you had the lens I wanted at a better price. I
was working as a Social Worker and had to drive miles out of my way to get the lens. The price was significantly better. I accused you of bait and switch." The man with the ponytail wasn't arrogant or angry; he was matter of fact.

"I learned something. And I avoided you. I saw your name on a course list at The University of Cincinnati. You're a professor." Arjunas make up things.

"No, that's my father."

"I looked at an apartment in Clifton and your name was on the mailbox, so I just left without even considering renting there."

"I come by it honestly. It's probably good you didn't take a course from my father. What are you studying?" Arjuna asks.

"Art History."

"I felt fucked; the adrenaline was pumping through me."

"I wish I was fucked," said the famous musician woman, tending bar.

"Me too," said the other man, a famous musician.

"Yeah," said the friendly woman sitting next to the ponytailed Social Worker.

They were laughing tense laughter.

"Sorry I was so hostile."

"Oh, that's OK."

"I'm glad I got out of the retail business."

"I've heard things about that camera shop. Stolen merchandise, you know . . . "

"The guy who owns it is a prick. He fired me for taking a vacation."

"Where did you go on your vacation?" asked the woman in the seat next to him.

"Skiing."

"Was it a good vacation?"

"Wonderful." (Expressively.)

"Where did you go?"

"My father had invited me to go skiing over a holiday."

"Where did you go?"

"Oh . . . I can't remember."

"You remember all that shit detail about this camera lens," said the woman writer.

"I want to hear about the vacation."

Sunday morning at the hospital Arjuna went to her bedside. Machines with lights and numbers flanked her. The room was glass and curtains. She opened swollen eyelids, a tube on her tongue and several in each arm. Her head looked puffed, inflated then partially let down; one eye stared off and didn't track, the other bloodshot and milky looked at him with a flicker of recognition. She reached for his hand with hers and squeezed weakly.

"Do you recognize me?"

"Arjuna," she slurred, nodded once, a small gesture.

He stood at the steel bed rail and watched her breathe. Black dried blood streaked her enlarged head, matted dark hair. They hadn't had a chance to clean her up in two days. He felt very bad and very relieved. His pulse ran in his ears. He talked to her a little, said her name, glad to see her and scared. Then he stood waiting for a thought or the moment to end; listened to her gurgling breath. When he left, he thought about, other things.

Arjuna went to see the Case Manager on Monday early and after talking a little about the visit he went back to his past.

"At Harding Sanitarium, I sculpted when I was imprisoned there. At first, we used Vermiculite and concrete. Do you know what Vermiculite is?"

"No."

"It's exploded mica. You know, mica. It's a kind of rock that's shiny like metal in layers, very light weight. They explode it for fertilizer. We would mix it in a wheelbarrow with concrete and pour the mixture into a mold then when it hardened, we would sculpt it with files and chisels. I was good at it. I enjoyed the process. I still have the first piece I did. I gave it to my parents. It's in their house. The breasts of a woman and a head on the other side. It's a figure without a head . . . and on the other side a head. King and Mona . . . I don't recall her last name, were the guards. He went to Otterbein. Big guy, beard, crooked lower teeth. I stayed late and mixed blocks for sculpting. I was trying to vent my anger at my father. One day I said I wanted
to kill him and then I cried. They took me out of sculpture after that. Mona had done a dissertation on Malcolm Lowry. She told me about his more positive writings. Something about a walk to a spring. I moved up from vermiculite to limestone. I had a huge piece of stone that someone else had started. I liked Lowry's disturbed writings. Lowry's character believed he was on a ship, then that he was a ship as he stumbled from one longshoreman bar to another.

"It wasn't such a bad place. We cut wood."

"How?"

"We had these six foot, long, two man, tree saws, sledges, wedges, and a maul. We spent several hours a week cutting firewood."

"What did they do with the wood."

"They sold it to the staff and families. It was a pretty good deal. Meaningful work, healthy exercise. I didn't like being locked in. But, I got out, played harmonica at a bar with the Bear Swamp Boogie Band, got high. I remember pink cigarette paper."

"How did you get out?"

"You know, privilege levels. You would go to the camp meeting and make your bed and go to your groups and they'd let you go out on a Friday night. The discouraging thing was that people would leave and then you'd hear they'd committed suicide. Kind of made you afraid to leave. Also, there was the guy I met when I first moved in who was in a wheelchair. He had jumped off the bridge over the stream on the way into the grounds. Scared me."

"Yeah."

"I guess it wasn't that bad of a place. I'm still sorting it out. It was kind of like a college. I did artwork, too. They even tapped the trees on the grounds for maple syrup and made syrup for an annual pancake breakfast. We played touch football, too."

"Sounds like a good place."

"Yeah."

"More comfortable than park benches."

The ponytailed man sat in silence. He knew that there would always be issues to discuss with the Case Manager.

"I think I'd like to reduce my medication level again. The last time I tried to reduce it I was still using alcohol, weed, cigarettes, and coffee. I haven't had any of those in years. I'd like to lose some weight. I think I would have more energy, could get up when I wake up instead of just going back to sleep after I first awaken."

"If you want to reduce the medication that's OK."

"Maybe a different medication. I hear of people on Prozac."

"Prozac is a different kind of medicine than what you have been taking. You've been taking an anti-psychotic, to control your thoughts, to control delusions."

I thought about that. I thought that I would always be deluded in the sense that I would imagine that I am important. I kissed a diplomat's daughter at Radcliffe. I thought that what they really wanted was to control behavior. The controlling of thoughts was secondary. Thoughts about the space-time continuum, gravity, entropy, infinity, Γοδ, yes time itself were what I wrote about. I unzipped my bag and pulled out a CD and showed it to the therapist. A distraction.

The man with the ponytail kept his mind from worry by listening to music, by hosting his radio show, by reading his radical poems at open readings in galleries and coffeehouses. He was afraid of his own outrageous energy and what might happen if he stopped taking meds. He also wondered what would happen if the stock market crashed a huge percentage and chaos gripped the city. These were only imagined ills. How much of his consciousness, and how much of the space-time continuum did the little orange pills control.

"Would there be any withdrawal effects from reducing the medication? Would there be a recurrence of the waves of emotion I felt in my chest as a child that I only feel now beneath a layer of numbness? Would I be less (more?) depressed and possibly need an anti-depressant like Prozac?"

"These are all good questions for the doctor. You take five milligrams?"

"Yes."

"I wonder what size pills are available." The therapist takes down the PDR and looks up the pills. "They come in one, two, five, and ten milligrams."

"I take five now."

"We could go to two twos."

"Let's   talk   to   the   doctor   about   it."

"Is there a reason you want to do this now?"

"Just that things are very stable. And, well, I'd like to lose some weight and have more energy. Since I'm working in a halfway house . . . I see others take their meds and doctors adjusting meds. I guess I think I'm ready. I don't think I want to take meds like this all my life . . . so I won't drink alcohol, smoke weed, cigarettes or drink coffee. Why not?"

1986

The older artist and the poet met over coffee at the bar. They also met at Fountain Square where the artist had set an easel and painted in black and white oils. Impasto. The details of the Probasco fountain always in black and white. One came to find out there were many versions. He altered the background. And the poet visited the welfare artist at the statue of beardless Lincoln in Lytle Park in front of the Taft Museum. The artist painted Lincoln in black and white. In his apartment painted walls, wild colorful oils with swirls, shapes, curves, imagination spawned multi-layered pieces. The artist offered reefer. Once stoned they drank tea with milk and honey at the kitchen table watching cockroaches, cats, and lifting the dictionary, pointing out words and speaking powerful knowledge about synchronicity. After a few minutes of intensity, the poet would have to leave, fear coursed through him with adrenaline as he walked the night streets of the urban concrete and brick ghetto. The artist sketched and wrote on pads of paper. Each pad contained the universe. The welfare artist vibrated with wonder of the universe. On the practical side he planned to paint and live in the ghetto and work at his own haphazard, yet dedicated pace, until the world recognized his genius. He had a well-trimmed beard, dressed always neatly, and was getting good dental work done on his General Assistance medical benefits.

He told of a rich Uncle. His rich Uncle was Sam. He never laughed when he said this. The poet snickered when the artist spoke of Sam, Uncle Sam. He hated cops.

The ponytailed man was a poet before he grew the ponytail. He was poet laureate of Over-The-Rhine, so named by the Recreation Commission and proclaimed by the mayor. Before he wrote poetry, he tried his hand at art. Starting with the van Gogh copies, made in the locked room. He was an experiment. They locked him in to see what he would do. He drew. Then later, after he was moved to suburban Columbus, he was gradually given more freedom. He had permission to ride the bus to the campus, found a job setting up bicycles, found an apartment in a rough neighborhood. He had help from a pal to move the limestone sculpture up the stair. In this apartment he drew. He drew bath water, ate pork liver and potatoes because it was the cheapest food he could find. He had no car, no bicycle, no bed. Slept on the clean, carefully waxed, hardwood in a blue sleeping bag.

When he showed the welfare artist in Cincinnati his drawings, he gave him one of the yellow devotee prints. The print shop had had an overrun because they were out of white paper. They had gone yellow and the artist had demanded fifty white prints and kept the yellow extras. The artist thought of them as the Harë Krishna ten-dollar bill. When he had money, he knew they would sell. As he grew, he would give them as presents to his dear ones and soon they began to appear in homes, in frames. He kept the original. The welfare artist took the print home to his cockroaches, tea and cannabis and put a crown on her as though she were liberty. By this time the artist was a poet. He gave spontaneous readings. The welfare artist walked Main Street with the poet in the tiniest hours of the morning when police drove clean white cruisers around corners. The poet did not expect the attention from the newspaper article about him.

The therapist seemed pleased for the poet. The poet rose up out of poverty and worked. The poet learned that the welfare

artist was hassled by policemen. So he said. The poet's artwork was critiqued by the welfare artist. The nose of the devotee was not right. The poet learned to listen to criticism and never to enjoy hearing it. He always felt the other was deriding, pushing, pressing him into more squalor that meant discomfort, perhaps park benches for beds. They often drank coffee. The poet began to get jobs in offices, wear ties and study with a writer. The press helped him to become a processor, a cleric. The welfare artist continued to criticize. They grew apart.

1996

Arjuna meets her at the crisis center in the city, but not downtown, where she is staying after the hospital, before moving back to her fifth floor room. A chaotic place, there are many ill clients sitting, smoking, milling. The doorways are wide to admit wheelchairs. Arjuna speaks privately with a staff member about her, both before and after he meets with her. Arjuna wants her in group housing. Not likely to happen.

"I'll never pull a stunt like that again," she says.

They walk, to a fast food restaurant, less scary perhaps because they are not "downtown." He orders orange juice at the counter and she follows. They sit to talk under the bright lights in the seats that don't move because they are attached to the tables and the floor. She cries, readily, freely grieving her father, a loss of long standing.

She thanks Arjuna for finding her. He is nervous curious about how it felt to be "gone," near death. He doesn't dare ask her but he wants to know.

The knife edge of life can be explored among the living when life is that miserable.

She suggests they walk. They make their way slowly around a large block, nearly half-a-mile, taking small steps.

She cries; misses her father; "He was told he was schizophrenic just before he died."

The Social Worker Arjuna is glad she is alive. He is finished visiting her.

1997

The poet knew they were destined to reconnect. The poet wanted the welfare artist to see success for both of them. The welfare artist was older than the therapist.

The therapist comes to the ponytailed man's apartment to visit. Are these home visits or house calls? Does the man house sit, or live in a home with a wife? We haven't met her yet. Tomorrow, in the early afternoon, the man will visit. He will come in his Volkswagen, park on the avenue, walk up the stone steps, across the tile porch, and enter the hearth.

The gopi out there waiting. When he stood that highway, Texas sun warming the bits of stone, tar, yellow sunrise, lapis lazuli fire dancing overhead as the cows lowed, he thought of those gopis who walked with sandals on scented feet, tens of toes tucked neatly. He danced his highway song, feet grabbing gravel, dust over leather, meeting his future faced backwards, walking, pacing the shoulder as now the residents at work pace the halls, corridor to entryway, stairs, to outdoor steps, cigarettes at their lips. He dwindles into their hearts and pulls up his bootstraps.

He is at home in the afternoon and he is going to tell the teacher, the mentor, the only therapist that has listened and been a friend for over fifteen years, that now, now he is able to function in home, job, yes life, for over three weeks on a dramatic reduction of his medication. And no malady has recurred.

A happy accident. The pharmacist had mistakenly filled his prescription with .5 milligram tablets instead of 5 milligram tablets before the ponytailed man left for his vacation. For two weeks the poet was taking his meds as usual, growing in energy and stamina, but noticing that his bowels had loosened considerably. That was the first clue. The pills were the right color but smaller; he didn't know if the pharmaceutical pill company people were simply reducing the size of their fives. He had seen the smaller orange pills at work, but that had been at another station. So, when he returned from the two-week holiday, he telephoned the pharmacy and asked. Sure enough. The pills were point fives. A happy accident, he was alright. Cycling more. Like in youth. Faster on a new machine. He reduced the fiber supplement. The tranquilizer slows the metabolism, constipates, therefore the reduction should loosen, no problem here. He reads a Russian folk cure manual. Suggested for constipation: knee bends, sit-ups, stomach massage, cucumbers with honey and lemon dressing. A very strict regimen. He tried. He could not keep it up. Like in college, he could follow the regimen to the midterm; yes, yes, yes then there are so many details, so many responsibilities, not enough delegates, not enough time, not enough energy, light like on the highway clear for so long so long long; then there is a breakdown of discipline, a variance from the regimen. He can remember to take the pills but to slice, and dress, and to sit-up and stand to squat. He did these things when he was younger. He knew how to do the mighty-flighty calisthenics. He had not kept the regimen. This man sometimes knew his past was of ill recruit. Swept out of that corps into psychiatry on the downside; don't think that he didn't want to become a shrink and hibit, instead of inhabit. The habit to observe was his, the calculate. (He could revise all this later. He no longer thought it out over a beer or toked it up into fine work with a cool chillum cupped to his palm. His was a simple regimen. He took the pills.)

So, when the therapist shows up at the apartment, he has a new car. A new Jetta, with six disc, changer in the trunk, and more speakers than the House of Representatives in every possible bit of space, and surface on the cloth and plastic interior of this gold car. By this time the ponytailed man has thought about the medicine reduction happy accident. They talk about rectal bleeding.

1982

When Arjuna left the first apartment in Columbus for the Greyhound to Cincinnati; being evicted, he left the two hundred pound, limestone sculpture on the second floor landing, a wool bluegray army gunner's sweater wrapped around, sleeves tied in a knot. The young bicycle mechanic had no bicycle, had a guitar, and this time in the yellow room (box) in The Jewish Hospital, back in Cincinnati, locked again by family, he strummed, hummed, juggled apples for visitors until they took his privileges away. They then moved him into the State facility, medications were introduced, and with time came no progress. He slept as the flies buzzed, he got bigger then, he cried, and they moved him back to Columbus. He lived a confined life. There were letters and tapes from Santa Fe. Beyond Texas was New Mexico. The lapis lazuli sky azure as bright as the diamond rug was tightly woven and meant to ease the peace. New Mexico, the woman. The daughter of the local Congressman, young and in love as well. Letters came from forgotten cities. What is so different from the youngman and the youngman he would later meet at the camera store? Are young men so different one from another? So, when he had settled a bit, his family returned some property recovered from that apartment. How it was recovered? Who recovered it? Unknown. The sweater with the elbow patches and the shoulder patches to rest the rifle stock returned. The sculpture?

Arjuna had been to an exhibit of Morgan Russell at the Columbus Art Museum. He remembered it as a field trip from the hospital. Synchromie en bleu violacé, 1913. The youngman sketched the ideas into his book, then taking over a piece of limestone already awarded, a ball shaped figure begun on one crumbling facet, he began to carve a Synchromic of his own. The problem: The movement was to use color to adapt shapes, the human figure, onto a flat surface . . . three dimensions reduced to two, with the use of light spectrae to imply the other dimension. The youngman took the shapes and sculpted them in three dimensions. To his mind it was a failure. He was not sure if it was finished when he left. He had no further access to sculpting files and chisels, hammers nor a shed. He could not have carried it down the stair alone. With a note, there might have been a return. He had thought about leaving it on the small Persian rug. A diamond prayer rug bought from a street vendor later given to the young lover (Congressman's daughter) when she visited Harding Hospital with an Associated Press reporter. So where is that sculpture?

Paul Thanas

Seeking & Finding Cleanliness

1984

Today I'm having a bourbon. Wild Turkey in a clear shot glass with six translucent slivers of glassy ice. Marlena is going to meet me later here at Joe's and we'll drink, I'll blow monica, and Lena and I will go home and fuck our bodies raw. I can see the whole evening opening like a tulip on a warm Spring afternoon, except, it's night, and I'm getting drunk early. I'm a spectator with an inkpen in my fist. The chestnut colored, ceiling fans beat my clinging, cigarette smoke out into clouds. I draw on an unfiltered Camel, and decide, I will become Ernest Hemingway but write songs instead. It feels like I'm in Key West. Panama hat, white trousers, a blond blazer, whiskey in the glass, man I'm gigging. I'm actually famous enough to blow with Katie and Leo on Friday night in Joe's bar. I smell the bourbon and whisk it with a finger, lick the finger, drift into the hazy past.

When I went to Draupudie in the thick of Winter off a train and saw that first snow of the year, I walked in magic time; my schizo walk began. I can dictate a song to this napkin on this deep walnut table in this booth in Cincinnati, Joe's Bar, peanut shells crunch as the skimpily clad cocktail waitress checks on me.

"Need anything?" she asks, cocking a pleasant smile.

"No," I say, I'm there.

She turns to go with an expression of the slightest confusion. She's not so confident as me. I write the song in a clear burst of slowly arched letters, gently formed in little dark pools like the puddles of Draupudie's pupils once seen. I see that night of transformation as a moment when my soul drifted into high seas on wild breakers. Arjuna is a tough motherfucker, I think.

One won't be enough. The inkpen rotates in my large hand. I'm going to write two songs. I'll give one to the bass player and one to the keyboard ace. They'll finally have some original material for Katie to sing. Sure she sings the standards, Billie Holiday, Duke Ellington, Who Could Ask for Anything More?, Summertime, The Boy from Ipanema. She belts, she croons, she scats, but nothing original yet. They all want to rise out of Joe's into some kind of career. I can sense these jazz artists won't put up with Arjuna and monica forever . . . but if I could write . . . and let Draupudie live in their music, the walking bass, the tinkling ivory, the blessed voice of Katie, more sacred in the city than the Northern Loon in Ontario, crooning cool and easy . . . two songs. "Someone's in Love" and "First Snow." I put that napkin on warning, I've dipped my nib in the liquor of choice, now, people, now, you'll hear what I have to say about my beloved Drap.

I'm going to be the ho! I'll sell my soul for these high-minded jazz composers. It is their gig. So, in not so characteristic diplomatic high-minded style, I decide how to handle my oh so competitive friends.

Leo arrives at Joe's, sucking on a Camel filter, sipping a gin and tonic, as he rustles into the seat opposite me.

"What 'cha writing, Arjuna?"

"It's a song."

"Yeah. A song?"

"For you and Leigh to compose for Katie."

"Lyrics?"

"Yes."

And I turn the napkin to face him, unfolding it with a low breath because I am awed by Draupsie's power of the muse. She seems to be in the room with me sometimes.

Leo reads, sips, smokes, reads, sips, more sips. He nods slowly and his clean-shaven face breaks into an early sweat. He pauses, "I like it Arjuna."

"Thanks."

"Does it have a title?"

"The refrain, 'Like the first snow.'"

"Call it 'First Snow.'"

"OK. But Leo, here's the deal. I'm getting drunk. I won't remember writing it."

He laughs. "Of course, you will."

"No."

"Uh-huh. Sort of a mystery song."

"You take the credit. Do whatever you want with it. Absolute freedom."

"I understand. Is that what you want?"

Leo's blue eyes dance about. We both light cigarettes and take long drags. He looks so good tonight, even his shirt is pressed. I'm feeling tall.

"Leo, if I ever ask who wrote it. Take credit."

"What if you insist?"

"Just say that it's a good song, but it would have been better if you had written it, Arjuna."

Leo laughs, finishes his gin and tonic, takes the song on the napkin and goes away.

When I was finished with my bourbon, I had a St. Pauli Girl and put the pack of smokes away for a while. Leigh came through the door carrying his upright bass, with a swagger. Leigh is the smallest bassman I've ever met. He plays with swagger. He propped the instrument on stage in its tan cloth case and I watched him take a seat that moments ago had been occupied by another patron. I am the observer. Leigh pushed the guy's corn beef, aside, and didn't even notice the bigger guy lurking behind him, forced to sit at another table and give up his deli sandwich or confront Leigh. A magical little man's swagger, I thought. Leigh sat and rolled a cigarette from a pouch of Drum, rudely called a waitress over in a high pitched but gravelly voice, ordered a Beck's dark and motioned me to join him. I had been standing, watching, uneasily shifting from wingtip to wingtip, tilting my Girl.

"Leigh," I said.

"Yeah?"

"I wrote some lyrics for you to put to music."

"Let's see," he said.

"Someone's in Love," I said and thought of Draupudie, even saw her black hair and blue irises in glassy white. I thought, I'm so fucking schizo.

He read over it and looked back directly, said, "Thanks Arjuna."

"It's yours," I said. "If I ever ask you about it just say, it was a gift." And I paused. He was unconcerned with me. Leigh caught the waitress and ordered a Rueben while I finished my beer.

Back when Arjuna started doing clean-up work was when they met. Arjuna started as a client worker, dirt poor and full of habits. Back then he'd been hanging in this urban ghetto where poetry flourished along with modern dance and jazz.

Leo, the piano player, and Arjuna, the poet, sat down in the poet's flat for Chinese noodles, grilled chicken, (Done to a savory satisfaction on Leo's Hibachi propped a floor up outside the window on the corrugated black painted iron fire escape between Leo's flat and his wife's dance studio with the mirrors, barre, and piquant fluorescent tubes hung on hardware store chain with plants courtesy of the community radio station's lawyer as barter for a meeting space.) carrots, green peppers, broth, mushrooms, with chopsticks. The chicken was four days old, torn into bites and tossed into this nearly vegetable soup.

Leo tipped the bowl to drink the broth, his lip brimmed with sweat. The nightly routine on a Wednesday included steamed milk in the espresso brewed on the gas burner in Cady's boyfriend's pot, lent in exchange for some long ago, forgotten favor.

Tonight, they had cappuccino, but it was Friday. During the week Arjuna struggled to hold a job in United Home Care's offices as a data-entry clerk. Leo had the ideal job in a cocktail lounge with an African American singer, Katie, Leigh, a vegetarian Buddhist bassist who composed in university, played a bass fiddle as well as a dangerous looking electric instrument, and tonight for the first time a drummer who had played with someone famous for a while. (George Benson?)

Arjuna exchanged his blue button-down shirts, cubicle and glare of fluorescent light, meetings about increasing productivity, nagging superiors, and terminal for leggy, lipsticked waitresses tucked into minis that were an inch short of topless, a regular supply of imported beer, a surplus of salted peanuts whose shells went underfoot, and the companionship of jazz cats, blues buffs, aspiring songwriters, and later, musicians who left their gigs to come hear the real thing.

Dark and mysterious as Katie, the singer, management kept the place full. Joe's Bar in the Netherland Hotel was the out of town, home for National League baseball's visiting teams when they faced the Cincinnati Reds. This weekend the Chicago Cubs were in town.

Leo drove his beat-up blue Pinto downtown at ten. The poet walked the sixteen blocks alone, blowing the blues harp. The poet was called on-stage to play with "monica" as a guest artist. This was the thrill of a lifetime, a white boy, in a seedy hometown bar, wailing the blues for Chicagoans.

Arjuna is taking a shower at Marlena's and he notices a heart with the initials "JP." drawn in the dust at the corner of the lime green tile stall. He feels the water cascade over him in a numbness from the Wild Turkey and codeine. *JP has been in Marlena's shower, he thinks. JP has been with her.*

Later, when she is slapping him across the face, when the dark beer combines with the bourbon and codeine, his anger releases. He challenges her to say JP was not here. "JP in your shower. Johnny Person naked in your house." She denies it and redirects, asking him about his hickey on his throat. His thoughts are clouded by drink and passion. He cannot be sure. *Did Lottie, the model at Ronald's Bar? No, no, too many days ago. Just, before; Marlena put the hickey there herself to catch him. When they were rolling around the living room floor with the cats and dogs she sucked on the side of his throat.*

Riley & the Poet

1986

Riley and the poet were sitting in Mullane's Café having Wallingford coffee. Riley's beard was neatly trimmed and light enough to show a slight tobacco stain at his upper lip. The poet drank his coffee with cream, savoring the buzz, the fragrance, the bean juice that seeded his thoughts, conversation, even making his Camel bullets and Gauloises unfiltered black tobacco sing within him like a message from somewhere beyond coincidence. The welfare artist, Riley, smoked Tops and Bugler roll-ups, which gave the fingers another activity between sips of black coffee filled with white cane sugar. Both were dressed for conversation, cords and shirts with collars. They shared the need for two brands.

"I was rounded up once," said the artist with the well-kept beard.

The poet started to reply, to ask, to mutter a "huh," but the artist was just beginning, and the whites of his eyes grew around his lenses. He had a small spiral flip pad and he flipped page after page of today's drawings of stick figures, key words, street signs, names of other people he'd seen today, snippets of conversation, where he'd seen police cruisers and vanity plates that had caught his attention as he had walked.

"I was picked up by the cops when I accused them of ferreting crime. See, it's illegal for them to ferret crime." Riley aggressively poked a finger at the black vinyl table-top, spilling a little coffee.

The younger man was scared a bit by the artist's anger, emphasis and jolting finger. The jolt caused him to push back in his seat, look around the restaurant to see if anyone had noticed the other heating up. The waitron was idling at the back, the cook was sorting spinach for washing, and the busser was smoking a filtered ready-made and having a beer with her. It was mid-afternoon and there were only two other occupied tables and Riley and the poet were there in the ether, invisible and inexorably present, the odor of their brands lingered as they did.

"Cops are allowed to stop you or check you out **if** you're breaking the law. I was walking across the Suspension bridge from Covington at four in the morning. I'd been painting then gone for a walk . . . I had my canvas on my shoulder, palette and paint box on my arm. I smoked and walked. They asked me what I was doing from their car window and I kept walking. They followed me. I kept walking. They stopped. They asked me to stop. I said, 'what for?' and they said, 'when a police officer asks you to stop, you stop.' I kept walking. Well, they arrested me."

"What for?"

"They searched me, illegally, and found a little weed. But they didn't take me to the station. I argued all the way and they took me to University Hospital and put me in Rollman's in restraints. The doctor there, the fucking shrink put me on some medicine." He spat the word out with venom. "Navane."

The younger man listened and reasoned with himself. This man was on the fringe of society. He had not worked at a job in years. The poet had seen the way bartenders treated his friend. No dignity for the welfare artist. One tender had insisted that the man should get a job. "He's a leech on society," Ned, the tender at Ronald's, had said.

They had coffee in silence for a moment. "I take medicine," said the poet.

The poet did not have his ponytail yet. He had dropped out of the university after three tries. During the third try he worked at the university as a clerk for free tuition. After dropping out he had quit his job. Unemployed but without welfare, he divided time between the library, research with the welfare artist . . . studying him, walking with him in the wee morning hours, sucking weed, lounging in bars and coffeehouses. One night they danced around the novel *Children of Light* while a copy of it sat on a chair in Ronald's Bar & Grill. Three fiddles, accordion, voices raised to beauty, to loving night and hedonism. This was their answer.

The poet of Over-the-Rhine spent time writing his novel and learning to use a Macintosh taking the early drafts of *A Razor, A House & A Wife—The Three Hardest Things to Hold,* from his first novel and typing them one modern page at a time. Riley was his contemporary but painfully without recognition.

"When they come to me, I'll already be discovered," said the welfare artist. He had no interest in agents, shows, exhibits . . . "life and painting is all I have time for," he said that night as they walked out of Ronald's. The artist had had his coffee and roll-ups. They had talked again about synchronicity. His fingernails were brown with the resin of synchronicity. His gait was even as the police cruisers' motors. They walked eight blocks up Main Street laughing large at the joke they were playing on society.

"We're the real artists, poet!" Riley shouted to the boarded up, buildings. "It's our city, our night."

The sidewalks were dry, Fall eased into Winter. The smell of dry itched at both of them, breathing dry air through big noses, giving their gaits a loping animated unevenness. Each step different than the one before, or after, so that the very rhythm they took was no rhythm at all. Arjuna, the poet, puffed at tobacco and stumbled a bit slower. He'd had a few draughts to celebrate the leaves coming down. He envied Stone the teaching gig at Harvard and the film deal on *Can't Stop the Rain*. Arjuna had no concept of the work he had yet to produce to write, publish, and profit. He walked the free walk of a poet in the city. What do poets think of as they walk the dirty night streets of the ghetto with their friends? They think of girls. As they age it's women, man . . . it's women.

"I wish I had a honey that would give me some money, money ain't funny, and playboy bunny," rattled the artist.

The poet scowled, "Rhyme is no good, man."

"I ain't got no money, I ain't got no honey; where's the bunny?" Riley made big faces showing gaps in his teeth. "I got bad teeth and no money."

Arjuna stumbled quiet and still, smoking a Gauloises, dangling from a long hand. "This is the richest country in the world," he said as they walked past block after block of boarded up storefronts, brown pressboard unpainted but for graffiti: ROSA SHE MY LIFE!

A police cruiser rolled past slow and silent. The traffic lights flashed yellow on a pulse. Empty forty ouncers, dead soldiers stood on each storefront locked door sill. A sad forlorn honking echoed over Fourteenth Street as Arjuna and Riley walked by the blind vacant alley, broken green glass glittered on the cobbles.

"She my life. That graffiti says it all, man," And he thought back to college when there were young girls, pretty and nice, and clean.

"I have a wife, and without without a life. I wrote four letters to my son this week," said Riley.

They passed Arjuna's home, "The poet's building! Yes, that's where the Over-the-Rhine poet lives!" shouted Riley to the street silent for now except for the clicking of the electric traffic signal boxes making their mechanical buzz.

Arjuna had not known the older man had a family. "Come home with me," said Riley. And they walked across Liberty against the flashing red 'Don't Walk' message, both enjoyed the dark river of street ribboning away from them into the night.

Through an exterior door that Riley quickly keyed, down an alley, over a wooden frame, up a creaking stair two flights, breathlessly; on one landing a round stained glass, porthole, for a moment it felt like a ship, wooden and creaking with age. Riley's apartment was warm, brightly lit, light brown, almost yellow carpet, wood furniture, table and chairs matching ladder backs. An orange striped tabby leapt onto the kitchen table chasing a brown cockroach playfully.

"Tea? Toast? I'm making eggs and bacon," said the artist flipping on the gas stove, opening the fifties style refrigerator with a heavy clunk.

"Toast and tea sound OK," said the poet, trying to decide where to sit.

Reading his body language, Riley offered, "Sit where you want . . . but think about it," he began a sort of lesson for the younger man on body language and in the stoned mindset the poet became anxious, felt unwelcome, fear and uncertainty in this man's home annoyed him vaguely, then moreso. He pulled back the chair opposite the icebox, in front of the white kitchen sink. Above the water taps was a wall mural of bright swirling oranges, yellows, browns; the artist had created abstract paintings right on the walls of his apartment. Riley's lessons were intimidating to Arjuna as he was never sure if he was learning or just being put through some agonizing test. He was reminded of his own father, who had often lectured, but had not been lost in the wildness of creativity like this man. The poet's father had attempted always to analyze and quantify creative work, as if creative writing was a science. Arjuna avoided contact with his father. Something about elders displaced Arjuna's confidence and shook him to his core. He distrusted his father deeply.

Arjuna imposed his larger, younger body on the room and he felt his power, his superiority over Riley. At the same time, he allowed himself to become the visitor on a friend's turf. He struggled with superior and inferior polarity and thought about talking to Riley about it then tucked it back in his mind to save for the therapist. Talking about the binary nature of the unconscious smacked of duality, which the spiritual knowledge from the therapist seemed to undermine. Riley had no car.

"Where are your wife and son?" Arjuna asked.

"The boy's with his mother and the girl. They live in the deep South," he volunteered almost nothing about them. "I've been sending him letters about the miracle of the universe. It opens up like a flower and dances down the street." Riley's voice took a singsong drama to it and he moved to and from the poet in the kitchen with large gestures. When he grinned, his face was huge.

In Riley's living room an easel stood in the center, the floor was black with stars painted in different sizes, swirls of color led to the bathroom and up the walls. He had a storage area he had built which held sixty or more canvases. On the mantle was a black and white rendering of the Probasco fountain on fountain square. Riley, as it turned out, had painted over sixteen different versions of the Probasco fountain, a stately Cincinnati icon on the central square, and the beardless Lincoln statue in Lytle Park standing in front of the Taft museum. Arjuna had run across the bearded man at each of these monuments on several occasions, day and night. The poet was drawn to the fountain like a moth to a flame, a convert to a temple, a seeker to a guru, or a writer to the page.

The barefoot Riley, his dirty white socks sitting on gym shoes tucked beneath a bench, brush in hand, wide thumb held to the sky, measured out Lincoln with a purpose both haphazard and deliberate.

"Why are you drawn to the monuments?" asked the poet.

"They have been here," said Riley, pausing, then walking back from palette box to easel.

"How long have you been here tonight?" asked the spirited poet.

"I arrived, sat for a while, as it came to night I began. I don't wear a watch. It's been several hours. Art takes time."

"You have the head . . . what is that on the hill?"

"The monastery in Mt. Adams," said Riley with a rapturous look.

"His feet are enormous."

Riley stopped painting, rolled a Bugler. The poet sat on the bench and pulled a Camel bullet from the pack, lit both men off a wooden match, flaring sulfur odor. The tobacco soothed them. The poet took off his shoes and socks. The street was quiet, lit with glowing globes.

Riley rubbed his well-trimmed beard with his large dry hand, then touched his yellow sweater.

They were in Arjuna's apartment looking at his artwork. The papers were spread at their feet on the green shag rug.

"Here's a poem about the drawings," said the poet. He went to a notebook and riffled through sheaves of worn pages and began to read:

Ashen sky blue faces peer forsaken through
wired glass only ten inches square
fixed stolidly in massive steel
painted yellow with a cool silvery brushed
aluminum handle on the outside.

Piss in a cold steel vessel
and hand it angrily to a steely-
eyed psychiatric technician
or nurse over a narrow space of
open door when the quiet room
bed is changed, quickly
antiseptic and lonely

304

This is where my artwork
flowered with beige, gray, black, white,
then titanium white, cobalt blue, lavender,
and all the myriad colors within me;
artist's crayons, watercolors,
brushed dipped heavily in leftover coffee
from the breakfast tray because coffee
in here only stirs me up.

I become Vincent van Gogh for several
days and shout at any footsteps I
hear. I was gone for a very long time.
Look at my product.

Arjuna finished reading, paused in the middle of the room, under the bright incandescent lights. At two-thirty in the morning they disturbed no one but one another.

"Too angry," said Riley. "You won't attract any honey with that."

Arjuna took a breath and wanted to bark at the older man.

"I feel pity for the numb fuck who takes the piss," said Riley. "Some of these do resemble van Gogh. Why did you stop painting?"

"It's too painful a process," Arjuna whispered. The older man came over and reached a hand to the poet's face. His dry touch was unwelcome. Arjuna pulled away. "You had better go now," he said loudly.

"OK, OK," said Riley. "This is for you." He handed Arjuna two joints. Arjuna managed a half smile. Arjuna walked Riley to the door, followed him down the two flights of stairs and locked the deadbolt behind the welfare artist.

Back in the apartment the poet lit up and quickly inhaled the marijuana. He felt horny, dizzy and sleepy. He went into the tiny cramped bathroom to brush his teeth. As he ran the cold water over his toothbrush he thought about Riley and shuddered. He wanted a woman, not this man. He spat the white-green paste into the basin. A bit of blood from his gums swelled in the sink and a very shiny, dark-brown cockroach appeared in the sink. For a moment Arjuna imagined he bled roaches from his gums.

It was afternoon and breezy, turning cold. In Piatt Park the leaves were down on the walk and the green park benches. Pigeons swept away from their feet chuckling. "Funny thing," said Riley. "Last election day I ate lunch in Hyde Park at a Woolworth's lunch counter," They were walking on Eighth Street toward Mullane's Café.

"Cheap laugh, Riley," Arjuna interrupted.

"No, no. Serious," said Riley. "I was buying groceries next door, had borrowed the neighbor's car, and I walked into Woolworth's, and there he sat. The shrink. The shrink who put me on that gunk."

"Shrink?" asked the poet.

"Fucking shrink I told you about. When they arrested me, that night on the bridge."

"Woolworth's?"

"In a shirt and tie with loafers on. Eating soup."

"Eating soup?"

"Yeah, soup."

"Same one?"

"He didn't recognize me at first."

"Not at first."

"No."

"I watched him for a minute. Walked up slow, sat down at his elbow. He looked up."

"He looked up?"

"From his big wide bowl of steaming hot soup."

"Could have been gazpacho."

"Hot soup."

"Oh."

"Then he went back to eating soup."

"Did he speak?"

"No."

Riley looked over. He stopped at the curb. They crossed Race Street. Mullane's was empty and they sat at the corner table. Riley tipped a hand-rolled jacket out of his tobacco wrap. The vinyl tabletop was dirty.

"So?" asked Arjuna.

Riley flared a wooden match and a bit of tobacco flamed, dropped to ash on the table. The busser came over, left a tin ashtray, cleared, then wiped the table.

"What'll it be?" asked the busser.

"Coffee," said Riley.

"Same," said Arjuna.

"Cream?"

"Yes."

Before the coffee was served, the older man leaned over, mouth to the poet's ear. "I put one hand on the back of his head and before he could jerk his head, I pushed his face bang into the bowl. Then I said, 'Don't ever do that again.'"

The waiter served steaming coffee.

Seeking the Wild Cleanliness

1989

A gray slop sink with four old frayed mops, knots hooked in clumps of filth, orange plastic handles laying at odd angles in a state of utilitarian neglect. The white tile halls of the Pauline Warfield Lewis Center looked neglected, too, barely cleaner than the maintenance closets, rags scattered, paper towels strewn, stacked with supplies. Begging, stuttering patients in ill-fitting clothes lurked with nicotine deprived and psychotropic drug induced tremors behind nearly every locked door. "Got a cigarette," was their halting mantra. Green walls, wooden doors with small, square wired windows swung into areas between the wards keyed only by staff or supervisor. In the odoriferous custodial closets, the new supervisor, Arjuna, driven to work by need for income found brass and rubber squeegees without extension handles, empty and busted spray bottles, spent orange aerosol cans in need of disposal, food wrappers stuck to yellow tile floor, orange and black vacuums clogged with dust, rubber belts broken, black cloth bags with damaged fasteners and no new replacement green liners. Stacked among boxes of toilet tissue, and paper towels were half-empty five gallon buckets of red, yellow and blue floor solutions each with a specific use. At the hallways' ends were brown steel doors without windows that, when keyed, swung into corners with external doors, also locked and windowless. This was a dark place to be walking with a cleaning crew of former patients pushing housekeeping carts of heavy brown plastic and bright yellow vinyl.

Churchill was the best of all janitors Arjuna ever supervised. Church with his flat face, and bulbous nose trained Arjuna to run a four man, cleaning crew at Lewis Center, a dirty, neglected state mental institution. Churchill had skills, a sense of duty, and kept to task steady as a soaking rain. Tile floors became endless corridors, a maze of doorways keyed by a fistful of master keys turning sometimes clockwise, and other times, counter clockwise. (Scratched in the paint or plain wood above each knob was an arrow to indicate key direction to the uninitiated.) Each supervisor carried keys, but workers could only borrow them. The patients waited by the locked doors begging for a soda or a cigarette. Arjuna shared with the crew but not the patients. One of the originals had been fired and when Arjuna saw him at the central office and supply center the worker stuttered that he wanted to be friends, "Could I have your number? Will you call me?" And Arjuna was cold and distant, had his own priorities. The worker knew trouble like the supervisor never could. Arjuna heard he leapt to his death from a freeway overpass. The poet turned supervisor could not face his former employee's funeral. Hoist a pint for him—someone. (Arjuna had given up booze and weed, now a college graduate, he'd had to beg for a job.) No name please . . . one of the lost janitors of the nineties. He never hurt anyone but by embarrassment of his pitiful nature. Ashamed to be pitied. Churchill was patient with Arjuna until Church was the last of the original four-man crew Arjuna had inherited. Church and Arjuna had had one night when they disagreed. Churchill had fight in him though mostly was gentle as a lamb. Arjuna had to call Captain Star, the neatly uniformed tough talker of the campus police. Everyone referred to them as security but Star, balding, short, and pudgy, fumed if it wasn't "Officer Star," or "Captain Star." A flash of eye and tooth and flaring tempers were quenched in a thirsty cool soda while Star stood by, his arrogant mustache bristled with calm, "A disagreement between two good men; two good workers."

Lisa, the other supervisor had been a problem. She had been in the habit of taking half the crew in the van off into the night parkinglot to smoke weed while we finished mopping the kitchen. Now that she'd been fired, Arjuna had responsibility for the whole crew, the whole building. Church had difficulty adjusting to the supervisory change, his job was no longer set, he had to face a team approach with Arjuna making more decisions. As many as fourteen workers might turn up on a given night, or as few as five. Arjuna's task was to settle things down and to clean the building.

Lallie & the Chocolates

1990

To the crew she was called "Lallie"– her full name was Lalliana and she was short, cute and proud of her tits.

"Hey, there's a wet T-shirt contest this Saturday at Joe's," she said as they walked through the tunnel-like corridors. Arjuna, the supervisor, listened, thought *would I announce my participation in a flash like that.* And the crew walked close as they dared to Lallie, her oval breasts bouncing below the small, cigarette sucking oval of lipstick. She smoked menthols with the crew in the black-floored commissary before they cleaned the patients' trash, filth, ashes and spills.

One evening she took him aside.

"My boyfriend likes to buy me chocolates," she said. "He's picking me up after work on his motorcycle."

"So you won't need a ride to the bus stop?"

"No."

They smoked in the commissary, Arjuna on Camel bullets, savoring, relaxing, breath meditation. Fat Chuckie was eating saus-meat. This gelatinous, fatty, tinned meat was new to

Arjuna. He'd never seen anything so unappetizing. Fat Chuckie offered it around. He ate with his hands, pudgy, unwashed, greasy, hands; slicing off huge slabs with a serrated plastic knife. The meat was pink, imbedded in cloudy translucent goo.

Fat Chuckie spilled out of his clothes – he shared butt crack when he filled mop buckets in the cluttered slop sinks. (Years later another supervisor told Arjuna of the nagging she'd had to give to get him to wipe his ass when he lived in a halfway house.) But generous, always sharing candy, meat, menthol smokes; he responded great to the supervisor. Fat Chuckie mopped with stamina.

So Lallie told Fat Chuckie, "My boyfriend buys me chocolates," and she giggled.

"Want chocolate?" Fat Chuckie said around a mouthful of icky meat.

Lallie giggled, ignored Fat Chuckie, turned her torso to the crew who smoked intensely, then more intensely, asked, "Do you think I'm built nice?"

White Bob was cross-eyed, swung his arms while he stood and talked loud to nobody in particular. He tipped his ash often and aggressively, ignored Lallie and said, "I'll be done early tonight, and I'll beat Sally home."

White Bob was married to Sally who worked the other site. Sally was pregnant and rode the bus while White Bob rode a moped to work, except when it rained. He never showed on a rainy day and was always getting suspended for poor attendance.

Lallie told White Bob, "My boyfriend buys me chocolates," and laughed.

White Bob said, "Who cares."

Black Bob was big-boned, light-skinned, with bad teeth and a pocked face from a metal and gas explosion. "Somebody fucked with my regulator," he told anyone who'd listen. "I had this oxy-acetylene torch blow up in my face. It almost blinded me.

That super never liked me. I know he set me up. He set it to blow. He hated me. He wanted to scare me off. That fucker."

"Bob, you got to move on." Arjuna said.

"I can't weld again."

"Give it time."

"That fucker. He could'a killed me with that regulator. I don't know why he hated me. I never did anything to him. I was making good money. Eighteen or twenty bucks an hour."

"Bob, you're a good worker. Just take it slow. You'll rebuild your confidence."

The break was over. Lallie headed for the offices and Arjuna keyed her in. She vacuumed and pulled trash. White Bob and Fat Chuckie dust-mopped and damp-mopped the halls to the commissary and the commissary itself with its fixed Formica and iron chairs and tables. Arjuna wiped down the buffer and put a fresh pad on it for White Bob. Black Bob was dust-mopping and pulling trash in the surgical and dental rooms.

Arjuna took a break outside in the night courtyard alone; smoked a cig and thought seriously about quitting cigarettes for the third time that day. A bronze fountain of a boy draining water out of his boot sounded in front of him in the dark. Arjuna thought about when his own shoes had been torn and his feet aching. He felt grateful for the job tonight, almost finished the Camel, stubbed the butt short and saved it. Back inside he checked on Black Bob. Bob was eating a chicken wing he'd pulled from the trash.

"Bob, what's this?"

"Nothing, Arjuna, nothing." And he dropped the bones back into the waste can, stopped chewing, gazing at the floor. Arjuna was more embarrassed than the older welder.

"You hungry?"

"No, no."

"Didn't you eat on break?"

"Yeah," he looked sheepish, grinned some, turned his head slowly from side-to-side then stopped.

"Anything I can do?"

"I was homeless for a while and I picked up some bad habits. I won't do it again."

"That's good. Sorry you were homeless. You could get germs, get sick."

"Yeah. I know. We're OK, right Arjuna?" Black Bob wanted to be liked. He brushed his pock-marked face with his hand and stared at the floor.

"We're cool Bob," Arjuna said and keyed himself out into the hall, took a deep breath, thought about what he and his crew had been through. Arjuna had been homeless too but had never eaten out of trash cans. He remembered sneaking into buildings at the university and raiding refrigerators. Life hadn't made much sense then. Today he was grateful to be working and wanted to talk to Nate, his boss, just to talk, but Nate would be busy, and Arjuna would not have known how to tell Nate about Black Bob. Nate would say, "Yeah, buddy," and that would end it. Somehow, Nate's smile was infectious. Nate had said he could hold his head high when he toured the Lewis Center these days. It had not been like that when Arjuna started. Arjuna felt the pride of having a good crew, each and every night getting the job done. He remembered when Nate had demanded that Arjuna clean the supply closets. He had felt boiling anger at cleaning up after Lisa, the other supervisor.

Arjuna checked on Lallie. She had finished pulling trash in the offices and ran the sweeper. Lallie shut down the machine, looked up at Arjuna with her face too red from make-up.

"Ya know," she said, "I could use another cigarette."

"Out here," said Arjuna keying an outer door. They stood side-by-side in the dark breathing smoke; the embers glowed as they sucked in unison.

"Chocolate gives me tee aitch owe!" Lallie announced to Arjuna, in an open and matter-of-fact way.

"What's tee aitch owe?" Arjuna asked.

"A titty hard on!" she laughed.

Arjuna felt his cheeks redden in the dark; glad she couldn't see. He puffed his Camel, said, "I'm gonna quit these," and flipped the butt into the grass.

"Is that funny, or what?" she continued.

"Lallie, I didn't need to know, that," Arjuna said.

She smoked her long thin cigarette patiently, conversing for a while yet in the dark.

"So, I'm a good worker, huh?"

"Yes, Lallie, you are. Let's get back to it."

"OK."

He keyed her into the offices, and she returned to the orange and black vacuum, and with deliberate motions, she began cleaning again.

In training, Arjuna, Churchill, and the freaky suicidal toilet man had cleaned half the building. Lisa and her crew cleaned the other half. Over a period of months, the job had expanded, and it became increasingly more difficult to finish in the allotted time. Arjuna had asked Nate, a thin white man who moved with the frantic energy of a speed freak to talk to Lisa about helping at the end of the night. At least, Arjuna asked, she could send some fellows over when they were through. Thin Chuckie was set in his ways, though, and Lisa didn't want to disrupt his routine, she claimed.

Once Arjuna was under the stars, smoking a glowing Camel, giving himself a break alone, when he saw Lisa driving around the parking lot in the company van. It wasn't even that late. Arjuna had mentioned it to Nate. "If she has time to drive around . . . couldn't she drive over to the far end with some crew members and help us knock out the kitchen and the kitchen hallway? It's not fair, Nate, she's finished and I'm still milking my cunt," Arjuna had heard the phrase from a Scottish folk singer. Nate had been stunned. He had talked to Lisa. Then she started sending her crew over to help for a while. A week and a half passed that were better. Tommy, her floor man, was cheerful, a laconic talker. "Arjuna, we understand one another," he said as he noticed Arjuna growing out his hair, wearing a headband and a short ponytail. Tommy did this handshake thing, with the fists and the thumb. Arjuna had the sense they were dopers.

"I caught Lisa smoking dope with Tommy and Thin Chuckie in the van while you were in the kitchen," Nate was waiting for Arjuna in the Lobby late. "Could you drive the van home and drop them off? You'll have an extra five hours a week." Arjuna had cracked his hardest habit. He was scared but had a sense that he was on the other side now. No more joints with Riley, the welfare artist, Arjuna had hung with before he got the job.

No more fighting Lisa. He told Nate he'd take the job. Nate agreed to bring him back to his car after he took the crew home. It was a clean sweep. Now he turned his back on Riley and the drugs; he headed for responsibility. Soon Arjuna would be a non-smoker.

The crew gathered in the break room after Nate left. Fat Chuckie broke a Hershey bar into squares and handed half to Lallie. She munched with her mouth closed and looked up at Arjuna. As they made eye contact Arjuna could see her nipples harden under the blouse. Lallie smiled, flashed her blues for the supervisor. He looked down at his tired feet and said, "Let's go, crew." And led them out to the van. Lallie's boyfriend drove up on his rattling Honda and handed her a helmet in the dark.

The next day Arjuna drove the van from the agency to Lewis Center. He talked to Thin Chuckie, who had a limp handshake and eyes that rolled away, never looking back. He carried pad and pencils, sketched cartoons of basketball players in motion. He waited in the lobby with soda and sketchpad, talking loudly in long-voweled "yaahs" at the other workers as they arrived. Arjuna had to ask Thin Chuckie to switch sites, starting tonight. Doing this felt extremely awkward to the newly promot-

316

ed supervisor. Thin Chuckie had been there longer than Arjuna. Thin Chuckie took it badly, saying, "Yah shit."

Lallie was there, too. She talked as if Arjuna had been with her all day. It was as if they were very familiar.

"You were hitting on me. All you want is to get into my pants," Lallie said, loud enough so that Arjuna had to get her out of the hall near the lobby. Churchill and White Bob were filling their buckets with an ear to Lallie. With Thin Chuckie gone the lobby was clear. There was a small alcove in the back. Arjuna steered her there, leading her with gestures.

"Lallie, you've got to go home." Arjuna could smell beer on her breath. She was drunk.

"You're just mad 'cause you can't have me." Her voice was plaintive.

"Lallie, you have to go home. You have to leave the grounds." Arjuna stayed directive, solemn, not angry.

"Arjuna, you like me, don't you? What did I do? I was a little late, that's all."

"Lallie, if I have to, I'll ask Captain Star to escort you from the grounds. You need to talk to Marie before you come back to work."

Lallie slurred her words, "Why are you doing this—you're jealous. That's it. I have more friends than you've got." She shouted. Arjuna and Lallie stood in the alcove. Lallie's face was flushed and Arjuna had a tremor in his hands.

"Lallie, don't make this difficult. I know you've been drinking. You can't come to work like that."

"So, I had a few. So. That's not it. You just wanted—" she shouted.

"Calm down."

"OK. OK." She stood there looking up at Arjuna and started to cry. "Will I lose my job?"

"JUST GET HOME. Call someone or take a bus. You have to get off the grounds of the Lewis Center, now. You're disrupting the crew." Arjuna was worried about White Bob and Churchill, but they would have to wait.

"How do I get home?"

She likes chocolate. Arjuna knows, according to Marie, that Lallie has a drinking problem. An alcoholic adolescent. He can remember some of that, but his denial system is still active, still active, but not as strong. Not as strong as young Lallie's, no doubt. Newly sober, to get this job, Arjuna remembers the fight with green-eyed Marlena that night three years ago when he had been a client worker at the Justice Center, back in the day. They had been at Cady's wedding at Leo's parent's roof garden. Lena flirted with Leo and his dad, with a drunken sway to her hip. Arjuna had had a bad headache and they went back to Marlena's five room house in Covington across the singing bridge from downtown Cincinnati.

Arjuna took a shower at Marlena's and he noticed a heart with the initials "JP." drawn in the dust at the corner of the lime green tile stall. The water cascaded over him in a numbness from the Wild Turkey and codeine. JP has been in Marlena's shower, he thinks. JP has been with her.

Later, when she slapped him across the face nine times when the dark beer combined with the bourbon and codeine, his anger released. He challenged her to say JP had not been there. "JP in your shower. Johnny Person naked in your house." She denied it and redirected, asked him about his hickey on his throat. His thoughts were clouded by drink and passion. He was not sure. Did Lottie, the model at Ronald's Bar? No, no, too many days ago. Just, before; Marlena put the hickey there herself to catch him. When they were rolling around the living room floor with the cats and dogs, she sucked on the side of his throat. Nine hard slaps and Arjuna did not fight back. He wanted to leave. He started up from the bed, dressed himself, buttoned the soft white cotton shirt and she grabbed the front, tore with her angry strength. As the shirt shredded, she shouted at him, "CUNT! CUNT! CUNT!" He had his keys wrapped in his fist, hit her hard on the side of her head.

He drove back across the singing bridge in the cool Spring night. The next day Arjuna took his swollen hand for an X-ray. Fractured the fifth metatarsal. "Did you punch a wall?" the resident asked. Arjuna nodded.

Paul Thanas

He'd had stout and Wild Turkey, and the bit about the hickey, the shower stall, all had been suppressed in memory until Lallie surfaced with her drunken flirtatiousness. If he could call it that. Arjuna knows he is a drunk. He's so newly sober, he doesn't know how to help Lal. Marie assigns the young worker ninety AA meetings in ninety days before she can return to work.

Trains pass at switches in the night--
head beams cut gleaming paths
like two janitors methodically backing mops--
one out of a room, arms in locomotion,
legs, patterns of moving oaks steady
over damp rag heads,
the room butts against a hall,
where the other works easily,
pausing to clear doorways.
I stand in the twinight of my struggle,
where they intersect--A rock,
between them and a hard place.

"Are you serious?"
"Yup," Ned answered.
"Quit."
"Spent the day in the park drinking wine."
"No painting? No writing?"
"No. It's OK till next month & the bills come due."
So I sidle over to the counter after thinking, "good luck," wouldn't want to be unemployed without support in this slush. Major slush raining from the sky. First time ever the plow driver lifted the blade so he wouldn't coat me in icy spray.
Coffee . . .
The dishwasher, a toast of a chick, says she quit her day job today, too.
"Finish the shift?"
"Yep."

319

She had worked at the movie theater. Go figure.

The bartender, Ned, he'll land on his feet, fourteen years on the job without incident. Ronald's Bar & Grill changed owners. Regulars beware. Things will be changing. Yep . . . change is in the wind.

Arjuna met Urban Rat and smitten by her brown fall hair full of highlights, a little fringe accenting her freckled forehead, her smile, and sexy lips, seeing her round eyes, he courted her. He caught her full stride, crossing the street toward him, surging off the curb into the frame. In a moment he wanted to remember how she dressed, the way she looked. He looked back into his memory each day.

Urban Rat, for her part, had heard of Arjuna. Handsome, big face, broad shouldered, stance like a boxer, only friendly, reached a hand up always, shirt tail flying, beige shirt, brown hair and eyes, warmer than Mom's. The two of them had met. And he remembered, the first time, maybe. Behind her, her ass, him walking toward, her fall hair, his face above the back of her hair, his working mouth, a flair of grin, him walking with her, her pirouette to keep aside, others surrounding, in the frame, in action. Stealing moments. Came within their purview.

Arjuna, an atheist, kept dancing to a minimum as he scared women with his shimmy. Urban Rat lingered in church driveways. She didn't like the atmosphere inside, she didn't mind the cookies, but the cook bothered her. The cooks always flirted. She didn't take to flirting. In the Christian circles of knotted pencil pusher typical bureaucratic middle-level-social worker types, the flow kept nubbed little efforts minimal. If he could get off the street into a building with old-wood frame windows, sashes, weights, rope. He might find tenement dreamed bliss. He landed in Over-the-Rhine.

She liked horse racing and didn't like jockeys. Trainers were all from hell. Breeders, holy, seers of mystic heights, and strange victims, marginally better than whisky brides, brewers from hell, and scenic bridges seemed to somehow escape into etherlike minefields above the tundra in exile. What did it mean to know how horses knew each other? What can anyone really honestly say about the lists of dams and sires? Mystic? Man O' War? Who Knew? Secretariat? Pennywhistle? When Urban Rat sat late at night, reading her slick green magazine called *Deep Horse Brood;* Arjuna, painted, detailed. She smoked, listed, pined, wept, kept figures hidden.

Her sobriquet came from punk sensibilities. She spiked her hair. She went to clubs where music thrummed into the morning. She grew toxic. Her toxic attitude sparked her call to be an angry dark urbanite.

He had good luck. Kept tools clean. Polished not much other than kitchen utensils. His glory wasn't going to make sure of much. Her defeatist attitude made it hard for her. His optimism encouraged everyone he contacted much to her chagrin. She competed with him. You know this feeling that he could get along without her and she couldn't manage with him or without. You couldn't exactly call him a body builder. He framed his athleticism differently than most men. He stood squarely, a little taller than most, boasted a shoulder line that loomed in doorways, even large openings. His hands seemed like they went from one end of the keyboard to the other when he touched a piano. He seldom did, embarrassed by the ringing tones, blending and tittering.

Uninterrupted Adjustment

I'm sitting in a lobby area of a downtown single room occupancy hotel with green walls, a two-tone black and white tile floor, wood grain tables with an aluminum edge. The setting is familiar, but nothing is solid in the dream. The chairs are brushed aluminum with green vinyl seats. I'm picking at cigarette butts and fooling with a harmonica. My beeper is on the table. I've been receiving signed books, memoirs from street musicians—a trumpeter with crippled fingers who could blow jazz blues like god or Buddha light or someone detached and out there. If I need a towel and a shower, I'm really just depressed and lonely and the beeper goes off. The message? I don't care.

In reality Dad has angrily reneged on his generous offer to pay for a wedding rehearsal dinner if I arrange such an event. He now is setting conditions, such as where—how many people? How much per person?

The beeper again please. This is the final and most important stage of recovery—uninterrupted adjustment. My therapist tells me this spontaneously without my having called. He has beeped my unconscious mind, to confirm my actions? Or to say change them? I had asked Dad to put his offer in writing and he has said no—I have said I don't trust him otherwise— that he just wants conflict, and I don't wish to argue or engage.

322

Paul Thanas

But in the dream, I am just above the edge. And before sleeping last night I have drifted into a dream of a straight razor then awakened to fear sleep. My parents have been more than generous. There is a woman painter, a luminous light in my life. (Here I am deeply diddled and disturbed. I have diddled the painter, a self-proclaimed Urban Rat as a necessary replacement for Draupudie, my muse, my heart's desire. My therapist has said to forget the Drap and take what is real.) I would despair to be reduced to cigs and harmonicas, beepers and books by soon to be famous dead jazz blues musicians. I felt despair in that dream. I also saw hope in the beeper message that I tried to write down verbatim from the beeper through tears and fears. Blurred, the vision ends clearly with knowledge that I can't predict, prevent, control the future. That harmonicas and cigarette butts, poetry and jazz are painfully part of my world. So is my father whose authority no longer controls me. I can marry the painter with or without his paying for the party. The Urban Rat came into my life at Ronald's. We met on the eve of my return to the university, a slow flower blooming, ten years of love and courting. I believe I can reject father completely or not. But this morning when I got up to write down the dream he was up and apologized, said he was wrong about last night and he was angry at my mother, queen Kunti. I asked for ten minutes to write in the early morning sun.

Note that I am a bit spoiled by my parents. They give where I cannot earn. Is this spoiled rich kid angry at his parents who owe him nothing? Is it greedy to accept gifts from Greeks and Jews? Is it wrong to care deeply about relationships yet fear responsibility—or is responsibility really only another hook–lie–trick of mind and consciousness. I'm lonely when I think I am alone on top or below. When I have social support around, I feel and see and hear all the light, warmth and musical intensity of the moment. Rain light on roof–electric hum of refrigerator. Lamp sheds light on page from above sofa–feet tucked under knees, right ankle, numb. Loose clothes: sweats and T-shirt. Comfort vacation. Comfort temperature perfect 72-74 degrees. Books around. I-Ching. I-Ching. Little purple blossom called heal-all or self-heal. An immediate lift for my emotional heart–soar like two bald eagles on shoreline seen from canoe. One led us to the other, paddles sweating lightly–clean, and bright day clear, calm Southeast wind rippling into bow. He was waiting–a little smaller, male. The painter, AKA Urban Rat, answers quiz about American Eagle–immature Bald Eagle looks like golden. White head looking around yellow beak, then looks at us. Waits a moment and launches into high green brown fragrant pine. Over blue water's edge, gravel shore– moving sound of wings rushing air–off off away. Wide span, yes, wide span.

Paul Thanas

S chizo Story

(When Arjuna is off his medication he hallucinates. He runs the past and the future together and thinks he sees visions. Arjuna's mind is not balanced without a daily dose. He hears things and sees things that are not as they are. We speak weekly.)

What is it about a woman who goes to bed with a syringe? Not the typical example, this Urban Rat, painter extraordinaire, tall, curvaceous, with a broad chin, Swedish features, and a deep rooted, need to control. Control is in her long pause. She has mastered the pregnant silence. I never believed she was shooting up because she once confessed her fear of needles. When the Urban Rat went to her physician, she never had blood drawn. Later I found many different sized syringes in our kitchen drawer.

I awoke in my tranquilized stupor on the waterbed, nude but for the oversized T-shirt. I smelled rubbing alcohol and I turned on her and saw the small plastic staff with the shiny needle. She had a Q-tip to sterilize my skin before injecting some poison. Now that she had been caught in the act, she could no longer deny she did this. I had suspected it of her, feared her torture. She claimed she kept the tools for dosing the ferrets.

325

And Then the Cow Was Drownded

In a previous life I was my wife. She wanted to be a man, a writer, and to love herself more. It just happened that I learned of it while on morphine for a root canal. I'll tell the details later. It surprised her when I asked for the divorce. I think I would have wanted a divorce even without the medication accident.

I lost my leg in a boating accident. Actually, yachting. After I sold my first novel, which preceded the sale of my second novel only by a few minutes, I bought a seventy-footer. Some years after Rigo finally withdrew his protest and stopped acting like a fuckhead, I asked him to sail with me in Florida. He was recovering from a tremendous loss. We never thought he'd be the same. I don't blame him for my tragic accident, nor would he dare blame me for the loss of his daughter.

I have a strange sense of premonition. Thankfully, often I'm wrong. It could be that his daughter never died. Well, yet. The loss of my leg may be an innocent lie as well. The truth is buried in the story, mine and yours.

There's a one armed man, sitting across from me in the library. One sleeve of his yellow shirt is tucked in. He has a heavy gold ring on his right hand. He is reading the funny papers. A gold cross dangles from a chain that mingles with his chest hair, visible over the muscle-T under his pale, unbuttoned shirt. I am thinking about losing a leg in an automobile accident, something that hasn't happened yet. I hope it never does. I imagine that is the way the man felt about his arm. Rigo won't talk to me to apologize for his nasty attitude. He is ashamed of me for accepting Social Security Disability. I am emotionally disabled. Have been for over twenty years. Rigo is my brother. He lives far away, and he is smug. His daughter has her whole life ahead of her and his life has never veered wildly. I told him on the phone that the risks I take every day make me more of a man than he will ever be. He (Rigo the fucker) is so fucking smug (fuckhead like) that I don't want to talk to him. If i hAD ONE leg . . . or if i were crazy like i am sometimes. . .I just started . . .

Two men sit in an office talking. The younger man, Arjuna, smokes an unfiltered cigarette and sips coffee with cream from a Styrofoam cup. The other man is Arjuna's Case Manager, he bows the fiddle of Arjuna's psyche. Framed photos of a small Asian man in simple robes stand on the desk.

"Who is that?" Arjuna asks, blowing smoke.

"That's Maharaj," says the therapist.

"Maharaj?"

"My guru."

"Where did you meet him?"

"In Bombay, India."

"My friend, Draupudie traveled and lived in India. Her father was a diplomat."

"A diplobrat."

"Yeah, I guess." Arjuna thought of Draupudie and wondered if she knew this guru, or if she knew the Case Manager. It seemed unlikely.

Molly, Draupudie's friend at college, had newspaper photos of gurus chanting "OM" posted on the wall of her room. Arjuna's breathing calmed him. He looked at the print of the walled village on the therapist's wall. He drew on the cigarette, watched and felt the ember grow red hot. Was the diplomat's daughter, Draupudie, a brat? Draupudie studied East Asian philosophy. Her focus was Buddhism.

Arjuna visits the therapist at home. Arjuna stays reserved and looks at bronze statues of Shiva and Vishnu, Hindu deities arranged on a chest of drawers. The therapist has incense burning; nag champa, the scent of nirvana and all holiness in heaven. The therapist is charged up, happily showing spiritual tools to the younger Arjuna—there is a Coffey indoor rower and a weight bench surrounded by mirrors tilted against the walls, resting on hardwood floors. There are two couches in the living room, one a futon with heavy fabric upholstery, the other has a heavy wooden frame. Both couches are solid and comfortable. The two men sit opposite one another, shoes off, feet tucked underneath them. Arjuna feels privileged to be with the nearly bald, graying man with the wire-rim glasses and thin mustache.

"I have a Dutch video of Maharaj." He plays with the remote—images scurry across the large screen while they listen to a glottal voice-over that is fast and indecipherable by these two. Maharaj is shown talking, kneeling at an altar—he speaks in Marathi and a man translates into Dutch. The therapist is able to interpret some of the dialogue from memory.

"Check this out," he says, as the video plays on—he walks over to Arjuna with a book.

"I took this photo!" He shows the photo to the younger man. Maharaj is climbing out of the shower, smiling. He looks good, obviously in his seventies, shirtless, a towel at his waist. He appears strong with a large fleshy nose, wide smile and large ears—a happy guru.

The Case Manager spoke of his Indian Gurus, "So you see, life is light, knowledge, pure being. Love & light & God. Concepts & the mind do not exist. Pure energy is timeless. Formless. Yeah, I took a lot of acid. Maybe 200 hits. I lived with Swami Muktananda, followed him to India. Maldy Shetty was fifteen when I met her—what does she call herself now? Gurumayi Chidvilasananda.

"So I left Muktananda & found this little guru in the whorehouse district of Bombay—a tobacco salesman who taught from his home. They called him Maharaj.

"Maharaj taught of giving up possessions and desires. Fear and desire cloud the mind. The guru taught of doing work without thought of compensation or reward. He taught compassion. The enlightened man feels neither cold nor heat, finds pleasure and pain to be the same, and is aware of neither honor, nor dishonor."

"I love to hear about Maharaj, but I feel unable to understand. I feel cold and heat, experience pleasure and pain, and am aware of both honor and dishonor," Arjuna says to the Case Manager.

Arjuna had been taking Haldol for his schizophrenia for fifteen years. Early September 1997 an accidental dosage change, from 5 milligrams to .5 milligrams interrupted Arjuna's stability. This began a ninety-five per cent reduction. The initial cause was a pharmaceutical error at the beginning of a two-week vacation out of the country. He noticed physical symptoms (less constipation, a brightness and increase in energy, especially on waking) within two days; he had suspected right away when he observed the tablets were smaller. Arjuna took them as prescribed as if they were simply "smaller" 5 milligram tablets. He noted in his journal that to correct the pharmaceutical error would have required contacting a pharmacy in Canada, and probably making several, long distance telephone calls, to Cincinnati. Likely it would have been necessary to drive one hour or so to a larger city (Sault Sainte Marie) and possibly would have involved re-crossing the International border to get medication. If he took .5 milligram tablets to maintain the prescribed dose, there was only a three-day supply in the bottle. (Thirty tablets.)

In a couple of days his energy increased, and his bowels moved more easily. He told his spouse, the former painter, who agreed to monitor behavior. The couple agreed Arjuna should discuss the change with his therapist/Case Manager upon return to Cincinnati. He suggested, at the time, she also see a therapist, as she voiced a concern that Arjuna might leave her behind.

She had painted portraits of the poet until she took a part-time job as a receptionist. After beginning to work, Urban Rat turned her brush to the lively weasels living with the couple. She painted dark canvases after Titian. First Pieta, then more boldly Danaë, and soon she was adding winged ferrets where cherubs and pups had been portrayed as demure elements of religiosity or domesticity by the master. She grew bolder and whimsical ferrets, rabbits and frogs walked on stilts around greenery. She imitated Sandy Skoglund, but the objects were weasels. Arjuna loved this expressive mimesis. She turned from the Modigliani cloned self-portraits which had agonized her. She could not see her own quirkiness and embrace it then. With the ferret art she had a new sense of victory. The Urban Rat and Arjuna collaborated on a show at Mullane's Restaurant in downtown Cincinnati. Between a jewelry store and a movie theater, the restaurant served the business crowd for lunch and sported a great vegetarian menu that attracted a diverse dinner clientele. It was a prestigious place to show. They called it "Ferretocracy." The Rat's *Dios Dos Muertos* was the hit of the display. The poet printed computer generated broadsides, framed in wood and glass. His ferret inspired raps were too far from the *urban naturals* he had written when in Over-the-Rhine. The couple had become middle-class artists—Arjuna, the ponytailed Social Worker—Urban Rat answering phones.

Then she got promoted to administrative aide. She worked over forty hours a week, closed her studio, fostered an interest in thoroughbreds—reclaimed from adolescence. The Urban Rat had grown up in South Carolina and had jumped show horses until her mother died when Rat was fourteen. Rat met Arjuna when she was in her mid-twenties. At thirty, she was a well-known community artist with direct ties to Arjuna, the poet.

She revisited her past melancholy and moped, slept, and took care of Arjuna's shopping and laundry. The increased domesticity timed to support the poet's efforts added to Urban Rat's depressed state. Arjuna's fieldwork hit rough spots. He found the older woman who had attempted suicide. Arjuna had a minor emotional collapse. He was demoted. Arjuna went into short-term therapy, for Post Traumatic Stress Disorder, in addition to his ongoing therapy, for schizophrenia. He had talked to the Case Manager about the woman's suicide attempt, had gone to see her at the hospital at the older man's urging. He became so overwhelmed with emotion that he resigned his job, then went to a department head at the agency and cried. The Case Manager became involved and helped the poet stay with the agency at a lower level position, in a group home. Arjuna saw a separate therapist for four visits to deal with the PTSD.

Arjuna managed a halfway house second shift. He struggled to write poetry—the Urban Rat sketched her pet weasels, knitted, and isolated. How could they stay compatible?

The athlete in Arjuna awakened in his trauma. He began cycling in the moonlight with his friends. The Urban Rat could not keep up. Arjuna thought his wife was depressed and angry—he had trouble working with her—and this all came out in conversations. Once, as they sat in the sedan in a cornfield her diversion that obfuscated his request that she seek a counselor was a difficult argument about cycling. She alleged he centered his attention too much on cycling. Rat had been supportive of Arjuna cycling with Elrenzo, who had driven up to St. Joseph Island from Cincinnati for the weekend (six hundred and fifty miles). The men had ridden forty-five miles on their high tech machines, around the remote island. Elrenzo had departed and the couple drove to a village to shop and happened upon another cyclist. Arjuna wanted to talk to the fellow. Urban Rat became a bit of a killjoy, wanted Arjuna to herself. He acquiesced. After they had lunch they returned to the island and stopped at a farm to buy fresh corn. The two picked ears from the head-high green stalks in a heavy drizzle before driving to the farmhouse to pay for the corn. They argued in the parked sedan while it rained, dousing the cornfield where they had walked and now watched a large terrapin plod. Arjuna felt angry because she wanted to restrict his pleasure cycling.

Return to Cincinnati, refreshed, feeling good and energetic. Contacted therapist and pharmacist. Picked up correct prescription. Negotiated with therapist/CM who contacted psychiatrist to maintain at .5 milligrams. It had been a topic of discussion for quite some time. I had been hitherto unwilling to risk the change. In this event, the opportunity was seized. (A happy accident.) I waited awhile and told some key people in my life, family and a small handful of friends. The therapist said that the psychiatrist sug-

gested 2.5 milligrams instead of continuing on the .5 milligrams. I asked to stay with .5. All agreed.

Things went well. I became more energetic. Difficult side effects of the medication all but disappeared. Hemorrhoids no longer aggravated me. I was losing weight, cycling more, working hard, accomplishing much. Family relations continued to go well. My spouse and I were planning to purchase property. We were in disagreement over a particular property that was commercial as well as residential. The property had a loft on the third floor, where we would live, two apartments on the second floor and a winery/restaurant on the first floor. I was excited about the possibility. My spouse was guarded, unsure, concerned about the risk. As were my parents on whom we were dependent for half of the down payment.

The whole family on my father's side, and my brother, his wife, my niece and of course my parents (who live here in Cincinnati) planned to travel to Boston to celebrate Thanksgiving. My father's sister was to host my spouse and myself. We were to drive to Columbus, Ohio to catch a flight on Thanksgiving morning. I was up all night. In the early morning, I showered, got ready and went for a walk intending to buy flowers for my wife, and bagels for breakfast. The bagel shop was closed. The flower shop should have opened at 8:30 or 9:00 and it did not. When I walked home, I found Urban Rat in tears, upset and very concerned that I was packed and missing. I had not left a note. It was, however, not a habit of mine to leave notes in such instances, and in fact it was a rather unusual occurrence for both of us. We then drove to Columbus, caught the flight and arrived in Boston without further incident, although my Rat seemed off balance.

In Boston, we stayed with my Aunt and arrived before the rest of the family. I don't remember much of the first evening there except that I believe we traveled to my cousin's in Norfolk, Massachusetts, to a rather suburban home where we had a huge dinner with the family. It seemed to pass much as these affairs do in my family, with turkey, walnut apple almond dressing, yams with brown sugar, spinach mushroom casserole, coleslaw, pumpkin, apple and rhubarb pie, buttered corn. I felt generally out of place and somewhat awkward, for my long hair and beard and general behavior tends to be a little more expressive than the rest of the family. My two and a half-

year-old niece seemed to have a good time and was the center of attention. There was a fellow who was a guest/friend/manservant . . . his role was unclear, but he seemed to be charged with carving the turkey and some of the more mundane cooking and cleaning activities. We engaged in conversation about a rock 'n roll band with whom I have a friendship called the "Ass Ponys" and this explanation on my part of some of their songs seemed to pique his interest although not in an altogether positive way.

If I remember correctly, the next day my spouse and I took a walk to a bus stop and took the bus to Cambridge. I proceeded to revisit some of my old "haunts." We walked to the Dudley Co-ops after crossing Harvard Yard. The Dudley Co-ops had hand painted signs over their doors: CENTER FOR HIGH ENERGY METAPHYSICS, which thrilled me to no end. We did not intrude upon the students at either location.

There were easily twenty rooms in the two houses. One was gray, wood paneled, boasted an industrial size kitchen with massive Hobart mixers, huge wooden cutting tables that made marvelous bread boards, a gas stove that had several ovens, a griddle half the size of China and a smaller one besides. The Wok was bigger than Lake Champlain, the pantry bigger than one of the rooms (known as the closet). In the entryway a Pogo cartoon had been started directly on the wall, copying Kelly's style in a wonderful likeness. "Don't spit in the soup, we've all got to eat," Pogo said. A second said, "Roun' here, cleanliness is next to madness." There were several large ancient refrigerators in the storeroom in the basement, as well as one in the dining area, a large medium high ceilinged room, with lots of windows around the back and a table with the stereo which was made of old Hi-Fi parts. The fridge in the dining room was for beer and milk only. The beer and milk could be checked off a list of names on the door. The honor system was operative. During my tenure there the industrial coffee maker became terminal and was put to death. There were many discussions on the relative merits of resurrecting a deep fry from a previous incarnation. I never saw it work.

To boast for a minute, I shall claim to have been in every room of each of the two houses, to have fucked in three, three distinctly different women, and I saw a naked womanin a fourth, which at the time was my own room. Further, I never made love in my own room. I slept at different times in at least nine different locations in the two houses, three in 1705 Mass Ave and six in 3 Sac St. (not including passing out on the couch, meditating in the laundry room and lying in bed to recover from my first LSD experience while still maintaining consciousness.) I do include the living room in 1705 as a sleep in room, because I "occupied" it during the end of my innocence.

Draupudie lived in the gray stucco building catty-corner from 3 Sac. Street above the massage parlor. Arjuna visited her there behind the door with the police lock. She sat and smoked filtered menthols
while he paced in front of the square mirror over the mantle and dictated. The yellow walls echoed his bold tone.

Urban Rat walked with me to a restaurant/bar called "John Harvard's" which had been once named "33 Dunster Street" its address. I had worked there for one week and had left there on the insistence of my family to return to Cincinnati for "treatment" in 1978. That had been the beginning of my unwilling incarceration in Cincinnati, then Worthington, Ohio for extended psychiatric treatment that had led to my being on Haldol upon returning to Cincinnati in 1982 for another hospitalization (this one voluntary) at a State facility. Certainly, the visiting of these "power places" held a strong impact for me. (These places changed my life.) On the return subway trip from Harvard Square to downtown Boston my spouse and I had an ongoing and rather difficult conversation. It was not possible for her to understand the impact that the places were having on my emotions. I think I began to remember the LSD experience, the closeness with Draupudie that had changed me, and the fear I had of my father. I may have been becoming paranoid. She was talking about how she was having trouble keeping up with me when I put a token in the subway turnstile for her and for myself, and she put one in for herself as well (wasting a fare), and she said, "Maybe I should take amphetamines . . ." and I replied in banter (which I now regret), "Or I should take tranquilizers." The Haldol I'd been taking all these years as an anti-psychotic is a tranquilizer. It was as though she were hinting I should go back on the old dosage, and I was resisting. I think I am more paranoid and impressionable with less Haldol. Just by saying I might need a tranquilizer so she could keep apace seemed a major concession. We were on the crowded train and exited at the wrong station. Then we got on a second train then transferred to another . . . if I recall correctly, we were on the third train when I felt faint standing in the crowd. At first, I thought that the suggestion of a tranquilizer was tranquilizing me. It didn't make sense as I struggled against dizziness. I knelt down, gripping the backs of my wife's knees and then her hand and stood, then knelt again at least twice. I blacked out as the train came into a station. I remember stepping toward a seat as I lost consciousness. When I came to, I was being attended to in a seat by my wife and a Metropolitan Boston Transit Authority (MBTA) official who was just arriving on the scene. I stated that I had thought something might have pricked my arm. My wife and the official ushered me off the train when I felt comfortable enough to stand. We sat on a bench at the station where an accordion player played to a small crowd. My wife answered the official's questions. He asked if I was on any medication and she said I was on medication for "schizophrenia."

I became concerned that my wife was disclosing unnecessarily personal information. She expressed alarm at the notion that I believed I might have been drugged on the subway. Next came two EMTs who checked my blood pressure. I stood and shuffled my feet, dancing as the sphygmomanometer was pressurized. The official brought orange juice and water. I drank. The EMTs wanted to take me to a hospital and I had the feeling that my wife wanted that also. It became apparent that my wife was interpreting the incidental fainting and my distrust of going to the hospital as "paranoid schizophrenia." They asked me to sign a form saying that I had declined treatment. I refused to sign. At this point I began to lose faith that my wife had my best interest at heart and in mind.

We managed to ride the subway then walk back to my Aunt's. Once I was seated on the couch, sipping some juice, my wife began to lobby with the other members of the family and soon sat down while others were coming and going and to tearfully confront me with her fears that I was losing my grip on reality and to insist that I keep my "promise" to take the medication at the dosage of 5 milligrams.

Sitting on the white couch facing the mantle under the giant, square, wall-size mirror that rises to the high, pale green ceiling. She said, "Arjuna, I have to talk to you." Her voice was husky, she took my right hand in hers, then wrung it, then was gently wringing her own pale hands, warm and sweaty. She was struggling to keep her composure.

"OK," I said.

"I know you had a fright on the subway."

"Yes. I don't know what happened. How long was I out?"

"Thirty seconds, or so."

"I had a sense it was longer. Was I in the seat?"

"The seat you were moving toward?"

"I was moving toward a seat?"

"Yes."

"I clutched the back of your knees. It was crowded. I felt dizzy. I listened to a couple talking in their seats."

I could see them. Their faces were next to each other by the streetcar window. I can't remember their faces, or their voices, but they were talking about school and their lives. I felt like I was part of their lives. I imagined I was a visiting poet in a big gray and red sweater, with a long ponytail and a funny colorful hat. I was wearing the Swedish Fiddler's hat that Rat had knitted for me.   The couple appeared mundane yet interested in one another's lives. I sensed a quiet common intellectual passion. They had to be college students. I sensed that Rat and I were in the middle of an argument and she had just let me have it with her ghostly magic. I truly felt my life was in danger. I didn't trust her. Her interests were not my best interests.

"I felt you grabbing my knees," she seemed irritated.

"I was losing consciousness. I was scared."

I looked around the room and saw my Aunt talking on the phone by the kitchen door. I couldn't hear her.

"You were only out for a moment."

"Where did the MBTA guy come from? He was on the train when I came to. How did he get there so fast?"

"I don't know."

"How long was I out?"

"I want you to take your medicine."

"No. I don't think so."

"You promised." She paused and her face became wrought with concern and charity.

I didn't trust her. She hadn't answered my questions and I didn't think she ever would. I had the sense that I was part of a Mafia family. And she was disrespecting me. I began to anger. Boston seemed a scary, dangerous place when touring with my family. A decision about where to have dinner was under discussion. Urban Rat kept me diverted away from this discussion. I had a sense that she was trying to control the conversation. She wanted to move me to the medical issue, and I wanted to know what had happened on that train that I had been kept from seeing. Rigo's daughter came in clutching a little fucking stuffed walrus with her mom trailing and Rigo talking, preoccupied. I wanted to talk to Rigo about blacking out on the train, but Rat had already put him on alert. Had I trusted her too much? Should I be grateful for surviving whatever happened and accept her explanation? Had I gone unconscious and killed someone with my lethal hands and feet? What in hell had happened on that train? I was talking about my paranoia. Had she protected me? Or had I protected her? Or were we working together, collaborating again. I felt our love had taken a serious blow. I wanted to know the truth. She looked me in the eyes and lied her ass off.

I left the room. First, I stood and surveyed the kitchen from a distance, then I approached my Aunt and asked her a question. She answered diplomatically, and I

thought for a moment that I was being left behind. I knew Draupudie would get all this down. I knew the muse would save my words. Urban Rat had committed to a script that I no longer approved. I wanted off the damn medicine. I pulled a harmonica out of my pocket and tried to interest Rigo's daughter in a little "Skip to My Lou." Grandpa was Lou. He'd been the patriarch until now. Kunti's husband, my earthly father was retiring. It was his turn now. I did not care for his attitude. He wanted me on the medicine. He did not support my desire to buy the loft back in Cincinnati. I wanted to connect my work at the halfway house to the restaurant at Κριστοσ ανδ Δρυϖακισ *The Urban Rat blocked this idea. She couldn't see me as a restaurateur. Kunti's father had run a restaurant. I managed the kitchen in the halfway house.*

Back in the living room, Urban Rat sat on the white couch with her shoes on the pale rug wringing her hands. Her diamond and gold band flashed in the warm bright light. As Arjuna crossed the room he looked up at the mirror and down at his niece. He wanted to finish the conversation. Her pause kept his logic from ever coming to completion.

"You promised," she began when he sat down.

"What?"

"Remember Riley when he went off his meds?" she asked.

"Don't compare me to Riley!"

"I'm sorry."

"I don't compare you to anyone. I wouldn't."

"Arjuna, I'm sorry. I didn't mean to compare you to Riley. You're right."

"He isn't a writer. He doesn't work a job. He hasn't worked a job in years."

"OK. OK. I'm sorry. I shouldn't have compared you."

"If you want to compare me to Riley, then I'd like you to talk about your mother. I want you to talk about something difficult for you."

"Arjuna, you're mentally ill. You have to take your medicine."

"Let's talk about your mother. Do you know how it hurts me when you publicly tell people I'm schizophrenic? You didn't have to tell that to the MBTA guy on the train."

Urban Rat's eyes pooled up. She looked at Arjuna and dabbed at her eyes with a tissue. "We were talking about your meds."

"Rat, I'm telling you I don't know how the MBTA guy got there so fast."

She turned away, frustrated, and when she turned back her voice was huskier. There was a scent of musk in the room. Rat's bangs hung limply on her forehead. Her eyes flashed with anger then softened. Arjuna glanced at their reflection in the mirror. Kunti, Arjuna's mother, stayed away from the couple.

"I can't reason with him," Urban Rat turned to Rigo, Arjuna's brother, who stood near her on the pale rug, next to the pale couch.

My head. My wife wanted me to take these meds because I blacked out. Did any of these people know me? I engaged Rigo.

"Rigo. I had a scare."

"I heard."

I read his face. He took the Rat's side.

"Rigo. I haven't heard from you in a while. I write to you."

"I know."

"Rigo, I'm pissed at you because you don't return my e-mails."

Rigo was doing this family thing. They're lying their asses off. He couldn't make this decision for me.

"Rigo, Rigo, Rigo, Rigo, Rigo," Arjuna said. He stood and walked past Urban Rat to Rigo. He rhythmically hit his brother on the shoulder with his palm.

"Don't hit me."

"Why don't you write to me?"

"All right. I owe you some e-mails. Don't hit me."

"OK."

"You had a scare."

"YES. I don't know how long I blacked out."

"Trust Urban Rat."

(Is that the lie? Did Rigo urge Arjuna to trust her? Had Arjuna blown his whole situation by being married? He understood that Urban Rat had wanted him to go to the hospital when the paramedics came. When Urban Rat and Arjuna returned from their vacation I talked to both of them. He obviously needed some medication. By then too much had passed to recon-
struct the events of the four days in Boston with any accuracy. By then I was dealing with outcomes of a human dilemma. By Arjuna's account it became an opportunity to adjust his life.

Draupudie held as his muse, while Urban Rat became frighteningly career oriented and moved out of the apartment. Before long she was living with Kunti and Arjuna's father.)

"If she can't honestly tell me how long I was out on the train . . ."

"She has told you. You won't listen."

"Rigo, there was an MBTA official in a uniform standing behind us."

"She told you."

I didn't agree with Rigo. Rat had not satisfied my question of the timeline. But, she wasn't going to budge. Urban Rat and I had never had an argument in front of the family.

Arjuna moved back to the pale white couch next to his wife.

"It's disrespectful of you to pressure me about my medication in front of my family. I won't pity you. Just because your mother died when you were young, I will not pity you. You're a strong, independent person."

I confess that I felt confused as the weekend progressed. As my wife pleaded with me, I asked for a divorce. We argued in the large living room of my Aunt's apartment facing the wall length mirror over the fireplace. As I paced around the room, I had the sense that we were acting out a larger drama. The next day when the whole family gathered again for another party, I thought of Draupudie and had a sense that I was moving toward her and away from Urban Rat.

Arjuna remembers being with blue-eyed Draupudie in her Cambridge apartment with the yellow walls, the square mirror over the mantle, Ossibisso on the turntable, and the typewriter on the table. He had been dropping out of Harvard at the time, consumed by love for this debutante. The third floor apartment, on the corner of Massachusetts Avenue and Sacramento Street had a police lock, and six rooms. Arjuna had once sat with Draupudie in her bedroom looking at her altar where she burned nag champa and candles. During most of their time together they engaged in lively conversation. Then, after twirling about the room in her blue jeans, she sat in front of the typewriter, waiting for him to dictate, and he did. He wandered the United States and Canada, dictating for her, the saga of Jack Acid. This was his youth and her maturity. Where they smoked from her roommate's plant in her small wooden bowl and they both had headaches. She had reached to the mantle for a small glass jar with a golden lid, turned the lid, revealed a red-brown paste. Tiger Balm with camphor and eucalyptus oil blended together. He had watched her swirl her white finger in the blend; he imitated her motion, then started to put his finger to his lips. She scolded him, rubbed her digit to her third eye. Arjuna checked her silver rings. He overheard a conversation with the blond roommate when they talked silver. The two had laughed at Arjuna's expense. About silver being a *gift*. His heart always returned to this room, the apartment where he lived with her later.

When *Jack Acid* was published, she was at the New York party. He was just divorced. His first wife, Urban Rat, was there at the party. Two important women. His first wife had been a painter. He did not want to remember her name. She never signed her paintings. He kept a drawing after they separated. Arjuna had schizophrenia and therefore was not responsible for a lot of his actions. His ex-wife and Draupudie had something in common. They both held Arjuna responsible for all his actions, at least in their hearts, and as we know, to a good woman, hearts and minds are not so far apart.

That night in the Cambridge apartment where Draupudie took dictation she told him she was a Gemini and shy about sex. He was an Aries and was sewing his wild oats before her eyes across the street at the CENTER FOR HIGH ENERGY METAPHYSICS. He had been a lightning rod, a catalyst, for the metaphysics of the mid-seventies. Baking wheat bread from the *Tassajara Bread Book* recipes with acknowledgments to his own Aunti Zen, eight loaves at a time on the massive wooden counters, his large strong hands were watched discreetly by feminists and all women of the place. There were lesbians and gay men, too. He loved Draupudie first but had others.

He knew there would be problems with modernity. Draupudie said, "I hate to cook. I love to do dishes."

Arjuna was having coffee from the Melita pot.

"I'll cook," he said.

She had an avocado. They rolled chunks of pale green ripe avocado in yellow hemp cigarette paper and ate them, with white daubs of mayonnaise falling to their shirts; what an indoor picnic, they took turns reading aloud from hardbacks.

Arjuna had been trained to live in a culture where women cook and men clean-up. Arjuna baked bread and washed dishes. Draupudie's needs worked well with Arjuna. In a sense, she never *took* dictation. In fact, she was as much the author as he. Her first husband had two children with his first wife, and he had written several Buddhist tomes with her vital assistance. Arjuna knew that Draupudie would be divorced before the party to celebrate *Jack Acid* and yet he did not know that he would be divorced from his first wife. Draupudie knew all of Arjuna's secrets. She could read him as he wrote. She knew which of their classmates he had fucked. She knew of each hitchhiking adventure, and of the rainbow miracle that had transformed his front tooth. (He had traveled by thumb to the Second Perennial Poetical HOOHAW in Oregon and on the magical journey had found the end of a rainbow springing from the magic lotus tree out of the California evening. The light had healed his broken tooth as he sat like Buddha in a puddle beneath the source of the mystical light.) She knew each of the mystics that Arjuna had met. He had no reason to keep secrets from her, as she performed the duties of muse and typist, ensuring the survival of his story. So, when he knew of her divorce, before she did, she perceived him as a wedge. Arjuna had whispered to her about the time he saw her with her ex in black leather walking the streets of Nob Hill in the nineties. Arjuna remembered this in '78; the schizophrenia allowed him this vision. He desired hope over any wedge. He believed he had a photo that someone took in the past of an event that had not happened yet. There was no explanation beyond his eternal hope for a love with the darling Draupudie. In the schizo mind hope was not eternal. It was conditional. He yearned for satisfaction, he prayed to her brother, Krishna, and to Buddha.

The Case Manager talked of Maharaj. "The real you is timeless, beyond birth and death. The body will survive as long as it is needed." This spiritual guide told Arjuna to build relationships and forget Draupudie—she was far away. She had rejected the poet before. Born out of Arjuna's anger for ridiculing him by sharing his love letters was a sudden affection for her best friend, Molly, which culminated in a one night stand, and a swim in the indoor pool the next day. Ultimately the resulting conflict rendered Arjuna a poet as he designated himself schizophrenic—in the midst of the struggle he asked Draupudie's hand in marriage. She rejected him. He ran.

Years later, after the Case Manager had taught Arjuna to meditate and medicate, Arjuna and Urban Rat went on their first overnight sailing cruise with his family. They departed Charlevoix, Michigan aboard the yacht Ruddyduck the same day Draupudie married her first husband in Montauk, Long Island. Arjuna's vision of the lake included the beauty of the blueness. Wide blue skies, leagues of water, white foam at play on the blue surface. The sound of wind, waves parted by the heaving bows of Ruddyduck and the drum drum of the diesel auxiliary provided a deep pattern for Arjuna's rhythm of life. This shakedown cruise let Arjuna's family draw together in a team as the six of them became a single unit, hauling on lines, bending sails, heaving anchors and chain day after day until they reached St. Joseph Island. Their course took them under the Mackinac Bridge where Arjuna's camera clicked a panoramic record, and past the straits they navigated Detour Passage under full sail. A glorious voyage for a family at play. Arjuna thought only of his vision of the lake. His parents and brother appeared, then disappeared from his view as he slept close to Urban Rat and dreamed of Draupudie. He could not fight his unconscious mind. Arjuna thought of the Case Manager back in Cincinnati and how he described the mind. Arjuna breathed the cool lake air in starlight, when he walked on the dewy deck to take a leak over the side as the yacht swayed gently on its mooring in a hidden harbor. He wondered where Draupsie and her new man honeymooned. Arjuna's mind was miles from Lake Huron, dancing with a young debutante, praying that she might clearly type each word. He was working on *Jack Acid* as the breeze blew through his graying hair.

They were all of the leisure class in America, though Draupudie and Arjuna shared a capacity to slum with the poor and impoverished and learn from the experience. Only Arjuna knew he was poor spiritually due to his thirst and craving for demon rum and the evil weed. These were some of the themes of *Jack Acid.* Arjuna wanted to give up this long distance, parallel universe dictation and finally be alone with Draupudie in the way he always desired. He was scared. She was married. Where and how to get a wedge? Would a photo displaced in tim—a photo taken before the event untangle time for him? Arjuna struggled with his dancing mind. He wanted to hope, and his spiritual guide taught him how. Draupudie's wedding was on an estate, elegant and formal, an outdoor ceremony, on a lawn without a tent. It was breezy and subdued. Arjuna saw it in his mental vision and they were all in black. *Could the bride have dressed dark for her own?* A wedge would dishonor the two lovers. No photo? Arjuna feared that Draupsie could not return his love with the ardor he felt. He prayed often to Jesus, to Buddha, to her brother, Krishna. Draupudie had been on the phone with her mother, complaining about Krishna's schizophrenia when Arjuna had come in out of the snowy dark. Arjuna had not known he shared this affliction with Krishna until they met later.

When he researched her later, in the Cincinnati Public Library, for *Jack Acid,* he found an account of Draupsie's wedding in the NY Times. He was pained that the day of the event he had been with the painter, his future wife, and not alone pining for Draupudie. Arjuna felt he deserved no happiness without Draupudie sharing it. She resented his happiness deeply as he learned when he was caught with brown-eyed Molly. Actually, Molly confessed to Draupsie (they were close friends) that she had seduced Arjuna with the green grass that was a harvest of plenty in the CENTER FOR HIGH ENERGY METAPHYSICS, a two-building commune in Cambridge, owned and operated by Radcliffe and Harvard. The quasi-scientific soft-porn novel *The Harrad Experiment* was one version of the Co-op's early history. From what Arjuna could tell, every fantasy of an intellectual and spiritual nature could be experienced within that metaphysical structure. There had to be intersecting stories for the keenest light in all of civilization among the residents. Forty years of existence were celebrated the Summer of Arjuna's biggest discontent, his fortieth Summer. Arjuna felt a recrudescence of his year at Harvard when they were seventeen at so many moments that he could only be a schizophrenic. He felt a certain terror at admitting this tragedy to anyone. He was handsome, with an aquiline nose, large brown eyes, a keen intelligence, well-educated by most standards, but his sense of reality shifted into a new dimension when he began to talk. He told stories. Not exactly a prevaricator, Arjuna was rich with the blood of art and aristocracy, skilled and talented as a harmonica player, a reed voice-flute that stirred folks when he played on it. When he wrote about his life everyday folks bristled with jealousy, scurried about, accused him of narcissism and blamed him for all that was wrong with the world. His confusion at being thus confronted was honest and vital. He did not want to run or hide from any emotion, and his compassion for those he spent time with in Insane Asylums at the mercy of nurses, doctors, orderlies, and social workers frightened him. When he felt most vulnerable, and powerless he also felt compassion.

Paul Thanas

Can the rocks protect you?

Can you have compassion for a flower?
Think of them, gathered among the rocks.
The picture of fragility like a wounded
animal that never had fight. Sunlight,
and rain protect a delicate life, if dealt
in moderation. Rocks shield the wind.

My friend, you move among us
with halting steps, a cigarette always pressed
to your lips, ember glowing and lengthening,
often nearly flaming with passion to breathe
smoke. As your steps weaken, as you cough,
and speak in a high-pitched strain I wonder,

Can the rocks protect you? Is there a way
to extend your days? I want to move you behind
a glass wall, feed you dung mixed with fiber
and give you well spaced drinks. When light
touches you a certain way I think of you gathering
in your glade, not watching, not thinking, just being.

And Then the Cow Was Drownded

When he heard screams from locked doors on his schizo walk he feared mostly for the discomfort of Draupudie and prayed that she was not suffering as he was, nor in fear for his safety. He imagined himself a prince, she a princess, kept apart by struggle and others, but always he returned to that yellow-walled Cambridge apartment with the mirror over the mantle, the girl waiting for him to state the next word. One word at a time, he breathed. Her black hair was natural. Blue eyes the color of sky with wheat in the sun flecked inside her irises. She spun with an hourglass figure that skated on the iced-over pond of all history. Draupudie typed with an imagination as colorful as her skin was pale. But these attributes are true of many women on the planet. Only Draupudie shone for Arjuna. She was leaving for India when he came back to see her. His imagined India became real in her watercolors. Arjuna must find the wedge. Yet not know the full truth. Arjuna knows the unfairness of his knowing too much. Arjuna believes that a photograph must be part of the plot. A photo that teaches her.

I wonder if I was locked up for the indiscretions in the commune. Once we had been stopped by an environmental cop in a red VW Rabbit for riding on the hood of a metaphysician's Cadillac hearse. Had this indiscretion been reported to some "higher authority?" Draupsie and I had been seated side-by-side on the bench seat of the hearse in sweaty Cambridge humidity. We bore the moment with dignity, though I had wanted then to say, "Go out with me." But I had no idea how to begin. Besides she had a boyfriend from the poker crowd. He was older, a country singer, a cowboy, from Washington Courthouse, Ohio.

Or was it the crimes of writing Jack Acid during the Clinton administration? I preferred a morality I had seen in film. I believe I am in a movie of my life. I just stare a lot of the time. I see people at all phases of their lives all at once in the same places. Draupsie knew karma. She ran around THE CENTER FOR HIGH ENERGY METAPHYSICS shouting, "Karma yoga is the only way! Buy karma yoga now, today!"

When Arjuna met the painter, they walked together in the Summer heat in downtown Cincinnati, from Ronald's where they met, where they later married and often partied. She had a studio in the Big Four which she shared with two other painters. This building housed many artists, some squatting, and even housed recording studios. With wide marble staircases five floors and no freight elevator, the building was ideal for the fringes of Cincinnati's artists. The fifth floor housed a commercial radio station's sound facility. The Big Four sat just off the Ohio River near the Clay Wade Bailey Bridge to Northern Kentucky. Urban Rat challenged herself by making eight-foot by five-foot stretchers and painting them in impasto-layered streaks of green and black. Imagine a canvas swirling with dark emotion, layer upon layer of the darkest colors built to a thick, lumpy texture, then put a random streak of bright green diagonally across from lower left to upper right. Moving them became a nightmare as each weighed thirty pounds and her space was on the fourth floor. When Arjuna saw her dark moody canvases, he knew instantly of a depth of emotion. He wanted to strip down and roll with her right then on the wooden paint-streaked floor of the tiny room with a high ceiling. Instead, he held back. They had not yet even kissed. On the way out the couple stopped and wrote graffiti with a black marker in the stairwell. "Killjoy was here!" with the cartoon. The two lovers walked in the heat. The young Arjuna paced himself alongside the tall pale-skinned beauty noting a red tinge in the perspiration around the fringe of her bangs. Her forehead shone in a mysterious auburn. He had to ask. The painter had colored her plain brown locks herself at home and the heat and humidity had caused the color to bleed. She held her head in a dignified manner despite the embarrassment. Arjuna's sympathy went to the painter and a bit of his heart was tied to her that day. Who knows why the young schizophrenic poet felt such passion at the girl's imperfection? It spoke to him of spirituality in a weird magical way and he did not question this attraction. She said she wanted a poet. He felt wanted and accepted in a way he had yet to feel from Draupudie. She was far away. The tall red-haired painter was here, by his side.

As they grew to love one another he quit drinking, putting aside the Wild Turkey as if it had never been meant for him at all. He remembered standing in Ronald's, the green and pink neon reflecting in the window, holding the clear brown liquid to the light, watching the world through its embers. The burnt sour mash flavor warmed his gums, lips and tongue. He had felt a glow in his gut then.   The painter's most unusual quality was her unwillingness to see her unusualness. Not that she didn't affect certain behaviors of the day, such as the violent punk music with its anarchic lyrics. She listened to the Psychedelic Furs, The Cure, Joy Division, Durum Column, and Siouxie and the Banshees. But, this was trendy, and kept her tight within a small clique of artists and museum workers.

When she began to paint in the new studio she turned to figurative work and with Arjuna as her beau she took a photo from before they met. He'd been photographed in a string hammock by a young playwright. When the painter saw the photo she chose to paint from it. Arjuna had a musician friend, Leo, whose wife was a dancer. The couple had a child, and at the christening, young Arjuna dressed in white with a Panama hat. And with a strong line, and impressionist touch, she captured the essence of the writer at rest above the forest floor. The painting featured rich foliage rendered in minute detail. Up close, individual sticks and leaves in varying hues of gray and brown stood out, but from a distance one sensed a forest floor beneath the reclining poet, and the white strings of the hammock stretched from Arjuna's white suit. The green leaves from the surrounding trees shaded the poet while light filtered on and around him in bright dapples. Arjuna knew her talent then. The unusualness was a strength of vision, a close tie to emotions of loss and dejection that kept her subtle and vulnerable to people and the artistic impulse. She could see a face and render it. Except her own. In the twelve years they were together, she had not had the ability to reflect her face accurately. A quirk perhaps, this inability to see herself, but hardly a flaw. She was terribly hard on herself and tolerated much abuse.

After she stopped painting, she took on more domestic chores to give Arjuna more time to dictate. He shouted at all hours. They moved in together, to a flat with a study for him. Both were thankful for the separate study. She did not understand Arjuna's passion for Draupudie. She hardly knew of their long-distance, schizophrenic connection. The painter would not willingly share her man, so Arjuna kept many writings from her. When she did read bits and pieces, she was always flustered by the naughty bits. Like Draupudie, she was shy about sex, but unlike Draupudie, the painter and the man co-habited for long years.

Are bodies young to look at or to touch, and feel, their skin taut and toned? Is youth wasted on the young?

Arjuna in his fortieth Summer knew less about the wedge than others. He could not even see the events that would build the wedge. He prayed that his vision would draw him closer to the love of someone, and that when the someone was *someone,* it would be like he wanted.

At the publishing party Arjuna's ex-wife would see how much Arjuna loved Draupsie and let him go. Feel happy for him. He knew that with all his heart. The painter would be a trusted friend in divorce. At the party she saw the way Arjuna looked at Draupudie and said to him, later, "when I saw the way you looked at her, I knew." And that let him know she supported his decision. She had read and helped edit Draupudie's typing of the novel. She put aside her painting in the struggle to understand him. She moved him from a collaborator to a compromiser. As a schizophrenic, he could no longer compromise. Arjuna asked himself: why am I here on this planet earth? *To be with Draupudie.*

The only answer that kept him working. To Arjuna work was always part of his life.

One day when he lived in the Over-the-Rhine ghetto under the dance studio, he walked home from his clerical job downtown in an office tower. As Arjuna crossed Fourteenth Street, burning embers were floating from the sky. Chunks of black soot, rimmed in coals, smoked and swirled between the tenements. A building burned downtown. At home, he flipped on the TV. Big Four was on fire. Arjuna called the painter at her apartment. The studio had been torched. Her huge dark canvases were water damaged.

He and Urban Rat had worked together at marriage, at poetry, at painting, at radio, and at social work. They had grown in stature as artists, then she had become obsessed with thoroughbreds. She began to question him. To doubt his passion for her. She saw his schizophrenia flower. They argued more and more. One morning he went out to buy flowers and bagels for her birthday and the bagel shop was closed, the flower shop was closed, and he waited for them to open. *Who ever heard of a bagel shop and a flower shop being closed on Thanksgiving?* He could not comprehend. When he returned empty handed, she was crying. His bags were packed. In one suitcase, he had packed every version of the manuscript for *Jack Acid*. He did not tell her what was in the bag. (His schizophrenic mind was taking that bag to Washington, D.C. for copyright purposes.) They were driving to Columbus, Ohio to fly to Boston, Massachusetts to meet his parents and his aunt, brother, sister-in-law, niece, cousins, and their wives. Actually, one of his cousins was gay and didn't have a wife. Arjuna hadn't touched the grass. She was a wreck. As she cried, he felt no sympathy for her. He did not identify with her fear. They made the plane, with time to spare. In Cincinnati, an urban Mecca, flower shops were closed. He could sort of understand a bagel chain being closed on Thanksgiving . . . and he could hear Arlo Guthrie talking about Alice's Restaurant and there was a certain irony to the whole ugly story.

When they arrived in Boston, they took a cab to his aunt's apartment in Brookline, in a wealthy middle-class downtown residential neighborhood, and then waited for the family to gather for a long drive to Norfolk, Massachusetts where everyone was to celebrate a holiday near and dear to the people of New England. Arjuna and the painter were vegetarians and planned not to eat turkey, but who cared? Arjuna chatted with the hired cook about a favorite Cincinnati band without a current hit. He had the sense that he was about to bust out and go back to his old haunts and could not explain why. Yet everything went well.

Arjuna wanted to live in that gray stucco apartment building across Mass Ave from the grocery with Draupsie. He'd self-medicate with a little Guinness Stout. He'd cook for her. With *Jack Acid* a bestseller he could teach writing, edit and take less Haldol so he'd lose weight and cycle daily from Cambridge. He didn't care about going out at night. She could go out if she wanted.

"So I wanted to thank her. It seemed like each woman was a vessel that held the secrets I craved. But, Draupsie was shinier, gem like, she shone in the desert of the Winter. Really, there was no desert around Draupudie. She was different. I thought about what my earthly father had said. The only thing about her was that she was here, not far away. But Draupudie wasn't here or far away. She took this dictation. She listened to every word my astral body wrote. Draupudie was the vessel for my schizo story."

"Stay."

"Never said that."

"Could have said, 'stay'."

"Never said that."

"Like a blues. A, A, B, B, only it's A, B, A, B—sort of. That's as formal as I get.

"Could have said, 'stay'."

It's all about Go. Trying to write a novel between meals, meetings, and seeing you. I have to work, you know. Go is this wonderful board game where . . . where one is always playing out the corners and then moving to the edges. Learning situations that are observed as predetermined. I could take this conversation and engage here. But if I do, I gain nothing—so. Time to get a meal. Choosing the battles. In the Gita, Krishna says: "Arjuna, you must fight." But, Krishna never said, "choose your battles." That was said by a supervisor.

"Never said that."

"Could have said, 'stay'."

Paul Thanas

Tool of the proletariat vs. Pawn of the aristocracy or
Pride of the proletariat vs. Tool of the aristocracy

I arrived in St. Petersburg, June 18, 2000; it's a full day later than scheduled. The hush as the plane landed erupted into murmurs of quiet anticipation, awe, perhaps fear. The pilot followed a dirty, yellow car with a flashing, orange light on top to the terminal where we disembarked in a cool, light drizzle onto the tarmac. The last one off the second of three rusty buses, I walked into the decrepit brick building with Cyrillic and English lettering on the outside. Officials in blue uniforms stood off to the side, their faces too young for such jobs. Inside we formed lines on the lower level of the two-story, beige, tile interior. All my thoughts were of fear at rumors. This was Eastern Europe, Russia, my ancestral homeland from a much earlier time. A whole era had come and gone between the exodus of my family and now. My reverie was broken by two men carrying a third in a wheelchair down the stairs, straining, banging, and grunting in deep voices. No ramps. I thought about my manuscript tucked in my bag and wondered if Jack Acid might be appreciated here. Would there be a way to get it translated? I wondered if I could be imprisoned in Russia for bringing such controversial art across an international boundary. A wide sign above detailed St. Petersburg as the Gateway to Russia, depicting the world centered here. Then I figured out how

355

invisible I was. The line moved. After a fifteen-minute wait in a queue I had to pull my wire-rims down and remove my Panama hat for the border check. Not a word was exchanged. The official was a woman who looked to be in her thirties. No nonsense, just gestures signaling me to pull down my disguise so I would resemble my passport photo.   I paid four quarters for a luggage cart, with no idea how far to a taxi. I wondered if I would ever find my bag as the antique, chrome carousel turned. Military police in gray with clubs and pistols paced by. Outside in the light, through an intense pressing crowd of greeters I found a man who spoke English. He offered a taxi. I told him Kazanskaya, Hertzen University. He thought for a moment and I repeated my question. Pedagogical Institute? He said, fifty U.S. dollars is a lot of money. I said, fifteen. He said, twenty. I said, let's go. He shouted, Sasha. A thick-browed fellow in plain black boots led the way to a gray Mercedes wagon. It ran very smoothly while he drove the unlined wide roadways bordered by wild looking green spaces. I saw a man throwing a stick for a big black dog. The huge gray high rise apartment complexes looked forlorn and industrial, a legacy to the sixties I guessed. As he drove, I thrilled. He edged out a faded Fiat tapped his horn securely and sped all over the roadway. A sport driver, fully concentrating. I noted the one wide windshield wiper and the huge convex interior rear-view mirror. The car ran like it had been designed for this purpose. I asked him his name, he turned, grinned, and said, Alexander. I had a sense of exchangeability. I could be any long-haired foreign visitor. Anonymous, yes, individual, maybe, distinguished? Who was? I wondered what made me different on the outside. People saw me. Khakis and a white linen blazer stood out as a novelty. But, what was different about me inside? I wouldn't have an affair with a married woman. A deference to duty. An appreciation for privilege. These were not outstanding traits. I had been taking photos all the way from the Midwest. My first photo in Russia was of the wonderful blue world map which hung in the terminal entry. At the center, St. Petersburg. What genre would this version of the trip fall into? What a long trip it had been to get through the airports out of the Midwest. When I began to see St. Petersburg proper, I was overwhelmed with a sense of difference. I had not tried to imagine it. I had seen photos, but my first image was the walls of buildings and the lack of smaller structures. Everything

356

seemed to be grand, large, dominating, and beautiful. Hundreds of windows on each of the structures, with so many rounded tops, and there I saw a palace, Eastern looking spires reaching into the gray. This country would bring me something new. A start, perhaps.

I haven't learned much Russian. My goal is to retain the names of the islands in the Neva before I leave. There are forty-two islands. I like to set attainable goals. I'd like to get angry once in Russia. I want to come back with a different view.

Today I walked past the yellow and white Grand Hotel Europe with its red awnings after changing dollars to rubles at its bank. Two things: The side street was unbelievable. Clean cars, a cat sleeping in the shade of a lamppost, shoe-shine available, people looking casual and wealthy, spending in two or three days what I'm spending in a month. Then I watched a motorcycle formation. When I looked back, I saw a set of motorcycles followed by a convertible with a movie camera. Action on the set.

That section of St. Petersburg evoked memories of Beale Street where I was alone and sure Draupudie, my muse, was up the street digging the other end. I had this sense we were working at both ends. Hoped to meet in the middle. But, that's a whole digression about what I did when Urban Rat and I first separated. First, I have to tell the story of our argument, and before that a moment of intimacy, that I was not meant to see.

They were fucking aggressively, loudly or he was chewing at her pussy, his liver spotted hands hard at her tits, the back of his gray head bobbing, his beard moving side-to-side, a shuttle-cock face.

I watched, be-torn. Fascinated with her head on the yellow-brown wooden, sharp-edged, rectilinear coffee table, inches above the hardwood floor. They were fucking in the living room and I could see this, torn from the closeness I felt for Father getting some from her, my mother, and that frightening taboo that I shouldn't see Mom and Dad going at it all that grunting hanging out as comfortable as the day in the sun on the deck by the lake, calm, blue, placid. Inside my heart churned for a look at my own frigid sex-life, my kisses smoke-less compared to their comfort with each other. They ought to have a medal for marital energy and big-thrill sexiness. I love my mom and pop, but I never would have sneaked a look, except that they left my dream door open. I look through that door and see snippets. I wonder that they are visions of the truth. This was hardly a vision, just a glimpse of a moment or two of tongue thrusting, before the shutter snapped shut on this moving, noisy twosome I love, as a twosome that fuck and fight and fuck and fight and fuck and fight until death.

The meaning in my life is anger. An angry woman who hates me for talking about my life. Urban Rat is angry about being left behind, but hell, she walked out when the going was the toughest. We were in Boston for Thanksgiving at my Aunt's house. I've tried to tell how we argued in the subway, but I couldn't get to the part about the divorce. Here it is. Then, if I can keep the time straight, I will try to tell, about Memphis and Beale Street. When I show these fragments to other writers, who are better, and know more about writing, they suggest making the whole novel about one scene, or one day. I don't think I can do that. My schizophrenia exists over a long period of time. My therapist claims that only the present exists. In a pure sense, we agree, but this is a novel and novels have many pages that can be leafed through back and forth, quickly or slowly. Novels also have linear progressions, so that if a reader follows along, page by page, then the author reveals what is necessary for the reader to know.

In any case, I sat on the my Aunt's pale couch with Urban Rat in the Fall of ninety-seven and argued.

"I want a divorce!" I said.

"You promised," she said.

"I want a divorce."

"You promised."

I'm thinking about how she said I promised to take this medicine and I didn't believe her. I knew things were getting better.

"You need to see a therapist," I said.

"I will. And, I'm moving out."

"We need to see a therapist together. But, first, you need to get your own."

"As soon as we get back, I will get a therapist."

"OK."

"Will you take your meds as you promised?"

"Just because I passed out on the train, you want me to take meds?"

"You promised."

"This is awkward. I can't call my therapist because he's in Scotland with his in-laws. I don't think the meds are the issue here. You did not have to tell the paramedics that I have schizophrenia. They didn't need to know that. You betrayed my trust."

"You thought you had been drugged."

I paused. The possibility had crossed my mind. I wanted to talk to my therapist. I wondered if I could call his supervisor? If I called long distance, I might get a number to call overseas and talk to him and get the help I needed. My family doctor had just retired. I could talk to him . . . but his heart was failing, and I had to choose a new primary care physician. All this seemed overwhelming as she sat there, confronting me, crying, wringing her hands, crying, and pleading.

"Yes. It's possible."

I got away and talked to the supervisor on the phone about the blackout on the subway. We went over the whole story after he assured me that there was no way to reach the therapist until we returned to Cincinnati. I stood in the bedroom where Rat and I were staying. Aunt's photos hung all around. In her place, I felt odd fighting so publicly. The rest of the family had paraded in and out of the pale room as Rat and I faced off. While I dialed the phone in the bedroom, I looked at a photo of Grandfather Lou, as a boy in Glasgow, Scotland, eight years old with his whole family. All the figures wore skirts and knee-high socks. The photo was taken in 1907. Great-grandfather Meyer was gray bearded, stern looking and surrounded by large women dressed simply in dark clothes. I couldn't tell if this was their native garb or if they were only a year in Scotland as Aunt tells. I trusted nothing but what I saw with my own eyes. I hardly trusted that. Lou wore a plaid kilt. Once he told me he crossed the Atlantic on the Numidian when he was eleven, in 1909. I thought he was born in 1899. Time stalled while looking at the photo, talking to the supervisor on the phone, Rat waited, chatting in the living room, and nothing added up for me. I knew that I wanted a divorce. I told the supervisor that I wanted to divorce Rat. We talked calmly. He suggested I put off any major decisions until we returned to Cin-

cinnati. I had disturbed his Thanksgiving. I tried to talk to him about his family. His voice seemed lighter then. We talked calmly. He agreed it would be disorienting to black-out on a subway. I felt weak mentally. I could not get the help from him that I needed. I had to face this alone. I held to my feeling of outrage and anger at her confrontation to secure my sense of self.

Arjuna left Cincinnati the second Monday in January. Urban Rat had moved out the day after their return from Boston. She had been methodically sneaking in and taking things when he worked at the radio station late Sunday nights. He finally got the nerve and spent a hundred dollars to have the locks changed. So, he was going to Memphis. His father-in-law had called, not knowing about the split-up and told him that Christmas would not be in Memphis, as Arjuna had wanted, but that the family would meet in Pigeon Forge for hiking at a condominium. Papa Rat had sounded drunk and Arjuna had agreed with everything he said and told him nothing. Arjuna had the phone number changed before he left. Papa Rat had been calling and letting the phone ring then hanging up. Arjuna was going to Memphis. Driving alone. He took several hundred dollars in small bills, only his street shoes and five days' worth of warm clothes.

On the drive he went faster and got crazier. His thoughts went into near hallucinatory experience. In Tennessee he got the Toyota up to a hundred twenty-one miles an hour in the mountains. He had the sunroof open. The car would go no faster. Fifth gear wouldn't redline, but he tried to push it to the maximum. He ran the engine in the power curve continuously, always revving and roaring. Fearing state troopers, after speeding, he got off the turnpike. On a back road he crossed in front of a train, spotting lit pink flares. For a moment he thought about what he was leaving behind and wondered if he had been hit by the train. Back in Cincinnati there'd be an obituary after an article about a gray car crushed by a freight train in rural Tennessee. He took back roads all the way into Memphis. He wondered if he passed the spot where Martin Luther King was killed.

In Memphis he found Beale Street. Home of the blues. He hadn't brought harps, a guitar, or any of his poems. He planned to check out the scene. Maybe he'd play tourist and come back later with an ax. Or, buy a harp at a music store. Memphis was a playground. He checked out restaurants. In a deli he tried to buy half a lox sandwich. He remembered his grandfather, Lou, arguing with his dying wife when she wanted half a sandwich. The guy at the deli said, "save half for later." He couldn't buy a half a bagel sandwich in Memphis. He camped on park benches on Beale Street talking to the natives. Knowing that he was a tourist, he talked to street people. These were black men who wanted money for booze. They repeated their demands as persistently as his family had demanded he take medicine. He wore his long gray hair down, dressed in black with a leather jacket, perfectly shined brown wing-tips, and his black hat with the ear flaps. The ties for the flaps dangled to his shoulders and blew back in the night air.

Arjuna spent two nights in the Holiday Inn. Otherwise, he lived on Beale Street. A tall dark-skinned black man, who resembled an older Michael Jordan, befriended Arjuna. The man asked for money intermittently. Dan listened to Arjuna describe his connection to Draupudie. Arjuna believed he had seen her in downtown Cincinnati five days before and had been afraid to say anything. They had walked past one another at night. She was with another man. Arjuna told Dan that he'd been carrying a torch for her for twenty years.

Arjuna said, "I think I saw her."

"You know you saw her," Dan said.

I didn't know. I thought about her and I prayed that she was still listening and typing in that room. I believed that she was there. Taking dictation about this. I imagined she worked the other end of Beale Street from me, dancing, singing, doing comedy, or just hanging with the street people just out of reach. Dan just wants money.

"Could you give me some money for a sandwich?"

"Let's walk up the street. I'll take you in one of these places and buy you dinner."

"They won't let you do that."

"Why? What do you mean?"

"These are white only places."

"No, I've seen blacks in those places." Arjuna and Dan were walking side by side up the cobbled Beale Street toward B. B. King's nightclub.

"I can't do that, Arjuna."

"I can't give you money."

"How about five dollars."

"No."

"Why not?"

"When I was thirteen, I saw B. B. King at the Ludlow Garage in Cincinnati. I live around the corner from where that club was. Now, it's a pizzeria. I haven't seen B. B. King since then. Twenty-six years. The blues bit me then and I've felt them ever since. Have you seen B. B. King?"

"No. I'm a poor man. I was in the army and now I can't work. I don't have money to go to no show. B. B. King is there tonight. I never seen him. If you've got thirty-five dollars you can see him."

As they walked, a man in a tux blew a trumpet to draw patrons into his bar. A sign said Rufus Thomas would sign records and sing in another club tomorrow. The picture of Rufus Thomas looked like Robert Junior Lockwood. Arjuna had seen him with Charlie Musselwhite and Alvin Youngblood Hart on the House of the Blues Tour in a huge hall in Cincinnati a few weeks before he left.

I tried to raise consciousness in Memphis. I saw these homeless men, like Dan, and thought of my struggle. They just needed room to breathe. Is it true that they were marked as beggars and would be thrown out of a club or restaurant even if they were with me?

Arjuna turned to Dan, "I was first bitten by the blues twenty-six years ago, and I've been carrying a torch for that woman for twenty. It's the blues that brought me to Memphis."

"Arjuna, my man, how about five dollars to get a chicken dinner."

"OK, Dan."

Arjuna peeled a five off his money clip, then walked into the red tent at B. B. King's. "I'd like a standing room only ticket."

"Thirty-five. And your name?"

Arjuna wondered why they wanted his name, but he spelled it for the white lady, who wrote in a ledger in black marker. A young blond man in a white shirt led Arjuna into the smoky club where B. B. plied Lucille in delicate bursts on a crowded stage full of horns and amplifiers. The music spun Arjuna's head, cigar smoke swirled, and he stopped at the end of the bar, near the bottom of a stair.

"Up the stair," the young blond shouted to Arjuna.

Arjuna stood mesmerized by B. B., whose upper lip moved with each finger placement on the frets of shiny Lucille.

"Up the stairs," the man shouted again.

Arjuna ignored the man who put a hand on his shoulder.

"Don't touch," said Arjuna.

"You can't stand there."

Arjuna pulled away from the man and stood, engrossed in the music, swept into a reverie with pure emotion.

Then, in a continuous motion, the man gripped Arjuna's jacket collar, and two other white men converged from the ether surrounding the bar, put their hands on big Arjuna's shoulders and steered him six large steps backward through the open door and tossed him bodily onto the sidewalk under the red tent. Arjuna walked back, resisting the men to keep the tension constant, fell on his ass, banged his head and elbow on a folding table, and laughed. He couldn't believe his luck.

"And stay the hell out," said the blond, looking like a young James Dean, shoulders framed by the doorway to the reclining Arjuna.

"Hey, can I have my money back."

"No fucking way."

Arjuna laughed, picked himself up and walked away, back to his Toyota.

(Arjuna has returned from his road trip. He did not call me when he arrived, nor had he notified me he was leaving. After he disappeared, Urban Rat contacted me and asked me to help her get her stuff out of the apartment. She knew he had a passport now and thought he had left the country. She was scared, upset and called while I was at work. She didn't mention anything about the Boston experience. She was angry with me when I refused to help her break into the apartment and wait with her in case Arjuna returned while she was moving. She was staying with Arjuna's parents. Urban Rat notified me on January twenty-ninth she had broken into the house and moved all her belongings, and some of his, to a storage area. Then on February second I got a call that Arjuna was in Christ Hospital, and when I visited Arjuna, and told him he'd have to take the meds to get out of there, he fired me on the spot and wouldn't talk to me.)

Paul Thanas

No Ritual Haruspicy for This Schizo

Thinking of the time when I was allegedly going crazy. That's what they said of me. I was losing it, so I changed the locks on the doors after the Urban Rat moved out. She had been sneaking in anytime she knew I was out. It especially hurt that she'd come when I was on the radio doing my weekly broadcast. So, so fucking unfair to know and listen while she'd take take take. She took photographs first. All of them. I had some out on the bed to sort. Thinking of her and looking at what we'd snapped together with the SLRs. She had these huge lenses. To her credit she'd moved out suddenly without taking much. To her credit? She said I was mental and couldn't stand to stay unless I took my pills. I suspected her of becoming pregnant and quizzed her when I saw her. Seldom. She denied being preggers. I may have been crazy to believe she might be knocked up. When I changed the locks, she had already taken a lot of the kitchen items. Divorce was on the horizon and it seemed we were ushering it in just like the winter. Cold nights, rain and snow. It's funny though, I think I cleaned the snow off the car a whole lot less that winter. Less than working routine. I had finished writing my first novel. I almost never write a page without mentioning that I had finished my first novel. It's important to locate the text. Now, that I'm in graduate school locating texts is more important than explaining why when I got back from a twenty-one day, thirty-five hundred mile road trip to Memphis, Tennessee, Cambridge, Massachusetts and Montreal, Quebec she'd cleaned out the house of all her stuff and a helluva lot of mine. I was charged up. She took the bait. Bills were a mess, she left pennies though and I threw them all over the floor. She left the pantry alone. There was food for months in there. The herring snacks were still in the fridge. The homemade baklava (even made the fillo) was untouched. I had worked on it for four days after Christmas (spent alone). I began to excavate the pantry with a Korean girlfriend in mind. She had been a Columbus lovely, originally from Toledo, with stunning Chestnut hair, brown eyes under slanted lids and a small slanted body with the chummiest, ymm, yummiest breasts I had ever touched and one time only. (In the introduction I promised to leave her out of this book. Sorry.) Yeah, once. This lovely had been on my mind as I raced through Michigan on I-75 past her Burt Lake summer home where I had once almost visited. Preying or praying on my mind. She knew I was a schizo. We met at a sanitarium in a sexual education therapy group in the late seventies. She talked to me alll the way down that highway, racing me in her VW and I heard her voice even back at home as I powered my way through the pantry and had the realization that the Urban Rat could not alone be responsible for all the clutter and the mixture of cultural and ethnic artifacts (skewers, cookers, steamers, ceramics, glassware, metalware) that I thought then I might might have described, but then was not writing but living living living and poured a can of grapefruit juice into a wooden cup and drank it before the cup split. Lickety-split. So when I found the bloody moldy yams, and thought of these women both fearing pregnancy so. The Michigander from Toledo was virginal and feared babies so so so. And Urban Rat was denying pregnancy and I was schizo and Draupudie took the dictation lithely with diligence and featured every bit of precision of language. I could see her as I imagined myself, mighty Arjuna, taking charge, and losing charge. My Tale of Genji spilling off the page and into the margins. I planned to have a blowout divorce, meet Draupsie and see the virgin somehow in between. What a fantasy. Then the miscarried yams and I freaked. I just freaked. I turned the cold water on in the brown kitchen

Paul Thanas

sink, clicked the switch on the garbage disposal, looked for a shovel outside, but hadn't the courage to toss the bloody mess down. Instead, I took a walk. A dead fetus in my kitchen pantry and shocking planes circling overhead with winking lights somehow tracking me back for thirty-five hundred miles of snow, rain, benzene, incense (nag champa burning in the car), yes tracking Arjuna from the skies to reel him in. Real him in out of the skies, the night sparkled sky. In my fear I studied on dismantling. I figured the old Pioneer Amplifier was transmitting. Unplugged and transmitting like the ticking in my head. A bomb. So I opened it and took it apart, board-by-board, transformer, wires, transistors, resistors, capacitors, screws, clips, all of it dismantled so it couldn't take me with it. The phone rang. I lifted the receiver and shouted the virgin's name and slammed it down. I had changed my number. Who else could it be, but a telepath. A wild ladder into the sky. I walked up that ladder clicked the switches. I climbed into bed after putting all my grandfather's (maternal) red cross pins (past pres and future) onto my army surplus coat . . . flight jacket, and ready for anything when the airmen land. Then I lay down, safe, on the waterbed after locking off the house from the dead baby yaammin the kitchen. Awakened later by police kickin' in my fuckin' door. No ritual haruspicy for this schizo.

Marriage Counselor

Three people are seated in a small room. There is a smell of fried onions. The floor is turquoise and maroon patterned carpet, the chairs are upholstered in light pink. They have beige wooden armrests. There is a sense that a larger room has been fitted into this small room without anyone's awareness being alerted. There are many diplomas on the walls, framed in wood similar to the arms of the chairs.

Two of the people are women, the other, Arjuna, is thinner than three months before. One of the women is Urban Rat her eyelids are large and hooded. Her hair is lighter brown, and shorter than the previous week. This is the second session with the marriage counselor. She is short, yet not petit, with very curly dark hair, flowing in a tangle from her head, her eyes are piercing, dark, full of confidence.

Also on the walls, are prints of over-sized, close-ups of interiors of blue-purple flowers with long, pale green stems.

The three are quiet until the short woman breaks the silence.

"Have you talked since the last time we met?"

"Yes," says Urban Rat.

"Not substantially," says Arjuna.

The three sit for a moment in silence. Arjuna remembers when the police came and kicked in the door. He can hear the officer shouting, Arjuna, we just want to talk to you. Open the door. Then the kicking sound, the wood cracking. Arjuna yelled back, GET THE HELL OUT OF MY HOUSE! Six officers watched him swing the heavy baseball bat in the air. He had hand-turned the poplar bat on a lathe at his brother's in Libertyville, Illinois. It was his Libertyville slugger. Then he had put the bat down when they asked him to talk. He had not wanted to talk to these blue-suited men. You've got bicycles, one said. You have a radio show, said another. Better bicycles than you boys have, he'd countered. Yes, there was a radio show. We have to take you out to the car. Your landlord's here, he tried to call you. You left the water running. We have to put these cuffs on you. What for? You're arresting me? No, no, we're just taking you in. We're not arresting you. What country is this? As the cuffs click. A wise-ass officer said, the United States of Russia. And from there to the car with the white door where he plead for a court hearing. This is arrest without reason. A federal judge this time. This should be illegal. Then to the hospital, with a dozen police officers standing around a semi-dark room. Asking names, trying to do a mnemonic. No way to remember names after the drugs were in his system. They put him in leather restraints and kept him overnight, strapped to the bed, until late the next day, after he'd been shouting, shouting, asking for a woman, he began to talk nice to the nurse. Sweet thing. Sweet thing. She was not fooled. Then he asked a man if leaving the water running was a capital crime. Soon he had been injected with Haldol and something for alcohol withdrawal. He hadn't been drinking this time. They didn't know for sure. Half-conscious they wheeled him on a gurney to an ambulance and they took him to Christ Hospital. The psych ward. What a marriage.

"I wish I could tell you what I've been through," he said. "They call it schizophrenia. My job gone. My radio program, canceled. You've taken a lot of my stuff when you took your stuff out of the apartment. I was going through the kitchen, finding all the shit you'd stockpiled that you'd never use when I just blew. I left the water running in the kitchen sink. Why did the police come?"

"The landlord called them. He got a call from another tenant about the water. I guess it flooded the kitchen or something."

"I had locked off the kitchen. I found rotten yams in the pantry. It looked like a bloody decomposed fetus. I carried it out back with a shovel, and it dripped like blood on the floor. I was so damn freaked out. Do you know you had seven different kinds of cocoa?"

"You're kidding," she laughed uncomfortably.

"In my mind you were pregnant and hiding it. I thought you had an abortion and left the fetus to rot in the pantry. I freaked out."

They sat in silence.

"You were very frightened and disoriented," said the therapist.

"And angry," he ate onion chips out of a bag.

"What are you eating?"

"Onion chips from White Castle."

"Ick. White Castle," she screwed up her face and looked superior.

"Want some?" he offered the bag.

"Yuck. No."

"Have some," and he flung a couple from his fingers to her lap.

"Hey, hey," she said.

"Have some," he flung more at Urban Rat who was looking shocked. Then he turned to the therapist.

"Want some?" he flung some at her, too.

She did not get angry at first, but Urban Rat started in her seat, scowled and started to say something.

Arjuna began flinging faster.

"How long have you been revving up for this?" asked the therapist, her brown eyes blazing.

"I'm angry. There's no passion in our marriage," Arjuna shouted.

"You've quit taking your meds," said Urban Rat.

"No, I haven't. I'm angry," he shouted and flung more chips at her and onto the floor. "You left me. All you cared about was the damn medicine."

"Stop throwing those things," her eyes flashed hot brown.

"Fuck you," he threw more at the therapist, too.

"How long have you been revving up for this?"

"That's a fucking loaded question. I'm angry."

"There's a lot at stake for you."

"Damn right. I lose my physical body by taking those damn meds. They fog up my mind, slow me down, I feel like shit. I can't cycle, or run, or think clearly."

"You quit taking the meds again. I know it."

"No. You're wrong. I don't have a choice. I'm angry. I've been in the fucking hospital. I've got to take these damn meds. I'm not violent. I'm just fucking angry." He stood and ground onion chips into the carpet with his foot. He tasted metal.

"Please don't," says the therapist.

"You're off your meds."

"No. You're wrong. I'm still adjusting to them. I'm just not afraid to express how I feel with passion. You're cold and distant and all you do is push me away when I feel passion. There's no passion in our marriage. You just go through the motions, then you cry. I don't feel pity for you anymore."

"Fuck you, fuck you, fuck you."

"That's creative, Rat," he flung more.

"I don't have to take this. I'm leaving."

"That's your plan. When you get angry, just walk out."

"Fuck you," she stared as tears started.

"OK. OK. How do you feel?" the therapist turns to the woman.

"Hated."

"Why do you care at all?"

"What do you love about him?"

"I love the way," she sobs, "he used to be," sob, "gentle, caring, holding me. Listening to me, giving me things. We used to talk and go out to dinner together. Like the way he was at our wedding. He wore his little wire-rim glasses."

She cried. He didn't offer her tissues.

"I don't pity you. You have everything you need. I wanted to be able to live. To live without these damn pills. I had to suffer. I had to take the damn pills. I'm the one that's schizo. But, you need therapy. You need to talk about your mother. At least now you're feeling something."

She cried and sobbed. Tears flowed, her cheeks reddened, the area around her lips darkened into pink. Her breath came in short bursts.

"I'm sorry I threw those things."

"That's OK."

He picked up onion chips off the floor, dabbed at the carpet with a tissue. She pulled them off her yellow blouse. They passed the trash can around plunking the chips in. He ate a couple from the bag in his hand.

Arjuna left before Rat and went down the stairs of the office building into the sunny cold day.

Mother called last night. She said her breast cancer has metastasized into bone cancer. At first, they thought she had a broken rib. I couldn't talk to Urban Rat about it. She had lost her mother to breast cancer. Urban Rat had been only fourteen. She would have been out of control with grief.

Oh, and the journey took me to St. Petersburg where I'm writing a book about us on scholarship from a Pedagogical Institute and my home university. I'm not fully supported yet, and I'll have some people to thank, but I'm not fully decided whose side I'm on. I think I'm alone, but with a lot of help, I'll pull through, just as I often did when I worked as a domestique for a strong but not tidy cycling team in a country that little appreciated what I had done. Odd, but the respect here is different. In our country they like to be pushed and tugged when they're on top. Here it's different and everyone is so respectful or neglectful depending on how you look at it. I'd tell you where I'm living, and the name of the Pedagogical Institute, but street names hardly translate, and although I like the music of "aya" this and "kazat" that, they describe districts that have poverty and wealth dividing them in ways I've never seen. That's why this painting thing of mine, the art world would obsess me as never before, and why, I think art is the world of the hardest workers, and the dimmest hopes.

I'm a volunteer for the homeless now, not a propagandist in the strict sense, but a writer who advocates for a better share, now and in the future, but through channels like public forums and weekly regional and local tabloids. I'm teaching at a private school, my needs are met, envy of the neighborhood in a social way. But nearly everyone can see it on my face, I'm in love, in a different way. That's why I try to dictate often to Draupudie, and wonder where she is. All my schemes are to win her back, as Draupsie's friend Molly often quoted the Beatles, the one about money, I knew I had to have more for Pudie to take me seriously.

When I teach, I include content about the homeless in my course material. We read George Orwell, well Eric Blair as they say in Britain. Here everyone knows that telephones shouldn't be used to call overseas from local connections. When the Spanish Civil War turned, Russia was too far away for a phone call anyway. The Lincoln Brigades were under trust fund money, with soldiers who were comfortable writers, but not equipped for the way things went. Everyone went to prison to become like others, or died, or fled. I don't know, really, there's a long debate there, but read Orwell or

And Then the Cow Was Drowned

Hemingway if you want that story. I say the artists and the homeless, and all the handicapped are most ignored in Eastern Europe, and the less we say about it the better.

I don't know who decorated my room, but I love it, except for everything. There are two seven inch square framed prints, one of two monks on a swinging bridge, a second of the boat on the beach facing the snowcapped mountain island (or is it a volcano). I think I could write a whole novel about these two pictures. Sometimes I feel like a monk on a swinging bridge over a vast chasm when I pray. Other times when I awaken from a nap I think of myself as a pilgrim about to cross the water to a more desolate place and I then go back to sleep.

On the opposite wall, six feet away, the lead glass mirror with the heavy maple frame, the stern military official, medals and ribbons on one lapel, and stars on the other. Really they're all on his chest, underneath, tattooed. A young Gorbachev with a full head of dark hair, perhaps. Under the watchful eye of several Saints and martyrs, the bed is OK and there are fake wilting roses, potted geraniums and mother-in-law's tongue, with cuttings from a large jade plant and another geranium on the sill.

It doesn't matter who I am. When I painted in a cell in a lunatic asylum in 1978, in America, I copied Vincent van Gogh. I set a copy of Lust for Life on the bed, propped a pad on my knee and with oil crayons in my fingers I painstakingly copied plates line for line, mark for mark. It took every bit of focus I could muster. The plate of Pere Tané was in sepia tone so I crafted the first version in black and white then I did a second based in green. Each painting kept me busy for several days. I determined to work eight hours a day, in the locked room. Really it wasn't quite a cell, just a bare room with a huge steel door. I had a window to the outside and a tiny square window in the door with wire-reinforced glass.

I'm standing by my art display in front of the blue-domed, yellow-walled, white, Corinthian columns of the Catholic Church between the Metro entrances on Nevsky Prospect. A man approaches. He is tall, wears
a beat-up, white, Panama hat with a black band, blue jeans, and bright blue sweater. He carries a brown ruck-sack on his shoulder.

The man sports a goatee with thin, graying whiskers on his cheeks. His hair is down his back gray and loose, too long for most men. He walks steadily, but when he sees my painting of the cottage on the hillside, he stops abruptly. Among the hundreds of people walking past on the wide sidewalk, his countenance appears warm and bright by comparison. It is summer in St. Petersburg, the time of the white nights. Summer snow, seeds from the topla trees fall from the sky and collect in white puffs against the gray curbstone. Cars roar past on the six-lane boulevard. He stares at my work as if he has never seen anything with such allure. He seems stunned, his jaw hardens, then he grins widely.

"What an honor," Arjuna whispers to himself. "My luck is incredible."

Think of my fate to be here now, in 2000, and to see a true Vincent. Blues and greens, a farmhouse low in the hills, orange fence, a white blotch of stones that close up looks like a naked woman from behind. But, I'm alone with no one to help me purchase it, and return to the states with it. I wonder if I can afford it. Does he know what he has? Did the Hermitage go out of business? Is it a remnant sale? Is it stolen? Is it a copy? I remember the book I gave Urban Rat for her birthday of van Gogh images recovered from the basement of the Hermitage. They had been misplaced after World War II, hidden from the Nazis and unknown until 1995.

What do we remember of our waking moments? Not all of what we see. Like dreams, some of the images, and some of the sensations stay in our memories. I think I am primarily kinesthetic, remembering body sensations, the touch of a foot in a bathtub, skin against skin, lips on lips. In dreams that are like so many slides in a mental slide show, there are physical sensations, confused between real memory and dream.

While I was in St. Petersburg, I figured it out. At first, I was scared of the underground. Riding it alone frightened me because of the remote possibility of another vaso-vagil contraction and a collapse into unconsciousness. I began to ride alone after the second day. The speed of the trains was smooth, fast, and made this wonderful electric iron on iron whirring

375

sound. There was an odor of diesel fuel in the tunnels. The tunnels are five stories down under the Neva River. The escalator ride is a tilting nightmare. I saw faces of thousands in one day. The Russians looked more defeated than I felt. As a train enters a station there is a whoosh of polluted air. I felt faint at times from the scent. It reminded me of the cabin of Ruddyduck with its kerosene lanterns. On a rough day I hated to go into the cabin because the diesel smell and the rocking of the boat would make me woozy. On Ruddyduck I'd feel like vomiting, on the train I'd feel faint. The trains had these incredible wooden window frames, varnished many times like woodwork on the yacht. The wooden trimmed trains were painted bright yellow inside with heavy drips along the edges above the windows. The paint must have dripped for hours onto drop cloths. In the tunnels, waiting for the trains, I could see the older ones were deep blue, like a computer screen, or the summer sky in St. Petersburg at two in the morning. During the white nights the sky was never quite as deep a blue as the train, which stop running late anyway.

Like I said, I figured it out. Maybe it was the distance from home, the fear, the remove from Urban Rat, and the need to simply watch and be. One day I was riding at rush hour in the morning and I got separated from Jorge, my instructor. He stepped out of the train at the stop with the maroon, mosaic, chipped tile and then stepped back onto another car, having been caught in the rush and then sucked back in like flotsam on an eddy. Then I started to feel it. At first it was disorientation, then a slight buzz, then dizziness. I fought and breathed. I looked around the car. I couldn't see Jorge at all. Let's posit the possibilities if I fainted. I could have been robbed. I could have been left alone for drunk. (Possible even at nine in the morning in St. Petersburg.) I could have been helped by a stranger. Or, I could be let to lie there, ignored until the end of the line. Perhaps an official or policeman would be called. I saw a lot of officers on the trains from time to time, but not on every car. The rush and struggle was so intense, that I felt convinced that my fate would be drastically damaged if I blacked out there. Then, in that moment of dizziness it hit me what I had known was curious all along. Urban Rat had been on my left, on the outside as I blacked out, as though she were going for the seat that was vacant behind me, as I lurched forward, she fol-

lowed. When I awoke, desperate and confused, questioning her and explaining to the MBTA official who had, to my mind, appeared miraculously on the spot, that I had been drugged or duped which she vehemently denied, she was on my right. That is, she had made it to the seat before me. I had not been able to remember this detail which had been disconcerting to me at the time, but just out of reach of my stunned mind. And, it must have been what she was hiding from me all this time. What's more, I was sure, when I returned from St. Petersburg, now two months divorced, several years after the incident on the Boston subway, if I told her of my discovery, my reconstructed memory, she would deny that I had recalled the facts. So, is there a way to get her to tell me what really happened on that train? I have lost hope. I only hope I live to tell about it, and to finish the novel that you are reading, so that we can finally determine if this is a mystery, or if it is a literary work.

Nick the Drunken DJ

I think it was the music that led me to success in the first place. It began with the harmonica, then the radio show, then I got this job as an extra in a soft porn flick called *chickboxin underground* sponsored by the people that make Tasty Buzz, a salt water taffy, wrapped in yellow wax paper, with ground up espresso in it. Available in three flavors, vanilla, chocolate, and coffee, go figure. They claimed that you could work around the clock and never need to piss. Invented by a computer geek, the product was being promoted for over-the-road truckers. But, it was a heavy-set, sweaty guy with a deep voice who ran that late night electric guitar wacky blues show who drew me into the tense dark world of porn. Well, I'd be lying if I said I hadn't seen porn, hell, I'd be lying if I claimed Nick had corrupted me, but now, tonight as I write in this coffeehouse, I want to help Nick, like he helped me. But, that's another story, about when my wife left, when the problem with the meds was at its peak and when my radio show fell apart. I'd like to think that story was well in hand.

378

My muse, Draupudie, whom I count upon to get the story down, was hard at work so I'm going to burden her with yet another side story, which will help my friend Nick who is in trouble now, bigger than me. From what I can figure Draupudie had been a go-go dancer thumping to techno music in Greenwich Village. I couldn't quite believe my muse would take a job like that. And, I didn't think she could find such a place in the Village. But, on authority, I heard, from a reliable source, no questions asked, that, deniability rests with her quarter. She could not have been into porn in NYC while she was taking dictation in the room over the massage parlor in Cambridge, Massachusetts? But a commute? Sure, she'd get on the train at Grand Central, spend the week with her red painted fingers snapping up and down the keys, flush with luster, faint with boredom, as she wasn't absorbed by my story yet, and hell, who can follow the story while typing pages, thirty-five a day. (She worshipped writers though, a top-shelf notch of a muse.) Like I say, she would head back to NYC where she'd dance, her tits bouncing in the cool club air to earn enough money to keep the place over the massage parlor in Cambridge and type the weeks away. She slept at her parents' Manhattan penthouse on the weekends, and never let them know about her clubbing. She'd started as a comedienne, telling jokes about broke novelists, like me, taking classy chicks, like her, to two-hundred dollar lunches, and then shirking the bill.

I was writing about Nick, the drunk. I was a drunk, too, but for today, I've got that one licked. The caffeine thing is killing me, though, and when Nick called, shouted at me over the phone, "Hey, Arjuna, wanna join me and be an extra in this soft porn movie my friend is makin'," I didn't ask questions. Hell, I'd been up for thirty hours, manic on cola and coffee and knew when I came down, I'd have a migraine that would lift my lips over my eye bones and peel the skin off the carrots in my vegetable drawer.

I had no idea that I'd be faced with Tasty Buzz at my peak moment of withdrawal. But it would come, that moment when the yellow wax paper wrappers would clutter in front of the color man on that brown table in the dark TV studio, calling that elusive boxing match, while a bare-breasted commentator used them for pasties on her over-inflated, saline implanted attractions. All I was seeing was a dull day with Nick smoking Camel bullets, smelling of cologne, telling me about his bad marriage, and wishing I could be with my muse, alone in that yellow room, dictating my story. Caffeine torture, I'd call it. An infinite, free source of Tasty Buzz, a mediocre view of the Tasty Buzz spokesmodel and a role walking back and forth behind her powdered naked back, wishing I was still with Urban Rat, my wife of thirteen lucky years. I was not focused enough to keep Urban Rat, that big, beautiful, pale body, out of my mind. More than anything, I dreamed of Draupudie, yet she lived far away, as UR did now. Help me! I wanted to scream. I desired to have the influence over the cosmos to swirl back into working steadily with my muse. But the music and the drinking brought me to porn, and all I can think about is a line from a Poi Dog Pondering song, *Spending the Day in the Shirt She Wore* about "putting my fingers on paintings to see the way they feel." Because all I could think about then was how much I wanted to be back with Urban Rat, the tall, brown-eyed, dark-haired, Swedish painter, touching her paintings, and how much I had fucked up my marriage, lost my job, and blown the radio show. I could imagine the chest of Draupsie, but I had seen the Rat's goodies. And so, I went to be in the porn flick with Nick, just to make me feel better, so I wouldn't be so alone. Even though by then I was probably back with Urban Rat in one way or another, in therapy, and working on re-stabilizing on the meds, and really quite sure this past crisis, with help of a couple of good friends, one of them Nick, would turn out to benefit me.

Now, I wasn't thinking then of benefits, or gains. Mostly I was stuck staring at losses. I wished I was staring at a lassie, and mostly Draupudie stuck to my mind the way those pasties, well, stuck to the nipples that were hidden from my view, but hadn't been long, it was soft porn, after all. Draupsie, she'd been coming and going in my prose for years, and more steady than I'd admit to anyone, even my friend Nick, to be stuck on someone like that, well maybe that could explain my schizo mind.

And that schizo mind is sort of the crux of my story, but Nick's story, well, that's about Crossroad Blues, and the Rainbow Bridge, a couple of beautiful outposts on the left end of the radio dial. A public university station let him show up twice a week, whether he was drunk or not, as long as he didn't smoke in the studio. And he could spin the discs, patter on about stuff that mostly made him sound like a stoner. Since it was late on the weekend, as long as no one complained, and the money came in okay on the bi-annual fund-raiser, he kept the transmitter humming and that guitar blues wafting and drifting over all of Highland Heights and its extremities. From the five-story gray concrete building with streaks of rust from hidden steel re-bar, Nick held court in a little padded studio, boom microphones all around, orange carpet, and a sound board that was small by industry standards. But adequate to spread blues, and late night rock guitar to nearly a million people. (Not that many listened. The GM figured that Nick had ten to twenty thousand listeners over a year, give or take a thousand.) He sat there in the purple cushioned swivel chair, sweating through his over-sized blue overalls, clicking buttons, flipping CDs, headphones over his ears, his mouth inches from the gray foam mic screen, doing what he loved, while fearing his wife was plotting against him.

The beauty in Nick's life was Cammy, wide as a bus, smoked like a tail pipe, and their three children, especially the youngest who studied piano. Cammy had been Nick's sweetie since her hair was short and dark in the sixties. They were in love then, and he longed to have her back. She had become a screaming Harpy, never close enough to touch, near enough to stroke, always just out of reach with a vindictive word and a plea to one of the children. Pam wanted to play music like dad. Nick had a Casio keyboard, and she hated how different it was from the actual ivories on her teacher's upright.

And Then the Cow Was Drownded

Nick loved to tell how he'd taken chubby Pam, his dear daughter just like Dad, to see B.B. King perform when he toured through Cincinnati. After a killer show, finishing with an encore of *The Thrill is Gone*, Nick had sneaked back stage, flashed his press pass, and snapped a photo of Pammy, her back encircled by the star. I had told Nicky of how I had been thrown out of B.B.'s when I was off meds, traveling in the South to Memphis. Nick favored B.B. in that story when he told it to another friend. The tale had circled back to me, and I had forgiven him. Nick's story was better, about how B.B. had said to Pam, "Watch your daddy, and have him bring you back to see me. I want a piano lesson next time I'm in Cincinnati." Nick had beamed when he told it.

Back in the early days on Friday evenings before airtime, Nick and I would snack on burritos while he'd quaff a couple of Bass Ales at the Kismet. It was a corner bar with a couple of pool tables, a coterie of tattooed and pierced pool sharks, and a kitchen run by a guy who looked like he'd been plucked off the deck of the Pequod. Cincinnati is a river town, and whales don't swim up the Ohio, but damned if I didn't think of harpoons every time I ate at Kismet with leopard patterned walls, men with huge silver ear-rings and long braided ponytails.

I'd become familiar with Kismet because I felt solace to stop in after my second shift at the halfway house where I'd been fired from, thank God. I think. Urban Rat worked days, and I never had dinner with her. Back then, I came to Kismet because the kitchen was still open and I wanted to unwind without drinking, but around drinkers, and maybe shark a little pool. I thought about having a positive effect on my universe. I wanted to be remembered and mean something to the people that most people called "mental." I wanted to come up with something better for myself. At times I thought I was a gambler and all I'd amount to was a guy who lots of times just stayed back, the perennial extra on the film set while someone else took the lead. I'd just go along and somehow, through some cosmic accident be thrust into the limelight. Does that ever happen? In Kismet the only special thing was the girls. Most of the female bartenders were in local rock bands. There was one who had great long dark hair but was always rude except for when I shot pool with her, once at another bar after closing. I had invited this svelte kitten to perform live on the radio back when I had a show. For a few months I was on her radar. Truth be told, she tended at several local cool spots. Like me, she worked where there were no TVs. But when she performed, she wanted them on, and she'd dive into her cups, hug and kiss any man but me.

Logan International

She stepped in front of a short, dark-suited man, with a swarthy complexion in line at the Delta ticket counter. The sun blazed outside. Arjuna sweated through his blue, button-down shirt from the walk between the bus and the terminal. It was unseasonably warm in Boston Thanksgiving weekend.

"Why did you step in front of him?" Arjuna asked his wife loudly, turned to the man.

Urban Rat looked at the floor. She wore black Reeboks, black cotton-stretch pants and a patterned blue and red vest with brass buttons over a yellow blouse. Why was he doing this? What possible purpose could he have for pulling this shit now, but she knew. He was off his medication. She knew this.

She wrinkled her nose, "Hey, it was the right thing to do. We have more luggage."

Arjuna sensed that she was making light. He lowered his brown rucksack to the blue carpet. If only she could always be this funny.

"Sir, would you like to go ahead of us?" Arjuna smiled showing his bad tooth and gestured to the swarthy man who stood behind them reading above the fold of his *Boston Herald*.

Miffed, she watched the swarthy man walk around them. Just one.

"He deserves to be ahead. He started ahead, he belongs ahead." Her husband was getting smug. She felt her dissatisfaction curling in her belly. The coil tightened and loosened in gentle spasms. She opened her black leather purse and fumbled for a Tums.

"Breakfast too fast?" Arjuna asked, shifting his feet in worn Asics, pushing the soft, dark bags forward on the blue carpet. He looked outside again and thought about his wife's inconsiderate nature. He tried to remember why he loved her, but he could not think of it now. She nodded agreement as she bit the antacid, her large jaw grinding. She did not want to fight with Arjuna all day, but she knew that this struggle had only begun. When the swarthy man reached the counter, he turned and smiled.

Arjuna looked at her red leather suitcase with the black cloth tape holding the handle together. Did she remember how helpful he was this morning, repairing the handle with tape he had with him? She had wanted to take a cab to the airport, and he had saved them thirty dollars by doing the repair. Then she was able carry the bag on the subway and bus.

Urban Rat approached the counter, put her picture I.D. and ticket in front of the reservations clerk dressed neatly in dark blue. The couple had even had time for coffee at his aunt's pale white apartment in Brookline. This aunt was his father's sister, mother of Arjuna's four cousins. Arjuna felt the fear and love between himself and his cousins as a troubling force.

As Arjuna stood at the ticket counter he thought about how much he'd rather be traveling with Draupudie than Urban Rat. He thought of Draupsie's sharp blue eyes, with the incredible whites, the pale skin, paler than Rat's, and the beauty of her curves, her black hair. Arjuna compared them in his mind, but he managed to focus on Urban Rat.

The ticket ordeal was over, they were walking through the off-white walled tunnel to the massive open door of the jetliner. His eyes were cast down, the pack cut into his shoulder. There was a break in the flow. The tunnel had a tear, a hole that let in humidity. Arjuna saw this disruption and started putting a word to it in his head. Feng Shui. There was no word in English that could explain this disruption of the flow. He was scared. Urban Rat walked on, her long stride cramped, by the flow of other passengers. Arjuna thought Draupudie could use this new element in the story to introduce her presence as muse and typist. Draupudie knew things Asian. Urban Rat entered the plane. Arjuna turned to the flight attendants at the door, "Do you see that?" he asked, pointing to the tear. He could feel the concern, he knew it crossed his face, he wanted to say, bad Feng Shui, but he couldn't find the word. The flight attendant looked where Arjuna pointed, the attendant was a black man, tall and well turned out in a blue uniform all crisp and pressed.

"It's OK," he said.

Arjuna moved on.

Urban Rat was waiting for the scene to start. She was pleading to herself, don't start, don't start. But she was ready.

They were seated.

Once they were airborne, Arjuna took a short walk to the john. She saw him converse with a stewardess but couldn't hear what was said. He was pointing, smiling, and shaking his head. She tucked her brown eyes back into the generic cheap mystery novel in her hands to avoid eye contact with her husband.

"I think I could teach," Arjuna said.

"Yes, of course," Urban Rat smiled tentatively.

"Teach writing. I want to. For a long time I've dreaded grading, but now, I really think teaching would be better than that fucking halfway house."

She listened and worried. She knew she was going to move out and leave him when they returned to Cincinnati. She didn't want to fight it out with him here, on the plane.

"Are you going to write another novel?" she asked.

He looked at her. She was acknowledging that he had finished the novel he had been working on. This was gracious. Often, she teased him about it. Just as Draupudie told jokes in New York City to patrons of a comedy club, she teased. Unfinished novels seemed to amuse women, he thought.

"Yes," he said, "but I can't decide what genre." He knew he and Draupudie quit reading trashy mysteries when they were both in tenth grade. He wanted to blurt that out, to articulate it to Rat. But, the words weren't there for Urban Rat. He could talk to his therapist about the muse and the wife, compare them. But even that scared him. He kept his thoughts about women to himself.

"Write a mystery," Urban Rat smiled. She knew it would itch at him. He hated her trashy mysteries.

"About us?"

"Well, you'll write about us when we separate, right?"

"Yeah, likely."

"Make it a mystery."

"I think I'd prefer a literary novel."

"You could write a mystery."

Arjuna thought again about the black out. That could be part of a mystery. But to write a formula novel on the heels of his twenty-year project! He imagined Draupudie giggling. Her mood would be lightened by this turn of events. Imagine a muse reacting to two characters trying to agree on the genre of a novel one would write. Self-conscious, it seemed self-conscious to write this.

"I'm going to teach about Eric Blair."

She didn't know Eric Blair, yet. She knew he would tell her who Eric Blair was. Arjuna thought about how he had been homeless like Blair, about schizophrenia, about marriage. Now, Arjuna knew, he wanted a family. He realized in the aftermath with his family when his aunt had listened so patiently in the pale Brookline apartment that he wanted a child.

"Urban Rat, I know we agreed not to ever have children. But we could buy the building with the restaurant, you could get pregnant, and I could get a job teaching writing."

She couldn't imagine all that. All that. She just—

I came to my senses for a moment as Joni Mitchell's voice swelled behind the clatter in the coffeehouse. I have these conflicting stories. I started with Nick, then introduced the muse, next came Grandfather, all that pool shooting—

It's the music. I'm tempted to begin a whole other story line about the music. And there are several. If I am schizophrenic, which I must be, because what else would explain my dependence on antipsychotic medications, then I must rein in my tendency to become tangential and irrelevant in our work; readers and writers work together of course, then I acknowledge that many readers are also writers. This keeps worrying me. I think Arjuna and Urban Rat are getting into a thread, this mystery versus literary argument, that I am open to, but as a writer, I don't want a mystery, that has my main character in yet more trouble. But, he's in a pool room, Kismet, where drunks can get angry when they lose. And I want very much for Arjuna, to reach one more room—

I'm a man of deep faith and I have been afraid to speak with my therapist honestly about the music. The music did not lead me to anything. It comes and goes like the madness. At times my penis gets hard. At other times, I pray. I pray that I don't kill someone. I fear that in my paranoid state I could fall into such a dark mystery. I've thought of killing Leo, the composer, pianist for leaving his wife and children. Remember Leo? I wrote a song for Leo. He had a trio with Katie, the black singer, and Leigh the Buddhist bassist with swagger. Again, this was a thread from the past. I wrote *First Snow* for Leo the piano player. The lyrics were about when I went to Draupudie in Cambridge in 1976 or was it

1977. It doesn't matter, you'll never keep the dates straight. And then I wrote *Someone's In Love* about Draupudie as I missed her many years later. Leigh took that one and Katie sang both. And I told them both that I didn't want credit. Now, it's eating at the plot of this damn book. I know I couldn't get that far into the underworld though. If I killed Leo in some time lapse and managed to vault through time like in some crazy sci-fi thriller to that subway in Boston. I wanted to re-experience the moment of blacking out and then to have another chance back with Draupudie. I think it is a thought crime thought. And remember all the discussion of Eric Blair?

See, my favorite EB novel is *Homage to Catalonia* but I am now teaching *Down and Out in Paris and London,* instead of *1984*. When I write the order of the chapters will be one way. But by the time a reader sees this they may be in a different order. Is this important for the reader to know? I think so. But readers can trust me. This novel is my second, my therapist will stick with me, even if I fire him. He did the last time. Anyway, if I admit Draupsie's control as moderate, right now, a socializing influence on me, a scholar, I'll have to say she wanted me to keep working at the halfway house after UR and I got back to Cincinnati. But I cannot tell that part. It involved Feng Shui, and the apartment complex with the restaurant and the loft and UR's absolute fear of Arjuna. Whenever I get Arjuna into scenes where I wonder how to comment, when I am in fact Arjuna, I get somewhat lost. Trusting my intuition, giving in to the internal voice that is whole scares me. I wonder if I write to be isolated, or if I am isolated by the time I spend writing. Some of this is fiction. So I guess I'll have to let it all sort itself out with time. It is also novel. But how could a schizo scholar who had a girl and then lost a girl have a novel unless he kills someone? I loathe gratuitous violence yet I don't mind some shocking sexuality. A long paranoia about an Orwellian character afraid to even speak Orwell's name for fear of being accused of thought crime.

Grandfather Lou, Piano man, Pool shark & Nick

I have been a student of the game since my Grandfather had shown me a thing. I remember back in 1985 the last time we shot pool together, I beat him with a trick. My dad had flown me down to Florida to see Grandma before she died. Grandfather stood a foot shorter than me, with slicked-back, black hair and a rotund body, a good, ruddy face, marked with watery brown eyes and a big Jewish nose that bristled at the nostrils right into a pencil-thin mustache. At the time my hair was cropped and dark, I wore a thick mustache and had been playing harmonica in Cincinnati bars evenings, with Leo. Leigh, and Katie. Grandfather and I wore the same shoes, heavy Florsheim Royal Imperials. Mine were brown wing-tips, his were black. He had worked forty years as a credit manager for Cristofori Pianos, smoking cigars, playing golf and schmoozing customers. He tracked the prices of strings, keyboards, pedals, frames, spruce soundboards, lacquered cases and wooden actions. In his looping script, Lou kept the records and knew the details of ebony, ivory, felt, and steel. He listed costs and could talk sostenuto, hammers, dampers, uprights, spinets, and grands. He had no talent to tune the eighty-eight pitches but listed octave after octave of the fifty-eight unisons and the thirty other two string sets. His labors for Cristofori were almost duplicated in the synagogue where he used his script to track the members, retiring as secretary only when he and my grandmother moved to Boca Raton, Florida when he retired. Born around the turn of the century in Russia, he had been retired longer than I had been working. He did not go in for that blues music, never had, and I think he harbored thoughts of straightening me out a bit, but he played the chum, offering big cigars, while I declined and puffed my Camel bullets. He loved introducing me to his fellow retirees, pool room cronies, who all said, "Lou's the best. Finest there is. Study on him, Arjuna."

We had shot straight pool in the retirement community down in Boca Raton, Florida. It was a gay place with sun streaming in tall windows, in sharp contrast to the grimness of Grandmother dying after a second stroke in an antiseptic and piss smelling nursing home with institutional green walls, floors and ceilings. Lou's second floor apartment with the darker green indoor outdoor carpet covered walkway that circled the off-white vinyl-sided building had an openness that kept him happy. The recreation area in a separate unit was a short walk across a blazing hot concrete and grass, sprinkler dotted plaza. I had trailed Grandfather through the hardwood-floored dance hall, up a medium-sized elevator, into a well lit, high-ceilinged room, with ten immaculate red felted pool tables. He chose one, put on his apron, chalked his hand and cue, which he carried in a compact black case, broken down. With years of hustling behind him, Grandfather Lou strung together runs, and led by twenty-five by the time I shot the second time. Then I was under thirty years old, and my game was eight ball, bank the eight, let the sucker screw up and scratch. Patience and defense didn't work in straight pool, and I think he saw my game before I suckered him. I remember with pride when he beat me at straight pool. I had fourteen balls in. He said, "you did a lot better than Rigo." My brother Rigo, he spoke of my handsome, intelligent brother. Something I did better than Rigo according to Grandfather Lou. My ego soared. Then I told him my game and suckered him clean. Sure, he cleared off his seven balls easily, but when it came to banking the eight, I kept placing the cue ball in great defensive positions. Eventually he scratched. He was pissed. I remember his gruff voice like my father's when he took off the apron, broke down the cue, laying it gently in the blue felt-lined case, and walked back to the john to wash his large good hands.

At Kismet, the tables were coin operated, and the sink was outside the john. That's what I call a pool hall. Grandfather Lou had hustled pool all his life. And I had suckered him. So, I'm a student of the game. I don't play bank the eight ball anymore, but I play eight ball, bar rules.

A year later at Grandmother's funeral, my mom was mean to me. I was skinny and hunger ruled. That was the last time I saw Lou. He recounted this incredible joke. He told it about my dad. I can't remember how it went, except the punch-line: "Better pull in your ears son, we're coming to a tunnel." I think it was about the birth canal, and I remember a lot of laughter and then he cried, laughing and sad. By then Dad had spoken proudly that Lou had an older live-in girlfriend.

But now, I think I'm taxing my blue-eyed, muse Draupsie, in that yellow walled room, her red fingernails flashing in the refracted light on Winter mornings. When I think of Draupsie I think of Mom. Both intimidate the hell out of me, always. Is that schizophrenia? Am I paranoid? Am I afraid of disappointing mother, and muse? That will drive me to finish this story.

Anyway, Nick didn't shoot pool, or even talk pool. We sat in a dark haze of his smoke, a long time after I had become a non-smoker, breathing deep the meditative breath of non-addiction, while Nick told me about how Cammy needed him. Needed him, my friend Nick, to be a better father, and he owed her money. And he kept saying it was about money. And I was trying to beg a burrito without a beer.

Okay, so between us, we didn't have money. And I think the jukebox at Kismet was the finest in town. John Lee Hooker was in a mood and sang, "The night time is the right time." (Crowing more, I'll say I tried that as a pick up line in a coffeehouse and it got me a free Tarot reading and a walk on Ludlow Avenue with a sweet lovely Greek girl, and I swear I was just thinking of Mom.) So, Cammy needed Nick, and Nick needed his kids, and I was worried about Nick then, cause he talked about divorce every time we'd get together. Nick has a beautiful head of wavy brown hair, a bushy mustache, and stinks like aftershave, sweats profusely and once we mimed the sound effects of his kidney stone passing at the end of a successful fund drive, live on FM radio. He poured water into a gray waste can, I tossed a dime, with a ping, and he sighed. Just like that, radio. All the magic, and we laughed loud. Nick had a spirit and presence on the air that pissed off the General Manager more than me. Often, he said, "stuff," and he'd play music for forty minutes straight, and back announce incompetently, with pauses, and a gravely voice. The worst thing he did, a pattern I had fallen into as well, was to back announce five or six songs at once, get flustered, correct a mistaken announcement, then realize the correction was mistaken, correct the correction, and altogether sound very unprofessional. Nick worried aloud about being fired. But he sounded so damn cool, I never worried about the ax falling on him. No, I'm lying. I worried all the time. I never expected to be the first one to lose a show. But I missed two shifts without contacting anyone, such a flagrant violation that I couldn't talk my way back, even after the hospital stay.

The day I went in to explain myself, after the hospital discharge, the first marital counseling session and beginning to re-tread the right road, I thought I saw a tear in the eye of the little GM, but he insisted it was business. Everybody else I talked to claimed to be on my side. God, I wished I could have organized them to fight with me against the GM. I might have hired a lawyer but didn't even know where to begin. Meanwhile, Nick took over my show, answered the phones and put people off. He had done what he had to do. I now will openly wonder if I think he's a drunk because he wouldn't fight with me against the GM. He probably believes something like that. Radio, even public radio, is where the ax hovers, daily, hourly, and even moment, to dead air moment. I've seen it happen over time to people who never fucked up like I did. And people who fucked up as bad or worse than I ever did have been hired back. There's no explaining radio. It's a medium that lives by ratings and members, and who knows what beat the GM hears.

I wonder if the worst thing that could happen to Nick would be to get more air shifts. Or if his wife moved out of the house. The thing is, he had lost a machinist job and had sued for wrongful discharge. I heard a lot of the details and they involved disability, carpal tunnel syndrome, and Nick's Diabetes. He seems to be on the edge of his physical tolerance, but always wanting to go later, do more, push the envelope. One fund drive he spun guitar blues three hours after sign-off to please a caller. As he tells it, the caller promised a three-figure pledge, and Nick stayed, got the pledge and the station turned down the money. He had been unauthorized on air, and it risked the radio. I don't know which part of this story to believe, and I don't want to get Nick, in any more hot water, I want to help him. Hell, just because he got me into the soft porn flick, and listened to me cry after Urban Rat left, didn't mean he didn't care. I agree I'm better off without the Rat, and the flick was small, and no one saw my face on camera. Actually, the funniest part was when I passed the skill-saw and the cord behind the head of the commentator. But that's what extras do in soft porn. They get soft-ons, and create silly sight gags for stoned viewers, who get up the next day, and hit the road, with a shirt pocket full of Tasty Buzz.

I meet Nick for a burrito at my home, a short walk from a Latin American restaurant. Nick looks upset. He has to be at the station in an hour for the blues show. "Arjuna, I'm not sure I have enough for a burrito."

"This time, I'm buying," I say.

"God, that would be great," says Nick.

Nick walks with me.

"Man, my back is killing me. I lost my keys. And I told my son to help me find them. I needed him to help move a speaker cabinet. And of course, he said sure. Then when I went to move it, he wasn't around. And of course, I moved it myself. My back went out. God, I ache. How far do we have to walk? Man, so the keys weren't there. And when I asked my wife for her keys to make a copy, she just glared. So, I have my son's keys to the car."

"New car?"

"This is relatively new. The other one's not running. God, my back is killing me." He talks on, and walks in short steps, arms hanging limply.

"You sure you can afford the burrito? I know it's a lot to ask. But it was a bit of a drive over here. And I don't know if I have enough gas to make it to the radio station without a couple bucks."

"Sure, Nick."

"Thanks, man. I finally got another shift at the station. Anyway, she moved out, but she comes back with groceries. She has. Man, my back. Is it much farther."

"There, Nick."

Nick's face fell when he saw the NO SMOKING sign. He didn't say anything. He sweated and smelled of cheap cologne. He was wearing these cool, rainbow sandals, and his T-shirt was clean, the overalls clean, too. I couldn't see his eyes under the shades.

"Tell me about this Russia thing you mentioned on the phone," Nick asked once we were in line. He pulled down the sunglasses, looked at the bright orange menu board."

"Whatever you want," I said.
"Always say 'spasíba!'" he said.
"Huh?"
"And 'pazhálsta.'"
"Huh?"
"Thank you, and you're welcome, in Russian."
"You know a little?"
"I took a year of Russian in college."
"Great Nick. I had no idea." The greatest thing about my experiences is they always brought me more from my friends. "If I had stayed married to Urban Rat, I'd never have had this chance."

He ordered the steak burrito. As the counter man asked him what he wanted to drink, I cringed. Nick was going straight for the booze. He ordered a hard lemonade. I thought about declining to pay for the drink, but here he was, gracious, broke, hurting, and I couldn't possibly make a scene here. I thought, I'm a writer, not a fucking Social Worker. He drinks, he drinks.

I think the consequences of being in the flick: *chickboxin underground* are minor. I find myself surfing the web looking at sex pics all hours of the day and night instead of finishing my novel. I did not tell Nick this. We talked about his wife moving out.

"She swung a heavy roll of wrapping paper at me the other night. I put up my arm to protect myself. She threatened to hit me in the head with it. I told her to go ahead. I lowered my hand. I turned to my daughter Pammy, who had walked into the room. And I said to Pam, if your mom
hits me in the head with that I want you to go call the police. Cammy stormed out of the room, muttering. I swear she wanted to hit me. I don't know if I can take this anymore. I can't pay the bills without her. And when she moved back in I thought maybe things would get better."

"You have radio shifts every night now?"
"Yeah, but I don't know how I'm doing it."

"Take it one day at a time, man. It's what you've dreamed of."

"That's another thing. They didn't send out a press release when they changed the schedule to include me."

"Don't sweat it, Nick. Make the most of it."

"Yeah," he smiled.

Then, Nick told me about a trick he did at another radio station where he had worked before.

"It's really wild, Arjuna. You take the same record, it has to be vinyl, and you put a copy on each of two turntables. You cue them up, but when you turn the disc back a rotation so they're up to speed when the music starts, one disc goes back a half-rotation more. Then, you hit both remote play buttons on the board at once, pot them up and presto, the song plays on both, slightly out of phase. It's the coolest effect."

"Nick, I have a couple of old jazz pressings from Leo, Leigh and Katie, this trio I wrote for in the eighties, *Someone's In Love* and *First Snow*. If I gave you two copies of each, could you play them like that for me?"

"It'd be my pleasure, Arjuna."

"I'd be grateful," I said.

And that was when I decided to get Urban Rat to give her old piano to Nick for little Pam. The Rat and I hadn't talked much for months, but I felt convinced if I worked it right I could make the deal happen. She had only taken it from my place because I was charging her rent for storing it. Kind of a mean thing for me to do, but I was really strapped since quitting the halfway house. I hadn't started teaching then. Now, I figured to offer her some cash for the old upright, and to pay the movers. I was sure the music would be on my side, if I could pull this off.

To Clear the Air

Dear Delta Airlines,

Don't get me wrong. I don't want to be a complainer. My ex-wife says I complain sometimes, well she did, we don't talk much now. Now, don't think I blame Delta Airlines, that would hardly be fair—but I want to tell you about this experience I had on one of your airliners, a Boeing 737 jetliner, I think. I'm sure it was all my fault, really, but then why would I be writing? OK, OK, here goes. I'm a paranoid schizophrenic. My ex-wife is a little off, too, but she'd hardly admit it. We took a family vacation to Boston over Thanksgiving. We flew Delta. OK, that's obvious, why else would I write to you? OK, OK, here's the thing. I was off my medication when we flew, so consequently a little more paranoid than usual. I was off the meds because the CVS pharmacist accidentally/mistakenly (choose your own word here) filled my prescription with point five milligram tablets instead of five milligram tablets. So, that wasn't my fault either, understand? But at the time, I knew I was on the lower dose, I just didn't understand that I was getting psychotic. My ex-wife could explain that better. So, imagine, here we are, fighting a lot, I'm kind of paranoid and in an accelerated state of illness, and I get on your jetliner and the stewardess (or flight attendant to be PC) talked to the passengers about flight safety. I had developed a sudden interest in Feng Shui and had noticed a big dent and a tear in the movable tunnel that went from the terminal to the jetliner. I pointed it out to one of the flight staff. It concerned me that if that was broken, well, I wondered what else might be neglected or damaged? Anyway, once we were in our seats, I read the plastic card with emergency instructions on it. (I listened to the flight attendant explain, too.) I read it very carefully. I looked at the diagram of the emergency door. Then, before the flight took off, I excused myself from my ex-wife in the window seat on the runway there in Logan International Airport while the sun streamed through the window. I walked down the aisle to the emergency exit, and I compared the picture on the card, you know, the diagram showing how to open the emergency door, the curved red arrow? —and turn it sideways and throw the door out, you know. Well, I noticed something. Something upsetting. So, I pointed it out to the flight attendant, and she looked a little concerned, but I don't think she did exactly the right thing, so to cover her ass, and mine, I'm writing this letter. Well, you're probably wondering what I noticed? Yeah, well, the arrow on the picture of the handle on the emergency door pointed to the left—counter-clockwise—and on the door itself, the arrow pointed to the right, clockwise. Now, as you may imagine, I was upset and scared. I kind of thought this was negligent and detrimental to the safety of me, my ex-wife and my fellow passengers.

Now, I didn't say anything to the guy in the seat next to the emergency door, but I told this flight attendant, a nice tall brunette named Sandra. Sandra said she would make sure the proper official heard about this and, real sincerely apologized, and said I was right and stuff. At the time, I thought I handled it real well; I went back to my seat and didn't tell my ex-wife because I didn't want her to worry. And well, now, now that we're divorced

and I'm back on meds and getting ready to take a trip—on Delta again—I just wanted you to know, just in case Sandra didn't tell anyone, I'm letting you know now—thanks for a great flight.
Sincerely,
Arjuna

Stunning Conclusion

I flew to St. Petersburg to attend a seminar. One night we went out.

Natalie had big green eyes, a crooked nose, wide lips, and long dark hair. I met her at the bar in the cooperative art gallery, Fish Fabrique. There was a crowd of Russians, but she spoke to me in English.

"Are you a student?" I asked.

"Yes, and I teach English lessons to children."

"I like your black corduroy jacket."

"Ah, yes. I got it in a second-hand store. There was a receipt in the pocket from 1982, before I was born. I took it for good luck."

"What do you study?" I asked again.

"Guess."

And her eyes flashed, she giggled, and I tried to figure out what her English accent was. I told her about Jorge, my host, whose English accent was Croatian except when he was being generous, then it slipped to Texan.

"Guess," she said again, "I mimic the English of anyone I talk to." It was true. She sounded Midwestern. She shifted to a British accent for a moment to prove she could do it.

"Art or Science?" I asked.

"Good. Sort of both."

"Social Science?"

"Yes. Social, but what?" She sipped her beer quickly and lit another cigarette. I wanted so much to be a drinker then. We sat outdoors under a temporary roof at benches and tables and she leaned in very close, our bodies touching. A friend of hers limboed under the fence to avoid the cover charge to a roar of laughter. I wanted food, but didn't know how, to order. She walked with me into the dark crowded bar and ordered chicken and rice with a side mushroom salad for me. I bought her another beer.

"Social Psychology?"

"No. Not Psychology, but that is a good guess."

"Social Philosophy."

"Yes, Arjuna, that's it. You have guessed."

"What is your thesis topic?"

"I am writing on the problem of the elite."

I thought for a moment. "Isn't that a religious question?"

"How?"

"People who believe they are chosen."

She looked startled, "Aha, you are right. I hadn't thought of that." Someone at the table asked me if I was a Jew. I said I was half-Jewish, which is true. A Russian Jew. There was a lot of chatter in Russian. Natalie leaned over and gave me a very wet kiss on the lips. "Let's go," she said, grabbed her black purse, pulled herself up, and took my hand. We walked out together onto Moscow Prospect. She had her beer bottle in one hand, her black purse on her shoulder and a firm grip on my left hand with her right. She hailed a light green, Russian Fiat taxi and pulled me into the backseat, negotiated the fare with the cabby in Russian, and as we pulled away from the curb, she drank. She lit a smoke.

"Smokes are cheap in Russia. Want one?"

She offered me a Marlboro. "No thanks."

She smoked, drank and then leaned in. I could feel the whole length of her body. Her leg felt great against mine. I hadn't had sex in two years and now the race was on. She leaned in and put her mouth very close to my ear, so I felt her words, her breath, her lips, she said, "I have condoms."

Not used to children, I didn't understand when the three-year-old joined me in my sleep. She snuggled up close, rubbing her pre-pubescent genitals against my leg and hand. Then she kissed me several times on the mouth. Her mouth, open against mine, convulsed with her little body against my bare, sweaty chest. A chunk of vomit in her kiss. I felt the thrust of bile and awoke choking, sweating. The child had entered my dream door. I wanted to know why she was there. Can my schizophrenia explain these slamming screen door dreams of parents fucking and a child puking while kissing me? I thought of re-writing these ideas. The parents could be strangers seen through a screen, or a knothole, some device must be available. The child could be a young Russian woman who drinks to excess and seduces me after a brash exchange in a bar and taxi. She goes into her cups and falls asleep against me after I am spent inside her pussy. Then in a sleepy moment, I kiss her out of my passion and loneliness, trying to wake her, probing with tongue. She catches herself suffocating slightly and gags, vomiting into my mouth. This is saner than my dream of a child crawling into my arms and trying to make love against my adult erection, hands, mouth. Failing, and childlike she gurgles and gags. The dream stories are in unconscious and bend my waking conscious with power. Repressed sexuality frustrates me and dogs my waking hours. In another scene I am in a warm pool with my brother and he tries to sodomize me. I attempt to return the favor. I feel so aroused that I wake to the dream door shaking and again the erection throbs. When I was off the medication, I had wet dreams with beautiful passionate women who were near my age and social status. I blame the Haldol for sucking me into perversion. Is that perverse? Is my fear of being sedated out of a sex-life what's rattling that dream door? I want to know. No, I don't. Does everyone dream of thieves in the night? Sometimes they take my bicycle, mostly they take my desire and twist it like a knot of hair around my soul and watch me feel ill and poisoned.

Dear Urban Rat,

I'm at Peterhoff sitting on the jetty. The Bay of Finland opens up before me. The hydrofoil is docked and loading. The sky is bright blue with high level cirrus, a fresh breeze blowing onto the shore, sea gulls soar above. Ducks, swimming, a man and a boy fishing and I'm crying in the salt air.

Oh Urban Rat, oh. I remember Boston, Thanksgiving and think of how I am still confused. When I blacked out, I remember heading for a seat and when I woke up you were in the seat ahead of me and there was an MBTA official on the scene. This did not jive with my memory of how—the time—how long—what happened while I was out? The truth? Can you explain moment by moment? How did the official get there so fast? Did I kill someone? Did I flip out as someone attacked me or you and go into a dark trance dance and use my Scarlet Belt powers and take a life in a matter of several instantaneous blows? Was I then sedated? And then you presented my documentation and had me revived back on the scene? Is that why there were different people around when I awoke? Is that how the official got there? Did it take twenty minutes or a half an hour, or even several hours or days? Am I part of some complex nightmare that the whole family knows about? Did I then have to face going back on the meds on my own? Is it the medication that keeps me safe in spite of my Scarlet Belt powers? Is this why you did not want to have my child? Am I just deluded again? Last night I didn't take my meds, because I stayed over at Jorge's after class and didn't have my pills with me. Are today's tears chemical? Do I truly miss you?

I love you. You are the closest friend I've ever had in my life. Even though Draupudie dutifully takes these notes and weaves them into a novel with my guidance across the telepathic sympathetic waves, you have been there. You talk to me. You listen. I look at you and feel everything. Everything I said to you in anger in the last three years was based on distrust from the incident on the subway. I know my medication helps me. I know you now have a better understanding of therapy—what works versus what doesn't—and medication—side effects versus help in dealing with emotions. I know you now have tried at least six different meds for depression without finding one you can live with.

I'm thousands of miles away and I think of you—St. Petersburg is a city for lovers as well as a tragic place. Architectural and natural beauty are embedded with a history of tragic violence.

The inner-conflict I feel at my new life—my terrifying loneliness, my fear that I have taken the wrong course—the muse whom I trust and long for versus the safety of our love. I have kept the spacious apartment in Cincinnati although it is a huge expense. I think of your difficult struggle with depression, which hurts and angers me—though not as much as it hurts and angers you—and your strength—you amaze and awe me. I pray for you. I want you to paint again—for your sake—for your joy—for you—and I want you to feel whole again.

I'll stop now as the tears flow,
Love,
Arjuna

When Urban Rat got the letter, she left a message on my phone machine. I think she thought I was pathetic. I called her back.

"Rat, I'm sorry to be such a sap."

"Yeah, Arjuna, I know."

"I've been working on the mystery novel, but I can't figure out the mystery."

"Oh," she laughed a fake laugh.

"But I have an idea for a wonderful redemption for both of us."

There was a pause on the line.

"Do you remember my friend Nick? The one I clowned with on radio once? He's having marital troubles and has three kids. The youngest is learning piano but doesn't have a real piano to practice on. So, I was hoping, thinking, praying really, that I could arrange to give her our old piano."

This time there was no hesitation.

"If you pay to move it, I'd be glad to get it tuned. My, pleasure."

"Thanks you, spasiba," I said. And that's how the music began to save my sorry ass.

VAMPS

I'm trying to become a normal human being. I meditate all the time, hunkering into half-lotus at any stolen moment. I feel I am a thief of schedules, having cast them away, opting for a timelessness that feels sacred and keeps me. I sense that I am in keeping. For a time, I felt truly that I lived as a kept man, when Urban Rat still held the leash, but did not act in my behalf. It seemed that our long time ability, to balance compromise and collaboration had folded into enmeshed anger, hate, imbalance, and fear. Now, I long to normalize a friendship with her. She avoids me.

I've been an extra in another soft-porn flick. This one has vampire girls that kill men, with a final kissing bite on the side of the neck, and at the final moment they expose their nipples in vigor. Imagine if you will, a tall, buxom blond in a flimsy, white, polka-dotted sun dress, no brassiere, spike-heeled, black, snakeskin boots, who disarms a dirt-bag in a faded green, army surplus jacket and blue watch-cap, knocks him to the floor of a seedy underworld strip club called VAMPS! and kicks him around, administers the death kiss after a wonderful head toss resulting in a flowing mane and the baring of hard nipples.

The last week has been a pastiche of mixed emotions. I've found the music, the bare flesh, the company of lassies of a variety of ages, and yet felt alternately blessed, and brutalized by dreams. My meditation grows peaceful and serene. I see mundane visions of dust particles suspended in my living room, and wonder if I can learn to make the dust materialize into a vision of Draupudie, my stunning muse. As I finished the last chapter she appeared in a calm dream, spooning with me on a daybed. Light filtered around the shaded bed. She wore thin, yellow and blue, paisley pants, tied with a drawstring, and a white scoop necked blouse. I had a gentle big hand against her hip where her skin was bare between the pants and blouse. Her eyes were closed, but I sensed blue behind the lids. Her black hair lay close on her neck. Draupudie's skin glowed white and shiny. In the dream I felt warm, calm, serene, totally satiated and satisfied.

Nights flash by, the time spent in nightclubs expands. I feel I'm taking a slightly less passive role, performing on 'monica, blues rippling the faces of customers, pursuing a poet's fate here in Cincinnati, trying to make the final chapters of this work a portent of good. I've played with a folk blues quintet at a coffeehouse bar. The two lead players are young red haired men. One of them was arrested observing a demonstration when a police horse slipped and tossed his man. The young red-headed folk singer spent a week in jail, accused of tackling a police horse. All one hundred thirty-seven pounds of him. I wrote the *Talkin' Cincinnati Trans Atlantic Business Dialogue Blues*, and we played it to loud applause. We played Johnny Cash's *Folsom Prison Blues* and Elizabeth Cotten's *Freight Train*. Monica leapt and wailed in my cupped hands, echoing back to the dobro and pedal steel.

His feet smelled like spoiled cheese. The black hair on the toe knuckles brushed against my lips and jaw. I wanted to curse out loud, but instead I sputtered, pursing my lips and blowing.

Sleeping head to foot under this thin, scratchy gray wool blanket on such a lumpy, narrow bed. This Russian poet slept soundly, while nits crawled from his furry crotch, over his dirty briefs, across a narrow expanse of sweaty, soiled, yellowed sheet to my briefs and then into my pubic hair. I could not sleep like this. St. Petersburg meant sweaty nights, chills and the stench of fungus. The sky never fully darkened. The mosquitoes bit my fingers while I tried to wave them away. I heard the high-pitched whine, and tucked my face back, against the Russian poet's feet. Crabs without any pleasure. Then with a start, I was awake alone in my sweat soaked bed in my roomy, high-ceilinged apartment in the gaslight district of Cincinnati.

I sense a possibility that I can forge this into memoir, fin d my typ-ing muse through some space time transcendence resulting in the reduction of the global village into

a closed system where all the players know one another. I know that my fate is not entirely in my hands. My voice booms through doorways while I try to wake Draupudie from her typing meditation. In reality I see her on television from my living room. Only a glimpse, but she is with her father as he bows out of politics and congratulates the new Senator of New York. I read in *The New Yorker* magazine that indeed I have caught such a vision. The Talk Of The Town mentions the outgoing Senator and his daughter. I do not stalk her, I dream of her and remember her. In this tale I have imagined her, too. As Arjuna, I believe we are always together. She lights the screen I carve my life from. I once lighted her smile.

In the film I think I know my role. I am a pool shark and a liar. Isn't that a consistent role for a novelist? I think of myself as a loser. I lose to entice others to play the game with me, that I might profit. I draw them in by my loserness. Then, the lie, perhaps is that I am a total loser. I don't fully understand this part. The first day of filming, I went through a drive-thru burger place on the way to VAMPS! The line was long. A dirty, black, Sports Utility Vehicle in front of me seemed to take forever. I had the moment to pull out exact change. (For years before going to Russia I had been a vegetarian, but now I have collapsed my ethics for convenience, beef and comfort food.) I had a two dollar bill, a single and eighty-four cents. When the window opened for cash, the young dishwater blond, pimples on her cheeks, took the bills and was marveling at the two. I put the change in her hand, and she closed the window as I moved to the second stop to get my bag of food. The heavyset girl with long, flowing, brown hair stood waiting for my burger. Ahh, it would be hot and fresh. Meanwhile I read the notice on the glass. "If you fail to receive a receipt, ask the manager and you will receive two dollars." She handed me the bag. I looked under the napkins, tugged at the wrapper on the straw, no receipt.

"No receipt!" I said.

"The other girl was supposed to give it to you."

"She didn't."

A pause while she asked the girl at the first window. "She said you drove away too fast."

"I didn't get a receipt."

A stern faced young woman with a green visor and a tight ponytail of straight, long, brown hair comes leaning to the window.

"She says you didn't give her a chance. But here's two dollars."

I took the singles. "I don't mean to argue, but she didn't give me the receipt," I said and pulled away. I had been eating the sandwich since the conversation began. My mouth full, breathing heavy, I shifted out onto the road toward downtown. I felt like I was already in character.

Later, at the strip bar, I stood next to the pool table where a tarp covered felt and a full spread of sandwiches and snacks lay available to the crew and extras. I wasn't hungry. The set had been built, in an after hours club, on Vine Street in Over-the-Rhine. At the outer door surveillance cameras monitored the stumble-bums.

The ceiling's acoustic tile, which had made a drop level was long gone. Fluorescent fixtures and incandescent spots were haphazardly built in above where the drop level had been. The framework was painted a dull red, and behind it everything was flat black, and looked dusty. The floor was concrete and sloped here and there. Along the walls brick was exposed intermittently with plaster. The plaster patterns were in faded green and brown, contrasted with the red brick it looked like someone had tried to map some almost familiar geography above the aluminum sheeting that filled the space under the brick from waist high to the floor. The bar was a dirty black Formica with cheap tube-chrome stools against it. Below the bar corrugated steel shone in the irregular glow. A foot rail was made from galvanized pipe. Above the bar were four TVs, all different sizes, tuned to different stations, sound muted. Figure skating, NBA basketball, XFL football, and auto racing filled the squares. Every so often a man would shout, "Quiet on the set!" and people would stop moving, hold their breaths until another shout of, "Cut!" I later found out there was a man on the crew, a squat fire-plug of a man, with big jowls, black hair, and a backwards cap, whose job it was to cry out instructions. A sort of cinematic town crier.

We watched the Daytona 500 with the sound off while waiting for our call to glory. There was a crash that included twenty-three cars or more. Or was it, car number twenty-three. In slow motion, a driver named Stewart, spun and spun through the air, his red car pirouetting on its left front corner, dancing over the hoods of one, then a second, then rolli ng over   one then a second, and finally a third car, spinning dar k, then red, into the infield pin-balling off other cars. Many   cars slammed into one another and the action reminded me of a person with Tourette's syndrome, a spitting and stuttering action that didn't want to stop and seemed out of control yet somehow part of the way things worked for this world of bouncing racecars. In the moments that followed, I wondered aloud if anyone was hurt. The other extras were playing computer games, cards, and sipping on beverages. I had been immersed, trying to get into character, and this whole car thing threw my balance out for a minute until I saw the driver, Stewart, climb out of the red car and walk to the infield. I wondered aloud again, this time what it would look like to roll and dance like that at a hundred eighty miles an hour. Then, the TV answered with a slow-mo view from inside the car. A view, but without the horrible sound and G-forces. I had a pocket Blake, *Songs of Innocence and Experience* and I fished it out of the inside breast pocket of my black leather jacket. The race resumed after a while. The last lap rolled around soon and now it was clear who raced in front from the animation. One of the announcers seemed ecstatic when his son won the race, but somehow another driver in a black car hit the wall moments before and died. A puzzling silent sport. Then before I could figure out who the winner and dead man were, we were called to the set.

Paul Thanas

A Reconciliation

When she talked to Arjuna in the drab Leesville Lodge, a low-slung bungalow run by an Indian couple (dots, not feathers) she told of living next door to an Asian man. She described how he spent eight hours cutting sticks and pounding roots in his side yard. She had observed through her tears, she said. When they were estranged Rat lived with a girlfriend in a neighborhood nearby Arjuna. Northside was poorer, row houses, and smaller rooms than the upper middle class rental where they had fought and loved. Urban Rat told Arjuna that the man didn't speak much English, but not how she knew this. She told of watching him with rusted hoe and ax working all day at tasks that she would never have attempted. "He saved so little money with so much work," she said. The couple had driven together to Leesville, South Carolina for her father's funeral. Pappy had died of a fall on a love cruise in the Aegean with his second wife. Arjuna believed that the fall and subsequent injury was complicated by Pappy's alcoholism. Arjuna had known of Pappy's struggle but

413

had never been able to broach the issue directly, to share his own struggle with his father-in-law. As far as Pappy had known, Arjuna and his daughter were still estranged. He died not knowing that they were reconciling. Arjuna's theory of how Pappy died was based on knowing that Pappy hid his addiction. If he had head trauma, and no one in the infirmary knew he was in late stage alcoholism, then the seizures could have been from alcohol withdrawal, preventable with medication. In Athens, Pappy had regained consciousness enough to talk to Rat's baby brother who had jetted across the hemisphere to watch Pappy die.

Arjuna's lust for Rat transcended his grief. Out of compassion he drove her the eight hundred miles through the Smoky Mountains to attend the funeral. In the drab motel room, the bed squeaked under her as they made love awkwardly. It had been over six months. She seemed anxious and sweaty. Spring in South Carolina was humid. After the two were spent and sticky under the white sheet, Rat got up and pulled on a T-shirt.

"There's no coffee in the room. We have to be at the funeral home at eight-thirty to finish the arrangements. If I call the desk and ask them for a wake-up call at seven, will you go out for coffee tomorrow?" she asked.

"OK," said Arjuna. He knew with the sedating effect of his tranquilizer and the relaxation he felt from climbing stairs together this would be a tough call. He wanted to please her. "Where do I have to go?"

"McDonald's," she said.

He got up, and pulled on sweatpants, and a sleeveless white T-shirt. She called the desk.

Paul Thanas

Vamps!

When they got onto the set the twenty-three men and two women saw a strip bar interior in the middle of a cavernous room. There were lights connected to scaffolding, lights on independent stands, two big tripods with digital video cameras, and about sixty other people in the room. A T-shaped runway, carpeted in pink ran out from a glittering curtain of tinsel that shimmered in blue, green and red hues. The curtain was lettered: VAMPS! Ten wooden, folding theater seats flanked each side of the runway. A woman in a short, dark ponytail and blue fleece zip up told us where to sit. There were some bar stools around barrels at the periphery. Smoke machines belched non-toxic fumes. Two grips waved rectilinear boards distributing the smoke evenly around the room. Then Lily came out in her glittering cape, bra, g-string and high heels. By her first turn she had shed the cape and bra. Her breasts were giant, almost balloon like, with noticeable scars on the underside from enlargement surgery. I decided to look at her eyes. Focus on her gaze. Blake's poem came back:

The Sick Rose

> O Rose, thou art sick;
> The invisible worm
> That flies in the night
> In the howling storm:
>
> Has found out thy bed
> Of crimson joy;
> And his dark secret love
> Does thy life destroy.

I would not be here if the reconciliation had succeeded. I stared at Lily and she returned my gaze. I had money in my shirt pocket for her, but I played hard to get. She swirled the runway, gyrating to the blaring music. I felt like I was in a seedy underground nightclub. I wasn't sure I wanted to be there. Then, without warning, she leaned down, braced her hands on my shoulders, tossed her long brown hair over my face and beard. I could smell the fragrance of her shampoo. Lily's breasts grazed my jaw. I was too scared to lean into them, and she stood waiting for me to tuck the bill into her g-string. I could feel my manhood. This was why men came to strip clubs. All of this was caught on camera. Am I a loser? A loner, yes, but a loser? She moved away through the pungent haze.

The Funeral

Arjuna heard the phone. He was too warm and dopey to answer. Urban Rat picked it up. She climbed out of bed, headed for the shower. Arjuna knew this was it. His twin callings were his dreams and McDonald's. He struggled to awaken. He heard Urban Rat start the water. Coffee. She needed coffee. He remembered this about her. At home she had the timer on the pot. But they were not at home. They had not lived together for six months. He tried to focus. Focus. He opened one eye and saw the brown wall paper. He could not force the other eye open. The sound of water swept out of his consciousness. The next thing he heard was the door to the room slamming. He got up. Arjuna stood barefoot on the coarse carpet. Then he collapsed back into bed. He was still in bed when she returned with her coffee. When she came in, he opened his eyes.

"Hey," he said.

"Shit, Arjuna," she said.

"I gotta get up."

He spun into the bathroom, showered, dressed for the funeral.

When he saw her, she was in her black linen dress. He had put on a black necktie. He never wore ties. He hoped she would notice.

"I'm sorry," he said.

"All I asked was that you get coffee."

"I guess you'll never forgive this one."

She scowled at him.

"Before you decide to start hating me, listen. I was so confused. Remember the syringes you got to dose the ferrets when they were sick? I found them in the kitchen, and I couldn't figure out why there were so many different sizes."

"The vet just gave me different sizes."

"Yeah, right. Well, I thought you were drugging me. I had dreams."

"Dreams?"

"Yeah. And after you moved out, I found that tiny bottle with the black liquid and the black stopper. I thought it was liquid opium."

"Yeah, right."

"I was very paranoid. Remember when you and Pete came over and I accused you of stealing my wallet?"

She stared at Arjuna as tears started.

"Moments before you arrived, I took some kitty litter and spread it on one of those square ceramic plates we got as a wedding gift. I put a small round charcoal on the litter. Then I lit the coal and sprinkled some of the yellow magic powder, the Frankincense, Myrrh, whatever that stuff was in the glass tube with the cork stopper, sprinkled it into the flame. There was a sparking WHOOSH! I was stunned. Then you came in through the front door. I followed you back to the bedroom to get some of your socks and stuff, I don't remember what all. The doorbell rang, I went to let Pete in. He was in the living room looking at his painting, the one he loaned us, and then I got scared, went back to check on you. Suddenly I knew you had taken something.

Your movements were furtive. I checked around and couldn't find my wallet. I never kept money in my wallet, used the money clip, you know, but that day I had stashed two hundred fifty dollars in my billfold. I accused you of stealing it. You approached Pete and denied it. Then I thought you two were in cahoots, so I accused both of you and called the police. Then I left. You said I was nuts. I think with all that was going on, I had changed a lot of routines about where I left stuff in the apartment. Anyway, I walked up the street to see if I had left the wallet at the automatic teller on Ludlow. I think I had just been there taking out cash. I don't know why I wanted all that cash, but I remember taking out cash. It wasn't there. I walked home. I called the police again.

This time I called 911 and they asked me some questions but nevertook a report. You, and Pete yelled at me, I don't remember what. I was really scared. You both left.

"I called our insurance agent. He said it was covered and calmed me down. He asked if I had a suspect and I told him about our separation and that I suspected you. He was real understanding. He said I had to make a police report.

"I drove down to the police station, made the report. I canceled all my credit cards. I went to AAA and got a new license, and while I was there got passport photos and had a International Driver's License issued. Then I drove up to Springfield, Ohio to get a copy of my birth certificate. I was sure you had stolen it, to prevent me from getting a passport. In Springfield, the office where they issued them was closed. I drove to the hospital where I thought I was born and tried to get one there. People were nice to me, but they couldn't help. I asked one lady if they had a footprint of every baby born there. She was really polite, but it was nearly five o'clock and she wasn't even sure I had the right hospital."

The dream door swings both ways now. Sometimes it is a vision other times I hear a voice that explains the deal. Like a kitchen door, on a weighted hinge, it props open against a sturdy cabinet. The words fly through, unhindered. Draupudie catches them with her flying fingertips, the red nail polish making bloody streaks, time lapses over keys, ink flashes on the page, and we have continuity where before only a steam hinge of cosmic sonic consciousness. This time the censor leaves the room when shyly Draupsie keeps it eternal.

"I remember one conversation in a lime green tile hallway where a lady said something to her child about me while I was standing there. Something about 'that troubled man' and 'we couldn't help him.' I had dinner in the cafeteria there while they had a big Christmas party. There was a live bluegrass band in this brightly lit hospital cafeteria with round tables, plastic and chrome chairs. The band was all made up of men in their fifties and older. I thought they were having a party for me. I knew it was Christmas, but I also had this sense that I was a visiting dignitary, being honored. I drove home at night with sunglasses on. I drove very fast and revved the engine all the way, racing cars through Dayton on I-75."

"Why are you telling me this now?" Urban Rat had taken a seat on the unmade bed. She dabbed her eyes with a tissue.

"I'm sorry. I'm telling you because I'm still scared, and I'm grateful as all hell. I was nuts. I'm still struggling. I'm thinking about your dad. I think when I get sad like this, I just start talking. I found the wallet in my dresser a couple of weeks later. I called the police and the insurance guy to cancel the reports."

"Pete was really concerned."

"I know."

Arjuna was hoping she would say something to reassure him. And Urban Rat desperately wanted Arjuna to comfort her. She was going to her dad's funeral and had to get her own coffee.

There's the trying to please Urban Rat that cannot finally ever work. In a moment of critical awareness another detail, a defensiveness, a determination that defines everything flavors the funereal coffee. It is this: The reason I felt so close to my Zen aunt was that Ken had fucked both she and Kunti on the night they met. One in bed, one later the Zen sister on the beach, Pescadaro, to be sure on the left coast 1952 just out of the military WWII, he rode an army motorcycle from one coast to another Boston, Ma to Eugene, Oregon fifteen days of blissful motoring. Then down the coast to Berkeley where he met them by a miracle, at a Greek restaurant the two sisters. Some months later both women delivered boys. A week apart. There was nothing to do but marry one of the women and raise the boys together. A Greek woman alone with a kid had no choice. They both wanted to be painters. One was better at it. Ken married the other. He loved Kunti. Only the three knew the truth. The boys were never told.

Did that make Dad a pervert? And if pomegranates don't fall far from the tree what did that make me? Or brother Will?

I slip into meditations all the time. When the world settles, it is usually late at night and I wonder why Draupudie is still taking dictation. I can see her blue eyes, her fingers paused above the keyboard, the mascara black on her lashes, the arched eyebrows. She listens with her whole head. Intent on getting every word I say, her body still and straight. Her posture is part of her readiness. I want her to take the rest of this down so that I can finally stop dictating and have the story's end. Do I have to go back to VAMPS! and tell of more dancers, more smoke, more anxious moments with my dick getting hard?

www.ingramcontent.com/pod-product-compliance
Lightning Source LLC
Chambersburg PA
CBHW070159310726
48976CB00001B/155